A PLACE CALLED HECLA

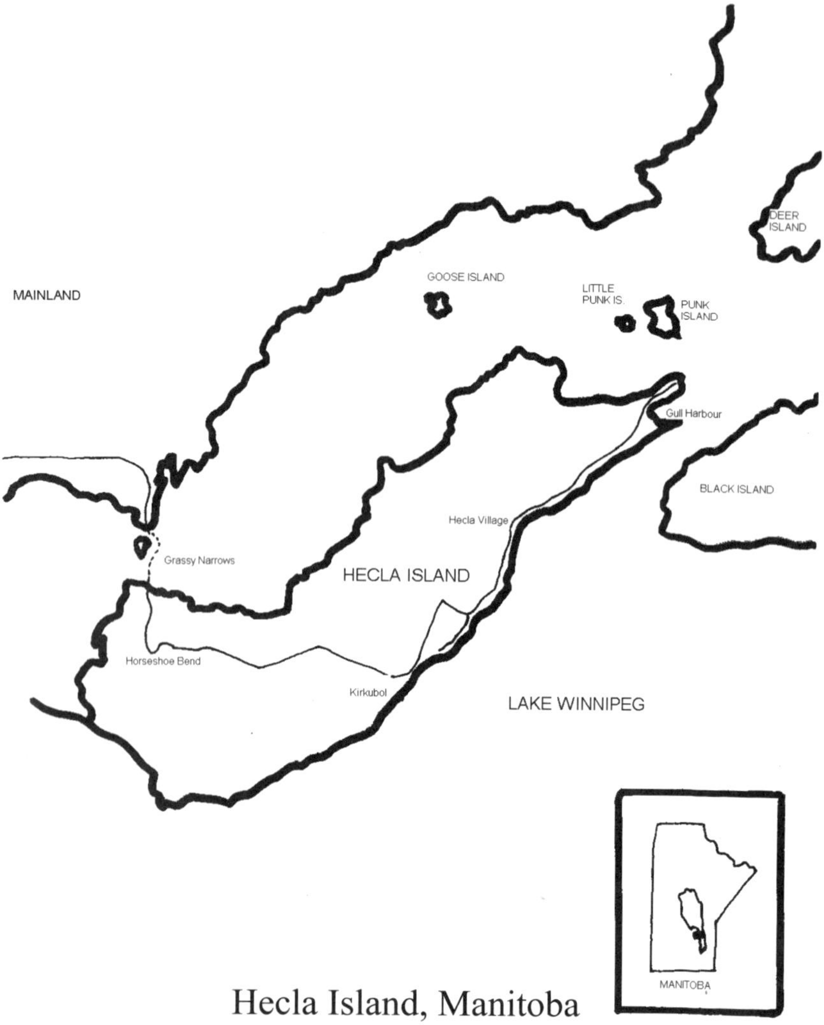

Hecla Island, Manitoba

A PLACE CALLED HECLA

Doris Benson

Second printing, 2008

Library and Archives Canada Cataloguing In Publication Data

Benson, Doris, 1949-

A Place Called Hecla/Doris Benson

ISBN 9780978302504

1. Hecla Island, (MB)--Fiction. I. Title.

PS8603.E577.P56 2007 C813'.6 C2007-902695-8

Printed in Canada by Friesens Book Division

Thanks to...

Roger – for your gift of storytelling and keeping alive the memories of your Hecla Island childhood. I couldn't have told this story without you.

Leanne – for your encouragement and honest assessments. I always feel confident with you in my corner.

Boyd – for your teasing way of keeping me motivated. It's amazing how many ideas come from our coffeepot chats.

The family of Pilot Officer Alfred Pratt, 408 (Goose) Squadron – for allowing me to use your father's rank and some of his WWII stories.

And to other family members (especially Jonina, Greg and Laureen) and friends – for listening, encouraging, proofing and above all, for never doubting the publication of this book.

Dedicated to my grandchildren...

Madeleine, Emily, Kelsey and Kyle

- may Hecla Island always hold a special place in your hearts.

Chapter 1

Hecla Island, Manitoba, September, 1953

With the breeze sifting through his dark brown hair, Ben Bergursson leaned against the ferry railing. The woollen jacket of his business suit strained over his shoulders, then tapered towards his slim waist and hips. He raised his hand to smooth the combed curl over his brow but gave up when another gust of wind rearranged it. His tanned face wore an air of determination as he straightened and gazed over the water. Crossing the Narrows on this new mode of transportation between Hecla Island and the mainland was still a novelty to the islanders. Prior to the ferry, the isolation had been broken only by boat during the summer months. Ben smiled, thinking how quickly the islanders were making the adjustment to the new vessel.

Lake Winnipeg, located in the prairie province of Manitoba, claimed the status of fifth largest freshwater lake in Canada. Situated in the south basin of Lake Winnipeg, Hecla Island spans twenty-two miles in length and six miles across the widest part. At one point on the marshy west side of the island, the distance to the mainland is under a mile. It was there that the islanders crossed.

In winter, people travelled off the island over the ice on a trail created by a snowplow. During the weeks of 'freeze-up' in the late fall and 'break-up' in the spring, people on the island were isolated from the rest of the world. The length of time it took to form a solid sheet of ice across the Narrows, which was strong enough to cross over on, was referred to as 'freeze-up'. 'Break-up' was gauged from the time the ice became too dangerous to travel across until the ice was all gone.

The summer of 1953 saw the new four-car ferry bring a sense of freedom and independence. Islanders were purchasing more vehicles now that road travel was more accessible.

Wiping some dust off the gleaming '52 Chevy, Ben recalled the day he brought the car home. It had been an impulsive buy but not one he regretted. He'd been looking for a sensible car, but the pale blue shade and shimmering chrome had been impossible to resist. His brother, Daniel, had shaken his head, trying to conceal his envy. A toss of the keys in Daniel's direction and the lure of a family ride for his wife, Rose, and their four children changed Daniel's mind about the foolish decision to buy such a car. Ben smiled in memory. They all enjoyed his car, including his mother.

The ferry captain, Kristjan Ebinsson, called out, "Will you be back tonight, Ben?"

The raspy voice brought Ben out of his reverie. The old sailor had a shaggy white beard and ample belly, giving the illusion of a jolly soul. His hearty laugh and sparkling blue eyes didn't dispel the image of Santa Claus. Large callused hands handled the ferry's wheel with gentleness and expertly guided the craft around the marshy island in the channel.

"Not until tomorrow. I'm meeting with the Manitoba Hydro guys today and hopefully we'll finish the plans for the rest of the power lines. Then, I'm going to the hospital to look in on Signey."

The men exchanged an uncomfortable glance. Everyone on the island was praying for Daniel and Rose's youngest girl, Signey. The polio epidemic made everyone nervous.

"It's been two weeks since Doc Johnson took her to the hospital."

"I remember when he came on the ferry with Signey in the car," Kristjan said. "He told me about Signey being the only one who had a low fever that never went away. I guess the others he looked in on had symptoms more like the flu."

"It was the fever and no strength. She couldn't stand by herself."

"What's the latest news of her?"

"When Rose talked to someone on the phone at the hospital yesterday, they said she's still paralyzed on her left side. It's killing Rose not seeing her, but the doctor thinks it would be too hard for Signey to have visitors and then be left there again. I'll stop in and find out how she's doing."

Because Hecla Island was a hundred miles away from Winnipeg, Rose wasn't able to make the trip on a regular basis. Hospitals weren't encouraging visitors to the overcrowded wards. In some hospitals, parents and other family members could only catch glimpses of their children through the window panes.

"I can't believe they turned Daniel and Rose away that day." Ben's eyes flashed in anger. Kristjan slowly nodded his head in understanding. "They drove all the way into Winnipeg only to be told they couldn't see Signey. I wonder if those doctors have any idea what it's like for people who live outside the city."

"Well, at least Rose is able to phone the hospital. That must help."

"It does. But we'll all be glad when Signey can come home." Ben studied the horizon, but his thoughts were of his little niece. He knew the loneliness of being far away from home surrounded by strangers. Signey was living that loneliness and he ached for her. Ben wasn't married with children, so Daniel and Rose's family was like his own.

Marriage had eluded Ben after returning home from his service in World War II. Claire, the English girl he'd fallen in love with while overseas, had refused to become a war bride. Since then, he'd dated other women but none had captured his heart like Claire. Earlier on, Ben contemplated a return trip to England to try and win her back. Then his pride kicked in and the plan was dismissed. Ben thought of himself as a man who believed in leaving the past behind and moving forward.

"*Litla elskan.*" The Icelandic endearment slipped out as Kristjan busied himself rolling tobacco into a cigarette paper. "Hopefully she'll be home soon and feeling better. Thora's niece in Gimli has been sick for awhile. They're calling it an epidemic, there are so many sick with it."

The captain left the wheelhouse door open so that he and Ben could continue the conversation, but both men left any other thoughts on polio unspoken. Kristjan swiped his tongue along the cigarette paper's edge, sealing the tobacco stick.

A pelican hovered over the ferry. Gulls and pelicans followed the fishermen, always looking for a handout. Any unsaleable fish caught in the nets would often become a meal for the patient birds. The ferry was still an unknown vessel to the birds and this particular pelican intended to be near if a net was lifted over the ferry's rail. It carried no cargo in its bill. Some gulls joined the watch. The forty-five-minute ferry ride across the channel usually attracted a large flock.

Kristjan scraped a match down the wooden doorframe and lit the cigarette. Settled in his captain's chair, he eyed the waves. "Starting to blow from the north. The boys will have trouble lifting at Black Island this morning." He exhaled a trail of smoke.

The channel of water separating Hecla and Black Island, where some fishing nets were set, was vulnerable to many winds. Deep with strong current, the channel had taught a healthy respect of the water to generations of island fishermen.

Ben appreciated the change of subject. "They'll be heading to camp. Jon and Daniel are lifting my nets today and tomorrow. If all goes well today, I should be back before the last ferry crossing tomorrow."

"Will this be the last meeting in Winnipeg for you?"

"I hope so. We set a goal for November. Then everybody should be hooked up. Come Christmas, we should be decorating our houses with electric lights."

The effort to bring electricity to the island had been challenging. The Manitoba provincial government commissioned a group of engineers to evaluate the possibility of supplying electrical power to Hecla Island. After studying the situation it was deemed an impossible task. The study advised that power lines could never be sustained across the water. With ice movement in the spring during break-up it would be impossible to secure poles to hold the lines. The engineers found the costly venture illogical and concluded it couldn't be done.

Ben, along with his brother Daniel and friends Sam, Fred and Jon, had taken up the gauntlet. Obviously, the government officials had underestimated the tenacity of the Icelanders. Saying it couldn't be done just fuelled the fire to succeed.

"The womenfolk will all be wanting electric stoves and refrigerators now. You boys are getting us into lots of trouble," Kristjan joked, but his gaze held the tremendous pride he felt in the young men who refused to be daunted by mere engineers. "It's been a long haul. Feels good though, doesn't it, to prove those fancy engineers wrong?"

"Yeah, it does." Ben smiled back.

The previous winter they had built wooden cribs deeper than the water. The poles at the lake bottom were longer to form a wider base for the four-sided structure. The men assembled the walls like a log cabin. Steel rods formed a floor. The towers were lowered through holes in the ice to the channel's bottom, then filled with rock.

Three cribs were strategically placed to accommodate the future electrical lines. The test came in the spring as the ice shattered along the shoreline and crashed into any immobile objects in the way. Tall and strong, the cribs stood through the assault and proved to the islanders and the government officials that it could be done.

Now, after much correspondence and many meetings, the line was strung across the channel and over the six-mile width of the island. The next stage would be connecting the lines to the dwellings.

At twenty-eight, Ben was a well-respected representative for his community. He had been a cocky and confident teenager with a sense of humour and sassy charm that endeared him to most people. His handsome looks and athletic build had touched the heart of many an island girl. Ben's face would light up with his broad smile and warm eyes. He had an insatiable curiosity which had earned him high marks in school and a stubbornness that made him a leader among his peers. Ben yearned to see the world and to a teenager in the early 1940s, he could see and save the world at the same time by enlisting in the war effort.

Ben grinned at the ferry captain. "I'm looking forward to having heat all night long without stoking any fires. When we get up in the morning there won't be ice on the water pail. A warm floor and a bright light to read by. It'll be heaven."

"You youngsters are getting soft. All these modern gadgets will spoil the whole lot of you." Laughter rang through the air as the two men bid farewell. Ben slid into the soft contours of the car's fashionable seat. As the car engine throbbed into life, Kristjan slowed the twin marine engines and brought the ferry to a standstill at the mainland landing. With a wave, Ben drove off the ferry and continued the trip to Winnipeg.

Following the gravel highway, he drove through the towns of Riverton, Gimli and Selkirk. These towns were familiar to the islanders and visited often for supplies or fish sales. Those who had moved off the island to seek employment elsewhere often chose one of the three towns.

Laura O'Neil adjusted the warm, moist cloths around the leg of one of her patients. She had only been on duty for an hour and already the strain was settling on her shoulders. She always tried to think positively, as did the other nurses on the polio ward, but three days earlier a six-year old boy had died. All the other children on the ward knew Charlie and were devastated when the dreaded disease claimed yet another young life.

Poliomyelitis hung like a dark cloud over them. The disease, which attacked the nervous system, caused inflammation of the brain and spinal cord. Because it usually affected children, polio was sometimes referred to as infantile paralysis. Transmitted into the body through the nose or mouth, the polio virus found its way into the intestines and then travelled to the central nervous system. There, in the nerve cells, the virus multiplied rapidly damaging or killing the cells. Fatigue and muscle weakness often resulted in paralysis. Sometimes, damaged muscles were known to regain strength, but many patients would leave the hospital with permanent disabilities.

Charlie's problems had centred around his respiratory system. He'd spent the past two months in an iron lung. Pneumonia then invaded his lungs, and his weakened body was unable to cope. Everyone who knew Charlie mourned his death.

"How are you today, Signey?" Laura turned the little girl on her side and rubbed her back. Big blue eyes met the soft hazel eyes of the nurse and a hint of a smile graced the youngster's mouth. "I'll just give you a little massage." Her long-fingered hands moved over the girl's arms and legs, gently bringing some circulation into the weak muscles. "There. Doesn't that feel better?" This time Laura was rewarded with a smile. She tickled the tiny chin and smoothed the blonde hair before moving on to her next patient.

Laura gradually made her way around the room, trying to meet the needs of her young charges. Tall and slim, she wore a crisp, white uniform, with white nylon stockings and white rubber-soled shoes. Her copper-red hair was pulled back into a bun and partially covered by her nurse's cap. Strands of the naturally curled hair threatened to escape the confines of the bobby-pins holding it in place. Nearing the nurses' station she reached for the charts and reviewed the changes occurring on the previous shift.

The staff at the Children's Hospital in Winnipeg worked as quickly and as efficiently as possible. Daily tasks took on a new meaning when the wards were bursting with patients. This polio epidemic was reaching record numbers and causing panic across the province. Considered a disease that spread during the summer months, polio had affected more than eight hundred Manitobans in 1952. The numbers for 1953 were already over the two thousand mark.

Jessica, another nurse and Laura's close friend, walked toward Laura. She leaned over and whispered. "Let's meet for lunch. You've got to fill me in on your date."

Jessica was referring to a disastrous evening that Laura wasn't sure she wanted to talk about. Lately she was too exhausted to have a social life. She raised her eyebrows and drew the corners of her mouth down, implying the subject should be put to rest.

Ignoring her friend's reluctance, Jessica pointed at her watch and silently mouthed, "Later."

Coming from an Irish-Catholic background, Laura's parents assumed she'd find a nice Irish-Catholic man to marry. Her last birthday cake had been adorned with twenty-four candles, and her family never missed an opportunity to remind her there wasn't any time to waste. Her sister, Hilary, had married Frank O'Sullivan after she attained her teaching certificate. Frank liked to boast of his family roots in Drogheda, north of Dublin. They had two children, putting even more pressure on Laura to move in the same direction.

The children on the ward had finished their lunch when the two nurses made their way to the cafeteria. They joined two other nurses at a table in the noisy room and exchanged the news of the day. As soon as the others went back to work, Jessica pounced on Laura.

"Okay, I want to hear all the details. How was Thomas?"

"Jess, it was a total flop. Thomas is a nice man, but –"

"But he's not the one for you. I know, I know, I've heard you say that about your dates at least a million times."

"He looked like a leprechaun. When you're dressed in green from head to toe, how can you expect to be taken seriously?" Laura frowned while Jessica tried to hide her mirth. She failed and drew a deeper frown from Laura.

"Isn't he a banker, or something along that line?"

"Yes, Jess, he's absolutely perfect – Irish, Catholic and a good job." Laura's tone was sarcastic. "I wish my family would marry him and give me a break."

Colin O'Neil, Laura's father, told her she was being too selective. There were several young men who'd expressed an interest in Laura that Mr. O'Neil would have been proud to have for a son-in-law. It didn't help that Laura's mother and sister had also taken his side.

"Your Mr. Right is out there somewhere. I don't want you getting married just to please your family."

"No, my sister Hilary has already done that. Not that Frank isn't nice enough, but I often feel there's something missing between them."

"So, is Thomas off the list, or will some new clothes make him the man for you?"

"Definitely off the list. It actually wasn't so much the clothes, but something he said that bothered me."

"What did he say?"

"He asked me, 'How can you work with those cripples?' The way he said it made my skin crawl."

"Dare I ask what your reply was?" Jessica's expression indicated she knew Laura well enough to know that she wouldn't let a remark like that hang in the air. She was too outspoken and too dedicated to her patients for that.

"I just told him that being a nurse was great, except for all the sick people." Laura replied smugly.

"You didn't."

"I did."

"And I suppose you said it with that delightful tone in your voice."

"Right again."

"In other words, you're not expecting a call from him, are you?"

"Not if he's half as smart as my father thinks he is." Laura sipped the last of her coffee. Her eyes sparkled in defiance. Her full lips broke into a wide smile, displaying even white teeth. "I guess I've read too many books and seen too many movies. I want the fairytale, like you and Jeff. Find me a man who looks at me the way Jeff looks at you. Maybe my father's right, and I'm living in a dream world."

"There's nothing wrong with dreaming." Jessica patted her friend's hand. "But, we better put our dreams aside for now and get back to work."

Back on the ward, Laura resumed her tasks of assessing patients and noting any changes on the individual charts. Dispensing medications would follow. Sometimes, Laura thought, it would be such a relief to run away from all her responsibilities. Maybe Thomas' remark had triggered this feeling of restlessness growing within her. Why did she want to work in these surroundings? A sigh escaped her lips as she gazed over the ward and looked at the many children. The answer was simple. They needed her.

The happy chatter of the children streaming home from school diverted Rose. Her mind was forever in a Winnipeg hospital with her four-year-old daughter, Signey. It seemed ages ago that Signey and her siblings were playing in the yard and arguing over who was 'It' in a game of Tag. The rambunctious teasing of just over two weeks ago had been irritating, but Rose would give anything to have those days back.

"Adam loves Beth, la,la,la,la," nine-year-old Karen chanted at her older brother as they burst through the back door.

Adam grabbed his sister and tried to gag her mouth. The slight blush on his cheeks brought a smile to Rose's lips. Adam certainly had good taste. Beth's parents, Jon and Elin, were good friends of Daniel and Rose. She hoped that Adam, at twelve years of age, would postpone the romance for a while.

Alexander jumped in to help his brother. "You've got a big mouth, Karen!" He'd been his big brother's shadow for most of his seven years and had no intention of sharing him with a girl.

"Yeah, Karen, you've got a big mouth." Adam echoed Alexander's words.

"Okay, that's enough. There's fresh tea biscuits for you." Rose disentangled the group with playful hugs. "How was school today?"

"I hit a home run, Mama. The ball flew over everybody's head. It went way out into the field."

Karen's excitement was short-lived.

"Not that far – if Edith had caught the ball on third base you'd have been out." Adam's translation of the event differed.

A stern look from Rose put an end to more analysis. "Good for you, Karen. *Pabbi* will be happy to hear about your home run when he gets home. I hope you still have some muscles left to do the chores." Many children used the Icelandic word *Pabbi* for father. English was spoken more frequently in homes with school-aged children but in most homes, Icelandic was the first language to be learned. English was taught before the school years started.

Conversation reverted to chores and homework. Each member of the family had chores. There were four cows to be milked by hand. Water pails for the house needed to be filled from the backyard well and wood blocks needed to be split for the woodstove, which held a prominent spot in the kitchen.

The kitchen was the gathering place in the house. Company would visit around the table close to the coffeepot. In winter, the kitchen was the warmest room in the house, with the woodstove providing a cozy warmth, as well as the aromatic smells of meals and baking.

As the Bergursson children spread home-churned butter on their tea biscuits, their neighbour, Margaret Gustafsson was riding by on her bicycle. The mail had come in and she was expecting a parcel from her daughter in Gimli. Margaret and Ingvar, Jon's parents, also had two grown daughters. The girls were both married, one living in Riverton and the other in Gimli.

Margaret enjoyed needlework and many of her homemade gifts were displayed in island homes and beyond. If there was a special birthday party, a new baby, or a bridal shower, Margaret's gift was always a handmade treasure. She was expecting some embroidery floss to finish a cushion cover. It was also a good excuse to hear news from Gimli.

Communication was minimal between communities. Most people had a telephone but all calls went through the one telephone operator on the island, with the exception of those sharing a party line. It was considered frivolous to use the telephone except for important calls. The ride into the village was just over one mile for Margaret. She used her bicycle as her mode of travel for the summer, visiting her friends on a regular basis. Biking by the two-room school in the village Margaret noticed the new teacher, Miss Taylor, descending the steps. Margaret offered a greeting with a friendly wave. The young teacher wore a stylish gathered skirt in a muted green cotton print. The co-ordinating button front, short-sleeved blouse was tucked neatly into the skirt's waistband. At the end of the school day Miss Taylor's hair was still well-groomed in a pageboy style.

Margaret stopped at the roadside. "Hello, Miss Taylor, it's nice to see you again. How are you liking our island?"

"Hello. I like everything very well, thanks." Miss Taylor had room and board at the home of the ferry captain, Kristjan and his wife, Thora. In the few weeks since school started, Miss Taylor had been busy getting organized and getting acquainted with all the families. She taught grades one to six in one classroom and an island lady, Mrs. Marinsson, taught high school, grades seven to eleven in the other classroom. This was Miss Taylor's first teaching position. Her classroom enthusiasm had won over her thirty-two pupils. Since the first day of school her students had gone home and told their families about the pretty teacher who wore beautiful clothes.

"Have you met most of the islanders?"

"I have met a lot of people. Everyone is so kind. Everywhere I go I'm offered something to eat. I'm afraid I'll outgrow all my clothes." Miss Taylor smiled and continued, "I'd never tasted *ponnukokur* before I came here. They're delicious."

"They are good. They're a traditional Icelandic dainty. We'll have to teach you how to make them."

Ponnukokur were thin crepes fried on a hot pan, sprinkled with sugar and rolled up. In Iceland, they were served with whipped cream and fruit.

"Oh, they look tricky to make."

The two women walked north towards Fred's Store, Margaret pushing her bicycle and Miss Taylor carrying a cardigan and school papers.

"Wait until after fishing season. We have a dance in the hall and everybody takes goodies to serve with coffee." With a grin and sparkle in her eye, Margaret said, "And you will meet all the fishermen. We have a few single ones who might catch your eye."

"Oh." Miss Taylor blushed, "I'm not looking for a fisherman."

A little high-and-mighty, Margaret mused, choosing to ignore the statement. She turned the front wheel of the bicycle toward the front of the store. "I'm hoping to find some embroidery floss in my mail today. My daughter in Gimli is sending some red and green, so I can finish the cushion I've been embroidering."

"I should check and see if Thora has picked up our mail. She usually does, but it won't take long to find out. Do you embroider a lot, Mrs. Gustafsson?"

"I like most needlework, especially knitting and crocheting. I often embroider on pillow-cases and tablecloths, and sometimes cushions."

"I'm afraid I haven't tried to do any of those things." Miss Taylor pulled the store's door shut behind them.

"We'll need to start a list of things to teach you." Margaret smiled.

The two women had reached the back corner of Fred's Store where the post office was located. Behind the wicket there was a wall of shelves sectioned off into cubbyholes. Each square cubbyhole was marked by family name. Three hundred and fifty people lived on the island and the postmaster had targeted each one to a family box.

Fred handed Margaret her mail which included a small parcel. "Here you go, Margaret." Passing the mail through the wicket, he glanced over at Miss Taylor. "Thora was in earlier and took a couple of letters for you."

"I thought she'd do that. Thanks." The teacher turned to leave.

"It was nice talking to you, Miss Taylor. See you again." Margaret eyed her speculatively.

Miss Taylor smiled and left the store.

"She seems quite uppity. I told them on the school board that hiring a city-girl was a mistake."

"Miss Taylor?" Fred raised his eyebrows at Margaret. "Everyone thinks she's an excellent teacher. The kids are always talking about her."

"Just wait until she starts encouraging the children to leave the island and see the bright lights of the city."

"We'll have our own bright lights in a few weeks," Fred reasoned.

"I'm not so sure that's a good idea. Mark my words, Fred, this island will never be the same again. We've got a good life here that's changing fast. Look at that ferry, for instance. There were people coming here this summer just to have a picnic."

"Well, Margaret, you won't hear me complaining about that. Most of the island visitors stop here at the store."

"You young people think you know it all. We'll see. I saw Ben drive by wearing his suit and tie this morning. I guess he's hoping to impress those engineers." Margaret slid a tin of Blue Ribbon coffee off the store shelf on her way to the front counter. Fred quietly shook his head and followed her. At the front counter he wrote up a receipt for her purchase.

Fred's store offered much more than a postal service. Staples like flour, sugar, coffee and tea were in constant supply. Fresh fruit and vegetables were seasonal, while canned goods were always available. A gas pump stood in front of the store.

Fred often told a story from the previous winter. One of the islanders had come into the store, stamping his feet and rubbing his hands together trying to shake off the winter chill. He had called out to Fred, "Fill 'er up." Fred had donned his fur cap, big parka, woollen mitts and big winter boots and headed out the door. A few feet outside, he looked up to see the old man's horse tethered to the gas pump.

Happy to have received her parcel, Margaret gathered her mail and tin of coffee for her return ride home.

"Give those twins a big hug for me, Fred. Bye, now."

"See you on Friday. Bye, Margaret."

Fred saw many of the islanders on the two mail days each week – Tuesdays and Fridays. Often they'd assemble and share news, tell a few tall stories or argue about politics. Lately, most of the discussions centred around the power lines. For the majority of islanders this progressive move toward electricity was welcomed. However, some of the old-timers argued aggressively against it. Once in a while tempers flew but usually by the next mail day any disagreements were forgotten. Unless, Fred thought, someone was in a disagreement with Oli. Oli tended to harbour hurt feelings longer than anyone else. He lived by the creed to stay mad until you got even. And so, some arguments lasted longer in Oli's mind.

Fred loved his store. It had always been a part of his life. His father had been one of the first store owners on the island. He remembered, as a boy, arranging stock on the shelves and packing groceries into bags and boxes. He'd spent many hours working alongside his father. Six years earlier everything changed. The man who he considered to be larger than life was left an invalid following a stroke. Fred's sister lived in Selkirk and to be close to a doctor, Fred's parents made the move there. The family home next door to the store became Fred's. So did the store. He married Kristine his childhood sweetheart and now they were the proud parents of four-year-old twins, Peter and Paul.

When Fred glanced out the window, Margaret was packing her mail and tin of coffee into the wire basket attached to the bicycle's handlebars. With one foot on a pedal and the other still on the ground, she pushed the bicycle forward stepping through the gap to settle on the other pedal, and steered onto the road. Fred grinned to himself as he watched the agile woman cycle out of sight. Margaret was a known busybody and if she felt it was required, showed no hesitation in offering advice and opinions. Fred's age group always said, "When in doubt, ask Margaret," but in fact would never dream of doing so. When the young men were building the wooden cribs for the power line, Margaret became a critic. "You boys think you're smarter than the government engineers?" In the end, proving an error in judgment on Margaret's part made success so much sweeter.

The back door of the store opened and Kristine and the twins came in with afternoon coffee. Refreshed from their nap, the twins were full of energy. They always enjoyed spending time in the store with their father.

"Hello, *Pabbi*!" the boys called out.

"Well, it's about time you came with my coffee." Fred half-wrestled and half-hugged the blue-eyed, blond boys. Kristine unwrapped some fresh cinnamon buns for a snack. In between customers, Fred enjoyed this family time. Often in the mornings Kristine helped Fred in the store. The boys knew how to stack things on the bottom shelves. They tried sweeping the floor but so far hadn't conquered that task. Fred hoped that in time, they would take as much pride in the store as he always had.

Waving a greeting to Margaret riding by, Rose saw Amma Anna, Ben and Daniel's mother, walking toward the children. Because the children had two grandmothers living on the island, they'd added the Icelandic title of 'Amma' before each given name. Amma Anna lived in the family's original homestead. Her husband, Ben Senior, had died as a result of an accident. Five years prior he'd been crushed at the sawmill when a stand collapsed. He had succumbed to his injuries before reaching hospital. Daniel and Rose built their home when they got married, leaving Ben and his mother in the big old house. Because the homes were close together, many things were done together. Ben and Daniel worked as a team in all their endeavours. Besides the fishing, they were amassing a beef herd. For personal use, they had four milk cows and raised a few chickens and some pigs.

Often, when Ben was away, Rose invited Amma Anna to eat supper with them. Amma Anna walked into the yard and saw Adam wielding the axe by the woodpile. Karen was pumping water into a pail and Alexander was heading toward the house carrying a basket of chicken eggs. Rose was going into the barn to milk the cows. Adam would help with the milking as soon as he had stowed the split wood in the wood-box by the back door of the house. When everyone helped, the chores didn't take long.

Later, the children circled the round oak table with their schoolbooks while Rose and Amma Anna cooked supper. Pickerel fillets sizzled in lard in a large cast iron fry pan. Each fillet was thinly coated in flour and sprinkled with salt and pepper. Potatoes and beans boiled in a pot next to the fry pan.

"Homework almost done?" Rose added sliced onion to the pan of fish. Affirmative nods and mumbles answered her. The youngsters cleared their schoolbooks off the table. Karen and Amma Anna set the table and Rose filled the serving bowls.

During the fishing seasons, the family ate fish often. Rose always fried the pickerel and sauger fillets. She boiled sunfish in a pot with potatoes. Whitefish was best roasted in the oven with bread stuffing.

Amma Anna heard about Karen's home run, Miss Taylor's nice hair and one of the boys falling off his bicycle and skinning his knee.

"I wonder if Uncle Ben has seen Signey." Alexander pushed the food around his plate, his appetite waning.

"Maybe he's with her right now." Karen spread some green tomato pickles over her potatoes.

"Why can't we go and see her?" Alexander's voice whined.

"The doctor said it would be best not to visit her because it will make her sad when we leave her again." Although Rose spoke in a patient voice, she had a difficult time accepting the doctor's recommendation. "We'll see her when the doctor says she's ready to come home."

"But when, Mama?" The whine was turning into tearful despair.

"When the doctor says she's ready,"Amma Anna repeated in a soft voice. "Signey needs to be in the hospital until she's better. I'm sure it won't be long."Amma Anna met Rose's gaze across the table. Rose realized they were both desperately wanting to believe her words.

"Let's hope that Ben is able to see her and bring home some good news." Rose tried to maintain a positive attitude about Signey's progress in front of everyone. It was late at night that she quietly wept into her pillow trying to alleviate the fear she felt. People had died from polio and others were left permanently crippled. Her faith was strong, but Rose questioned how her God could let this happen to a child, her sweet little Signey who had done no wrong. She'd been taken away from all that was familiar and it broke Rose's heart that she couldn't be with her.

Chapter 2

"Congratulations, Mr. Bergursson." The government engineer extended his hand. "Can you imagine all the lights shining in Hecla?"

"Thanks. And yes, I can see the glow already." Ben's face beamed with satisfaction.

It was nearly four in the afternoon when Ben concluded his meeting with Manitoba Hydro officials. The final stage to electrification for every islander was planned to completion. Ben stood tall as he arranged his papers and slid them into an envelope. His calloused hands and the weathered skin on his face spoke in contrast to the tweed suit he wore. He was obviously an outdoor man. In the government office he looked very much at home while presenting his ideas.

The boy who had joined the air force with the excitement of a tourist had returned two years later, weary and disillusioned, with no travel plans in mind. His wanderlust was replaced with a deep commitment to the island. The cocky confidence had become proud assurance. He wasn't easily intimidated.

"It seems we've found answers to all the questions." The senior official's eyes met Ben's with definite approval. "I've got to say, though, I really never imagined we'd reach this stage."

"Well, we didn't have anything to lose by trying. And, it didn't hurt that we were stubborn Icelanders."

"I think it took more than stubbornness to build those cribs. I'm glad everything is turning out well for you."

The man's admission spoke volumes for Ben. Throughout the negotiations, Ben had sensed the official's lack of confidence in the ideas outlined by the islanders. But, he wasn't about to rub their noses in that. With the diplomacy of a statesman, he'd met with them several times to discuss the necessary steps in bringing electricity to his community.

Ben drove the few blocks to the hospital, where Signey was a patient. His mind was still cluttered with details from the meeting.

He was mentally mapping out the next steps and plan of action. He parked the car and entered through the front door of the hospital. The receptionist at the front desk steered him to the flight of stairs that led to the ward Signey was on. Walking into the second floor ward brought Ben to a sudden halt. His preoccupation hadn't prepared him for the scene before his eyes. There were beds and cribs everywhere. One nurse was distributing medication, another was exercising the thin legs of a little boy. A volunteer read a story to two patients. The forlorn cries of one child reached his ears. But it was the hospital smells, smells he associated with sickness and pain that caused him to pale.

In an instant he was back on an English ward during the war. His leg injury had been minimal in comparison to those of his friends. It had been eight years before, but the memory was crystal clear. It might have been yesterday.

During his training in Shilo, Manitoba, Ben had become friends with George Meyerton. George hailed from Stonewall, just north of Winnipeg, and he and Ben quickly became inseparable. The two young men were members of the 408 Bomber Squadron, nicknamed 'Goose'. After six months of training in Canada, they were posted to England and stationed at RAF Linton-On-Ouse in Yorkshire, where they completed their training.

Ben was a pilot officer. Because George had some previous flying experience, he earned his pilot's wings. For several months they lived a relatively charmed life. Their crew was all-Canadian and all their flights were conducted at night. Their missions had been successful, and they'd returned safely to their base in England. Until the last time. They dropped their bombs and were navigating into their homeward flight when they were hit by flak. Three men were hurt, Ben's injuries being the least serious. George was the worst. His unconscious body slumped in the seat next to Ben. With only one of its four Rolls-Royce Merlin engines working, the Halifax Bomber limped home with Ben at the controls.

The next morning, the airfield ground crew stood in amazement when they saw the plane. Flak had pounded the bomber, resulting in holes of varying shapes and sizes. One hole was large enough to crawl through. The one working engine had been sputtering when they landed.

Ben camped out beside George's bed and the nurses gave up trying to keep Ben in his own bed. When George died on the fourth day, a part of Ben had died too. He'd been overcome with grief and the guilt that he had lived when George had died.

The war ended two months later, but victory came at a price. Amid the cheers and toasts to freedom, thoughts always went to the fallen comrades that were buried on foreign soil. Victory had come too late for George. When Ben had boarded the Lancaster that would fly him home, he'd left without the friend who'd always been at his side, and the girl who held his heart.

Eighteen-year-old Ben, who enlisted looking for glamour and excitement in 1943, had turned into a twenty-year-old in 1945, longing for the peace and quiet of Hecla Island. He returned to the island and pushed his painful memories into the recesses of his mind. He never spoke of his war experiences, except the good times the air crew had enjoyed when on leave. Although he was a trained pilot, Ben vowed never to set foot inside an airplane again.

"Can I help you?" The nurse's voice jolted Ben back to the present. She eyed him warily, noticing that he was visibly shaken.

"I'm here to see Signey Bergursson."

"Just one moment, please." She walked to the nurses' station and spoke to another nurse. After several minutes, the other nurse approached Ben.

"Are you Mr. Bergursson?"

"Yes, I wanted to see how Signey is doing." Ben looked directly into the nurse's hazel eyes. A sprinkle of freckles over her nose were the only markings in her otherwise flawless complexion. She hastily tucked a truant tendril of her curly red hair behind her ear. A small brass pin identified the nurse as Laura O'Neil RN.

"When I spoke to your wife," the nurse's voice was sympathetic, "I explained why we don't recommend visits to the young children. It can cause such homesickness. It could mean a longer recovery time."

"I know what Rose has been told. I'm Signey's uncle. I need to check on her to ease everyone's mind at home. Is there any way I could see her?"

The nurse maintained an air of authority and Ben thought it wouldn't be possible to see Signey. Then, the nurse's all-business facade softened and she said, "Come with me." Ben couldn't help but notice the dark, curly eyelashes outlining her expressive eyes. Creases lined her straight skirt and a tiny run had appeared in one of her white nylon stockings. With quick, short steps she led him to a window with a discreet lace curtain. He peered into a large room lined from wall to wall with more beds and cribs, separated only by enough space to walk between. "She's in the crib over there." The nurse pointed out Signey's crib near the far wall.

Ben's eyes looked at his little niece. She was lying on her back, her body still. Her large eyes stared into the ceiling. The gaunt lines of her thin face were circled by a blonde bob. Her head moved slightly when a nearby child spoke to her.

"Her left side is paralyzed." Nurse O'Neil said. "When she sits up, her head rests on her shoulder because her neck muscles aren't able to support the weight. She can stand but only if she holds onto something. I'm sorry that I can't give you better news."

"I understand, thanks for being so honest. The family's pretty scared."

Ben was moved by the compassion in the young nurse's voice. She explained some of the procedures used in revitalizing the weakened muscles. He could tell she didn't take her job lightly.

"We've had many successes. Some children regain their strength. There's always the hope that Signey will be one of those." Her positive attitude conveyed the message that Signey's condition wasn't hopeless. Ben appreciated her no-nonsense and optimistic approach. He was captivated by her alluring eyes and spontaneous smile.

Having found his equilibrium again, he observed her hands, noting the neatly clipped fingernails and the absence of a wedding ring.

Laura drew his attention to the attendant helping Signey to her feet. Unaware of her audience, Signey smiled at the therapist assisting her. Her head hung to one side and her left leg didn't have the strength to support her body. Her left arm was motionless. With gentle coaxing, the therapist stimulated her arms and legs with exercises.

"We try to give each child as much exercise as possible." Laura stated. "We use bathtubs for water exercise, but we don't have enough time or bathtubs to offer that daily. In the water, they have a buoyancy that gives them more movement with less exertion."

Ben's sideways glance caught the nurse assessing him. A faint blush coloured her cheeks.

"She's doing well." Ben's face softened. "Look how hard she's trying. That's my *litla elskan.*" His voice swelled with pride.

He was glad he'd come. Daniel and Rose would be happy to hear that Signey was responding well to her surroundings. The staff had impressed him also, especially the redhead standing beside him.

"Would it be alright if I spoke to her for a couple of minutes?" Ben understood the restrictions but he also wondered if a little contact from home wouldn't be a positive part of her recovery. He remembered the isolated feeling of being far from home and how seeing another

Canadian had helped to bridge the gap for him.

Laura hesitated. "A few minutes should be okay. The therapist is finished with her now."

Together Ben and Laura walked toward the crib. Up close, Ben noticed that Signey's limbs were even thinner.

"Hello, *elskan*. How's my big girl doing?" Ben reached his hand through the bars of the crib and held her tiny hand. Signey opened her eyes wide and a smile appeared on her face.

"I saw you doing your exercises. If you keep that up you'll be feeling better soon. I see you have a pretty doll to play with."

Signey's eyes shifted to view her toy. Then she smiled brightly at her uncle, dimpling her cheeks. She held the doll in the crook of her right arm. Ben stroked her left arm and noticed the muscle in her left shoulder was shrivelled and only skin and bone remained.

"Does your shoulder hurt?"

Signey slowly moved her head from side to side.

"That's good." Ben smiled at his niece, hoping to coax another grin from her. "Your pups told me to give you a kiss."

The girl's face lit up at mention of Dixie and Spike.

"Do you know what those dogs were doing yesterday?" Ben asked. "They were chasing a rabbit in the pasture behind the barn. The rabbit zigzagged and confused them so badly that they ran into each other and rolled on the ground." Ben acted out some of the dog's antics and drew the attention of some of the other patients. Signey smiled but the sadness in her eyes weighed heavily on him. He wished he could scoop her up and take her home. She hadn't spoken a word to him but she seemed to enjoy his stories from home.

A girl propelled a wheelchair in their direction. "Hello, my name is Donna. I read stories to Signey."

"That sure is nice. I know Signey loves to hear stories." Ben knew he should take his leave. Donna wheeled closer to the crib with a storybook in her lap. "I have to go now, Signey. I think Donna has a story for you." He leaned over the side rail and kissed his niece on the forehead. "I'll see you soon, when you come home. Keep working hard on your exercises." Ben was distressed when Signey's eyes filled with tears. He stayed beside the crib until Donna had captured her attention. He then slipped away with a wave and a smile. Signey responded by slowly moving the fingers of her right hand.

Ben found his way back to the nurses' desk and the pretty redheaded nurse. He wanted to thank her for allowing him to visit with Signey.

In a lighter mood, he said, "She's a strong little Icelander. She'll be just fine."

Laura responded to his smile, "Does she have any Irish background? Then there would be no doubt of inherited strength."

In an exaggerated Icelandic accent, Ben retaliated, "Our Vikings were masters of the land and sea – second to none!"

They shared a laugh and then Laura looked uncomfortable. His eyes asked the question before his voice found the words. "How late are you working tonight?"

Appearing to be taken aback, her face flushed. "I – I work until eight."

"I was wondering if I could buy you supper after your shift. You've been very reassuring and I'd like to thank you. What do you say?" His heart lurched, anticipating her answer. A room full of government officials hadn't frightened him, but this red-haired Irish lass was causing some churning nervousness.

He realized that several other staff members were starting to notice the time she was spending with him. Aware that there would be many tasks to be completed before the end of her shift, Ben hoped she would make the right decision. Still, she hedged.

"There is no need for that, Mr. Bergursson."

"I bet you don't go out with strangers." He laughed as he realized they hadn't even introduced themselves. "I'm Ben and I see you are Laura." Ben was in his element now, his charm working its magic over Laura.

There was a slight pause then she said, "There's a restaurant at the end of the street called Tipperary. I could meet you there."

"Tipperary....hmm... Maybe we can order some Irish stew." His smile indicated his approval with her suggestion. "I'm staying about three blocks from here so that'll be perfect."

His attention reverted back to Signey, who was lying on her side. Donna had wedged her wheelchair in between Signey's crib and the next bed and was still reading her a story. Signey was listening in earnest.

"I'll be going home tomorrow to Hecla Island. That's where I'm from. I had some business in the city and promised I'd check up on Signey. Everyone at home is worried about her."

"She's a popular girl. We have volunteers who come in to read to the children or play card games. And older patients, like Donna, are helpful when it comes to entertaining the younger ones."

"Thanks again. I'm glad I saw Signey. I know she's in good hands."

"We do our best." An appreciative warmth gleamed in her eyes.

"See you after eight at the Tipperary."

"See you then." Laura blushed. Ben walked toward the exit.

"I saw you hogging that gorgeous guy, Laura. Tell all, who is he?" Jessica demanded of Laura.

"His name is Ben and he's Signey Bergursson's uncle." Her cheeks flamed as she added, "And I'm meeting him later."

Jessica nearly fell over. "Aren't you the sly one – want me to come along? I'll just call Jeff..."

"No, I'll have enough babysitters. I'm meeting him at the Tipperary." Laura didn't need Jessica and her husband holding her hand.

Jessica laughed. "The Tipperary? Does he know what he's getting into? God, now I feel sorry for the poor thing."

Laura laughed, too. It probably was a mistake to meet someone she knew nothing about, but her Irish cousin would take good care of her. Sean O'Neil owned the Tipperary and was protective of her, since she didn't have any brothers. She knew his eyebrows would arch when she introduced the handsome Icelander.

It was time to distribute the evening meal to the patients and then it would be time to prepare for the night. By eight o'clock when the shift changed, the ward should be settling down. During the night shift, nurses had more time to catch up on the necessary paperwork and resupply the inventory, but the hospital never really quieted down for the staff. Many of the sick children suffered pain in their affected muscles and were unable to sleep well.

While the stainless steel kettle heated water on the woodstove to wash dishes, Rose and Amma Anna stacked the plates and fed the few leftovers to Dixie and Spike. The family pets tried to look hungry, but their plump bodies told a different story.

The unused milk in the jug was stored in the cellar under the house. The cellar was cool and acted as a refrigerator. Before Daniel and Rose had built their house with the cellar, the family had used an ice house in the backyard for cooling milk and cream and preserving other foodstuff.

Ice houses were made with large blocks of ice covered with hay or sawdust for insulation. Some were makeshift structures, while others had walls, a door and a roof. More hay and sawdust was packed around the building to maintain the ice blocks throughout the heat of summer. Some moose and deer meat was salted to keep it from spoiling, but most meat was canned to be preserved for the summer months.

"Are you going to Thora's tomorrow?" Amma Anna reminded Rose about the 'Knit-A-Bit' Club scheduled to gather in the afternoon.

"No, I already told Thora I wouldn't be coming. Daniel will be coming home and I want to hear news of Signey as soon as Ben is back."

"I have that new sweater pattern I wanted to show the ladies..." The older woman's voice faded. Rose could tell Amma Anna's heart wasn't in it. But life went on. It didn't seem to matter what a person's troubles were, housework and chores needed to be done and families needed to go on.

In the two weeks since Signey had gone to hospital, Rose had lost weight. She hadn't been sleeping well. She just hoped Ben would have encouraging news.

"They'll love to see that pattern. You have to go, even though I'm not going." Rose hesitated a moment, then continued, "I'm just tired of everyone asking. I know they all mean well and are anxious, but it's so hard..." She swallowed a sob. Amma Anna hastened to give her a comforting pat on the hand.

"I know, I know. She will get better. I truly believe that."

Rose pulled herself together. She didn't want to upset the children. They were scared too. Rose knew she would feel better when Daniel came home. She could always draw strength from him. Usually, the fishermen stayed in camp for several days at a time. This fall, however, Daniel was coming home more often.

"The kettle is hot." Rose poured the hot water into an enamel dishpan. "Karen, it's time for dishes." Amma Anna took Karen's place in a card game with Adam and Alexander. Washing dishes was part of the evening ritual – the girl time in the kitchen. Rose and Karen had many discussions over the dishpan. They both enjoyed the sharing of ideas, confidences and light-hearted gossip.

Daniel and Jon had finished their evening clean-up, which was similar to the home ritual. The fish camp, shared by Ben, Daniel and Jon was a crude building but provided many of the creature comforts of home. The wood heater was central in the one-room structure, and served as a cookstove. They had an old table, some wooden chairs, and cots to sleep on. The camp was situated east of Hecla Island on the southeast shore of Black Island. The fishing grounds in the vicinity had been held by their fathers before them. There was no paper to declare the area as theirs. It was simply an unwritten code to respect another fisherman's space.

"Hopefully this wind will die down by morning." Daniel watched the swaying treetops around the camp. "We were lucky to finish lifting all the nets."

Strong winds meant the fishing skiffs stayed anchored in the harbour. There was no fish that was worth risking a life over.

"Good thing you came to my rescue. That squall looked kind of ugly for a few minutes." Jon spoke with a distinct Icelandic accent. His facial expression and slight shake of his head emphasized his words.

The squall had blown up quickly, just as all squalls do. It hadn't seemed menacing and Jon continued to pick fish from the net he'd just begun lifting. The sudden wind hit with the impact of a small hurricane, sending everything in the fishing boat askew. Jon pushed the full fish boxes toward the boat's centre to prevent the boat from capsizing. He bailed water with a pail as wave after wave threatened to plummet the skiff. The strong wind lashed at him, throwing him off-balance.

Something grabbed the boat, turning it swiftly, and pulled the back of the boat downward. Too late, Jon realized he'd forgotten to tilt the boat motor's propeller up and it had tangled in the anchor line of the net, holding the boat at a fatal angle. Frantically, he bailed water but was no match for the pounding waves. As suddenly as the squall had hit, it blew over. Exhausted, Jon scooped pail after pail of water out of the skiff and tried to reach the anchor line. Daniel could see from the angle of the boat that something was amiss with Jon. Daniel sped over the short distance and was able to untangle the propeller from the anchor line.

Daniel, too, experienced the squall first-hand but had fared better than Jon. A small bay had provided some shelter for him, diminishing the effects of the storm.

"Yeah, we sure were lucky." Daniel met Jon's serious look. "I know I'll always respect the danger of a squall after that one."

Jon nodded in agreement. "I wasn't sure we'd get all of Ben's nets lifted this morning, but I'm glad we did. I wonder how things went with the government guys?"

"Ben will have the deal done. I'm sure we can count on that. They'd better send enough workers to hook everyone up. Everybody's getting impatient, now that we're so close. Imagine... a switch for a light, a switch for heat, a switch to cook. It wasn't long ago that the only switch we knew about was the willow switch across the backside." They both laughed at the joke and at the same time, winced at the memory.

Ellen Taylor daydreamed between marking exercise books piled on her desk beneath her room's solitary window. The spacious upstairs room in Kristjan and Thora's house, where she had room and board, bore many accessories she wasn't accustomed to. The bed had layers of sheets and blankets topped with a handmade quilt. Other furniture included a washstand, an armoire and a chair. A filled water jug and soap dish stood beside the fancy basin on the wash stand. Under the bed, a chamber pot with a lid was discretely stashed to use instead of the outhouse during the night. Appalled at the bathroom facilities in both home and school, Ellen had hidden her displeasure to the best of her ability. It hadn't occurred to the new teacher that a school within driving distance of Winnipeg would be without basic amenities. Rather than admit defeat and return home, she was determined to tolerate these uncivilized conditions.

"Ellen, come for supper." Thora's voice carried up the stairs.

"Coming." Ellen welcomed the distraction. Apart from the obvious discomforts, she was surprised to be enjoying her teaching experience on Hecla Island. Her family lived in Winnipeg and had questioned her desire to teach in such a remote community. She didn't expect to go home until Christmas. But since she'd lived on her own while obtaining her teaching certificate, the separation wasn't a problem.

"Supper smells delicious, Thora." The teacher took her seat in the dining room. The bay window in the dining area offered a view of the village similar to the one from her upstairs room.

"I made a meat pie. It's a change from the regular fare."

"What's wrong with the usual. I'm a meat and potatoes man, myself." Kristjan teased Thora. "I'm used to being outnumbered by women, but don't forget who's the boss around here." His eyes sparkled as he passed his plate to be served a helping of the meat pie. Their two daughters were married and living on the island. Elin was married to Jon Gustafsson and Gudrun was married to Sam Austmansson.

"Moose meat with potatoes and mixed vegetables in gravy. I'm serving it in a different way, that's all." Thora placed a wedge of pie on each of the three plates before sitting down. Thick gravy oozed out of the flaky crust.

"Thanks, Thora." Ellen looked over the contents on her plate. She wished Thora wouldn't elaborate on the ingredients. Why did she have to name the animal they were eating?

"What's going on out there?" Thora's attention diverted to a car stopped in the middle of the road. "Someone must be having trouble."

Kristjan and Ellen joined the watch, but all three kept eating the evening meal when another vehicle slowed down. After a brief discussion between the two drivers, the second car was angled so the car hoods faced each other.

"Looks like battery trouble," Kristjan said. "It's Oli. And right in front of the church. He must've fallen asleep during the last service."

"Behave yourself, Kristjan." Thora's smile took the edge off her words.

The church was just to the south of Kristjan and Thora's house. It had been built in 1927. One carpenter had been hired, Thora had explained, and the rest of the labour came from the islanders. The Lutheran faith ran deep among the Icelandic community and a great deal of love and pride went into the construction.

"There goes Oli. His car battery must have just needed a boost." Kristjan was now able to concentrate on his meal.

The rest of the buildings in the village were strung out along the bay's shoreline and were visible through the dining room window. Fred's store, the school and the community hall faced the lake on the land side of the road. The sawmill stood across from the store, and the fish packing shed bordered the harbour dock. Scattered houses dotted the remainder of the scenic landscape.

"Ben left this morning for Winnipeg. He said everything's still on time for hooking up the electricity." Kristjan helped himself to a second wedge. "I told him he's getting us into lots of trouble."

The older couple shared a smile as the trio finished their meal. Ellen failed to see the humour. Surely everyone wanted to modernize their homes. But, she surmised, I guess if you don't know any better, you simply don't know what you're missing.

She'd been engaged to be married. Richard had been perceived as an excellent catch by her parents. He was a lawyer in his father's law firm, handsome, and a gentleman. Ellen's friends didn't share her parents' viewpoint. He was 'boring and full of himself,' they would say and gradually they spent less time with her.

When Ellen realized she would be sacrificing teaching to become a society wife, she broached the topic with Richard. He failed to see that being his wife would not be enough for her. Arguments ensued and she called off the engagement. Ellen cancelled the wedding plans and focussed on her dream of becoming a schoolteacher.

When she applied for the teaching job her closest friend Sara had been supportive. She encouraged her to make a fresh start. "Don't think of exiling yourself, just think of it as a grand adventure." In fact, Ellen planned on exiling herself. She wanted to get as far away from Richard and her parents as possible. She wanted her own life, not an extension of her husband's. Looking back, Ellen was both amazed and proud that she'd found the courage to stand up for herself. Her mother was accustomed to others always falling in with her plans. Ellen applauded her own defiance, even if it meant adjusting to a primitive way of life in these backwoods.

Teaching grades one to six was a challenge but also rewarding. None of her students lacked discipline and they were eager to learn. There were some conflicts in personality, but generally speaking, they were well-behaved in school. Ellen was humbled by the high regard her young pupils held her in. She noticed how the girls admired her clothes and hair and took extra care not to disappoint them. Each morning she methodically brushed her shoulder-length hair, turning the ends under in a soft curl. The short brown bangs were pin-curled every night and combed into swirly curls in the morning. The pageboy hair style was popular in Winnipeg and complemented the angular shape of the teacher's face. Ellen had fine features that would be considered 'plain' if anyone saw her without her make-up. She artfully applied mascara and eyeshadow to emphasize her brown eyes. A hint of rouge gave colour to her pale cheeks and bright shades of lipstick caught the onlooker's eye, drawing attention to her small mouth. Her two front teeth were slightly overlapped, adding character to her otherwise straight smile.

During the lunch recess one rainy day, the girls wanted to do some hair styling. Ellen showed them how to make a French braid and a vertical roll. Thora's granddaughter Aldis was thirteen years old, with long hair, which Ellen dressed in a sophisticated bun. The boys left their game to watch and tease the girls, but laughingly returned to the game when Ellen thought she could try some styles on them. She enjoyed the friendly rapport she had with the children until word got back to her that some parents thought she was far too easy on them and was spoiling them. They expected discipline and learning the three Rs. Ellen took the remarks as advisory and while she still maintained a friendly nature with her charges, there would be no lack of education.

The Tipperary was a lively place, filled with Irish music and happy laughter. As soon as Ben walked through the front door he was engulfed in the atmosphere. A long oak bar ran the length of one wall. Behind the bar, mirrors covered the wall and reflected an elaborate collection of bottles on glass shelves. Photos of Ireland set the decorating theme throughout the restaurant. One photo in particular over the fireplace at the back of the large room caught Ben's attention. It was an enlarged picture of Ireland's green countryside. He'd often heard Ireland referred to as the Emerald Isle when he was overseas. The words *Erin Go Bragh* were painted into a mural on one wall along with shamrocks and Ireland's flag. In Gaelic, the ancient language of Ireland, the words meant 'Ireland forever'. In one corner, three musicians stamped their feet in tune with their flute, fiddle and guitar.

Sturdy stools lined the front of the bar. Most of the stools were occupied and the conversation carried an Irish accent. At the far end, a young man doted on the girl at his side. They seemed oblivious to the raucous men sharing the bar stools. The four men were swapping jokes and were well into their glasses of stout. Ben guessed they'd met here after work when he noticed the lunch kits stowed at their feet. Many of the dining tables were occupied. Ben was sure a special occasion was being recognized at one table where the eight patrons were attired in fancy dresses and suits. Other diners lingered over dessert and tea. At the table nearest the bar, a group of four women raised their glasses in a toast and let out a cheer.

With a hearty "What's yer pleasure, lad?", the bartender welcomed Ben into the fold.

"I'm meeting someone here." A quick survey over the crowd did not locate Laura.

"Time fer a pint? Who yer meetin'?" The bartender glanced around the tables.

"I'm meeting a girl named Laura O'Neil. Do you know if she's here?"

As the bartender poured stout into a large glass mug, Ben felt his scrutiny. His dark eyes studied Ben's face and didn't appear impressed by what he saw.

"She isn't here. How'd ya know our Laura?" The question was asked casually, but Ben sensed an air of ownership that didn't sit right.

"I know her as a nurse. How about you, is she family?"

"Aye, she is that." His eyes continued to study Ben.

The bartender placed the glass of stout in front of Ben as he settled on a bar stool. Ben hadn't ordered the drink, but he knew it was a test. The bartender's eyes scanned Ben, assessing the tweed suit he still wore. The glint in his eye annoyed Ben. Who did this guy think he was? When it came to tipping a liquor glass, an Icelander could keep up with an Irishman any day. Maybe it was his meeting with Laura that put the scowl on the barkeep's face. Ben hoped he wouldn't have to fight the man to his death to be able to dine with the pretty nurse.

With an attempt at casual conversation, Ben glanced around the room and commented, "Nice place you have here." He motioned to the picture over the fireplace and continued, "I was overseas during the war and that reminds me of some of the places I saw."

The scowl vanished and a new appraisal seemed to take place. The bartender's features softened. Ben wondered if the transformation occurred because of his praise of this man's homeland or his reference to the war.

"M'brother served overseas as well. I was blessed w' flat feet, so they turned m' down." His tone of voice altered with this confession.

Just as Ben wondered if the Irish lilt was put on, the bartender's face lit up. "Aye, here she is now. Laura, m'girl, this gent says he's here to meet ya'. Mind, lass, he has the look of a pirate."

"Behave yourself, Sean." Laura smiled as Ben's guffaw drew a few looks.

"I've never been called a pirate before, although I do have a boat."

"Here ye go, m'bonnie lass. A cuppa tea befittin' the finest nurse this side o'Dublin."

Ben could not help but openly admire Laura. Out of uniform, she had changed into a cotton print dress with a gathered skirt. Accenting the blue print, a blue belt cinched at her slim waist was the same shade as the thin cardigan. Her red curls were drawn together by a clip at the nape of her neck. Her large, sparkling eyes and bright smile caused a tightness in Ben's stomach. There was no doubt in his mind that she truly was a 'bonnie lass'.

"Don't worry about Sean. He's my cousin, and since I only have a sister, he's delegated himself as my older brother."

Ben let out a heavy sigh. "At first I thought he might be your boyfriend the way he was eyeing me." His relaxed grin softened his handsome features.

They found a table near the fireplace at the back of the dining area. For two people who had met only a few hours earlier, Ben and Laura fell into conversation like old friends. She told him about her work and her family. He described Hecla Island and his life as a fisherman. Laura learned more about Signey's family and about the islanders' quest for electricity. Before he realized it, he was commenting on the picture above the mantle that had appealed to him earlier and had reminded him of his time in Europe. She explained that her cousin Aiden, Sean's brother, had joined the armed forces.

"Most families had someone over there. At least your cousin and I were lucky enough to come home." Ben drained the coal-black tea from his cup. "That was good. How about some more dessert?" He steered the conversation away from the past.

"No thanks. That was great," Laura replied.

Throughout the evening, Sean had found several reasons to stop by their table. Instead of being annoyed, Ben chuckled with Laura as they tried to guess what his next excuse would be.

"If the Tipperary didn't exist, you wouldn't have met me tonight, would you?"

"No," she answered.

"I'm glad you did." His eyes shone with sincerity. "I feel like I've known you all my life."

"Me, too." Suddenly shy, Laura gazed into the burning embers in the fireplace. Ben's hand reached out and covered hers.

"I want to see you again, Laura." His voice was not questioning but stating a fact.

"I'd like that." Her eyes met his as the pact was made.

The hour was growing late. They had talked through the best Irish stew 'this side of Dublin', they had talked through an Irish bread pudding, which Ben still argued was his Amma's recipe, and they had talked through several cups of Irish tea, which Ben said was exactly like a tea blend his mother brewed. Ben hadn't laughed so much in a long time and he knew this Irish girl across the table was the reason for it.

"I guess Sean will be asking us to leave soon. Even Irishmen need their sleep."

Ben settled the bill. He took Laura's arm and they walked to the exit. At the bar, Sean joked with his patrons, "The Irish would've ruled the world if t'wasn't for whiskey. See ya again, Ben." With a big wave, he continued, "G'night, Laura, m'love."

Inside the car, Laura gave Ben directions to her home on Wolseley Avenue, where she lived with her parents. At the restaurant, Laura had mentioned her father was a newspaper editor with the *Winnipeg Tribune* and her mother was a primary school teacher.

Ben walked Laura to the front door. The windows were darkened. Her parents had obviously retired for the night.

"Did you say you need to be at work at ten in the morning?"

As she nodded in confirmation, Ben went on, "Let's have breakfast. I'll bring it. Is there a park near the hospital?"

"Yes, very near."

"It isn't an Irish park with a cousin on every bench?" His face lit up with laughter.

"No, but I can ask Sean to come if you'd be more comfortable."

When he kissed her, he drew her into his arms. Then he whispered into her ear, "I'll be here at eight to pick you up. Goodnight, *kaerasta min*."

He was gone before she could respond. She stood on the step watching the car go down the street. Laura didn't know the meaning of his last words, but she would bet money that they were Icelandic words of affection.

What had happened today? It seemed that one minute she was lamenting to Jessica about her pathetic social activities, and the next minute a handsome knight charged into her life. The car was blue, but in her eyes it was a white horse. Was she a fool? Probably. But how could dreams come true if you were afraid to dream? At least he hadn't been dressed in green from head to foot!

Was this real? When she had left the house that morning, she hadn't known Ben Bergursson existed. Now she couldn't wait until morning to see him again.

Chapter 3

The cuckoo clock in the O'Neil living room was announcing eight o'clock. Ben stood on the top step and knocked on Laura's front door.

Wearing cotton pants and a blouse, Laura opened the door and welcomed him. Because she kept her uniforms at the hospital, she was able to dress casually for the park.

"Good morning." Laura's sparkling eyes were a clear indication that she was happy to see him.

"Good morning." Ben winked at her. "We have perfect weather for the park."

"I'll just grab my things. My parents have left for work and the dog has finished his outdoor business." Laura counted off the mental list of things to do before locking the door. "Did you need me to bring anything for breakfast? Maybe some coffee?"

"Taken care of. I hope you like what I brought." Ben smiled, returning her admiring gaze. His business suit from yesterday had been replaced with navy twill pants and matching shirt.

The couple picked up the comfortable conversation they had enjoyed the night before. Laughter and a teasing banter came easily to both of them. They continued an argument over city living versus country life.

Laura guided Ben to the park, which was across the street from the hospital. They found a bench near an oak tree and Ben started unpacking the big brown paper bag. Few people frequented the park at this hour.

"I didn't know what you liked, besides Irish stew, so here goes. We've got muffins and fruit, buns with a ham and egg filling, and sausage rolls."

"You really didn't need to bring juice, milk *and* coffee. I can't believe it. Do you really expect me to eat all this?" Her jaw dropped in astonishment.

"Well, I thought I'd help you."

"Of course," she giggled. "Where should we start?"

They ate at a leisurely pace. Laura smiled at an elderly man who ambled by with his dog in tow. The dog was quick to sniff out the food but his master shortened the hold on his leash to prevent him from becoming an uninvited guest.

Ben was surprised to find himself oblivious to the city noises. In his experience, cities were a mass of traffic, cement and general mayhem. It was certainly not like lifting nets on Lake Winnipeg in the peace and quiet that nature offers. Here in this park, he felt at home. The trees and grass seemed to block out the traffic. He could hear birds. People walked by enjoying the flowers in an unrushed manner. But he also suspected that his sense of well-being at the moment had a lot to do with Laura.

"Try this sausage roll." Ben leaned closer, holding the roll up to her lips. When she opened her mouth and took a bite, he grimaced. "Watch the fingers. I need them for picking fish."

She covered her mouth with her hand, trying to suppress the laughter bubbling in her throat.

"Okay, your turn. Try this blueberry muffin." Laura delicately fed him the tasty morsel.

His eyes remained on her face. Some of her lipstick now adorned the edge of her cup. A copper-red curl fell over her cheek and she quickly brushed it back with her fingers. She glanced at her watch to check the time, then met his eyes.

"What are you thinking?" Laura asked.

"That I wish we could spend the whole day together. You're very comfortable to be with." Ben's arm lay on the back of the bench behind Laura. His hand toyed with her red curls. "Actually, I'm thinking of throwing you over my shoulder and taking you home with me." His face was both amused and sad.

"Ah, spoken like a true Viking." Laura laughed. "I'm afraid my patients would have something to say about that, not to mention the other nurses who are expecting me to work."

"Will you write to me?" Ben suddenly felt like a schoolboy.

"Only if you write back," was the quick rejoinder.

This time, when he kissed her, she melted into him. He held her tight, wishing the clock would stop.

Later, they cleaned up the debris from their breakfast and he walked her to the hospital. While Laura was changing into her uniform, Ben walked to the window and located Signey in her crib. She was lying there playing with a doll. He fought the urge to go to her crib and rescue her.

"She must feel like a baby again, lying in a crib." Ben spoke his thoughts when Laura came to his side.

"It's safer for her. Because her left side is paralyzed, she could fall out of a bed and hurt herself. She needs the crib rails for support when we stand her up."

"Take care of her, okay?"

"You know I will."

With promises of letters and another visit soon, Ben left the hospital. He picked up an engine part for Ingvar and a yarn order for his mother before leaving the city. Then it was homeward bound. Was it just yesterday that he had come to Winnipeg? Something told him that his life had changed dramatically in the last twenty-four hours. How would the future unfold? What reaction could he expect from his family when he brought an Irish girl to the island? In his heart he knew his mother and Daniel's family would be happy for him. Laura mentioned a Catholic background. He foresaw religion presenting a problem if Laura wasn't open to his Lutheran faith. The nearest Catholic church was inland west of Riverton. Ben knew the islanders would have plenty to say about her religion.

By the time he neared Selkirk, Ben's instincts told him that everything would fall into place. He smiled the remainder of the way home.

Ellen arrived at the school much earlier than her students. At home she'd prepared original copies of the worksheets she planned to use for the day. The first sheet she pressed on the hectograph was a geography quiz for grades five and six. The special ink on the original copy was absorbed into the gel. She carefully peeled the copy off and then smoothed a blank sheet of white paper over the gel. A gentle rub over the paper transferred the impressions of the questions onto the white paper.

Ellen studied the sky through the wall of windows as she continued the copying process to the required number. Rain clouds were moving in even though the air had been still when she walked to school. Ellen was becoming more familiar to the quick changes in the weather. For most people living in the city, weather was noted when making wardrobe choices. On Hecla Island the weather dictated much of the daily activity. It still surprised her when someone would say, "It's starting to blow up." The trees would be motionless but the islanders could almost smell the incoming breeze that within minutes formed whitecaps on the lake's surface.

The young teacher yearned to overcome the stigma of being an outsider. Small communities often tended to be close-knit. Remote communities were even more so. She wondered if she would ever be really accepted here. Everyone was kind, even though she knew some had voiced a low opinion on her teaching methods. She appreciated their involvement. At least it showed that the islanders cared about the children's education.

She looked forward to the social activities and meeting people on a different level. So far she'd been visiting parents of students to introduce herself, always in the capacity of 'teacher'. Although she enjoyed her elevated status, she longed to blend into the community.

It seemed that everyone here had an island history. Some of her pupils were great-grandchildren of the pioneers. Every islander could trace his or her background to the early Hecla homesteaders, or they'd married into a family who could. How did anyone break into a circle like that? Ellen hoped to find the answer. In the few weeks she'd been at Hecla Island, she'd grown accustomed to the scenic landscape and the industrious, hard-working people of the island. Winnipeg was far away, not only in miles but in general life. She'd been unaware of life in remote areas. Some of her family and friends had questioned her sanity when she'd accepted this teaching position, while others admired her adventurous spirit. She wondered if any of them would understand her affection for this place and the role she played in it.

Ellen peeled the last copy off the hectograph. Now she had the geography questions for the children to do, as well as a health test for the grade four students. She washed the gooey gel off her hands and put the hectograph back in the storage cupboard.

The clouds dissipated and the sunshine poured through the east windows. In a few minutes she'd ring the school bell and the children would settle into their desks. One of the older boys would raise the Union Jack on the outside flagpole. Then the morning assembly would begin with the singing of *O Canada* and the bowing of heads for the Lord's Prayer.

The mirror by the door reflected Ellen's image. She smoothed her hair in place and arranged the papers on her desk in preparation for the school day.

Rose sat at her treadle-driven sewing machine, busily making a new skirt for Karen. Daniel had given Rose the second-hand sewing machine for Christmas shortly after they were married. Rose pressed her feet on the large foot pedal in a back and forth motion which turned the belt, setting the machine into a rhythmic hum. The fabric she was using had first been sewn into a skirt for Amma Anna, who chose to believe the woollen fabric had shrunk rather than admit the tight waistband came from extra inches around her middle. Rose was adept at remodelling and creating her own patterns.

Amma Anna was at Thora's with the Knit-a-Bit ladies, the children were in school and Daniel hadn't come home yet, when a knocking on the door interrupted her sewing. Elin stood on the step. Elin and Rose had always been good friends and their husbands' families had always been good neighbours to each other.

"Hi, Rose. Are you going to Knit-a-Bit today?"

"No, I'm sewing a skirt for Karen. Daniel should be home soon –"

" – and you didn't want to be in a crowd of women," Elin finished and smiled at Rose's tired face. They chuckled together as Elin stepped inside. Dark lines were drawn where Elin's eyebrows used to be and dark mascara gave the illusion of thick eyelashes. Blue eyeshadow coordinated with her blue floral-print blouse. Her fingernails were painted to match the lipstick she wore. A brush of rouge on her cheeks completed her daily ritual of applying makeup. "I'd feel naked without it," she always said. Daniel called her 'the Makeup Queen of Hecla Island'.

"If you don't want company, I understand, but if you're in the mood for a cup of coffee, I'll stay."

Rose knew that if she told Elin that she wanted to be alone, Elin would understand. The two women joked that they were kindred spirits and were as close as twin sisters. Often the two couples – Rose and Daniel, and Elin and Jon – socialized together with a card game and a visit.

"Coffee sounds good. I can't do much more on this skirt for Karen. I was measuring pleats for the waistband but I need to make sure it fits before I sew the next seam in." Rose ladled water into the kettle with a long-handled dipper and placed the kettle on the woodstove.

"I didn't feel like going to Knit-a-Bit today. I'm not working on any needlework right now. You know how well that will go over with the older ladies," Elin said. She had always been a bit of a rebel, which wasn't appreciated by some of the ladies, especially her mother-in-law, Margaret. For all her good intentions, Margaret could make Elin feel inadequate in the housekeeping and child-rearing departments. Rose always sympathized with Elin as she knew Margaret very well. Elin often told Rose how lucky she was to have Amma Anna as a mother-in-law.

"Before I forget, you won't believe what Margaret is cooking up now. She thinks Ben and Miss Taylor would make a good couple. Should we warn Ben or just sit back and enjoy the entertainment? She might be right. They might be a good match, but lord love a duck, can you imagine what Margaret could do to them?"

Rose truly laughed for the first time that day. "Maybe we should let Ben and Miss Taylor decide on their own. They would be a good looking pair, though. Mmm, Margaret may be on to something."

The two friends chatted on about the other schemes Margaret had come up with over the years. They were sure a book could be written on the many escapades of Margaret.

When the kettle boiled, Rose poured the boiling water through the 'sock' in the coffeepot, which was a rectangular bag made of heavy cotton. The bag was sewn onto a copper wire ring and shaped to fit the top of the coffeepot. Twisted wire ends formed a handle for the coffee filter. Rose spooned coffee into the sock and poured boiling water through. Some people liked very strong coffee which meant either adding more coffee to the sock or pouring the coffee through the filter twice. Bjossi, their old, bachelor neighbour, was renowned for his tar-like coffee. It was said that Bjossi's coffee would either clean out your arteries or completely clog them. It was a risk most islanders had taken at one time or another and so far, all had lived to tell the tale.

Elin watched Rose pour coffee into two china cups with matching saucers. Amma Anna maintained that the best coffee came from china cups and Rose agreed.

"I guess the guys should be home soon," Elin said as she spooned some sugar into her coffee. "Jon has been happy with the amount of fish. It's turning out to be a good season."

"Daniel is already making plans for a new oil heater and refrigerator. He thinks we should get an electric stove right away but I have mixed feelings. I love my old woodstove. I've never cooked on anything else."

Elin chuckled, "I know what you mean. I hate to admit it but I feel the same way as Margaret when it comes to the stove. I'd rather have an electric wringer washing machine."

"Me, too." Rose smiled. "We must be getting old, Elin, to be thinking like the old ladies on the island."

"Well, I guess we're lucky that the fishing season is going well and we may have a choice of electrical appliances."

"That's what I said to Daniel. We should keep our feet on the ground. We can afford a furnace and maybe a refrigerator, but I can wait for a stove and washing machine. We've made it this far without those luxuries, a little while longer won't hurt." Rose pushed the plate of cookies closer to Elin. "An electric kettle and electric hotplate will be nice to have for next summer. Then we won't need to heat the house up with the woodstove."

Elin nodded her agreement.

"So tell me more about the matchmaking. What is Margaret planning?"

Elin rolled her eyes. "Oh, you'll hear all about it. She's going to be talking to you. She thinks you could invite Miss Taylor over for supper and have Ben over at the same time. Devious, huh?" The two friends laughed.

"I'm not sure Ben would welcome any interference in his love life. And I have a hunch that both Ben and Miss Taylor are smart enough to see through any plots we might come up with. We'll try to get them together at the Hallowe'en dance. That might just work."

"Good grief. You're actually thinking about it. Margaret will be so pleased." Elin said sarcastically.

"Speaking of the Hallowe'en dance, do you have your costumes ready?" Rose asked.

"I do. But I'm not telling you about them."

"Well, I'm keeping mine a secret then, too."

They sipped their coffee and ate some oatmeal cookies. The happy conversation continued. Rose was able to escape from her worry just as she knew Elin had intended. They were still at it when Daniel and Jon walked in.

"I saw your bicycle outside. I knew what you two were up to." Jon sat down beside his wife. Two cups and more cookies were added to the table setting.

"How was fishing today?" Both wives asked the question in unison.

"Good," Daniel answered. He joined the others at the table. "We sent nine boxes in with Ingvar on the pick-up boat this morning and then we brought in six more boxes when we came in."

The pick-up boat went to each fish camp every day to transport the fish to the packing shed at the Hecla dock. Ice was kept all summer in the packing shed in a similar manner as the ice houses. The huge ice blocks were chipped into ice pebbles which was packed into the boxes with the fish. The refrigerated fish was shipped to market in Selkirk by freighter.

Ingvar Gustafsson, Jon's father and Margaret's husband, owned and operated the packing shed and the pick-up boat. He paid the fishermen for the fish and then in turn, received payment after shipment.

"But we sure notice the difference without Ben. It takes quite a bit longer to lift and there's more chance to get stabbed by those fins." Daniel turned his hands palm up, revealing the red swollen wounds. All the fishermen bore similar markings. "Don't tell Ben we missed him, though. It would go straight to his head."

The Knit-a-Bit Club began as a social get-together for the women. They took turns hosting the monthly assembly. It was a time to show handwork currently in progress and to share ideas. Most of the women brought knitting needles and yarn.

Some worked on embroidery or other fancy needlework. Each year, by late fall, the winter woollen mitts and socks needed for the fishermen were already made. Then it was time to set the needles to creating Christmas gifts.

When they gathered at Thora's that day, it was to see many varied projects from mitts, toques and scarves to fancy sweaters. Margaret brought her embroidered cushion while other ladies were crocheting or tatting doilies in fine crochet cotton.

Everyone looked forward to hearing the news of the day and spending time with the other women. When Olivia and Malla, the elderly widows who were sisters, knocked on the door, Thora greeted them with hugs and a warm welcome.

"Hurry up before all the flies get in." Olivia tried to quickly usher Malla through the doorway. The black flies were in the hovering stage. Evenings were cool and the flies clung to the door screens in the hope of spending a warm night indoors.

"This darn hip," muttered Malla as she limped inside. Even though her hip gave her problems, she still split her own wood and carried in her own water. Both Olivia and Malla were fiercely independent. No one even dared guess at their ages. Since their grandchildren were grown it was safe to say they were 'getting up in age'. It was rumoured that they enjoyed a glass of homemade spirit each evening to stave off insomnia. Because their homes were less than a half-mile apart, they saw each other often.

"Come in, ladies, don't worry about the flies. I'll swat them if they get in," Thora joked as she opened the door wider. "What have you got here Olivia? You didn't need to bring anything." Thora unwrapped the package Olivia handed her to find an iced square of *vinarterta*. "But I'm glad you did. Mmm..."

"It's nothing." Olivia tried to sound gruff but was pleased with Thora's response.

They made their way through the kitchen and into the living room where other women were finding chairs. There were two sofas and some armchairs. The chairs from the kitchen had been arranged around the sofas so that all the seating was in a circle.

As soon as the two sisters saw Anna, they asked about Signey. Everyone listened to Anna describe Signey's condition and how anxious they were to hear if Ben had been able to see her.

"Rose phones every day and talks to the nurses. They have been good at explaining everything but we'll all feel better if Ben can tell us how she is really doing."

"Poor Rose, it's so upsetting and scary." Malla summed it up in a few words. "All of you are in our prayers, especially little Signey."

Electricity was a favorite topic. Opinions varied among the different age groups. The younger women were very enthusiastic and eager to have the conveniences that electrical power would bring. The older women were more set in the traditions of the past. To some it was an extravagance, while others feared it would change island life for the worse.

"There's nothing wrong with hard work."

"There will still be lots of work to do by hand."

"The youngsters will get lazy."

"The chores will still need to be done, just differently."

"The wiring in the walls could start house fires."

"I'm sure the wires will be safer than burning wood."

The debate went on. Knitting needles clicked in rhythm as the dialogue continued. Talk turned to plans for the Hallowe'en dance which coincided with all the men coming home after the fall fishing season.

"I wonder what Sam will dress up as this year?" Malla smirked and reminded them of the previous year's dance. "Maybe he still has that dog suit from last year."

Sam was a fisherman and a good friend of Ben's. Last year he'd married Gudrun, Kristjan and Thora's daughter, and they were expecting a baby in March. Sam had caused quite a stir at the dance when he wandered around the hall on all fours in his dog suit. He would sneak behind people's backs, lift his back leg and pretend to mark his territory. It had earned him lots of laughs and the prize for the best costume.

Malla's face glowed. Everyone laughed in remembrance. Prim and proper had its place, but to have fun you had to be a little naughty.

Thora made coffee and arranged the baking on plates. She had made *ponnokukur* and sugar cookies. Olivia's layered prune cake perfectly complemented the coffee lunch.

After coffee, the group dispersed. Some needed to be home before their schoolchildren came back from school. Everyone had chores to do and supper to prepare.

The afternoon bustle was well underway on the hospital ward when the female volunteer made the rounds with the toy cart. Each day the children could pick something different to play with. The toy selected on the previous day would go back on the cart for another child to enjoy.

Signey held the rubber-faced doll tightly in her right arm. The doll had a frilly gingham dress with a satin bow tied around the waist. When the woman bent over to take it, Signey shrank into the crib, still clutching the doll.

"Look at all the toys to pick from. What would you like today?" The volunteer attempted to reason with the quiet child. "You have to give me the doll now. Someone else will want a turn with her."

Because it reminded Signey of a favourite toy at home, the doll was like a lifeline. When the lady reached farther into the crib to wrench the doll from her arms, Signey wanted to cry out. Defeated, her right arm empty, she suffered in silence as tears trickled down her cheeks.

"What would you like to pick?" The woman was growing impatient. "If you don't say, you won't get anything. I have to let the other children choose too." No answer was forthcoming.

Signey's sad, tear-filled eyes followed the woman's progress around the room. Another girl asked for the coveted doll. When the woman came near again, she once more offered Signey a choice. But the only toy Signey longed for was gone.

The doctor arrived to make his rounds on the ward. When he stopped at Signey's crib he asked her to sit up and then to stand up. She needed assistance with both. Concern marked his face when her head tilted to the side due to the weak neck muscles. Any questions directed at Signey went unanswered. The nurse said she was very quiet. As a thought occurred to him, he looked into her eyes and very gently asked, "Where is your voice? Can you say something for me?" He held her eyes in his gaze and after a pause, Signey shook her head. The doctor surmised that the muscles in the neck that controlled her vocal chords were paralyzed. Signey was unable to speak.

Adam and his friend Andrew planned to meet at their fort after chores were done. The fort was located in a willow bluff that was alongside the road between their homes. The previous week, Oli had been backing down the driveway at Andrew's home, misjudged the distance and cranked the wheel too soon. The car careened off the road and into a telephone pole. The pole snapped at its base but the line remained intact.

Bracing the pole at a slant held the lines high enough over the driveway so no one would be inconvenienced. In the willow bluff fort, the once high telephone line sagged just above the walls. The boys pondered various ideas as to how they could use the sagging line to their advantage. Before they came to any decisions, fate lent them a hand.

Bjossi, the bachelor who lived on the other side of Andrew's, owned a few cattle and a very poor fence which offered few challenges to an adventurous animal. His herd was the bane of the community. As often happened, Bjossi arose from his afternoon nap to see his cattle venturing out of the fence. Summoning help from his trusted sidekick, he sicced his dog Chopper after the wayward group. Eager to earn praise from his master, Chopper leapt into action. So determined was he, that he failed to plan ahead. Tails in the air, the eight animals stampeded in every direction, causing mayhem everywhere. One of the cows, in her haste, ran into the line where it sagged at the lowest point. When the dust settled, the cow had pulled down three more poles.

Now four poles were braced to hold the line over driveways and out of harm's way. The line hadn't been severed. A crew from Manitoba Telephone would be coming out in the next couple of weeks to install new poles. This new development opened up a whole new plan for the boys. The line now sagged right through the fort.

Johannes, Andrew's father, was trained as an emergency telephone repairman. He was seldom called on to repair anyone's telephone, but he had supplies that were kept in a storage shed. Among the rolls of wire and tools was a box phone. On each side of the box were wires and clamps. By clamping the phone on a telephone line, the repairman could determine if the line was working or not.

Protected in the willow bluff, the boys blew the dust off the box phone and gained access to the telephone line. Over the weekend, they spent hours listening on the phone. Most of the calls they heard were boring – sharing recipes, ordering supplies and inquiries about trips into Riverton. Their patience was rewarded when Andrew's cousin Linda, who was dating a young man from the mainland, was on the phone. The boys suppressed many giggles while listening to the steamy conversation.

After evening chores, the two friends planned to sneak the box to the fort again with the hope of hearing more interesting news.

Alexander was dawdling with his schoolwork. He usually faced all his lessons with the same eagerness that he relished playing games at recess. Ellen appreciated his good natured approach that had been evident since school began. Today was different.

Ellen thought back to the lunch recess and remembered that Alexander had come in ahead of the others and he'd been unusually quiet. Because her day was busy, with all six grades to teach, Miss Taylor failed to recognize the change in attitude until school was nearly over. Something was definitely amiss.

"Class dismissed. See you in the morning. Alexander, I need your help with something. Please come here before you go home." Miss Taylor stacked the exercise books she needed to mark. Afraid he was in trouble, Alexander shuffled to her desk.

"Don't worry, Alexander, you haven't done anything wrong." His teacher reassured the young boy. The other children were on their way to the door, some glancing over their shoulders to see if Alexander was in trouble. One of the older boys tittered on his way outside.

"I noticed that you were quiet this afternoon. Is something bothering you?"

Alexander's nervous eyes shifted to see who was still in the schoolroom.

"It's alright, you can tell me if someone hurt you. Is that what happened?" Ellen's soft voice reached out to the boy. He was still reluctant to open up to her.

"If you can't tell me, Alexander, that's fine. I just want you to know that if there is something I can help you with, please come and talk to me about it."

Finally, Alexander found the courage to ask, "What's a cripple?"

It was suddenly clear to Ellen what had caused such worry in her student. Thora had told her about the Bergursson girl who was in a Winnipeg hospital suffering from polio. Ellen hadn't seen the girl but she understood that the girl was paralyzed on her left side. Reflecting on the knowledge she had of the situation, the teacher chose her words carefully.

"A cripple is someone who can't use their arms or legs or some part of their body because of sickness or maybe because of an injury from an accident. It just means that a part of you doesn't work the way it should. Are you thinking about your little sister?"

Alexander nodded his head, his eyes betraying his fear.

"They said Signey was just a cripple." The scene was played out as he recalled hearing the older boys. "Adam didn't hear them or he would have beaten them up." The misery etched onto his face lessened with admitting the cause of his distress.

"Sometimes, when people say hurtful things, it's best to ignore it and walk away. I know you're worried. I wish I could explain polio to you. The truth is, I don't know very much about it myself. What I do know is that lots of children who have been sick with it are getting better. Maybe you should ask your mother about your sister."

"Mama is sad. She looks like she's going to cry if we ask."

The teacher resisted the urge to hug him as she considered his words. Often parents protected their children by shielding them from the truth when in fact the truth would end the scary speculation going through their minds.

"My Uncle Ben was going to the hospital yesterday. He's coming home today."

"Maybe he'll tell you how she's doing." Alexander seemed to brighten to that idea. "Remember, Alexander, cripple is just a word. When Signey comes home she might not be as strong as she was, but she'll be lucky to have a big brother like you. Try not to worry so much, and keep in mind that I'm here if you want to talk about it."

The young boy seemed relieved that he had shared his dread with his teacher. He picked up his schoolbooks, smiled at her and left the classroom.

Alexander had needed an ally. Ellen hoped he'd found one in speaking with her. She resolved to keep a closer eye on things, especially if the comments Alexander had heard were meant to be hurtful. The children may have heard adults talking about the Bergursson girl, and inadvertently spoken out without realizing the impact their words would have. Tidying up her desk, she hoped that Alexander's uncle would have good news for the family.

An expectant hush fell over the six people surrounding the kitchen table when Ben walked into Daniel and Rose's home. It was just after four o'clock in the afternoon. Daniel was home from the fish camp. School was over for the day and Amma Anna had joined them for afternoon coffee. Ben's smiling face was a welcome sight.

Rose poured him a cup of coffee and set a plate for him to share the coffee lunch. Ben's arms were laden with shopping bags. There was yarn, two new filleting knives and some candy that had magically found its way into one of the bags.

Ben had just settled into a chair when Karen asked the question on everyone's mind.

"Did you see Signey?"

He nodded and smiled, bringing relief to his audience. Ben had decided on the long ride home that he would use Laura's approach and explain what he had seen through her eyes. When Signey came home, it would be with weakened muscles. There was no point in glossing over the facts. He described the hospital ward and the treatment Signey received. He talked about the exercises and about the other children.

"I told her the story of Dixie and Spike chasing a rabbit." Ben smacked his hands together. Everyone laughed remembering the dogs' crash.

He mentioned the girl in the wheelchair who read a story to Signey. Recovery stories that Laura had relayed to him, he in turn passed on to them.

"She did all her exercises. Laura...er, the nurse told me that Signey is very cooperative and liked by everyone."

Alexander leaned back in his chair. "I'll help her when she comes home."

"That's what she'll need, Alexander, help to get strong again. We'll all do what we can," his eyes encompassed the group, "but it will be up to Signey to help herself get better." As the words tumbled out of his mouth, Ben realized the truth of his remark. With help, we heal ourselves. "Signey's a trooper. I'm sure she'll win her battle." When she came home, she would begin to heal the wounds and erase the memory, just like he had. Or had he? Some of his war memories had left deep scars. The light-hearted chit-chat and laughter he'd enjoyed with Laura had lain dormant within him for many years.

Ben decided to keep his friendship with Laura a secret for now. They had fun and he was definitely attracted to her. He was sure the feeling was mutual but something he couldn't explain compelled him to remain silent. Laura could change her mind about him. Another man might romance her away from him. Maybe she belonged in the city. Was an Irishman planned in her future life? Ben, he said to himself, you are being paranoid. If he was bent on healing his well-hidden insecurity, he vowed to himself to keep in touch with Laura and see what would unfold in the days to come.

Around the table, conversation moved to Ben's meeting with Manitoba Hydro and to Daniel and Jon's two days on the lake without Ben.

"It's time for chores. Ben can't have two full days off." Daniel slapped his brother on the back.

"I wasn't exactly twiddling my thumbs." Ben rose from the table. "I'll meet you in the barn. I need to change clothes."

Everyone stood up and left the table. Thanks were echoed for the shopping purchases Ben had brought. Ben gave Rose a hug and said, "I'm sorry, Rose, I didn't bring anything for you."

Misty-eyed, Rose returned his hug. "Yes, you did. You brought me the best gift of all. For the first time in over two weeks, I feel hopeful about Signey."

"She's going to be fine, Rose. She's a real fighter, and as I told the nurse – we Icelanders are far too stubborn for anything to keep us down. It will take time, like she said, but Signey has lots of time to get over this."

Early the next morning, Ben slowed the eight horsepower outboard motor as he neared the buoy on the first gang. Each gang of two or more nets was stretched in a straight line and held by anchors at each end and one anchor between each net. Stone or lead weights were tied to the lower edge of the net and wooden floats were laced on the upper edge to keep the mesh as extended as possible.

Ben cut the motor and allowed the boat to drift up to the buoy. With a practised ease he swung the marker into the boat. His hands grabbed the net lines. In a smooth motion, he tossed the buoy back into the water on the opposite side of the boat and slid the lines between his body and a wooden peg on the boat's bow. As he tugged the lines, the end of the net appeared. The nylon mesh was pulled in one side of the boat and slipped back into the water on the other side, after picking out the trapped fish. Each net was fifty fathoms or one hundred yards long. He didn't miss the old nets of cotton and linen. Every week they had to be pulled out of the lake, cleaned and cured with bluestone to prevent them from rotting. Ben, Daniel and Jon were now completely converted to nylon mesh nets which could withstand the lake water throughout the fish season.

The eighteen-foot skiff bobbed on the water, following the net's path. There was a steady roll to the waves, indicating an upcoming wind. Usually, the wind increased at this time of day rather than decreased.

Lake Winnipeg had many faces that determined how the fish would run. In a short while, a shift in the wind could fill an otherwise empty net. Ben had already lifted four nets and was rotating toward camp again. Three fish boxes were full and another was nearing the halfway mark.

Ben came from a long line of fishermen. His grandfather had come from Iceland before the turn of the twentieth century in the hope of finding a good life for his family. Iceland had suffered hard times with drought and a decreased fish supply. Volcanic eruptions had spewed lava and ash, rendering much productive land useless. Back then, the future seemed grim. Many Icelanders made the sea voyage to Canada and travelled by train from the east coast to Winnipeg.

In 1876, the first Icelandic settlers came by boat to Hecla Island. The first winter presented many challenges, from keeping warm in inadequate housing to learning how to fish through the ice. Smallpox claimed many lives. A few years later, when Ben's grandfather came to homestead on Hecla Island, those who had come before him had learned how to adapt to the variations in fishing practices and extreme climate.

This fishing season had proved to be fruitful for most of the Hecla Island fishermen. Good fishing would be a real boon this year with the electricity coming. Any money that could be spared from everyday living would likely go toward updating homes. Electric lights and regulated heat were high on everyone's list. But, many islanders were so entrenched in their ways that it would be difficult to adjust to new methods. Ben grinned as he thought about Margaret and her resistance to change. He guessed she was still nursing her chagrin over the islanders' success in getting the power lines across the channel. One would think she'd learn to keep quiet, but Ben knew that wouldn't happen anytime in the near future. Margaret was Margaret. There was no changing that. Ben was sure that Olivia and Malla would be far more receptive to changes than Margaret would. He admired those two old widows. They had been behind the young men all the way in the challenge of stringing power lines across the channel.

Malla had been unimpressed with the engineer's report. "What do those educated city boys know about Lake Winnipeg? I think our boys have a better idea of how the water runs through the channel. They'll find a way."

Malla and Olivia always showed an interest in other people. They particularly enjoyed young people. The genuine concern and interest they demonstrated were reflected in the many visits they received from students and young job seekers who were home on the island for a weekend. Ben was one of their regular visitors. The old girls had relished hearing about the antics of his youth. They had been upset and worried when he left to enlist in the war. Ben recalled how excited Malla had been when he sent her clippings from the London papers. She had a few drops of British blood in her Icelandic veins and had a yen for the monarchy. She adored King George and his family. The queen had been filmed walking through the debris of bombed London and, sympathizing with those who lived in the devastated neighbourhoods. The two pretty daughters of the royal family were often photographed for the tabloids. Malla loved to follow the stories and treasured all the correspondence that arrived from Ben. What she especially had treasured was the thought that Ben took the time to write to her. He didn't realize, until he'd come home, how much Malla had read between the lines when he described what he was doing and how he felt about the war. Malla had been fearful for his safety and prayed every day for his safe return. When Ben returned from England, he visited her shortly after arriving. He remembered thanking her for all her letters. She'd written to him regularly, relating the events of the island. In her amusing way, she'd joked about the rumours and gossiped about everyone. Her letters were light-hearted and intended to make him laugh. Olivia had also sent notes in Malla's letters, mostly criticizing the gossip Malla was writing about. On many of the bad days overseas, Ben remembered pulling out those letters and letters from his family to feel closer to home.

Ben turned to drag the wooden fish box closer. His 'oilers' crimped noisily. The rubber canvas pants worn over his work clothes kept him warm and dry but made movement difficult. A hooded rubber jacket offered the same warmth and dryness. Early morning mist held a distinct chill and if accompanied by wind, could be cold.

He tossed two sunfish into the bailing pail. They were the perfect size for Malla and Olivia. He smiled as he anticipated delivering the fish to them. He regularly dropped off fish for their supper. The two women represented the true grit needed to survive life's curve balls. Each of the women had known her share of tragedy, but they stood firm and carried on. 'Face it, deal with it, then get on with it,' was the creed they lived by. Some islanders considered them to be too blunt and too opinionated, but to Ben that was what he loved about them. Olivia was less likely to offend but Malla seldom stepped down from a good discussion. Ben remembered the day he'd won her heart when she'd witnessed him in an argument several years before. Ben and some other teenage boys were involved in a dispute over a baseball game at the annual Spring Picnic.

Their older rivals attempted to intimidate them and take the victory in a controversial run around the bases. The base runner clearly was tagged out at third base, but he'd knocked the ball out of the player's hand and proceeded to home plate, where the game-tying run was celebrated. Not everyone noticed the play on third base, but Ben had. He wasn't going to stand back and accept defeat. Ben hadn't yelled or displayed any animosity. He simply walked up to the celebrators and told them the runner had been out on third. Angry faces glared at him. "Get lost, don't be a sore loser." In response Ben had repeated, "Ted knows he was out, you didn't tie the game." As his opponents approached in a threatening way, Ben stood his ground and looked Ted in the eye. Words were spoken but Ben continued his steady stare. Finally Ted capitulated and admitted that he 'probably was tagged on third' and he 'may have bumped the players hand as he ran by'. Chaos ensued as victory changed hands. The third base tag was the third out in the ninth inning.

After the game, Malla had singled out Ben. At that time, Ben was wary of the older lady who was famous for her verbal thrashings. She made eye contact and he wasn't able to escape.

Her steely blue eyes bore into his as his pulse quickened. "I saw what happened on third base." Malla had noted the defiance in his eyes and so she reassured the fifteen-year-old. "Good for you, Ben. It isn't always easy to stand up for what's right." The wrinkled face had crinkled into a smile. "And I wanted you to know that I'm really proud of you for making things right."

Ben knew his face was flushed when he thanked her. Over the years, a kinship had developed between them. Ben listened to adults discussing politics and other topics which he then argued with Malla. He could credit her with challenging his thoughts, inciting his imagination, and being able to present a well-informed opinion when necessary.

Yes, Ben reflected, Malla was quite a gal. He'd love to introduce Laura to her. He knew the two women would get along well. They both possessed strong characters and common sense. Although Ben had just met Laura, he was sure the impression she'd left him with was an accurate one. It was only yesterday when he last saw her, but he was anxious to make contact with her. He vowed to write a letter to her soon. He'd love to show her the island and introduce her to his way of life. His thoughts went to his pen and paper and what he'd write to her. Would it be too soon to invite her to the fall dance? He could suggest that she bring a friend in case she was nervous about coming to Hecla Island on her own.

As he picked more fish out of the net, he mentally planned his words. The more he scribed in his head, the longing to see the Irish nurse grew.

Rose finished washing up the breakfast dishes. She carried the dishpan of used water and depleted suds out the back door. Near the edge of the yard, she dumped the dishwater into the tall grass. Since Ben had come home with the news of Signey, she believed her daughter would recover. She decided to sweep the floor and then make her daily call to the hospital.

Rose tried to soothe her anxiety as she rang through to the operator. She recited the Winnipeg phone number from memory and waited for the connection to be made. Eventually she was put through to the second floor ward. A nurse answered the call and introduced herself as Nurse O'Neil. Rose had spoken to her a few times and she quickly identified her name and her reason for calling.

"Hello, Mrs. Bergursson. Did Ben get home and tell you about visiting Signey?"

"Yes, he did." Rose was taken aback at the familiarity with which the nurse spoke of Ben. "We were happy to hear about how she looked and the things being done to help her. How is she today?"

"She's doing well, but there are some changes. Signey is a quiet child but we think she may be struggling with her voice. As you know, her neck muscles are weak and we think the muscles that work her vocal chords are affected by that weakness."

"Are you saying that she can't speak?"

"I don't want to alarm you, but that seems to be the case. She isn't able to speak right now but we are hopeful that it will right itself. Her left leg is stronger today, stronger than it's been since she came to the hospital. That's a good sign."

Rose raised a hand to her forehead. A strangled breath came out in a sob. Tears trickled down her cheeks and the hand holding the telephone receiver trembled as she sniffed into a hankie. She pictured her child, all alone and unable to communicate.

"Mrs. Bergursson, I'm sorry to upset you. Signey is happy and, honestly, her leg has improved. That's good news. We've seen other children start to improve like Signey and the improvement continues throughout the weakened muscles. We have to be prepared for a long wait."

"Thank you." Rose was grateful to the nurse for trying to reassure her. "I appreciate the care Signey is getting. I just want her to come home soon."

"I feel I know you, Mrs. Bergursson, after Ben told me about your family. I don't mean to upset you, but I think you want to hear the truth. I believe Signey will steadily improve and she will be able to come home before too long."

Puzzled again by the casual reference to Ben, Rose questioned the nurse about Signey's ability to stand, if she was eating her meals, and if she was able to swallow. Satisfied with the answers and feeling a closer connection to her daughter through this nurse, Rose's emotions settled down.

"Thank you again, for all the information. I'm always glad when I can talk to you. You must be a mother yourself, to be able to understand what I'm feeling."

"No, I'm not a mother." The nurse hesitated. "But I know that if I were a mother, I would be feeling alienated if I were in your position. And I know that I would want to be aware of everything going on."

"When we are able to bring Signey home, I hope I can thank you in person."

"I'm looking forward to meeting you, too. And, I'm sure it won't be long until Signey will improve enough to go home."

"That's what I'm praying for. I'll telephone again tomorrow."

"Good-bye for now, Mrs. Bergursson."

"Good-bye, Nurse O'Neil." Rose wanted to feel elation over the renewed strength in Signey's leg but the question regarding her speech cast a dark shadow over any celebration. Hopefully, the change in Signey's leg was the beginning of her full recovery.

Daniel came home in the afternoon by himself. Jon and Ben had stayed at the fish camp.

"We have to think positively Rose. The improvement in her leg has to be a good sign, as the nurse said." Daniel was encouraged by Signey's progress. "Let's try not to worry too much about her voice. It will come back. If her leg is getting stronger, then she'll get stronger in her whole left side. I'm sure the next few days will tell the tale."

Rose always felt better when Daniel was home. He saw the silver lining in every cloud. And he was usually right, which often irritated her, but this time Rose prayed he was right. The nurse had hinted at the same thing on the phone.

"Oh, Ben asked me to give you this letter for the mail going out tomorrow." Daniel pulled an envelope from his jacket pocket and set it on the corner of the cupboard.

Rose glanced at the envelope as she reached into the cupboard for coffee cups and then abruptly looked back at Ben's distinctive writing. The recipient was none other than a Miss Laura O'Neil at a Winnipeg address. A smile formed on Rose's lips as the pieces of the puzzle fell into place. She had some questions to ask her brother-in-law when he came home.

"I'll meet you in half an hour." Adam turned to walk into his driveway, on his way home from school.

"Sounds good. See you at the fort," Andrew shouted over his shoulder. "I should be finished my chores by then." Like Adam, Andrew's family had a variety of livestock that needed tending. Chopping wood and filling water pails were common chores for all families. All the children were required to assist with the daily chores. It was simply part of each day.

"Maybe we'll hear some good gossip today."Adam's eyes searched the neighbourhood after the two boys climbed into their fort. The co-conspirators didn't want to be caught as they huddled over the box phone. The fort was situated in an advantageous spot. From the willow bluff they could monitor any traffic on the road and see into both their families' yards. The willows also provided dense cover for them, so they could hide unseen from any passerby.

The rings on the line alerted the eavesdroppers. Thora answered the phone and was told that Miss Taylor had a call. Anticipation heightened as the young ears listened attentively. When the popular teacher's voice came on the line, the boys scarcely breathed. It was a call from a woman.

"Have you come to your senses, Ellen?" The unfamiliar voice was stern. "I think Richard would still take you back. He was here last night looking for you."

Miss Taylor quickly answered, "I know what I'm doing. Richard will find someone else."

Adam and Andrew glanced furtively at each other. They hadn't heard their teacher use such an angry voice before.

"That's what I'm afraid of. He'll find someone else while you're hiding out in the middle of nowhere."

"Mother, I am happy out here in the middle of nowhere. I signed a contract for the school year."

"Running away doesn't solve problems."

Adam and Andrew couldn't believe their ears. Was Miss Taylor in trouble? How could anyone be mean to her? And who was Richard and why was he looking for her?

Afraid they'd be detected, the guilt-ridden boys unfastened the box telephone from the telephone wire. They hastily packed it into the wooden container to carry back to the shed.

"Should we tell someone?" Andrew's eyes were as round as saucers and his mouth was agape in worry.

"No, not a word. We're not supposed to be listening." Adam spoke with an authority he didn't feel.

"But, what if she needs help?"

"Let's not do anything yet. If we keep our ears open, maybe we'll find out more."

Chapter 4

Rose stacked the clean dishes in the cupboard. Freshly-washed floors gleamed throughout the house and she'd planned the day's menu. She'd completed the outside chores, mechanically going through the motions of her morning routine.

"I just know that tomorrow will be a good day." She'd confided her premonitions to Elin the previous afternoon.

"Soon, Rose. Signey will be coming home soon." Elin had hugged her friend.

In her heart Rose knew today was different. It was over two weeks since Nurse O'Neil first told her about Signey's voice. In that time, Signey had regained more strength. She was now able to stand, although only for short periods of time, and her neck muscles were improving. The last phone call had been very hopeful. The doctor had suggested that Signey would likely be able to return home this week. Rose had kept herself busy so the time would pass quickly and she could put her phone call through to the hospital.

Cool October winds whipped the autumn leaves off the trees. The fish harvest had dropped and the fishermen were pulling up some of their nets. The fall season was coming to an end. Ben had only two nets left in the water. Daniel and Jon had a few more but they, too, had pulled up most of their nets. On that morning, the three fishermen lifted the remaining nets and then headed homeward to the Hecla dock. Tonight would be spent at home.

The *Lady Canadian* was docked in the Hecla village port when the three men arrived. The freighter made regular stops to load the fish bound for market. Boxes of fish were moved from the packing shed at the dock to the cargo hold on the boat. The *Lady Canadian*'s crewmen were hard at work loading when Ben, Daniel and Jon joined the line. Jon was familiar with the loading procedure. When he wasn't on the lake or in the fish camp, he helped his father in the packing shed. Ice chips surrounded the fish to maintain the quality of the meat for the remainder of the journey to Selkirk. From the time the fish were picked out of the net until it reached the processing plant in Selkirk, special care needed to be observed to protect the product.

"What's the news from north?" Ben was curious about the fish catch from the north basin of Lake Winnipeg.

"It's dropping off at Norway House but Berens River is still pulling in quite a bit." The first mate addressed the question. "It's nearing an end, though, in other parts, like Matheson Island and Grand Rapids. They've nearly quit for the season. The fish have gone into hiding."

"Yeah, we only have a few nets still in. How many more trips will you be making?"

"Probably two more for fish. We still have plenty of supplies to haul up north, so it may be more."

The remote communities farther north relied on the lake freighters to supply them with food staples and other goods needed for the winter ahead. During the winter months, caterpillar trains would deliver fuel, food and other wares to the far-reaching communities but these trips were few and were hampered by the rugged terrain.

With the last boxes of fish stowed on board the *Lady Canadian*, the big door on the freighter's side was locked into place and the crew prepared to leave port. They still had stops at Hnausa and Gimli before reaching their destination of Selkirk.

The three fishermen retrieved the empty fuel cans and their jackets from the skiff and climbed into Jon's truck for the ride home.

Daniel was welcomed by the tear-streaked, beaming face of his excited wife.

"We can bring her home tomorrow." Rose flung herself into his arms. "Our baby is coming home."

Rose had been ecstatic ever since phoning and receiving the doctor's confirmation that Signey was ready to leave the hospital. Signey's voice was still silent but she had progressively improved and there was hope for more progress.

When the other children came home from school that afternoon it was a lively group that assembled around the kitchen table. Ben and Amma Anna joined in with the coffee lunch.

"Is there a nurse we should give your regards to, Ben?" Rose's teasing question brought a sly grin to Ben's face.

"Maybe."

"Well, if she's as nice in person as she sounds on the phone," Rose paused for effect, "then, I might even put in a good word for you."

Later, Rose tried to prepare the children for Signey's return, but she found difficulty explaining the situation when she herself wasn't entirely sure how things would be. With all the excitement Rose was still aware that there would be trying days ahead for all of them. But at that moment she was thankful that the next day she would hold her baby in her arms again. It had been five weeks since Signey had been hospitalized, the longest five weeks of Rose's life.

At eight o'clock the next morning, Daniel drove Ben's car onto the ferry. Amma Anna was going to get the children off to school so Daniel and Rose could cross on the first ferry trip and be on their way to the Children's Hospital in Winnipeg.

Rose had packed Signey's favorite dress and her woollen coat that Amma Anna had sewn for her. The matching woollen hat had a narrow brim on the front and lace-thin ties that secured under her chin. For late October it was a mild day, but Daniel heard on the radio forecast that they could experience rain showers before they reached home in the evening. Signey hadn't been outside since the beginning of her hospital stay. She'd be aware of the chill in the cool autumn air.

They arrived at the hospital and were directed to the second floor ward. A nurse met them and ushered them toward the wide doorway opening onto Signey's ward. Rose didn't realize she was holding her breath. When she found Signey in the overcrowded room, she gasped and quickly went to engulf her daughter in her arms.

Rose and Daniel were shocked to see Signey's thin limbs and unsteady neck. The quiet mouth beamed in a smile that reached her eyes. As Rose told Signey about the dress she had brought, another nurse approached.

"Hello, I'm Nurse O'Neil. It's so nice to meet you both."

Her warm smile appealed to Rose.

"It's so good to meet you in person. I'd recognize your voice anywhere. This is my husband, Daniel."

"You must be the Laura O'Neil that we've mailed those letters to." Daniel smiled and formally shook her hand.

The telltale crimson flush creeping into Laura's cheeks was answer in itself.

"I do know your brother. He's told me so much about Hecla Island and the people there that I feel I know you, too." Laura said she'd like to spend more time with them but she knew they had an appointment with the physiotherapist to learn about the exercises Signey would need. Later the doctor would speak to them about the child's progress to date and what they might expect in the near future.

Laura assisted Rose in dressing the girl. "I love your dress, Signey," Laura said. "This shade of blue is beautiful on you. I'm so happy for you to be going home today, but I'll miss seeing you every day."

Laura guided Daniel and Rose into a room to meet with the physiotherapist. The woman sat Signey on a cot and demonstrated the many exercises that would help restore circulation in the damaged muscles. She wrote everything down and drew diagrams to clarify some of the movements. Rose went through the drill to ensure she knew the workout. Signey meekly tolerated the lesson and appeared glad when it was over.

After a short wait, the doctor was ready to see them. Signey clung to her mother, not wanting to be separated from her again. Beady eyes in an unshaven face was the first impression that Rose had of the doctor. Then she noted the shadows under his eyes and the white shirt that had lost its crispness hours ago. The poor man probably hadn't slept for days. He introduced himself and then studied Signey's chart. His tired voice abruptly explained the diagnosis. "She's stronger throughout most of her left side. The left shoulder muscle, though, probably won't come back. There are some options you may want to consider. Surgery seems to have helped many polio patients. In your daughter's case, we could explore the idea of straightening the arm at the elbow. It may give her more upper arm movement."

Rose held Signey snugly on her lap. She just wanted to escape from the hospital and take Signey home. Daniel assessed the suggestion. "We'll need to think about that. Is surgery something that would need to be done soon or can we wait a while?"

"As long as she's improving, we should wait. Actually, right now the best medicine is rest, home-cooked meals and her exercises. We can always evaluate and consider surgery later. Her neck muscles have improved although they are still very weak. I think her voice will return but I can't guarantee anything. I can tell you we have seen miracles happen, but there will also be many young people who'll always be crippled."

"Signey will work hard on her exercise program and time will tell, I guess." Daniel rubbed the thin leg. "We are grateful for all the care she has received here."

A smile transformed the doctor's unkempt face. "It is a very scary disease, this polio. The wards are still full to overflowing, but every time we are able to send someone home..." he smiled at Signey, "then it's a good day. I would like to see her again in a month." They all rose from their chairs as he continued, "I'll ask you to make an appointment at the nurses' station and in the meantime we'll hope for the best." Daniel and Rose shook the doctor's hand and thanked him again.

At the nurses' station, they waited a few moments while Laura was explaining a procedure to a volunteer. Rose scanned the ward and for the first time, realized how busy it was. Rows of beds and cribs were home to so many ailing children. The nurses and volunteers went about their tasks, displaying efficiency and competence. Upon closer examination, she could see the tired lines on the faces of the staff members. She watched as patients were helped to sit up or lie down. Some children were enjoying storytime while others played quietly on their own. What impressed Rose the most was the kindness and warmth with which all these tasks were performed. It gave her a sense of calm knowing that Signey had been among these caregivers.

"Sorry to keep you waiting." Laura made her way to the desk. "Do you need to make an appointment?"

"Yes, we do. The doctor said to come back in a month." Daniel calculated out loud. "That should be before freeze-up."

"I know about freeze-up. Ben said the island is cut off from everyone for a few weeks. What do you do in emergencies?"

"Oh, there's always a way." Daniel spoke with the same optimism as his brother. "We walk on the thin ice, pushing a boat for security, or take an airplane. Remember, Rose, when Mundi had appendicitis and they flew him to Gimli?"

Rose nodded and added, "It's isolated during the fall freeze-up and the spring break-up, but it's just a part of our life on the island."

Laura had opened the appointment book and flipped the pages to the appropriate date. They agreed on a time and then the Bergurssons prepared to leave. Rose reached out to Laura and gave her a hug. "Thank you so much. You'll never know how much the phone calls meant to me. Maybe one day I'll be able to do something special for you." Her eyes twinkled as she said, "Ben has been very secretive but I have a hunch we'll be seeing you again."

Daniel hoisted Signey into his arms and she rested her head on his shoulder. They said their goodbyes and made their way to the car in the parking lot. Signey sat in the middle of the front seat, snuggled between her parents. Rose had packed a lunch. When Signey spied her mother's oatmeal cookies, she quickly pointed and smiled. They were happy to leave the hospital and the city behind and be on their way home.

Signey's stomach was still churning with excitement when *Pabbi* drove the car through the streets of Winnipeg on their way home. It was a dream come true to the child after all this time.

Earlier, she had looked up at the people coming through the doorway and there they'd been, her Mama and *Pabbi.* Mama wore her gray tweed coat. On her head, a burgundy hat with a little gray feather on the side coordinated with the coat. *Pabbi* wore his dark woollen coat and matching hat. Although she was only four years old, Signey knew she'd never forget how her parents had looked as they walked toward her.

Signey hadn't been able to speak for over two weeks, but in her mind the words were clear, "Mama, mama, you came."

She munched on a cookie, then nestled her nose into a fold of her mother's coat sleeve. It smelled like heaven. It smelled like home.

The Bergursson house was abuzz with activity when the car drove into the driveway just before six o'clock. Right after school, Signey's siblings had pedaled their bicycles home as fast as possible. Alexander spread paper out on the living room floor. He drew and coloured a special welcome home banner. Karen helped Amma Anna make a batch of *ponnukokur* while Adam and Ben had completed the outside chores.

Signey had slept for part of the ride and then had become increasingly excited as they neared home. Daniel lifted her out of the car and set her down. She walked on the path to the house holding her mother's hand. Dixie came racing around the corner of the house. When she spotted Signey, her tail wagged so hard her whole body was in motion. As her tongue washed the girl's face with kisses, a happy chortle gurgled from Signey's throat. The sound erupting from her mouth was the first indication that her voice might return.

Signey was welcomed home into gleeful chaos. Hugs and kisses and tears were the order of the day. After a feast of fish with potatoes and a dessert of *ponnukokur*, Signey was tucked into a quilt on the living room sofa. She fell asleep to the wonderful clamour of home. Knitting needles clicked, the newspaper rustled, the static tones of the battery-operated radio offered a play from the Lux Radio Theater, and Karen asked Adam for help with her arithmetic homework.

"With lots of love and your Mama's good cooking," Ben whispered loudly, "you'll be as good as new before you know it."

Bjossi was patting his dog's head when Chopper's ears picked up and he eyed the landscape between Bjossi's house and Ingvar and Margaret's home. Only about three hundred yards separated the two homesteads.

Bjossi's eyes followed Chopper's stare and they both focused on the figure coming toward them. Margaret strode toward them, her skirt flapping in the breeze. A cloud of flies accompanied her, but Bjossi was sure that none of them would risk settling on her skin to bear her wrath. Bjossi smiled to himself as he rose from the stoop. He and Margaret often had a difference of opinion. She would fly off the handle at the drop of a hat and he enjoyed baiting her anger. Today she looked as if she was already in a temper, so he wouldn't need to goad her.

Bjossi had a billy goat, aptly named Billy, who followed Bjossi around the farm like a puppy. Billy also arose when Bjossi stood up and the trio – man, dog and goat, all slowly ambled toward the oncoming visitor.

Twenty strides away, Margaret yelled, "You keep that mutt of yours at home. It nearly killed my cat."

Bjossi started to respond but the wad of chewing tobacco stuffed around his gums impeded his speech. With a practised motion he grabbed Billy's goatee in one hand, the goat's horn with his other hand and pulled the goat's mouth open. Bjossi spat the soggy tobacco mass into Billy's mouth. Margaret recoiled, as she always did when witnessing this scene.

"Chopper wouldn't kill your cat. But I saw the cat near my barn this morning so he was just chasing it home."

Bjossi wasn't sure which offended Margaret more – the brown spittle on his teeth, Billy chewing the tobacco in obvious contentment, or his easy dismissal of his dog's behaviour.

"Maybe if your barn wasn't full of mice, Cuddles wouldn't be tempted." The sarcasm in Margaret's voice irritated Bjossi.

"Are the rats in your barn too big for Cuddles to play with?"

Throwing her hands in the air, Margaret stormed back to her house. She couldn't resist having the last word. "Keep that ugly mongrel away from my cat."

Bjossi smiled as the angry woman stalked back to her yard. He fondly scratched Chopper's chin. "Don't pay any attention to her, I know you wouldn't hurt a flea."

The three friends resumed their positions at the stoop. Bjossi picked up his binoculars. He was an avid birdwatcher and made a hobby of documenting all his bird sightings in a journal. Sometimes, the distance glasses were aimed toward the neighbours' yards. Bjossi was aware of most of the activity in the area by observing from his stoop. It amused him that Adam and Andrew had put the box phone to such good use. At first he'd wondered what those boys were up to. Then he'd put two and two together and come up with them listening on the party line. He was proud to have played a part in this prankish scheme. His cow had pulled the line down. If those boys decided to blackmail someone, he would ask for 'hush money.' Chuckling, Bjossi kept his eye on a bald eagle gliding over the trees. Eagles had been in the area all summer, but this particular one was the largest, with its impressive wing span and menacing talons. Margaret's cat would be better warned against the eagle instead of fearing Chopper.

Ellen looked up from the papers on her desk to see Alexander burst through the door.

"Miss Taylor, my sister Signey came home yesterday." His face was flushed with excitement.

"That's wonderful, Alexander. How is she?"

"Not very strong. She can walk though. And can hold her head up. Mama says her voice will come back. Even use her arm again."

"I'm sure she'll get stronger each day. You must be so happy to have her home again." Miss Taylor wondered about the recovery. She hoped the little girl would regain her voice and muscle strength. With the limited knowledge she had of polio, Miss Taylor was reluctant to offer assumptions on the recovery.

Karen had followed Alexander into the school. Overhearing the verbal exchange, she also came to speak to her teacher. "Good morning, Miss Taylor."

"Good morning, Karen. Alexander is telling me about your sister. Does she need to do some exercises?"

"Yes, I'll be helping her after school. Mama has a list of exercises that she needs help with."

"How about you, Alexander?"

Alexander looked at his feet, then said, "I don't know. I can play with her, but she can't do very much yet."

"You could read to her and draw pictures for her."

The boy brightened and decided he would do that.

Chapter 5

Like a mirage on the lake, the city of Winnipeg appeared on the horizon. Throughout the entire drive from Hecla Island, Ben struggled to curb the desire to press his foot down on the gas pedal. The last time he'd seen Laura was their initial meeting in September. In the four weeks since then, they'd exchanged letters each week and spoken on the telephone a few times. With his nets out of the water, Ben was able to justify a holiday. When Laura invited him to Sean's birthday party at the Tipperary, he was quick to accept. Mrs. O'Neil had invited Ben to join them for dinner before the party.

The '52 Chevy merged into the traffic flow. Stopped at a red light, Ben scrutinized the nearby vehicles and their inhabitants. Next to him, a woman pulled her hair back over her shoulders and tried to ignore the noisy children in the back seat. The hairy head of a dog arose out of the confusion and happily licked all the young faces. On the other side, a man dressed in a suit impatiently tapped the steering wheel with his fingertips. Probably had a long day, Ben surmised, and he was anxious to get home. Ben was glad when the light changed to green. He felt hemmed in after being on the lake.

Making his way through the city, Ben was pleased to have estimated his arrival time correctly. Laura was to be home after four o'clock and dinner was scheduled for six. His watch read five-fifteen – not too early, but early enough to meet Laura's family before mealtime.

Ben had joked on the phone after Laura issued the invitation. "I'll try to be on my best behavior."

"Just be yourself." Laura had laughed.

She was a gem, his Laura. And that was how he always thought of the Irish nurse – as his. He'd only known her for a month but it felt like much longer. Now his days were full of thoughts of her, anticipating her next letter and longing to hear her voice on the telephone. Whenever he heard a good joke or any newsworthy tidbit, he would smile and think,

"I'll have to tell Laura."

He parked the car in front of the O'Neil home. When he was halfway up the front walk, the door opened and there she stood. Ben hastened up the steps, grabbed her arm around the wrist and whirled her into his arms. Laura laughed and clung to him, relishing in his warmth and spontaneity.

"My Viking, you're back at last."

Ben's heart melted with her words. "You're even more beautiful – if that's possible. It feels so good to hold you again."

A loud throat-clearing sound brought them back to reality. An older version of Laura approached. Her graying hair was waved in a short coiffure. Behind wire-rimmed glasses, her hazel eyes crinkled in amusement. She wiped her hands on the floral apron tied around her waist.

"Enough entertainment for the neighbours. Bring Ben inside, Laura. Hello, I'm Katherine O'Neil, Laura's mother." She returned Ben's firm handshake and ushered him indoors.

"Thank you for the invitation. I'm looking forward to meeting all your family." They moved toward the kitchen where Ben was firmly instructed to take a seat and enjoy a cup of tea while the women continued with dinner preparation.

Colin O'Neil, Laura's father, was next to arrive. He joined Ben for a cup of tea and the group fell into conversation about the day's events and Ben's trip from the island. Ben studied the kitchen with all the conveniences that electricity made possible and envisioned his mother enjoying the same luxuries. Mrs. O'Neil checked the leg of lamb in the oven, then pulled the roaster out and set it on the top of the stove. Potatoes boiled on one electric element and mixed vegetables on another. Laura cut up the ingredients for a green salad. Ben admired the crisp apron covering her cotton dress. He had usually pictured her as a nurse. This domestic side of her was new to him. It suited her. Of course, in his eyes, everything suited Laura.

The dining room table was set with crystal wine glasses and fine china placed on a linen tablecloth. A large oil painting of a rural landscape hung on the wall over a mahogany sideboard. A family portrait adorned another wall. Both were displayed in ornate frames. A quick glance hinted at the affluence this family was accustomed to. How would Laura fare away from the everyday comforts she had always known? In their teasing arguments about country versus city, he hadn't seriously considered what a girl of Laura's background would have to give up to live on Hecla

Island. Or what her family would think if she was asked to make such a move.

Hecla Island was paradise to him. He couldn't imagine living anywhere else. Looking at Laura, her red curls dancing, her large eyes glowing, her sassy mouth smiling, he couldn't imagine living without her.

The arrival of Hilary, Laura's sister, along with husband Frank and children Audrey and Michael, brought a spirited energy into the home. The preschoolers wasted no time in captivating their grandparents. The happy chaos reminded Ben of Daniel and Rose's family. It was evident to Ben that Laura had spoken of him to her family. The interest and knowledge they revealed about Hecla Island and the fishing industry pleased him.

Although the atmosphere appeared amiable, Ben was aware of underlying tensions as they sat down to dinner. He caught Laura's father eying him suspiciously. Hilary had a snooty air about her. Laura seemed agitated and Mrs. O'Neil flitted around the room like a fairy godmother trying to sugarcoat everything with her magic wand.

"What do you do on the island for fun?" Hilary's question carried a judgmental tone.

"We have dances in the community hall and there are other gatherings for special occasions."

"Community dances, how quaint! Is there a school?" She accompanied this question with a patronizing look.

"Yes, and a store with a post office, the hall, and a church." Ben was careful to keep a matching edge out of his words.

"What kind of church?" The abrupt question came from Mr. O'Neil.

"Lutheran." Ben sensed there was no point in elaborating.

"Is everyone ready for dessert?" Mrs. O'Neil jumped up from her chair. "I've made Laura's favourite, a cherry cheesecake."

Hilary and Laura removed the dinner plates from the table to make room for the dessert.

"It's nice to be together. I haven't seen Audrey and Michael for so long." Laura smiled at her niece and nephew as she stacked the plates.

"You're working with all those sick polio kids. I'm not eager to take chances with my own children." Hilary seemed to accuse Laura.

Ben realized he wasn't the only bee in Hilary's bonnet. The threat of contracting polio was very real to her. She feared for her children and Laura's profession was a direct link.

Ben knew there were hurdles to overcome if his relationship with

Laura was to flourish. He was very proud of his roots, but, the O'Neil family certainly had its share of pride, too.

After dinner, plans were made to go to the Tipperary for the birthday party. Frank and Hilary would only stay for a short time. The children had to be in bed at a reasonable hour. Mr. and Mrs. O'Neil knew the younger partygoers would outlast them. They agreed to travel in three cars to the Irish restaurant.

"What happened to daughters who listened and obeyed their fathers?" Colin O"Neil ranted as he backed the car out of the driveway. "My father must be rolling in his grave."

"That's a bit harsh, Colin." Katherine sighed. "Ben seems like a fine young man. Laura's happy. She's just like you, you know, headstrong and outspoken. Didn't we raise her to stand on her own two feet and make her own decisions?"

"Kate, for the love of God, he's an Icelander *and* a Lutheran."

"And like it or not, our girl is smitten with him. I'm not saying I disagree with you. I'd welcome an Irishman, who's Catholic and has a good job. But, I must say, Laura has good taste. I like Ben."

And that was Colin's biggest problem with Ben – he liked him. In spite of this, he hoped Laura would come to her senses and find a more suitable man as her partner. He had to admit that Ben was a fine young man. Just meant for someone else's daughter.

"It won't be easy changing her mind." Colin pressed down on the sedan's clutch and shifted gears. Katherine was right, Laura was headstrong and outspoken. Whether nursing a bird with a broken wing or taking the role as referee in a playground argument, Laura as a child, had approached everything in calm determination. This trait had carried into adulthood.

"She's twenty-four and he's twenty-eight. They're not children, Colin. Give it some time and see what happens. They may discover on their own that their worlds are too far apart."

"Admit it, Kate, you're already planning the wedding supper."

What was a father to do? Other families had dealt with mixed marriages and seemed to get along. It just hadn't occurred to him that it could happen in his family.

"The wind blew stronger and the Icelandic travellers had to struggle with the oars. On a raft behind the boat, the cow was fussing. The poor cow had never been on a raft and certainly never on the lake before." Amma Anna spun her tale. Signey listened with rapt attention. While the rest of the family was outdoors tending to the chores and cooking the evening meal, Amma Anna stayed with Signey. The girl was progressing. Her thin limbs were getting stronger and her skin was losing the sickly pallor she'd come home with. On occasion, sounds were heard from the challenged vocal chords. Hope was very much alive that she would speak again.

"All of a sudden, they heard a splash and realized Bessa, the cow, had loosened the rope and had jumped overboard. What a commotion! The men had been watching the shore, trying to find a good place to land for the night. Bessa made their minds up for them. Afraid they would lose the cow, they rowed toward the shoreline and searched for a site to set up camp." After a slight pause, Amma Anna asked, "Do you think they found her?"

The girl nodded and smiled. Amma Anna always asked questions to make sure her audience was listening. Signey's head was propped on her grandmother's lap at one end of the sofa. She was tucked into a warm quilt to rest, after her exercises that Karen did with her after school every day.

"The people in the boat were very tired. Not just from that day of travel but from the long voyage they'd been on. You see, they had left their homes in Iceland – that's a country far, far away. They had heard that life was good in Canada and decided to come. It had taken them many months to make the trip. First by steamship across the ocean and then by train from the east coast to Winnipeg. From there they came by boat, stopping in Gimli before settling in Hecla. Back to Bessa. They saw her run up the shore and into the thick brush and tall trees. They had small children who needed milk. They had to find her." Amma Anna heard the others coming in the back door. Supper would be ready soon and there was more story to tell. "The travellers found a clearing and set up camp. They lit a fire so they could cook their supper and be warm. Their clothes were damp from the mist on the lake. Smoke from the campfire discouraged the pesky mosquitoes from coming too close. But a few steps away from the fire, the mosquitoes were very thick and very hungry..."

"Don't forget to tell Signey how big they were. What was it now? Nearly as big as my hand?" Daniel interrupted his mother's storytelling. He laughed as he remembered how he and Ben had loved to hear the stories of the early settlers.

Amma Anna chuckled and gently covered Signey's ears, "Don't listen to his nonsense. The mosquitoes weren't quite that big! Anyway, the settlers were sitting around the fire, trying to think of a plan to find Bessa. They could hear an owl hooting and a wolf howling deep in the woods. The wind was blowing so hard the waves crashed on the rocky shore."

More ears had perked up toward the living room. The older children had heard this story before, but Amma Anna always varied the telling so it was still interesting. Her voice altered to a near whisper as she continued.

"There was a thrashing sound in the brush near the clearing. All the children were huddled in the protection of their mothers' arms. The men reached for their weapons, fearing a bear was coming toward them. Suddenly, a large beast burst into the clearing. It was Bessa. She was so happy to find them. Her eyes were as big as saucers and she panted like a very tired dog. Everyone was happy as they settled down for the night. And in the morning when they explored the clearing and shoreline, they decided that Bessa had chosen a fine site for their home. They had intended to go farther north but that spot had everything they were looking for. And that is the story of the first permanent settlers on Hecla Island in 1876. The first one wasn't an Icelander from Iceland, but Bessa the cow from Gimli."

The children laughed and the adults joined in at Amma Anna's conclusion. She loved to spice up her stories. The children all learned the Hecla history at her knee.

"Supper's ready. Come and eat." Rose had everything on the table. Signey and Amma Anna joined the others in the kitchen where the adventures of Bessa carried into mealtime conversation.

The Tipperary emitted the animation of an energetic crowd. The music and Irish dialect was reminiscent of Ben's first visit to the restaurant. This time, streamers and other birthday decorations hung everywhere. Children were dancing near the large birthday cake. When no one was watching, the children took turns dipping a finger into the icing and sweetening their tongues.

Ben was hanging up his and Laura's coats when Sean shouted a greeting from behind the bar. "Ah, Ben, m'lad, ye had the good sense to come back again."

"Couldn't miss wishing you a happy birthday. It's good to see you again, Sean."

The party was in fine form. Every year, Sean invited his family and friends to the Tipperary on his birthday. He considered it a thank-you to them for supporting the restaurant all year. There was lots to eat and stout flowed freely all night. Sean joked that the watered-down stout only tasted that way.

Laura introduced Ben to various family members, then she led him to the end of the bar. "Ben, I'd like you to meet my cousin Aiden, Sean's brother." Aiden was taking a break from bartending duty. As the men shook hands, Laura continued, "Actually, the two of you have a lot in common. You both served in Europe. Maybe you saw some of the same places."

The two men exchanged details on their service overseas. Aiden had been part of the Canadian Army going through northern France and Belgium in order to liberate Holland. Although their war experiences were very different, there was an unspoken kinship that drew the two men together. For both, it had been a time that had changed their lives forever. Some of the unspeakable tragedies they had known were mirrored in each other's eyes. Laura excused herself to visit with her aunt. When she returned twenty minutes later, Ben and Aiden were still huddled together at the end of the bar.

Sean needed help behind the bar and Laura was motioning toward the dance floor when the two war veterans stood up.

"Next time you're in town, let me know and I'll take you to the Legion. You'll like the guys there."

"Thanks again, Aiden, I'd like that. I'm glad I met you. See you later."

Ben led Laura to the dance floor. They swayed in unison to the slow beat of the music and just as Ben was thinking how well they moved together the tempo changed in the next song. Ben guided Laura into a cross between a foxtrot and a two-step. She was quick to follow his lead and within moments he directed her around the floor. He had a unique backward kick as he whirled her around. Soon they were gliding like seasoned partners and they began to attract attention. The crowd circled them and clapped in time to the music. The music ended with loud cheers.

"That's some fine steppin', lad." Sean beamed his approval.

"On Hecla Island, we all grew up dancing." He wiped his brow and gestured to Laura. "But, here's my fine stepping partner."

The party continued into the wee hours of the morning. Laura's family had left hours before. The last revellers were reluctant to call it a night. Ben had been welcomed and treated like a close friend. He was completely at home with the teasing banter and amiable chatter that created the atmosphere in this Irish establishment.

In the car on the way home, Ben pulled Laura across the seat to sit beside him. He held her tight as she nestled her head against his neck. They both dreaded the evening's end and his leaving in the morning.

"Remember the Hallowe'en dance? Will you be able to come?"

"Yes." She responded softly.

"You can bring a friend or one of your Irish cousins to protect you." Ben laughed at the reference to the first time they had been together.

"You'll be there, won't you?" she asked.

"Well, yeah, of course I will."

"That's all the protection I need." The kiss she planted on his cheek along with the spoken trust in him set his heart thumping.

They quietly crept into the house. Ben brought in the overnight case he'd packed. Laura's parents had offered him a bed for the night. Ben and Laura weren't ready to go to sleep yet. Laura raided the refrigerator, finding juice and cake. The humble picnic was carted into the living room where they resumed what they'd started in the car. The snack was quickly forgotten.

In the morning, Ben thanked the O'Neils and accepted Mrs. O'Neil's invitation for another visit. He wrapped his arm around Laura's waist, when she walked him to his car. "I had such a good time. And thanks for introducing me to Aiden. I know you wanted to get us together, and you did. He's a nice guy, we'll probably be good for each other." He grinned at her. A blush reddened her cheeks as she realized he knew of her plan for the soldier and airman to spend some time together. "Will you always look out for me, and all your family too? Take good care of us?" He tickled her and drew her into his arms.

"Please don't be upset with me. It's just that I've seen the same sadness in both your face and Aiden's. Both of you put up barriers when the war is mentioned. I realize that the rest of us can't fully understand what you experienced. We weren't there, but Ben, if you never talk about it, how will we ever know what really happened and what you survived?"

The passion in her voice drove into Ben's heart. He held her tightly. "I'm not upset with you, Laura. I don't think I could ever be upset with you. Guys like Aiden and me, we need you to be patient with us. It isn't that we want to shut everyone out. It's just easier to talk about with someone who's been there. But believe this, you're the first person that I want to tell the stories to. Laura, I want you to know me and all about my past. I want to bring down the barriers for you." He pulled her back away from him to look into her face. Tears glistened in her eyes and spilled onto her cheeks. He wiped them away. "Please don't cry. Don't be sad."

Laura shook her head at his words. "I'm not sad, Ben. I'm happy that you want to tell me."

"God, I hate to leave you." His eyes bore into hers. "It's nearly two weeks until the dance. Could you stay for a few days? My mother would love that."

Nodding, she said, "I have some holiday time and I switched a shift. I can hardly wait to see your island and meet your family and friends."

"Let's give the neighbours one more show." He gave her a lingering kiss and hug. "I love you, *kaerasta min*."

"What does car...., what you just said, what does it mean?"

"My love, my dear one...., and no, I've never called anyone that before." Ben had read her mind.

He was in his car and turning the key when he saw her lips say the words back to him. "I love you, too."

And again he smiled all the way home.

Chapter 6

The ferry engines loudly propelled the vessel into the channel. Laura felt the vibrations throughout her body and clutched the railing. It was the end of October and she was on her first ferry ride. Noisy gulls escorted them across the choppy waves.

A brisk breeze tugged at the scarf covering Laura's hair and threatened to loosen the knot tied under her chin. Seeing the channel gave more credence to Ben's explanation on freeze-up and break-up. Laura could only imagine how nerve wracking it would be to cross on the first ice of winter and the last ice before break-up in the spring.

Ben had spent the night in Winnipeg visiting with Laura's family and then first thing that morning they'd set out for Hecla Island. Laura was excited to see the island and to meet all the people that Ben spoke so fondly of.

Ben pointed out the many mallard and teal ducks that were still in the marsh. "The male ducks are colourful and so they're easier to see. Female ducks are more muted in colour to camouflage themselves in the spring, while they sit on the eggs in their nests."

"When will they start migrating south?"

"Soon they'll be gone to seek a warmer climate for winter. Many have left already. Because the weather's been warm this fall, the ducks and geese are taking their time."

"Look, is that a beaver?" Laura pointed towards something swimming in the water leaving a wake in its path.

"No, a muskrat."

"Aren't those beaver houses in the marsh?"

"No, they're muskrat houses. But, you're close. Muskrat houses resemble beaver homes. They're shaped the same, but beavers build with sticks and mud while muskrats favour bullrush reeds and moss."

"What exactly, is a muskrat?" Laura shivered in distaste. "They don't sound very appealing."

"They're big, chubby rats with long, shiny hair." His head swooped down and he stole a quick kiss, hoping to erase the look of repulsion on her face. "Maybe you've worn a muskrat-trimmed coat?"

"I don't think so!" A tremor rippled up her spine.

"It wouldn't have been called muskrat, though. It usually goes by the name 'Hudson seal'."

"You're joking."

"Sound familiar?"

"Yes. I once owned a coat with a Hudson seal collar. Actually, I've seen quite a few coats like that."

"It's often mistaken for mink, seal, or sable."

"Are the muskrats, here in the marsh, trapped and sold for fur?"

"Every year Daniel and Jon come out here and trap. I usually go for a few days with them." Ben slowed the car for the last bend in the horseshoe-shaped road skirting the marsh. Laura nodded, then her eyes followed the road toward the island's interior. The marshy terrain of the west side of Hecla Island soon changed to lowland trees as the road veered eastward.

"I didn't expect the road to be so smooth. Is it a new road?"

"It was built in 1945, replacing what the Heclingers called the 'Mill Portage'. They used to haul the lumber from the sawmill by horse and sleigh along this trail in winter. Not in summer though. Then the lumber went by boat from the east side of the island. They used to haul supplies from Riverton on this trail, too."

Ben named the trees as they drove along the narrow road – swamp spruce, willows and tamarack. Nearing the interior of the island, the higher elevation offered foundation to tall spruce, birch, poplar, balsam and ash. Ben continuously studied the whole landscape, bringing Laura's attention to any visible wildlife.

She gasped when they sighted a bald eagle and she sighed at the vision of four deer on the road ahead. Ben stopped the car in hope that the quartet would dally to entertain them. One doe perked her ears up, her head twitching from side to side. Her wariness alerted the others to the bright blue car and its potential danger. They flitted into the forest.

Some autumn colour was still evident in the tree coverings, but most of the leaves had already fallen. Ben described how the branches, laden with leaves in the summer, dipped over the road keeping any wildlife well hidden from sight. The forest was home to deer, moose, timber wolves, foxes and coyotes. Smaller animals like rabbits, weasels and mink also maintained abodes in the woods.

They travelled northward and then eastward again. Laura noted the open brightness ahead and realized they were nearing the east side of the island.

"I can't believe it!" Laura was amazed at the expanse of the lake when they reached the beach road. There was water as far as she could see. "It's a different world from one side of the island to the other."

The east shoreline varied from sandy beaches to craggy cliffs. Rock formations dotted with vegetation could have sprung from an artist's canvas. Laura was captivated by the raw beauty unfolding before her eyes.

Ben waved a greeting to everyone they saw as they drove past houses. Laura was intrigued by the fact that everyone on the island knew each other. A close-knit community was unfamiliar to her. She had lived her entire life in Winnipeg.

When Ben turned into a driveway, Laura admired the two houses in the yard. She knew that Ben shared the older, two-story house with his mother. It was painted white with dark brown trim around the windows. A veranda stretched across the front of the house, offering a clear view of the lake and Black Island. Rose and Daniel's house was situated on the other side of the driveway. Two dogs came charging around the side of the house, their tails wagging when they recognized the vehicle.

"Guard dogs on duty!" Ben warned of the impending attack. "Actually, you don't need to worry about these two. When they show their teeth they're just smiling."

"Remember, I have one of those vicious kind of beasts at home. Our Lady's greatest flaw is wanting to rub up against everyone, leaving clumps of dog hair all over. It isn't always appreciated."

Ben opened the car door for Laura and retrieved their luggage from the backseat. The dogs were quick to circle and were anxious to sniff out the stranger. Ben's command to 'stay' was in conflict to Laura's outstretched hand. Cautiously, the two dogs approached and were instantly won over by her soft voice.

"Like I said, guard dogs on duty. You two hounds are pretty pathetic, but you have good judgment." Ben ruffled the hair on the dogs' heads and ushered Laura toward the backdoor of the house.

Amma Anna met them in the doorway. "It's so nice to meet you. I've heard so much about you, from Ben and also from Rose." As it was customary in most Hecla Island homes, Amma Anna held her arms wide and gave Laura a welcoming embrace. The warmth and aroma emitting from the kitchen urged the couple inside.

"Smells good in here, Mama. What's cooking?" Ben strode over to the woodstove and tipped up the pot lid.

"There's soup and the bread is fresh from the oven." Amma Anna had made the soup with moose meat and vegetables. The table had been set for their anticipated arrival. Laura felt at home immediately. The spacious kitchen was painted in a pale yellow with coordinating frilly print curtains at the windows. An oak table and spindle backed chairs were varnished in a light hue to enhance the rich grain of the wood. The table setting was simple and inviting.

"Ben, show Laura where she can wash up before lunch."

In a room off the kitchen, Ben poured water from a pitcher into a basin on the washstand. The cool water was refreshing.

"You must be starving. Here Laura, have a seat. Everything is ready." Amma Anna ladled the thick soup into bowls which she served with slices of home-baked bread. The kettle simmered on the woodstove for the coffee that would go with apple pie for dessert.

"I didn't think I was hungry, but your soup smells so delicious." Laura enjoyed both the meal and the conversation that accompanied it. Ben and his mother were both strong-minded individuals, but it was apparent from the way Ben had spoken of his mother and the way they treated each other that they had a mutual understanding.

Amma Anna was interested to hear about Laura's work as a nurse and about her family.

"Hello, anyone home?" Daniel shouted as he, Rose and Signey came through the door. They found the threesome chatting amiably, surrounded by empty dessert dishes and half-filled coffee cups. When Laura turned to face them, Signey shrank back, clutching her mother's pant-leg. Not understanding the reason for the child's shyness, Rose tried to draw her forward. Signey tightened her hold, her eyes large and fearful.

Laura understood immediately what had happened, and she gently slid from her chair to kneel on one knee in front of her former patient.

"Hi, Signey. You remember me from the hospital, don't you?"

The little girl trembled and nodded.

"I'm not taking you back to the hospital. I know your Uncle Ben, and he invited me to the dance tonight." Laura tried to ease the panic she knew Signey was feeling. "I'm just here for a visit so don't worry. I'm not going to take you away. Please don't be afraid of me."

Signey loosened the hold she had on her mother, but she still stared wide-eyed at the nurse. Laura knew that trust wouldn't come easily and she'd have to continue the reassurances. As the other family members looked on, Laura reached out for Signey's hand.

"I hear you're doing all your exercises and getting strong again."

Signey let Laura take her hand. By this time Rose had knelt beside her daughter, realizing that her assurances were needed as well.

"Laura is Uncle Ben's girlfriend." This remark was said in a conspicuous whisper. As Signey's face softened, she smiled at her mother and then at Laura. Rose continued, "I wonder if she has a costume for the dance?"

Ben arose from his chair. The two women stood up. He put an arm around Laura and said, "There's no way my girl is wearing a mask. I'm showing her off to everyone."

Laura cheeks were flushed. Rose came to her rescue. "Don't scare her, Ben. Honestly Laura, we aren't too bad, but be prepared for a lot of attention. There are some other bachelors on the island, so let me know if Ben gets too irritating!" Rose shrieked in laughter as Ben shook her by the shoulders. All these antics had lightened the atmosphere and Signey giggled.

Signey's speech was slowly improving and there was evidence of renewed strength in her damaged muscles. However, there had been no improvement in the left shoulder muscle. Her left arm still hung motionless.

Ben lifted his niece into his arms and said, "You'll have to help me tonight. Laura has never done the 'Butterfly' dance. I bet we could show her how it's done." The girl smiled and nodded. Ben held her in a dance position and whirled her around the room, much to Signey's delight.

Signey followed the women as Amma Anna and Rose showed Laura the rest of the house. In the living room, well padded cushions on the sofa and armchairs, sheer drapes and handmade accessories were pleasing to the eye as well as looking comfortable. A chess game and cribbage board on a table gave an indication of how evenings were spent. The battery-operated radio and overstuffed bookshelves hinted at other diversions. Coal oil lamps were scattered around the house. The Bergurssons were still working on the wiring required to have electric lights. Laura had stopped to gaze out the front window. Two rocking chairs on the veranda caught her attention. She imagined how wonderful it would be to sit there with such a stunning view.

"It's beautiful, isn't it?" Rose grinned as her eyes followed Laura's gaze.

Laura nodded. "How do you get all your work done? I"m afraid I'd spend half my time daydreaming."

"I grew up on the island, so I guess I take my surroundings for granted. It's good to have someone remind us."

The two young women joined Amma Anna on the stairs. Rose carried Signey, who was still unsure of their visitor. The second floor of the house was divided into four rooms. Amma Anna and Ben each had a bedroom. One room was used as a guest room and the fourth served as an office for Ben. Although sparsely furnished, the office provided adequate space for the mass of paperwork that Ben had accumulated while working on the power project.

Laura followed Amma Anna into the guest room. The lone-star quilt covering the bed took her breath away. Amma Anna modestly accepted credit for the fine handwork. The walls were a pale green and matching cotton curtains adorned the window. Rose pointed out the water pitcher and basin on the washstand in one corner. She also lifted the edge of the bedspread to reveal a chamber pot.

"I guess you aren't used to outdoor toilets and carrying in your bath water." Rose's voice sounded slightly apologetic.

"I may not be used to that, but I haven't got any problem with using a chamber pot or carrying water. This is a wonderful room." She turned to Amma Anna and said, "Your whole house is beautiful, Mrs. Bergursson. Thank you so much for your hospitality."

"You are very welcome. I'm so glad you were able to come. And, please, just call me Anna." The genuine warmth in her words and on her face reached out to Laura. She was relieved that Ben's family was so welcoming. Maybe they just hid their concerns better than her family.

Laura felt that she knew Rose after the many telephone calls. Her involvement with Signey had provided a personal link to her. She wanted to impress Ben's family and friends and be accepted as the special person in Ben's life. But she was well aware that many obstacles were apparent. They were from different cultural and religious backgrounds. They had grown up in different worlds.

Bjossi was dressed for the dance early. He always enjoyed social gatherings when music was involved. His violin was stowed into its carrying case. The case was worn and the clasp was unpredictable. Crude twine wrapped around the case and tied in a rough knot provided extra security for the precious violin.

Chopper looked on with sad eyes. He recognized the clothes as a sign that he wouldn't be accompanying his master. Sometimes when

Bjossi changed his clothes to go to Riverton, Chopper was invited along and he would sit in the cab of the old truck while errands were run. When his master put on the fancy tie and woollen suit, Chopper knew that he didn't have a chance. He flopped down on the floor and lay his head on a paw. Misery was etched into his sorrowful eyes.

"Sorry, Chopper, you'll have to stay home tonight. I know you'd behave yourself, but you should see the heels on the shoes all the women wear. They could kill you if they ever stepped on you. Those heels are like nails." The old bachelor patted the dog and tried to conceal his excitement from his furry friend.

Bjossi had played his violin at Hecla dances for three decades. A band was never hired for these events. Islanders who played a musical instrument brought it to the dance with them. The musicians took turns on the stage so the music never stopped for long. They simply rehearsed as the party went on.

Reaching into the cupboard, Bjossi brought out a flask of whiskey and tucked it into the inner pocket of his suit jacket. A swig now and again helped to keep his fingers nimble. The band members imbibed alcoholic beverages during their breaks when they could slip outside. They didn't bring liquor into the hall. Inside the hall, the women served gallons of coffee and juice with trays of baked dainties and sandwiches.

"Guard the place while I'm away." Bjossi instructed Chopper and Billy. "See you later." Bjossi climbed into his truck and drove to the hall in the village.

On the other side of the village, north of Kristjan and Thora's, Oli sat at his kitchen table, grumbling about having to attend the dance. His wife, Hilda, knew that he was anticipating the goading he would be subjected to over the telephone pole incident. Islanders had long memories and loved nothing better than to tease. Oli was famous for bringing up embarrassing moments in front of people, but when the shoe was on the other foot, it was a different story.

"Put your shoes on, Oli. They're right behind your chair." Hilda wasn't about to listen to his whining. She was anxious to get to the hall and help the other women set up the lunch.

Oli glanced behind the chair and turned to reach for the shoes. They'd been polished and buffed to a glossy shine. He tied the thin laces and rose.

"Are you ready? I'll get the car out of the garage." Resigned, he walked toward the back door. The sooner they went to the hall, the sooner the ribbing would be over.

"I'll be right there." Hilda sympathized with her husband. She knew Oli could 'dish it out' a lot better than he could take it back, but he was a good man and she loved him dearly. He had a hard time reining in his temper, but Hilda would always stand beside her man. Because his anger was seldom aimed at his wife, she could usually make him see reason.

As they drove to the hall, Hilda picked some lint from the collar of Oli's suit and smoothed the front of her woollen skirt. She wore a hand-knit sweater that had been featured in a needlework magazine. The red worsted yarn complemented the plaid skirt of gray, black and red.

Several vehicles had arrived already. Everyone, with the exception of Oli, was eager for an excuse to have a good time. The completion of the fall fishing season certainly was reason enough. This fall they also had the electricity success to celebrate.

"Isn't that Ben with his new girlfriend?" Hilda spotted the couple in the parking lot. "My, look at that red hair. Anna said she was Irish, and a nurse in Winnipeg." Squinting to get a closer look, she said, "She's pretty. I guess he was doing more in the city than meeting with the government. I'm not surprised to see him dating an outsider. He thinks he's too good for the island girls."

Oli scanned the parking lot. He spotted a group of men sharing a laugh. He wasn't paying attention to Hilda's words.

"Look at him strutting around like a peacock." Disgust laced Hilda's speech.

Oli assisted his wife with the food tray. As they turned to walk toward the hall, a male voice shouted, "Oli, have you fixed your car?" Oli frowned. He handed the tray to Hilda. "They could have waited a few minutes." He muttered, gritted his teeth and headed in the direction of the amused men.

Polka music was radiating from the hall when Laura stepped out of the car. In the parking lot two men shouted a greeting. They were leaning against a car. The open trunk revealed a case of beer, which the men had started on. There were groups of people all around, on the hall steps and in the parking area. Everyone waved and yelled greetings to Ben. All eyes seemed to be focussed on Laura.

Inside the hall, the music had attracted several dancers. Laura had never seen a polka danced before. She'd grown up with the Irish jig. Both styles of dance required quick steps and lots of stamina. At the front of the dance floor, by the stage, a group of children were creating their own dance moves. A woman grabbed Laura by the arm. She was turned toward a woman who gave her a quick hug and a kiss on her cheek.

"Hello, and who are you?" The woman stepped back and smiled at Laura.

Taken aback, Laura smiled and before she could say anything, another woman approached and gave her a similar hug and kiss. Ben laughed and introduced Thora and Margaret to Laura. As he led her away he whispered, "Remember my first time at the Tipperary? Well, this is your first dance in Hecla!"

Sam's wife, Gudrun, was the next person to come forward. Under the new maternity top, her pregnancy was visible. "I'm so glad to meet you, Laura. Ben has told us about you." Then she leaned close to Laura's ear and whispered, "Thanks for putting that big smile on his face."

Laura smiled. "It's so nice to be here. I've been anxious to see the island and meet everyone. Ben has told me about you, too. He said you're expecting your first baby. Congratulations."

"Thank you. Yes, we're very excited.

While they were talking, Ben was eyeing a witch that seemed to be hovering around them. Then he burst out laughing. "Laura, I want you to meet my best friend, Sam."

The witch swung 'her' broom at Ben and then took Laura's hand. In a cackling voice, 'she' said, "Welcome to Hecla Island." From inside 'her' cape, the witch withdrew a bottle labelled 'Love Potion' and offered it to Laura. "You'll be needing some of this if you're going to put up with this guy all night."

"Hey, stay away from her, you old hag. I can imagine what's in that bottle."

"Sam, go bug someone else. Besides, everyone will guess who you are." Gudrun had come to the dance alone saying that Sam wasn't feeling well. Of course, no one had believed her. They all knew he'd be dressed up. His witch's costume covered his identity perfectly, but Ben knew his friend very well and had seen through the disguise.

Jon and Elin arrived with their children. They were all in costume. Jon and his son Stefan were scarecrows, while Elin and the two girls, Aldis and Beth, were dressed up as a queen and her princesses. Fred and Kristine were right behind them with the twins in tow. Kristine had cut and painted cardboard cartons from the store to portray characters from a deck of cards. Fred was the King of Hearts and Kristine was the Queen. The boys were the two and three of Hearts.

A group of circus people walked in. Laura recognized Daniel, Rose and their children. Daniel carried a chair and a whip in his role as a lion tamer. His attempt at subduing the witch failed. Sam merely put a hex on him.

Laura was impressed by the effort and enthusiasm that the islanders put into making this event such a success. Whether preparing lunch, playing in the band, dancing, or just visiting, everyone was having a good time.

Ben took Laura's hand and guided her onto the dance floor. The band was playing an old-time waltz. After Sean's birthday party, Laura easily fell into step with her partner. She noticed that the other dancers glided along in similar movements. When Ben had said that everyone on Hecla Island grew up dancing, he hadn't been joking.

Benches lined the wall around the dance floor. Ben led Laura over to the side where Malla and Olivia sat. They were delighted to meet the Irish girl that they'd heard so much about.

"Take good care of our boy. He can be a rascal, you know!" Malla had a twinkle in her eye, communicating the deep affection she had for Ben.

"It's a big job." Laura laughed, winning approval with the two women.

"You'll have to bring her over for coffee, Ben."

"Will your coffeepot be on tomorrow afternoon?"

"You know it will." Malla beamed, anticipating the visit. "Now get on the floor for this polka. I don't want to see any dust settling on your shoes."

The couple joined the throng of dancers on the floor. The quick stepping polka required perfect harmony between the couples. One wrong move could result in a pile-up. As they raced around the floor, Laura concluded that the islanders addressed the polka the same way they addressed all challenges, head down and at full speed.

When the polka ended, all the dancers were short of breath, with beads of sweat on their foreheads. The men shed their suit jackets and rolled up their shirt sleeves. They loosened their ties and mopped their brows. The ladies rested their feet, since they weren't accustomed to wearing high heeled shoes. As soon as the band was ready for the next tune, so were the dancers.

Laura noticed one of the old fiddlers get a tap on the shoulder indicating it was time for a break. Another fiddler took his place as he made his way outside. From her position on the floor, she watched as he joined one of the groups of men. Pulling a whiskey flask from his pocket, he enjoyed a few sips as he contributed to the ongoing conversation.

At the front of the hall, the children played and spun in little circles. Signey was dressed up in a clown costume and sat on a bench with the twins. They were watching the dancers and playing with their friends. Signey shyly looked at people staring at her, but the twins seemed to keep her mind occupied. Rose had told Laura that this was Signey's first social gathering since her illness. Signey appeared to be thoroughly enjoying herself.

After another heated polka, the men ventured outside. Gudrun entertained Laura with stories of other island events. They'd formed a quick friendship. Laura sensed the protectiveness toward Ben by those close to him. If she didn't already suspect how his family and friends felt about him, she certainly knew now.

"Laura, I should introduce you to Ellen. She's a teacher at the school and she's from Winnipeg. She has room and board with my parents. This is her first year of teaching and the first time she's lived so far from home."

Gudrun and Laura made their way over to the teacher. Ellen Taylor, Laura learned, was also attending her first dance in Hecla.

"I don't know where everyone finds the energy to keep dancing. Obviously, they play as hard as they work." Ellen nodded her head in admiration.

The two city girls discovered their homes weren't far apart in Winnipeg. Ellen's family home was down Wolseley Avenue, along the Assiniboine River, on Sherburn Street. They had both attended Laura Secord School. Because Ellen was younger than Laura, they hadn't known each other in school.

"Do you know the Tipperary, a restaurant just off Portage Avenue?"

Laura gasped at the coincidences in their lives. "My cousin owns it. I go there all the time."

"It's my favourite place. I get such a kick out of the bartender."

"That's my cousin."

"It's a small world, isn't it?"

When the men returned, they all decided to go for coffee. Laura couldn't believe her eyes when she saw the lunch that had been prepared. There were trays of sandwiches and more trays filled with baked dainties. Many of the dainties were new to Laura. She had never seen *ponnukokur* or *vinarterta* before. Ben insisted that she try everything. Someone had made Calla Lillies. They were sweet sugar cookies that were pinched on one side to form a little cup in the centre. This cup was then filled with whipped cream and topped with a piece of fruit, usually a piece of orange. On the woodstove, kettles were keeping the coffee hot.

A wood heater had been lit earlier to take the chill out of the building. As soon as the women arrived to prepare the lunch, they kindled a fire in the wood stove, which provided auxiliary heat to the hall. Body heat and polkas provided the remainder of the warmth indoors.

After eating their lunch, Ben and Laura refilled their coffee cups and ventured outside. They skirted the various clusters of people in the parking lot. With the help of the new lights in the village, Ben and Laura walked across the road, past the packing shed and to the end of the dock. On the way he had grabbed his jacket which he draped over her shoulders. They sipped the coffee and Ben pointed out the different buildings in the dim light.

"Tomorrow I'll show you all over the island. The road goes north to Gull Harbour. There are some summer cottages there and the old fish hatchery. At the end of the road there's a park, right on the northernmost tip of the island."

"I can understand your love for Hecla. What a beautiful place."

"It's pretty special, alright." Ben set their empty coffee cups on the ledge that circled the outer rim of the dock. He gathered her into his arms and feathered her face with kisses. "I've been waiting all night to steal you away."

Although Laura was enjoying her Hecla dance experience, she couldn't argue with Ben on this privacy on the dock. In his arms was, by far, the best place to be.

"I guess we should get back, before they send out a search party." Ben bent over to retrieve the coffee cups.

"Don't fall into the water!" Laura warned, looking worried as Ben was tilted so near the edge.

"I'm okay, don't worry." Ben laughed as he remembered a story. "One Sunday in the spring, it was Confirmation Day at the church. Adam and his friend Andrew were in the class. Some of the other kids had come down here to go swimming, and when the boys came out of the church, they headed straight for the dock. They were both on their bicycles, and," he paused for effect, "in their best clothes. Andrew rode his bike along the edge of the dock, talking to the kids in the water. Just as he was asking them if the water was cold, he put his foot out to stop the bike. He had planned on setting his foot on this ledge, but he miscalculated and slipped over the edge." Ben's laugh was infectious. "He went overboard and the bicycle right behind him. They fished Andrew and the bike out of the water. There was no need to tell him how cold the water was. He walked his bike off the dock, his soggy leather shoes squelching water. Poor Andrew. We heard the commotion all the way to the church."

Ben's stories always made Laura smile. She was sure that Andrew's mother probably saw the humour in the escapade, even though she wouldn't have been too happy with him at the time.

Walking back through the hall's parking lot, Laura overheard an angry shout. "What's going on over there?"

"Some guys spend more time drinking beer than dancing. Looks like those mainlanders are getting into a fight. Don't worry, they're too drunk to hurt anyone."

"Do many people from the mainland come to the Hecla dances?"

"There's usually some visitors. But those guys," Ben motioned to the brawlers, "they come on their own. Nobody invited them."

"How late does the ferry run? Will they get home tonight?"

"No, they'll sleep in their car."

"Why wouldn't they just stay closer to home if all they're interested in is drinking?"

"It isn't just the drinking. They like some of our island girls. That's likely the cause of the fight."

On reentering the hall, they could see the party was still at full throttle. Ben and Laura were just about to sit down with Gudrun and the witch, when the band announced , "Get your partners for a Butterfly." Ben looked for his little niece. When he spotted her, he grabbed Laura's hand and went to meet Signey. Ben was in the middle, with one arm around Laura's waist and the other around Signey's shoulders. They strutted together to the beat of the music until the tempo changed to a polka tune and Ben circled, first around one girl, then the other. The pace altered from the walking beat to the polka beat. Signey's thin left leg was dragging at the end of the dance, but her face glowed.

Laura had several dance partners throughout the night. It was a wonderful party. In between dances, she loved gazing over the crowd. She could see with some scrutiny, that there were many distinctive personalities among these people. But however diverse they were, they melded together to form a strong and vibrant community.

A slow waltz was just beginning when Ben leaned over to Laura and said, "I'm going to dance with my smallest best girl." Laura nodded, understanding his intention.

Signey looked hopeful when she saw Ben coming toward her. His eyes met hers and he beckoned her to the floor. He lifted her into his arms, placing the little left arm on his right shoulder and clasping her right hand in his left. Ben waltzed around the dance floor, cheek-to-cheek with Signey. As the waltz ended, he tipped her over into an elaborate dip, sending her into gleeful laughter. It was a sight that brought a tear to many eyes.

Later, when Laura was slow dancing with Ben, she noticed the fiddler lean over. With his fiddle bow, he flicked a guitar player's tie over the man's shoulder. She guessed the guitarist had taken a few too many breaks in the parking lot, and didn't realize his tie had lain on top of the guitar strings. His strumming was completely muted by the tie. The guitar player never missed a chord. The bow's quick flick brought the band to full capacity again.

It was past two o'clock in the morning when the hall fell silent. Many islanders were reluctant to go home. Sam had won the prize for the best costume again. He considered himself to be the undisputed King of Hallowe'en.

Ben had been instructed to 'bring Laura over' by so many people that Ben told Laura she would have to stay for a few weeks. Before Laura got into the car, Gudrun gave her a hug and confirmed the card game they had planned for the next evening.

"We'll be partners and show those men who knows how to play cards."

"Actually, I don't play cards very often. I might not be a very good partner."

"I have faith in you. We'll show 'em!"

Later, as Laura snuggled under the covers in the guest room, she was still too excited to sleep. What a day this had been. She grinned as she closed her eyes and recalled Ben's words, "Sure you can sleep in. The cows don't have to be milked until 7:00."

Chapter 7

Sunshine peeked through the window when Laura awoke in the morning. She gazed out to see the waves rolling in a leisurely fashion with the sun glistening on the water crests. The lake was a murky gray in colour. Ben had told her how the shades of the water changed with the seasons. In spring it was a sharp, icy blue. In summer it became a softer hue that sparkled like sapphires. And then the lake wore the dull colours of autumn, before slushing up to form an ice cap that would cover the lake all winter.

Noises from downstairs alerted Laura that she wasn't the first riser in the house. She felt the chill in the room as soon as she pushed the covers off. A colourful braided rug beside the bed didn't feel nearly as cold as the floor to her bare feet. She poured some water into the basin on the washstand. A cozy green towel had been left beside the basin. The water was cold but refreshing, and completely woke her up. Not wasting any time, Laura quickly dressed in thick socks, woollen pants and a pullover sweater. She brushed her hair and gathered it into a ponytail.

She found Amma Anna stirring a pot on the stove.

"Good morning, Anna."

"Good morning. Did you sleep well?"

"Yes, like a log! When we came home last night, I was still so excited that I didn't think I'd sleep a wink. But I think I must have been asleep as soon as my head hit the pillow."

Amma Anna smiled in response to Laura's eagerness.

The back door opened and Ben walked in carrying two sticks of wood for the stove and a jar of milk.

"Well, look who's up. I thought you might sleep all day."

"What time is it?"

"Nearly eight o'clock. You must think you're on holiday or something. Here, I've been slaving away for hours."

"Stop it, Ben. He's only been up since seven, Laura."

Laura laughed. She enjoyed the camaraderie between the mother and son. They obviously teased each other often.

"The porridge is ready. I hope you like it, Laura." Amma Anna spooned the oatmeal porridge into bowls as Laura nodded and took her seat at the table. Ben gave her a secret grin and the flash in his eyes put a blush on her cheeks.

The hot cereal was delicious. The rich milk that they poured over the porridge still contained some cream.

"Mmm, this is so good. This milk is nice and thick."

"When we milk the cows, we pour the milk into a separator and the cream is taken out. After the milk sits in the cellar for a few hours, excess cream rises to the top of the jar."

"The milk you drink has quite a bit of cream in it," Laura said.

"Just for porridge. The cream is skimmed off the jars for the milk we drink. But porridge needs that extra richness."

Toasted bread slices were served with the porridge. In order to toast bread, an element lid on the top of the stove was removed to expose the coals inside. Amma Anna placed a slice of bread in a two-sided wire rack with a handle, and held it over the coals until the required crispness was achieved.

"What are your plans for today?" Amma Anna asked.

"Well, we have a lot of ground to cover. First, I want to show Laura the village. It was too dark to see very much last night. Then, we'll go to Gull Harbour and the park at the end of the road. This afternoon Malla has invited us for coffee, and tonight Sam and I are going to show the girls how to play King Pedro."

"That sounds like a busy day. I'll make some sandwiches for lunch. Then it won't matter what time you get back. Rose wondered if we could come to their place for supper tonight."

"We should be able to manage that." Ben glanced at Laura with a raised eyebrow.

"Everyone is going to so much trouble," Laura said. "I'm embarrassed over all this attention."

"No, Laura, everyone just wants to get to know you. We Icelanders are curious by nature." Amma Anna hastened to put Laura at ease.

"That's why we're so smart." Ben puffed up his chest. Laura gave him a playful nudge on the arm as they both laughed. "What are the Irish noted for?" Ben continued, "Oh, yeah, I remember – red hair!"

This time the playful nudge carried a bit of a sting on impact accompanied by a sassy smirk.

Laura helped Amma Anna with the dishes. Water had been heated on the woodstove, then poured into the dishpan. Amma Anna transformed an aluminum bake sheet, used for baking cookies, into a drain board for the washed dishes. Laura dried the dishes and then placed them in the cupboard.

"I'm going to check with Daniel before we leave to make sure he doesn't need me for anything this morning." Ben grabbed his jacket and cap as he left the kitchen.

Laura spread her arms, holding up the dish towel. "This is beautiful embroidery. Did you do it?"

"Yes, I like doing handwork in the evenings. And I like to make use of any cloth that comes my way." Amma Anna said.

"This is such a big tea towel, and the fabric is so soft."

"It's just a cotton sugar bag that I opened up and hemmed on the edges. We buy sugar and flour in one hundred-pound bags. They make good-sized drying cloths.

"You have so many beautiful, handmade things in your home. The only handwork I've ever done is some embroidery and I haven't done a lot of that."

"I always say, 'if you can hold a needle, you can learn to sew'. Have you ever used a treadle sewing machine?"

"No, my mother has never owned a sewing machine. But after seeing the clothes and costumes you and Rose make, I would love to learn. And the quilts and curtains. Is there anything you can't make?"

"Oh, now, you're going to make me blush." Amma Anna was flattered by Laura's words. "I guess we've learned to do the best with what we have. I think my treadle sewing machine is the best gift I've ever received."

"The first settlers built their homes south of here at Kirkubol." Ben gave Laura a detailed report of the community's beginnings. "All that's left there now are the graves of the people who died during those first years after 1876. There was an outbreak of smallpox, which claimed several lives. Then some of the pioneers decided to move to this location. It's a natural bay with higher banks and I guess they felt it would provide them with more shelter and a good place to dock their boats. You've already seen the hall, and the packing shed. Here's the school," Ben motioned toward his left as they drove slowly northward through the village. "You were talking to the teacher last night, weren't you?"

"Her parents live about five blocks from my house. She even knows

Sean at the restaurant. I think she was very glad to talk to someone from home."

"I believe that. When you're away from home, it's pretty special to run into someone from the same place. I remember when I was overseas, if you met someone from Canada it was like seeing a next-door neighbour."

Laura nodded. But Ben erased the melancholy expression from his face and continued the tour.

"Are there two classrooms? I love all the windows facing the lake." Laura admired the school.

"Mrs. Marinsson teaches in the other classroom. She's been teaching for many years. We played a few pranks on her, but she managed to give us all an education."

"I can just imagine some of those pranks. What I want to know is, how did you get your schoolwork done with this gorgeous view?"

"Laura, I've lived here all my life. I love the view, no question there, but it's in my head. I don't have to look at it to see it."

"I guess that's true. I'm sure I'll be able to see it in my head after this weekend. Now when I read your letters, I'll be able to picture what you're doing and where you are." Laura's eyes locked with Ben's. The dark brown eyes that could be brooding and cool were sparkling with warmth. If she hadn't already been head over heels in love with him, the way he embraced her with those eyes would have clinched it.

Ben motored along the beach road, pointing out the store and the abandoned sawmill across the road from the store. He explained how his father had died as a result of an accident at the mill. He also told her how the islanders had skidded the logs out of the bush to the mill.

"After the logs were processed, the lumber was transported by barge on the water in summer, or across the island and ice in the channel in winter."

"Was island lumber used in all the buildings on the island?"

"It was. Our church is probably the greatest standing tribute left to us by our ancestors. My father was one of the workers when the islanders built it in 1927. They hired a carpenter and provided the rest of the labour themselves. The people here have always had a strong religious faith. They sure needed that faith when you think of all the struggles they encountered."

"It's absolutely breathtaking. And in 1927, they probably didn't have a lot of tools to work with."

"They had the sawmill and handsaws, hammers, levels and hand planes. But, you're right, they didn't have a lot to work with. What they had though, was determination and plenty of elbow grease." The pride Ben felt in his forefathers was evident in every word. "I was planning on taking you to the church service tomorrow morning. We can go inside now, if you like, or wait until tomorrow."

Laura looked at Ben with a glitter in her eye and said, "Can we see it now?"

Ben steered the car to the side of the road and stopped. Before he opened the car door, he slid his arm around Laura's shoulders and leaned over to kiss her. "Are you enjoying the tour, so far?"

"Mmm, it's even better than I expected." She snuggled into his arms. "I love your island, Ben, and I love you, too."

"That's good, cause the island and I kind of go together." He stroked her hair and held her close. "I love you, too, *kaerasta min*."

Inside the church, Laura was in awe of the elaborate detail on the altar. The railings were shiny and smooth. Rays of coloured light shone through the stained glass windows. Walking down the central aisle, Laura looked into the face of a young Jesus. The mural adorned the back of the altar. Wooden pews formed rows on either side of the centre aisle. Everything spoke of the deep love the islanders had for their Lutheran faith. Laura stood still and drank in the beauty, thinking of the men who had created such a masterpiece. Ben showed her a staircase at the back of the church that led to a balcony. They climbed the stairs and Laura stood at the balcony railing. She looked at the pews and altar below. Turning her around, Ben brought her attention to the bell tower with the heavy rope.

"Tomorrow you'll hear the bell ring. I get the feeling that you'll want to come to the service tomorrow."

"I do."

"That's a dangerous thing to say in a church. But I like the sound of it." Ben's eyes danced in his face as he chased her down the stairs. They left the church with their fingers entwined and laughing about Laura's protests regarding the crimson tinge in her cheeks.

Adam and Andrew were worried about Miss Taylor. After eavesdropping on their teacher's telephone call, they'd tried to understand the conversation they'd overheard. Since then, a crew from Manitoba Telephone had replaced the damaged poles and the wires were well out of reach again. Their days of listening on the line from the willow bluff were over.

"What could she have done?" Adam asked Andrew as they went out to check on the traps they would be setting in a couple of weeks.

"It must be bad. Remember how sad she looked the day after we heard her. She was probably really scared."

"I wonder what that man called Richard will do if he finds out that she lives here?"

"Did you see her talking to my Uncle Ben's girlfriend. She's from Winnipeg, you know. What if she knows that Richard, and tells him where Miss Taylor is?" Adam hoped that Laura wouldn't cause any trouble. "Uncle Ben and Laura are coming to our house for supper tonight. Maybe I can ask her without her knowing why."

"What are you going to say? You have to be careful that they don't find out about us listening on the line. My mother would kill me if she found out."

"I'll be careful. I'll just ask her if she knows Miss Taylor." Adam was confident that he could practice a little espionage without being found out.

The boys pulled out the traps they used on their winter trapline. They set traps for squirrels, weasels, mink, foxes and coyotes. All the traps' springs were tested as the young trappers took careful inventory.

"What if she knows Miss Taylor?" Andrew had difficulty hiding his concern.

"We have to hope she doesn't. If she does, maybe I can convince her not to tell anyone about Miss Taylor living here."

"Just watch out. We could be the ones in trouble."

"I know. It'll be okay. I wish we knew who this Richard was. He might be a policeman or something. Then what?"

"Then you will have to make sure your Uncle Ben's girlfriend doesn't go blabbing to everyone in Winnipeg." This conversation wasn't helping to alleviate the upset in Andrew's stomach.

As they finished sorting the traps, the boys hoped they could keep Miss Taylor's dreaded secret from getting out on the island.

Back in the car and heading north, Ben and Laura proceeded to Gull Harbour. Along the way, the road was flanked with homesteads. Whenever they espied someone working outside, Ben honked the horn and waved a greeting.

At Gull Harbour, Ben told Laura about the fish hatchery. It was a large two-storey building that stood close to the shoreline and near the dock. The harbour itself was large and protected against the elements of nature. Toward the channel between Hecla Island and Black Island, a lighthouse stood on the east side of the harbour, directing water traffic safely through the channel or into Gull Harbour.

"What a pretty picture. Are those houses, or cabins, in the trees over there?" Laura was looking southward, scanning the shoreline in the harbour.

"Yes, there are a few cabins there. The beach is sandy in that part of the harbour, and you can see how protected that area is from high winds and the erosion that those winds can cause."

"Do the cabins belong to people who grew up on Hecla?"

"Most of the 'summer people', as we call them, are from Winnipeg. We don't see that much of them. They come on the *Keenora*, a passenger boat, which docks here. Things are changing now, though, with the ferry. They'll be able to drive by car after this. All the Gull Harbour campers are nice whenever we see them, but there are enough of them to have formed their own community here."

"So they don't come to any of the dances? I can't imagine being on the island and missing a Hecla dance."

Ben smiled, "They haven't made a habit of attending our social events. They have a social life of their own. They have church services and dances down here." His hand tightened around hers. "I'm glad you enjoyed the dance last night. That's a part of Hecla I really wanted you to see."

"I loved it. And meeting your friends. Everyone is so welcoming. But I know that the way I'm being treated is definitely a reflection on you and the feelings everyone has for you. You're pretty popular around these parts." She lightly tickled him. He drew her into a hug.

"As long as I'm popular with you. That's all that matters to me."

"Remember that day you walked into the hospital and made it clear that you weren't leaving until you saw Signey? That was the day I joined your fan club." She smiled up at him. "And I remember thinking later that day how happy I was that you were Signey's uncle, not her father as I'd first thought."

"I remember the sinking feeling I had when Sean glared at me, before you got to the Tipperary that first night. I was sure he must be your boyfriend. Then you walked in and like the perfect nurse that you are, you made it all better." Ben wanted to hold her like this forever. Everything about Laura seemed so right for him.

"I think you're forgetting about the tour we're supposed to be on."

Laura was reluctant to leave the comfort of his arms, but they had a busy schedule to keep and time was slipping by. "Tell me more about the fish hatchery. What kinds of fish were hatched here and how was it done?"

Ben kept his arm draped over her shoulder, maintaining a physical connection. "It was mainly a hatchery for pickerel and whitefish. But other types of fish were tried as well. They even tried to raise some sturgeon. You know, the boneless fish which dates back to prehistoric times. Sturgeon have an armour of bony plates that protect their heads and bodies, which is very different from the other fish in the lake."

"How did the process work? I mean, what is involved in running a hatchery?"

"You see how close the building is to the water. Lake water flowed through aluminum pipes that went into big glass jars in the hatchery. The spawn were raised in the jars. The water flowed out into the lake again through other aluminum pipes. The hatchery manager regulated the water temperature in the jars hoping that the majority of the spawn would hatch."

"Did the hatchery have a wood furnace?"

"That's right. The water had to be carefully monitored for temperature and also for freshness. It wasn't allowed to get stagnant. The manager always aimed for lots of healthy fish."

"How did they put them in the lake?"

"In the spring, the small fish went from the jars, through the pipe and into a large holding tank that was just outside the hatchery in the lake. The tank was then towed out farther into the lake where the fish were released."

"Why is the building so big?"

"The spawning equipment took a lot of space. Each jar was about three feet tall and probably a foot across, and there were several of them. The pipes were pretty big too, and then they needed to have room to work around all the equipment."

"Where did the spawn come from?"

"Trap nets were set in the spawning ground – whitefish spawn in the fall and pickerel spawn in the spring. The spawn was squeezed out of the captured fish and then the fish were released again."

"Is that ever interesting."

Ben nodded and laughed. "Okay, it's time to move along. I want to show you the cliffs at the north end of the island. It's just a little farther up the road."

"One more question. What was the second storey in the hatchery used for?"

"The hatchery manager lived there. The upper floor was all living quarters. Now the building isn't used regularly. It was closed as a hatchery in 1936."

Thora went about her morning chores as usual. Kristjan had already left for work. She was thinking about the previous night's dance and all the new developments. It had been nice to see Signey dancing and playing with the other children. Her left arm still needed to improve and she was so thin, but Anna had said she seemed to get stronger every day.

Ben's new girlfriend had livened up his life, Thora mused. It had been a long time since she'd seen Ben so happy. She'd have to ask Gudrun about this new romance, since she had spent lots of time with the new girl.

And, thinking about new romances, it seemed that Ellen had made a conquest, too. Mrs. Marinsson's son, Matthew, was home from his fish camp and Thora saw him dancing with the young teacher. Thora couldn't recall Matthew ever showing an interest in a girl before. Better late than never!

Thora reached for a plate, cup and saucer, and cutlery when she heard footsteps on the stairs.

"Good morning. I can't believe I slept in so long." Ellen still looked sleepy.

Thora noticed a new sparkle in her eyes.

"Good morning, Ellen. Did you enjoy the dance last night?"

"It was wonderful. I can't get over how everyone pitches in. The band, and the costumes, and the lunch, or should I say the feast! What a community effort! And my students were having so much fun. I'm sure we'll be talking about the dance for weeks."

"You're right. Everyone does pitch in. The costumes are always good for a laugh. That Sam, my son-in-law, gets the craziest ideas. Gudrun said he was full-of-himself now that he's taken first prize two years in a row." Thora smiled as she remembered the witch riding 'her' broom around the hall.

"You must be hungry. I made some tea biscuits and there should be some coffee left. Actually, there's probably two cups. I'll keep you company."

"Thanks for saving breakfast for me. Us sleepy-heads don't deserve to be pampered." Ellen often said she was very fortunate to be living with Thora and Kristjan. They'd taken her under their wing and treated her like another daughter. Elin and Gudrun also included her as if she were a member of the family. Because Gudrun was closer to her age, Ellen had more in common with her.

"Don't be too hard on yourself. This isn't pampering and I believe this is the first morning since you've come that I didn't hear you bustling around in your room when I woke up." Thora served the coffee. Ellen helped herself to a biscuit. Cutting the biscuit in half, she applied some butter and homemade strawberry jam before joining Thora at the table.

"I had such a good time last night. I met Laura O'Neil. She's dating Ben, one of the fishermen on the island."

"This is the first time she's been here. Ben met her at the hospital when he went to see Signey."

"That's what she told me. I know her cousin at the Tipperary, a restaurant in Winnipeg. It's a popular place to go, even if you aren't Irish. My friends and I used to go there often." A wistful calm settled on Ellen's face. Speaking with Laura had left her with a touch of homesickness.

"You have to tell me. I was watching Matthew whirl you around the dance floor. Should I be expecting him to come calling?" Thora had noted the sadness creeping into the teacher's soft features. She was rewarded with a sudden flush on Ellen's cheeks. "So there is a story there." Thora couldn't keep the teasing out of her voice.

"We only danced a few times. I enjoyed meeting him."

"Matthew is nice. He's always been on the shy side. I must say the two of you make a striking couple."

"I'm not sure I'm looking for any romance." Ellen's voice and flushed cheeks betrayed her words.

"Do you have someone waiting for you in Winnipeg?" Although Thora wasn't one to pry, she had developed a close relationship with her boarder and felt comfortable asking her a personal question.

"No," the young girl hastened to reply, "I don't have anyone." Her eyes gave away her sadness. Looking into Thora's anxious eyes, she decided to confide in her. "I had a boyfriend. Actually, we were planning a wedding. We broke off our relationship just before I decided to come to Hecla."

"I'm so sorry, Ellen."

"It was really for the best. Richard and I disagreed on several things. The most important was my longing to be a teacher. He thought my having a career would interfere with our life as a couple. That argument seemed to bring out a lot of other traits in him that I'd been blind to before. I don't regret the decision to call off the wedding, but it makes me sad sometimes that Richard wasn't the man I wanted him to be."

"Things happen for a reason. I've always believed that. You were meant to come to Hecla Island and become a much loved teacher to the children. And, if you find a new romance along the way, well, what's wrong with that?"

Ellen smiled. "You always know the right thing to say. What would I do without you?"

"I don't think you realize what you've brought into our home. After Gudrun married Sam and moved into her own home, this house was far too quiet. Offering room and board to the new teacher was the smartest thing I've done in a long time. And before you get me off track – I like Matthew and if he comes calling, I'll hold the door wide open."

The two women chuckled and finished their coffee.

Laura opened the passenger door and quickly got out of the car when Ben parked at the end of the road. They were at the north end of the island. Clumps of birch trees were scattered throughout the park area. There were several picnic tables inviting island visitors to stop and enjoy the view. Through the trees, the lake was visible. Some small islands dotted the horizon.

Ben took Laura's hand and walked with her through the woods in a westerly direction. Watchful of protruding tree roots and rough rocks, they descended to the shoreline. Ben directed her along the stony beach until they were near the base of the cliffs they had just been standing on.

"I've never seen anything like this before." Laura said with a hushed awe.

Layered limestone created the rustic ledges that rose vertically out of the water.

"See how erosion has caused a shift in some of the layers of rock. The way the rock formations tilt and hang over the water looks dangerous," Ben explained. "But, the cliffs take years to record any amount of change."

"We shouldn't get too close anyway." Laura was cautious.

Retracing their footsteps, they continued along the shoreline until Ben was able to point out the spot where rocks had been taken from the quarry.

"For a few years before World War I, many barges of limestone were hauled out of the quarry and into Winnipeg."

"Over in that bay?" Laura pointed southward at the vacant beach.

"There isn't much left to see now, but at one time it was a thriving part of the island. They dislodged the rock with explosives and then used train cars to transport the limestone to the docks, where it was loaded onto barges."

"What happened to it after the war?"

"Limestone was found closer to Winnipeg. It was less expensive to bring in and more accessible. Operations were never resumed after World War I. The docks and buildings are all gone now."

"It's amazing how the resources of the island have been used. Not only were the pioneers able to adapt to a new life in a foreign land, they had the courage to try their hand at skills which must have been foreign to them as well."

"True. I think they realized very quickly that life on Hecla Island would bring many new challenges to them. We Icelanders are always ready for a challenge!" Ben's eyes twinkled in amusement as he and Laura made their way to the car.

"Or too stubborn to give in!" Laura said.

"That, too!" Ben laughed.

Laura smiled. She had never been so comfortable with a man before. Her mother had warned her about being too outspoken and 'scaring them off.' But she was grateful now that she'd always been true to herself. With Ben, she could be completely relaxed and speak whatever was on her mind. He appreciated her opinion and treated her with respect. At the same time, he coddled her in a protective way that made her feel very special and feminine.

Her father had voiced his opinions, as had others in the family, about her relationship with Ben. What could a 'hick from the sticks' offer her? The jokes about 'horned helmets' and 'barbarians' struck a nerve, as did the derogatory remarks about rural life and fishing. She understood some of their concerns. She and Ben came from different cultural and religious backgrounds, and from two different worlds. She hoped her family would come around to her way of thinking, because this was a romance she wasn't walking away from.

Come in." Malla opened the door and welcomed the couple inside.

"It's going to cool off by tomorrow. I hope you brought a warm jacket. That sweater isn't going to keep you warm enough." The old lady put her arm around Laura's waist and walked beside her into the kitchen.

"That's my job! I'm better than a jacket any day." Ben's reply brought an instant look of glee to Malla's wrinkled face and provoked a retort from Laura.

"I have a cozy plaid coat with a warm lining. So, don't worry about me, Malla!" The teasing lilt in her voice and the sparkle in her eyes were music to her hostess' ears. Laura winked at Ben. "It's nice to know you're available."

"See what I'm up against?" Ben circled his arm around Malla's shoulders and whispered loudly, "Maybe you can put in a good word for me."

"He's always been naughty. I can see that hasn't changed."

"That's not a 'good word,' Malla," Ben murmured in the old lady's ear.

"But it's the truth," Laura quickly added with laughter, "and we wouldn't like you any other way."

Malla was a contradiction of sorts. On one hand, she chopped wood and could handle any outside chores On the other, she could serve an elegant lunch. Malla had arranged delicately cut dainties on fancy plates and set them on the table along with fine china cups and saucers. Embroidered forget-me-nots bordered the linen tablecloth. It was a table setting befitting royalty.

Malla's home was plain but efficient. She wasn't one for frills and had never had the finances to indulge in many whims. However, she had everything that she needed and was content with that. The tablecloth and fine china had been gifts and were used sparingly.

Laura took an instant liking to Malla. She was an interesting conversationalist and had the ability to draw comments and opinions out of others in a relaxed manner.

"I promise to bring her back for another visit." Ben hugged the old lady as the couple was leaving.

"I don't think I've ever seen you so happy. I like her, Ben."

Laura smiled at her words and gave her a hug.

"Are your feet still sore from all that dancing last night?" Daniel welcomed Laura with his mother and Ben.

"Yes, they are raw. But it was worth every step!"

Rose stirred the deer meat simmering in the large cast iron frypan. She'd sliced the meat thinly and fried it with onion. Then she pushed the pan to the edge of the woodstove where the heat wasn't as extreme. The meat was soaking in the gravy that Rose had just made. Potatoes and carrots were boiling in separate pots. Karen and Signey were setting the table.

"You've been busy today. What do you think of our island?" Rose asked. She motioned Laura to a seat at the kitchen table.

"I'm amazed at the interesting history of the island and how hard the settlers worked."

"I guess every place has its story, but we like to think we're special," Daniel commented. Everyone was seated and the bowls of food were passed around the table.

Light hearted conversation about the day's activity accompanied the meal. Adam fidgeted in his chair, looking uncomfortable. Finally, he asked Laura, "Do you know Miss Taylor?"

"I do now. I met her last night. I discovered that she grew up near my house and she knows my cousin."

"Are you going to tell your cousin that you saw her?"

"I probably will. She told me that a friend of hers is a nurse and works at the same hospital that I do. I told her that I'd look her up and tell her about seeing her here."

Adam tried to hide his anxiety. Ben wondered what this was all about. His nephew certainly was agitated.

"Maybe, Miss Taylor doesn't want anyone to know where she is." Adam blurted out the words without thinking.

"She asked me to say 'Hello' to her friend and my cousin." Laura was surprised at Adam's outburst.

"Adam, why do you think Miss Taylor wants to keep her whereabouts a secret?" Rose was curious about her son's behaviour.

"I heard her talking on..."Adam gasped when he realized what he'd said. "I just heard her talking about hiding in Hecla."

Ben had been quietly listening. The pieces of the puzzle started to fall into place. The telephone wire hanging through the willow bluff. Adam and Andrew running to the bluff concealing a wooden box. Andrew's father storing telephone repair supplies. He realized the boys had probably used the box phone to listen on the line.

"She was likely just making a joke. I know she wanted me to talk to her friend at my hospital. And she didn't sound like she was hiding to me. She loves it here."

"Sometimes words just come out wrong. You might have just heard part of what was said. It's probably nothing. Don't worry about it." Ben tried to end this subject and move on. "We need to keep going, Laura. Sam will have the cards polished up and ready." He rose from the table. "We have a card game waiting for us."

"Thanks so much, Rose. Supper was delicious." Laura joined Ben at the back door, where he helped her into her coat.

As soon as Ben and Laura were inside the car, Ben burst out laughing.

"What is it – what's so funny?"

"Adam." Ben had difficulty speaking. "He's been listening on the phone with his friend, Andrew." Ben told her that he'd seen them going to the bluff with a wooden box. He hadn't given it much thought until Adam clumsily questioned Laura about his teacher. Then he understood what must have happened. He thought the boys were very clever to come up with the plan. "I think they got themselves into trouble by listening to part of a conversation."

"Are you going to tell Daniel and Rose?"

"No, it's not a big deal. Most of the people on the island listen on the telephone at one time or another."

"What do you mean? Do people listen on the phone? How do they hear each other's conversations?"

"There are a few homes connected to each telephone line. It's called a party line. Each home has a different ring. We have two long rings and Daniel and Rose have one-long ring, one-short ring. There's four other houses on our party line. There's only one main line going off the island. Often, when you pick up the receiver, someone is talking."

"Are you saying that someone might have listened to our conversations?"

"Very likely."

"Why didn't you tell me?"

"Would you still have whispered all those sweet nothings in my ear, if you had known we weren't alone?"

Laura smiled and cuddled up beside him. "So that's why you sound so casual on the telephone. I wondered why you saved your sweet-talk for your letters or when we're alone."

He grinned into her upturned face and kissed her.

"And that's just the way I like it," she said.

Later that night, Ben and Laura snuggled together on the couch. The living room was dimly lit with a coal oil lamp. On the table in front of the couch was an open picture album. Ben showed Laura photographs of his family and old pictures depicting early life on the island.

"Is this a wedding picture of your parents?"

"Yes."

"You look just like your father."

"That's what everyone says. My grandmother used to say, when I was little, that I looked more like him than he did at that age!"

Amma Anna was in bed when the young couple returned. Lights were off in most houses early on the night after a community dance. It had been fun visiting with Sam and Gudrun. The ladies had squeaked a win over the men in King Pedro. The men maintained that they'd been such gentlemen letting the women win.

Although Ben and Sam could have stayed up late, Laura recognized the fatigue in Gudrun. "I know we could stay awake all night, but there's a baby here that needs some sleep."

"Nurse O'Neil speaks – and I've been on her ward. We better listen!" Ben said.

Laura loved Sam's sense of humour. The battery-operated radio had been on while they played cards, and at one point, Ben was singing along with crooner Perry Como.

Sam had interrupted him, saying, "Ben, you should sing on the radio." Laura had looked at Sam with a question in her eyes. She didn't think Ben could sing as well as Perry Como. Then Sam had clarified, "Then we could turn you off!"

Now, back at the Bergursson home, Patti Page's voice wafted through the room. The music was set at low volume so Amma Anna wouldn't be awakened.

"Some of these pictures are of relatives living in Iceland." Ben had turned the page in the album. "Mama writes to them every Christmas. Even though we've never met them, they're still family. And I think our great-grandparents would like to know that we always stayed in contact."

"I agree. My parents do the same. They keep in touch with our relatives in Ireland. I've always dreamed of some day standing on the same soil my ancestors did."

"I'll make you a deal. On our twenty-fifth wedding anniversary, I'll take you to Ireland and Iceland."

"Deal!" Laura attempted to shake his hand and seal the promise, but Ben sealed her lips instead.

The gravity of the words swept over them. A thoughtful silence followed the kiss.

"Hey, are you trying to back out on our deal?" Laura strove to lighten the mood. "Because I'm already planning our itinerary."

Ben smiled and stroked her hair, tucking it behind her ear. She could feel him moving away from her, although he remained in the same spot. It scared her.

"Ben, what's wrong? Did I say something..."

"No, Laura." He stopped her in mid-sentence. "You didn't say or do anything wrong." He thought for a moment before he explained. "It's not you, it's me. My life is here on Hecla Island, fishing and farming. I can't offer you the nice things that you've grown up with, like crystal wine glasses and beautiful oil paintings."

"I don't need those nice things, Ben. I thought you knew me better than that."

"I'm saying it badly. It's so different here, compared to the city. Daily routines in your house in Winnipeg aren't at all like ours." He gently caressed her hands. "These hands have never chopped wood or washed clothes on a washboard."

"Okay, now I'm mad!" She pulled her hands from his grasp and stood up. "I'm not some spoiled little girl who needs to be pampered! Is that how you see me?" Angry sparks glinted in her eyes. Her cheeks were washed in a heated blush.

Ben got to his feet and reached out to calm her. "That's not how I see you." He wrapped his arms around her, diffusing the cool stiffness in her limbs. "I don't want you to wake up one morning and have regrets about marrying a fisherman from an isolated island."

"Don't underestimate me. Just because I haven't lived here all my life, doesn't mean that I can't." Her anger was threatening to come back.

"That's not what I meant." A strain in his voice caused Laura to tilt her head back and look into his face. A painful vulnerability was etched in his eyes. The arrogant, self-assured man who had demanded to see his ailing niece was not standing before her now. "I guess what I'm trying to say is, I don't want you to be sorry you married me. I know you love Hecla. But, twenty-five years from now, will you still love me? I know there are lots of men in Winnipeg who could give you a better life than I can. And there isn't a hospital here, where you could be a nurse."

"Are you breaking-up with me?"

"There are plenty of reasons why we shouldn't be together."

"Are you breaking-up with me?" She repeated in a muffled voice against his chest.

"No, I don't ever want to lose you."

Laura gently broke from the embrace, took his hand and led him back to the couch. Her outspokenness might scare some men off, but she decided that Ben needed to get a few things straight.

Laura held his hand and began. "We're still getting to know each other. I'm sure there are many couples who have been married for years and are still discovering quirks about each other. When you said 'twenty-five years' it never occurred to me that we wouldn't be together. I realize now that ever since that night at the Tipperary, I've thought of you as my future. Am I making you nervous? My mother thinks I talk too much, especially when I'm nervous."

Ben grinned. "No, you're not making me nervous at all. And I don't think you need to be nervous either."

Laura smiled back at him. "I love my work as a nurse. The polio epidemic is scary and it seems our work is never done, but it's so rewarding. When you see children improve and go home, like Signey, then all the hard work is worth it. But, I want to be a wife and mother some day. One of the reasons I became a nurse was because it was a vocation that I could take with me wherever I went. What I've learned as a nurse should help me in raising healthy children of my own."

"That would be 'our children'." Ben had curled his arm around her, finding comfort in having her near.

"There's something else I want you to know. The house my parents live in belonged to my grandparents. My mother was an only child. She inherited the house and everything in it. Most of the furniture we have now was there when my parents moved in. My parents didn't raise Hilary and me with a big fortune, but we had what we needed. My mother has only been teaching since I was in high school. Before that she was looking after our home and raising her family. Ben, maybe we aren't so different after all."

"Keep talking. I love to hear your voice." Ben nuzzled her neck, tickling her.

"Are you sure I'm not talking too much?"

"I'm sure. Are you sure I can make you happy enough?" His eyes held a glimmer of arrogance again as he snared her in his arms.

"Ben," she held his face in her hands and looked directly into his eyes, "don't you know by now – I'd go anywhere with you."

Laura knew they would have challenges to face, but she was confident that together they could handle anything thrown in their path. The strength, respect, and love they each brought into their relationship already exceeded what many couples strive for years to achieve.

Chapter 8

"Hello, anyone home?" Elin had knocked on the door and then hastened inside to get out of the cold. She stamped the fresh snow off her boots before removing them and placing them on a mat beside the stove.

"Good morning. Are you ready to get to work or should we finish off the coffee first?" Rose noted the cool redness in Elin's cheeks and shivered as the cold blast of wind from the open door hit her. "Let's finish the coffee."

"Sounds good to me. Why is it that every year we have to get used to this freezing weather all over again. You'd think we'd remember from one season to the next and not have to get acclimatized each time." Elin rubbed her hands together over the woodstove, trying to warm her fingers.

The early December wind that had brought a fresh snowfall before dawn still held a distinct chill. In the past month the Heclingers had experienced many changes. Most homes were enjoying the comforts of regulated heat and the bright, consistent glow of electric light bulbs. Christmas was nearing and many islanders were asking Santa Claus for gifts that until now had been futile.

The two women were meeting to 'seam on' a new net in preparation for the oncoming winter fishing season. Usually this task was done outside in the summer months when they could string the net length between two poles and weave the seaming twine to form the upper and lower edges of the nets. However, when the men were taking inventory of the fishing nets, they discovered that mice had damaged some of the mesh. One net needed to be replaced. The mesh or 'web' was purchased in bulk of five hundred yards and cut in one hundred-yard lengths to make five new fishing nets.

"You've got the net set up already. This shouldn't take long at all."

Rose laughed. "Do you think we just sit on our hands over here?"

The outside edges of the mesh was doubled to form a selvage for extra durability, and it was on these edges that a side-line was attached by looping the seaming twine through the square net mesh and around the side-line. At equally spaced intervals special loops and knots were added to accommodate the wood floats on the net's top and the lead weights on the net's bottom.

Rose stretched two rows of side-line across the living room. Daniel had brought in the winch they used for this job, as well as a wooden box to house the finished net. Turning the crank on the winch pulled the completed net evenly and kept the lines taut as the 'seaming on' process progressed.

"Which side do you want?" Elin asked as she wove the seaming twine onto the big eye of the seaming needle.

"I'll take the side closer to the kitchen door. That way I'll be able to check on our lunch."

Both women fell easily into the routine of looping and knotting. Over the years they had developed a steady pace at which they worked. Their hands adeptly wove in unison. A guide string was draped down the centre of the net marking the placement of the weights and floats. The weights and floats were placed directly across from each other so that the net would remain straight in the water and not twist or sag.

"How serious is Ben over the nurse?" Elin, like many other islanders, was very curious about the new girlfriend.

"He's pretty serious about her. I've never seen him this 'ga-ga' over a girl."

"Isn't she Catholic?"

Elin was a dear friend, but Rose didn't want to hear negative criticisms about Laura. Conversations in the store and at 'Knit-A-Bit' were censored when Rose appeared. Although she thought the world of Laura, she too, had concerns about the couple and how they would meld their backgrounds.

"Yes, she's Catholic. I hope they can find a compromise, because she's perfect for Ben."

Elin didn't get a chance to respond because Amma Anna arrived to keep Signey occupied while they worked on the net. Signey's voice, although very weak, was gradually coming back. The muscles controlling her vocal chords seemed to be limited in strength. She spoke in soft tones that quickly tapered off into silence. The muscles on the left side of her body had regained some of their pre-polio strength. As the doctor had cautioned when she was released from the hospital, her left shoulder muscle hadn't shown any improvement and wasn't expected to after all this time. Signey's left arm was very weak in spite of her daily exercises.

"Tell me about the *Huldufolk*, Amma Anna." The girl loved her quiet time with her grandmother. Since returning from her hospital stay, Signey had spent a part of most days with Amma Anna. Reading from a book or spinning a yarn from her head, Amma Anna never failed to entertain her young granddaughter.

"I wonder what Brinki and Baldur are up to today. Could they be hiding here in the living room? Do you think they can hear us?" Amma Anna's eyes twinkled as she questioned Signey. Rose and Elin smiled while their hands automatically continued to fasten the mesh to the side-line.

"If those guys are around here, they should be helping us. This is no time to be hiding." Elin laughed at the stories about the *Huldufolk*. From Icelandic folk lore, the *Huldufolk* were naughty little spirits that played tricks on everyone. They especially enjoyed misplacing things in people's houses and causing havoc wherever they went.

"They would probably put the knots in the wrong places just to play a joke on us." Rose said while she stood up to pass a section of seaming twine across the width of the net to Elin. On every ten-foot span of the winter nets, a ten foot piece of twine was stretched over the fifteen-foot width of the mesh causing a billowing effect. Because of the ice cover on the lake, water currents and general water movement differed from the wind and waves of summer. Open water fishing nets in summer didn't require the crossover twine since the natural wave action kept the net extended in a billowy fashion. Because the same nets were used in all seasons, the crossover lines were removed for the open water seasons.

"I don't know if they are here now or not." Amma Anna began. "I know they were at my house yesterday." Signey's eyes grew large as she snuggled in closer on the couch beside the animated storyteller. The story went into detail about the mysterious disappearance of a knitting needle. It had been in the knitting basket with the wool that Amma Anna was making a sweater for Alexander. After a thorough search, the missing needle was found between the cushions on the couch. "It's just the kind of mischief that Brinki likes. I know I left that needle in the basket, so it must have been him. Then later I was baking cookies and I couldn't find my heart-shaped cookie cutter. I gave up looking and used a cup to make round cookies instead of the heart ones. The last batch was in the oven when I spotted the cookie cutter in the back of the cutlery drawer. I'm sure that Brinki and Baldur were chuckling somewhere."

The net was completed before lunchtime with other stories of the escapades of the jolly, Icelandic spirits in the background. No one feared the *Huldufolk*. They meant no harm. And when things went awry, it was handy to have them around to blame.

At the school, Ellen was happy that the oil heater had been installed. It kept the classrooms at a comfortable temperature without all the work of starting a fire each morning and then remembering to add wood throughout the day. Ellen had joked to Matthew that she hadn't been taught the fundamentals of teaching in a classroom without electric power. That course hadn't been covered in her teacher training.

Since the Hallowe'en Dance, Ellen had been seeing Matthew. She was learning more about the fishing industry from his stories on the lake. As the months went on, she was feeling more at home on the island. Now she was a part of the community that went beyond her role as school teacher. Matthew had introduced her to his friends, and because they were too young to have children in school it was easier for her to fit in.

Ellen was looking forward to the weekend and Saturday evening at Gudrun and Sam's. Hockey season was well underway and a favourite winter pastime was tuning into Saturday's *Hockey Night In Canada* on the radio. She had been invited with Matthew and some other friends for the following evening. Although Ellen had been to Gudrun's home before, she had never been there with Matthew and his friends.

"Is everyone learning their lines for the play?" Ellen smiled as all the children nodded their heads. The school was in the midst of planning the Christmas Concert. Each year they performed a play, sang Christmas carols, and also entertained with recitations and readings. It was a very exciting time for the children because it heralded a special holiday that they happily celebrated. The concert was also an educational production. Memorizing lines, singing and speaking in front of an audience were all valuable learning skills.

"We will need to look for some clothes that will match the characters you're acting in the play. Adam, maybe you can borrow some of your father's clothes for the role you're playing. And Beth, you could wear something from your mother's closet." Snickers and giggles interrupted Ellen and the cheeks on both Adam and Beth turned red. The young couple was taking on the roles of the parents on a Christmas shopping trip with their family. Ellen hastened to divert the attention away from the teasing and instructed the remainder of the cast what their requirements would be.

"Before I dismiss you for the weekend, I want the grade two class to come forward and practice your recitation. Then you can lead us in singing *God Save the Queen* at home time."

Adam and Andrew met after Saturday morning chores. Each day they checked their traps for the fur they sought. Yesterday's snowfall had buried all the traps, so they had to reset most of them after school. Today they hoped the extra work in resetting all the traps would pay off.

Armed with their rifles, they trudged through the snow toward the first traps. Both boys carried their firearms with care. They'd learned at an early age to respect the power of guns. There wasn't any room for carelessness when in charge of a weapon. The consequences could be very unforgiving. After respect for the guns was learned, the next lessons taught were gun-cleaning and loading procedures followed by target accuracy.

In most homes on Hecla Island, firearms were visible and stored for easy accessibility. Most island men hunted and trapped. Hunting deer, moose and rabbits, for the meat served in every home, and trapping for the income the plush mink, wolf, fox, coyote and squirrel pelts could bring at market. Predators of the farm livestock were never given a second chance.

Into the woods, the trappers caught sight of rust-coloured fur. Earlier in the week they spotted the prints of a fox. In a dense part of the trail they'd set a snare. Snares were made of thin wire that was looped to form a noose styled knot, then secured to a branch. The loop was camouflaged in the branches, hidden from sight. When an animal ran along the trail, the loop would snare its quarry and quickly tighten for an instant kill. They found the red fox dead in the trail, with no sign of a struggle.

On Saturday mornings the boys spent more time in the woods, making sure the traps were properly set, and scouting for new places to set. They could name all the prints left behind in the snow. They recognized signs of timber wolves or moose. A flattened area near a thicket had been a bed to a deer the previous night.

A loud clicking sound erupted in a nearby tree. Adam espied the source and raised his rifle, taking careful aim before squeezing the trigger. The clicking sound stopped and the squirrel fell to the ground.

"Nice shot, Adam. Look at the size of him, that's gotta be the biggest squirrel so far this year." Andrew praised his friend's sharp shooting.

"Yeah, he is pretty big. He might be worth fifty cents. We'll get rich this year if our luck holds."

The young entrepreneurs carried the furs home. Besides the squirrel and the red fox, they had also trapped a mink. It had been a successful day. On many days the traps were empty or set off.

Back at home the trappers' job wasn't done. Each pelt was skilfully skinned from the carcass, then the inside of the skin was scrapped to remove excess fat. The inside-out pelt was then stretched over a wooden slat that had been whittled into the shape of the pelt. Tacked in place, it was set aside to dry. After the skin was dried, the pelt was turned right side out and was ready to be sold.

In the sunroom off the living room, Bjossi studied the skies around his house and over the lake. The sunroom jutted out at the front of the house and had windows on three sides offering a wide expanse for viewing. For a bird watcher it was ideal.

When Adam and Andrew came out of the bush with their fur stash, Bjossi had focussed the lens on them. The red fox was easy to recognize in the distance but he had to guess at the rest. It looked like a marten or a mink. Bjossi was proud of the youngsters. They were carrying on the old traditions that he remembered well. Bjossi still trapped, but not to the extent he once had. Pain in his joints was difficult to ignore when the snow deepened in the woods. By the end of December the snow could easily be two or three feet deep, and by February much deeper depending on the snowfall. His legs couldn't handle the struggle of a long trap-line.

"Chopper, look over there." A movement had caught the corner of his eye. Two 'whiskey-jacks' flew into the front yard and settled on the woodpile. The gray jays had earned their nickname from the manner they boldly stole food. The shades of gray plumage stood out against the snow. Beady eyes were watchful as the strong beak poked into the logs, hoping to locate a tasty morsel.

On the driveway, a flock of chickadees chatted and scratched the ground. The gray and white bodies were easily recognized by the distinct black caps on the top of their heads. Later in the day, Bjossi knew the grosbeaks would come to visit. The evening grosbeaks featured yellow bodies while the pine grosbeaks were feathered in rose-red and gray hues.

Chopper's eyes followed in the direction that Bjossi indicated. The dog had learned that his master only meant for him to watch the birds, not to chase them off the property. The two friends had traded the outside stoop for the comfort of the sunroom. Billy spent the winter close to the barn where he could seek shelter with the cattle. The old goat was satisfied with this situation although he would have preferred to spend the winter in the house with Chopper and Bjossi. The cows didn't show as much respect for his importance as his two summer friends did.

Atop a telephone pole in front of Ingvar and Margaret's house, a great gray owl rested quietly in wait of darkness. Through the binoculars, Bjossi studied the broad head with a ruff of feathers outlining the large eyes. A strong, hooked beak and sharp clawed feet presented a clear danger to any prey caught in its vision. The owl would likely stay on its perch for most of the day as it was considered a night hunter. Known for their keen night sight, owls could swoop down on their quarry from above the trees. Rats and mice were a favourite meal so farmers welcomed the presence of an owl.

The old bachelor's eyes followed Ben working in the barnyard. He hoped Ben wasn't offended by his previous day's conversation. People on the island were gossiping about Ben's new girlfriend and Bjossi knew first-hand the problems that could arise from those rumblings.

Many years earlier, Bjossi had fallen in love with a girl from Shorncliffe, a farming community northwest of Riverton. She was Ukranian and Catholic, and his mother had made her feelings very well known that their home wouldn't welcome the outsider. People on the island talked and Bjossi felt shunned. If only he could bring those days back, how differently he would act. Broken hearted, the couple had ended their relationship. His beautiful Lena had married someone else, and to this day resided in Riverton. His heart still quickened its pace whenever he'd see her on trips into town.

When Bjossi broached the subject with Ben, he'd been pleased to see the young man's reaction. Ben made it clear that he wasn't going to let any 'narrow-minded bigots' rule his life. He and Laura could take care of their lives without intrusion from the islanders. If they wanted to talk, let them talk. And he had thanked Bjossi for telling him.

"It must be time to make coffee. Or maybe we should go over to Daniel and Rose's for coffee. That way we could find out what the boys caught in their traps." The old bachelor spoke to the dog as if it was a human being. In many ways, Bjossi considered the dog a better companion than other alternatives. Imagine being married to someone like Margaret! He gave the dog an affectionate rub behind the ears and then pulled on his boots for the trek down the road.

Chapter 9

"It's been way too long!" Angela said when she met Laura and Jessica. The three friends tried to get together for a "girls'-night-out" as often as possible, but over the past months they'd found it difficult to plan many outings. Laura and Jessica saw each other regularly at work. They didn't have much opportunity to visit but at least they were able to keep up with each other's lives. Angela worked as a secretary in a different area of the city. She had recently become engaged to be married and was anxious to show off her new diamond ring.

"That's for sure." The other two concurred. "Let's see that ring."

Angela beamed. She held out her hand for examination. After hugs of congratulations and gushes over the fine taste her betrothed had, the girls walked toward the movie theatre. *Roman Holiday*, starring Gregory Peck and Audrey Hepburn had just opened in Winnipeg. With all three off work for the weekend, the trio decided to see the movie in the late afternoon and then have some dinner at the Tipperary.

Laura was grateful for the night out. She'd spoken to Ben on the telephone at least three times in the past week. During freeze-up there wasn't any mail delivery or any chance to see each other. She already missed receiving his letters, and it had only been a week since the ferry had ceased to cross the channel. Normally, it took approximately three weeks for the ice to become strong enough to travel across.

Laden with popcorn and soda pops, the girls found seats in the dimly lit theatre. There were a few couples in the crowd, but most of the movie-goers were women who couldn't resist the heartthrob Gregory Peck. His classic good looks and gentlemanly charm filled movie houses everywhere.

"Is he ever gorgeous." Jessica's stage whisper reached all the ears in the near vicinity. Peck's role as newspaper reporter, Joe Bradley, provided a suave, charismatic background for the screen star. "Does your father have any reporters like him at his newspaper?"

"None that I've noticed." Laura replied.

"I guess none of us are looking anymore, are we?" Angela whispered the question in Laura's direction. "You'll have to tell me all about Ben after the movie."

Laura nodded and then they settled in their seats to watch the remainder of the movie. Filmed in Rome, Italy, the movie captivated the audience with sights of the city. Cathedrals and the Colosseum, as well as street markets and sidewalk cafes were visited in the black and white feature. Joe Bradley escorted Princess Ann who was concealing her true identity after dodging security guards to have a day alone in Rome.

"I'm getting a haircut like the Princess'," Angela announced as they left the theatre. Her hair was very similar to the style Audrey Hepburn had worn in the beginning of the film. To alter her looks the Princess had gone to a hair salon and changed from her long, straight hair style to a short bob with short bangs.

"That style would look great on you. I liked the way she had it pulled back over her ears and pinned. Then the back was sort of sticking out on the bottom in little curls." Jessica had also studied the new hairdo.

"You're right, Jessica. I think Angela resembles Audrey Hepburn. Doesn't she?" Laura teased as Angela strutted down the street, one hand on her hip, with the air of a great actress. Flipping a strand of hair over her shoulder from beneath her felt hat, Angela enjoyed her moment of stardom.

"I want that outfit she was wearing." Jessica was referring to the blouse and skirt the Princess had worn. The blouse was buttoned down the front with cuffs folded just off the shoulder. The full gathered skirt had a wide belt circling her waist, drawing attention to her petite form. A scarf knotted at her throat completed the jaunty ensemble.

"I just want her figure." Laura surveyed herself in a shop window.

"None of us will ever have that!" Jessica stood beside Laura in the reflection of the window. The fitted seam lines of their winter coats hugged their bodies, but the bulk of the fabric added inches to each waist.

"But close. Look again. We're not bad." Angela had lined up with her two friends and they all giggled as other pedestrians wondered what the joke was.

They were still laughing when they reached the Tipperary. Sitting down on three bar stools, they waited for Sean to finish serving a customer.

"Aye, m'lovelies, what's your pleasure?"

"We want to look like Audrey Hepburn." Laura answered.

"Who? Why I wouldn't change a thing about any of you. Next you'll be telling me I should look like Gregory Peck!" Sean straightened his shoulders and gave his best impression of the idol. "How about a pint on the house? That will cheer ya."

"Thanks, Sean. What's your dinner special tonight?"

"Tonight we have succulent lamb served with a dab of mint jelly, potatoes in a spice sauce which is a secret recipe not to leave the premises, and green beans sauteed in the best butter this side of Dublin. 'Tis a meal befitting the princesses you are." The jolly bartender was familiar with the new movie the girls had just seen. The beautiful young actress had been mentioned several times by his patrons.

"Sounds wonderful." The other girls nodded at Jessica. "We'll order three dinners right now."

"Are you lasses out on the town tonight?"

"We are." Angela acted as spokesperson. After swooning over her description of the movie star, she told Sean about her evening mission. "I have to hear all about Laura's mystery man."

"Aye, that'll be our Ben."

"Does everyone know him except me? I can't believe it!"

"I only saw him once. He's quite handsome." Jessica recalled the time Ben had come to the hospital. "Laura nabbed him before anyone else had a chance."

"He looks like a pirate."

"Sean, he does not!" Laura quickly sprang to defend Ben.

"Okay, so he's a pirate living on some God forsaken island. And handsome, you say?" Angela summarized the observations of her helpful friends. "And now he's caught in some kind of freeze-up. Sounds fishy to me."

Everyone, including Angela, laughed at the unintended pun. In telephone conversations Laura had told Angela about the fisherman who had walked onto her ward. Angela had learned a few details of his life and Laura had spoken of her trip to Hecla Island.

"The next time Ben comes to Winnipeg I'll get everyone together. How about Christmas? He'll be bringing me in on Christmas Day and spending a few days."

"The party'll be here." Sean ordered. "Invite everybody."

"Are you going to his place for Christmas Eve?" Jessica asked.

"Yes. They have the school Christmas concert on the twenty-third and on the twenty-fourth there will be a service in the church. Ben's family gets together on Christmas Eve, which works out perfectly since my family opens gifts together on Christmas Day. I'm taking some holiday time, but I'll be working two days before New Year's Eve and then going back with Ben for the New Year's Dance on the island."

"This is sounding pretty serious to me. Tell me more about the people out there." Angela was surprised that things had progressed so quickly between Laura and her pirate, while she had been romancing with John.

The girls were seated at a dinner table and Laura was still regaling her companions with anecdotes of the island and the people who lived there. They soon were acquainted with Ben's friends and his family. She described Sam's witch costume and the card game she had learned. Special mention was made of Malla, who had quickly earned a place in Laura's heart. As she spoke, her affection for Ben was obvious.

"I think we're going to lose her." Angela sighed and glanced at Jessica.

"I think you're right." Jessica said to Angela.

"Just make sure your house is big enough for all of us. We'll be coming to visit."

Following a whipped pudding for dessert, the three friends made plans to meet again. Sean had been by the table a few times during the evening. Each girl had updated the others on the most current events in their lives. Angela and Jessica were looking forward to the holiday party that Sean would be hosting for Ben.

"I hope you don't scare him." Laura remarked.

"Not ta worry, love, I don't think Ben scares easily!" Sean had been passing by and overheard Laura's remark.

"Let's make it a 'double for your money' party. Meeting Ben and celebrating Angela and John's engagement."

Jessica was on board. "Great idea, Laura. What do you say Angela?"

"Fine, as long as we remember the real reason for the get-together which is meeting your potential Mr. Right. I mustn't get sidetracked from my mission of thoroughly scrutinizing your pirate from a mysterious island."

"Okay, never mind scaring Ben, now you're terrifying me!" Laura laughed, knowing her friends would never do anything to embarrass her. She knew Ben wanted to meet all her friends, just as she had enjoyed meeting his.

"Romance is in the air." Angela admired her engagement ring.

"Blame it all on Joe Bradley and Rome!"

He shoots! He scores!" Foster Hewitt's deep voice was muffled in the cheering which erupted in Sam and Gudrun's living room. It was always a high tension game when the two Canadian teams met on the ice. The favourite team by far was the Toronto Maple Leafs, but Fred was still basking in the glory of the previous season when his Montreal Canadiens had claimed the Stanley Cup. Matthew favoured Detroit and top scorer, Gordie Howe. The remainder of the group assembled on that Saturday night were Maple Leaf fans all the way.

Sam and Ben could still describe the play-by-play win in 1951 when Toronto skated to capture the coveted first place in the National Hockey League. They nearly fell off their seats when Ellen had spoken of the abilities of Toronto players Max Bentley and Ted Kennedy.

"You're a hockey fan?" Sam was shocked.

"Sorry Matthew, as much as I like Gordie Howe, I've grown up cheering for Toronto." Ellen turned toward Sam, nodding. "I always listened to the games with my father. He's been a Maple Leaf fan forever."

"Give it up, Matthew, cross over to our side." Sam punched his friend in the arm.

"You'll all be sorry when Detroit wins this year." Matthew grinned at his new girlfriend. "I'll have to talk you into changing your loyalties."

"Well, I must admit that Detroit's Alex Delvecchio is really cute."

"Now there's the woman talking," Sam butted in, "cute has nothing to do with it!"

By this time the entire group was laughing. Gudrun ushered the ladies into the kitchen and away from the hockey combat. Kristine checked on the twins. They had fallen asleep in the bedroom off the living room. She tucked a blanket under their chins and went to join Gudrun and Ellen.

"I guess you're busy preparing for the Christmas concert?" Gudrun asked Ellen.

"Yes, it's fun. All the children are excited and happy to learn their lines. I'm really amazed at the singing. Those kids sound like a well-balanced choir."

"Part of that is wanting to please you," Kristine said, complimenting the teacher. "I know you are very popular with them."

"Oh, thanks for saying that." Ellen blushed at the praise. "I'm lucky to have such a nice bunch of students and, after the library concert last month, I can see where they get those singing voices from. I was surprised that a community of this size would put on a play. Everyone knew their lines and the vocal parts were excellent."

"It's a good way to raise money for more books. We'll be doing the same kind of concert in March for the Help-In-Emergency fund."

"I know the library committee was formed to establish a public library for all the islanders. I've been to the house where the library is and I saw several books that I haven't read yet. Then there are all the Icelandic books. It may be a while before I'll be able to read those!" Ellen chuckled, then asked, "What is the Help-In-Emergency fund?"

"It's money set aside for emergencies. At this time of year when travel across the channel is very dangerous, the victim of an illness or accident would have to resort to hiring an airplane to land on the island and escort them to a hospital. It can be extremely expensive. In a case like that, the fund helps to pay for the costs."

"What a great idea. When someone needs help, it's readily available and also it's in a fund that everyone has contributed to."

"Exactly. It isn't used very often but everyone appreciates its existence."

"Maybe you'd like to have a part in the next play?" Kristine was on the planning committee for the fund-raiser.

"I don't think I'm much of an actress but if you need help with the planning I'd be happy to volunteer."

"I'll let you know when we have a meeting."

"Are you going home for the holidays?" Gudrun set the filled kettle on the woodstove.

"Yes, I am going for part of the break. Matthew has invited me to spend Christmas Eve with him and his mother. Then I'd like to come back in time for the New Year's Dance. I'll have to see what kind of arrangements I can make."

"Talk to Ben. I know Laura is coming for the concert and Christmas Eve. Then I think they're going to Winnipeg for Christmas Day with her family. Hang on a sec." Gudrun walked to the door leading into the living room. "Ben, you and Laura are going into Winnipeg on the twenty-fifth, right?" Ellen and Kristine assumed they were when she continued, "Ellen might need a ride."

"Sure, that would be fine. We're coming back for the dance on the thirty-first." Ben had risen from his seat and walked into the kitchen. "I could give you a ride both ways if you like."

Ellen was overjoyed. "Great, that was easy. I wasn't sure how I could be in all the places I wanted to be. Thanks, Ben. I really appreciate the offer and if you're sure you don't mind, then I'll take you up on it."

"I don't mind at all. We'll be leaving first thing on Christmas Day. Laura mentioned that your folks live near to hers. We can easily drop you off at your home." Another victorious shout from the living room caught Ben's attention. "I'll talk to you later about it, but you may certainly have a ride with us." He was gone.

"Everyone on the island tries to be accommodating when it comes to rides or picking up some needed supplies. Most of the time all you need to do is speak up and there will be someone who can help." Kristine had often organized errands for Fred's trip into Riverton. He made the two trips into town for the island's mail every week and often came back with a machine part for a tractor or boat motor.

"You must have to overstock your store with everything during freeze-up. How do you know what everyone will need ?"

"That's a good question. We try our best and if we don't have it, then you have to improvise. Heclingers are very good at that. We've learned long ago to make the best with what we have. Just like at the school, if you run out of glue you mix up a paste of flour and water until you can buy more."

Ellen smiled, thinking of the saving measures that Matthew's mother had taught her in the classroom. Nothing was wasted. The school supplies were purchased on a tight budget, so each dollar was stretched to the limit.

More applause was heard from the other room. Toronto had scored to take the lead in the game. With the game nearly over, the goal could be the game winner.

In the kitchen, Gudrun set the table for a late lunch as the women visited. Coffee was ready and was served with egg sandwiches and oatmeal cookies. When the men joined the women, Gudrun put her arm around Ben's waist. "You're missing your Laura, aren't you? What is she doing this weekend?"

"She was meeting two of her friends and going to a new movie."

"Is it *Roman Holiday*?" Ellen had heard the movie was a big hit.

"That's the one. Apparently, Gregory Peck is in it."

Kristine and Gudrun immediately sighed as if they were under a spell. Ellen laughed and agreed with their opinion of the actor.

"You should be worried, Ben." Gudrun warned. "Not too wise to let her out with Gregory Peck."

"Her cousin, Sean, will put their feet back on the ground. They were going to his restaurant after the movie."

"I know the place, the Tipperary. It's such a fun place to go. Many of my friends meet there."

"We should all go there some time," Ben suggested. "You'd all enjoy it."

Although it was unlikely to happen, they tentatively planned a day in the big city. Then, they finished the coffee and dressed in their winter coats to go home. Ben carried one of the sleeping twins to Fred's car and laid him on the back seat, careful to leave enough room for his brother. Sam and Ben shared one more victory cheer in the frosty night air, amid groans from the others, and then they left.

Margaret finished tidying up her kitchen after breakfast and then decided to take inventory of the gifts she had planned for Christmas. She created many items during the year that would be wrapped up and put under the Christmas tree. With only three weeks until the holidays, it was time to decide who would receive each article. She had knitted sweaters for each grandchild. She was able to set that bag aside. Margaret wanted to give Elin a tablecloth that was dominated by the colour blue. It would clash with the colours Elin had chosen for her kitchen, but Margaret thought the room could use a fresh coat of paint and this gift might hasten her to apply a new, more attractive colour to the walls.

For her sister in Riverton, she had decided on the embroidered cushion that she'd completed. For her daughters, she had made some pillow cases with embroidered floral designs on the ends and crocheted lace trims on the edges.

She'd give Bjossi jars of her homemade jams made from fruit picked on the island. Margaret picked wild strawberries and raspberries in summer. In the fall, she'd picked moss berries after the first frost. Each kind of berry made a delicious spread. Several jars lined the pantry shelf in Margaret's kitchen. She clicked her tongue in disgust musing that Bjossi would probably share the sweet treat with that ugly, old goat. But her giving nature would rule and her neighbour would enjoy the gift, however he chose to use it.

Many pairs of socks and mitts were packed in another bag. In her head she calculated the destination of each set and concluded that there were enough pairs to go around.

Margaret was going to visit her two daughters. She liked to stay for at least two days at each household. In Riverton, she planned to do some baking for her younger daughter whose pre-school children dominated most of her time. In Gimli she would also bake, but because those grandchildren were in school during the day, they'd shop for the extras that Margaret wanted. In particular, she was looking for books for all her grandchildren. Reading was a favourite pastime in most Icelandic homes. Poetry and stories from Iceland were very popular.

Mentally noting the things she would need to buy, Margaret decided to start a written list so she wouldn't forget anything.

Hunting for the family's meat supply provided a diversion for Ben. He missed Laura's letters. Due to the party lines, their conversations seemed censored and left him dissatisfied. The ice was thickening on the lake. Not fast enough for Ben. In another week it should be three inches thick, which was the precedent followed in the safety requirement to walk across the channel. The ice would have to be six inches thick before an attempt would be made to drive a vehicle across. Some vehicles were left on the mainland side, so when the ice could be walked on they could drive into Riverton.

Ben and Daniel had cleaned the rifles and packed the bullets in their jacket pockets in readiness for hunting. Each held a thermos filled with coffee.

"Should we check in the bush behind the barn or should we drive to the west side of the island. I'll leave the decision to you, Ben."

"Fred shot his moose close to Horseshoe Bend and I know Sam was saying he had seen lots of tracks on the west side. Why don't we start there?"

In agreement, the two brothers set off. As they drove, they watched the woods for any sign of movement. They noticed several moose tracks crossing the road in various places. They'd nearly reached the curve into Horseshoe Bend when Ben broke the silence.

"Over there," he pointed to a thicket edging the marsh. "Do you see it? It looks like a yearling. Should we take him?"

Because there were several moose on the island, the brothers could be selective. They possessed confidence in their shooting ability. Not only were they looking for a clean shot, they also aimed to kill with the least damage done to the meat.

"He's a nice size. Is he yours or mine?" Daniel questioned Ben. Ben cautiously climbed out of the truck. He leaned over the hood and took careful aim. The yearling thought he was camouflaged in the brush and made the mistake of peeking out to see if he was in danger. The sound of the rifle shot echoed in the marsh as the moose was struck by the fatal bullet. Hit in the neck, the yearling dropped where it stood.

Ben and Daniel retrieved the sharp knives from the truck. They waded through the snow to reach the carcass. With deft accuracy, the two men bled and eviscerated the animal. Before carrying it to the back of the truck, they skinned and quartered the carcass.

At home again, each quarter was then taken inside to the warmth of the house and placed on the paper covered table. Again the sharp knives were put to work. With practised skill, the meat was cut away from the bones. Rose wrapped each chunk of meat in freezer paper and packed the parcels in a box. The meat would be stored outside in the shed where the freezing temperature would preserve it.

Signey sat quietly on the seat between her parents in Ben's car. They were on their way to Winnipeg for Signey's second appointment with the doctor. It was the week before Christmas and travel was now possible over the ice on the lake. The snowplow had cleared a path to follow across the channel. Signey had brought her doll with her for moral support and to play with in the car.

"Ben said that Laura would be at work when we get there. I'm looking forward to seeing her." Rose said.

"Poor Ben. I think he wanted to come with us. Can't say that I blame him. Those two are pretty serious about each other. He said he'd be seeing Laura next week and she'd be working today. There wasn't much point in coming along. He looked kind of sick when we left though, didn't he?" Daniel grinned at his wife.

Signey squirmed in the seat. The trip was long and she was unable to see outside. Mama had told her that they'd be seeing the doctor and then they'd come home again. The last time they'd been to the doctor, Mama had taken Signey's clothes off, leaving only her panties on. The doctor had asked her to walk back and forth many times. Then he had stretched her left arm in all directions and it had hurt. *Pabbi* and Mama had thought the quiet tears expressed her fear in seeing the doctor. It was true that she feared the doctor and the hospital, but her tears reflected the pain in the damaged muscles. When he probed her back and neck muscles, her body trembled in painful spasms. The doctor recognized the spasms and must have known he was causing her discomfort. He'd looked at her and said he was sorry for hurting her.

The more Signey thought about her last visit to Winnipeg, the more agitated she became. *Pabbi* had just said they were getting close and would probably see Laura soon. When they stopped in the parking lot of the hospital, Signey's anxiety was reflected in her big eyes.

Rose tried to pacify her daughter. "You know it won't take long to see the doctor, Signey. Then, maybe we'll be able to visit with Laura for a few minutes. Won't that be fun? You can tell Uncle Ben about seeing her."

Making their way to the familiar second floor ward, the solemn trio scanned the area in search of Laura. Signey clasped her mother's hand tightly. As soon as they walked toward the nurses' desk, an excited Laura came to greet them. Having adopted the Hecla tradition, she held her arms out and gave each of them a warm hug.

"It's so nice to see all of you. I can't wait for Christmas. How about you, Signey?"

Signey tried to hide any indication of her inner turmoil.

"After your appointment with the doctor, how about meeting me for lunch? There's a cafeteria on the main floor. They have good soup. It won't be as good as the soup your mother and Amma Anna make, but it's good."

"That sounds like a fine plan." Daniel answered the expectant look on Signey's face.

"We were hoping to be able to visit with you for a while. We have a letter for you from Ben." Rose handed the envelope to Laura.

"I have one to send back with you. It's in my handbag. Oh, the doctor's office door just opened. I don't see anyone else waiting so maybe he's ready to see you."

They left Laura, promising to let her know when they were ready to go for lunch. Before they had a chance to ask if the doctor was ready for them, he appeared in the doorway and summoned them into his office.

Signey clung to her mother as the instructions came to remove her clothing. The girl's eyes grew big when they met the dark stare of the doctor. Similar to the first visit, he told her to walk back and forth in front of him. Then he asked her to come closer so he could examine her back, neck and arm. She tried to be brave, but the trembling in her limbs gave her away.

"How high can you lift your arm?" The doctor nodded his encouragement as Signey slightly bent her left forearm. There wasn't any movement above the elbow.

"Let me hear your voice. Can you sing me a song?" His attempt at joviality was lost on the young patient. Her mother urged her to speak, but Signey couldn't make her mouth move.

"Tell the doctor about the Christmas ornaments we made." Rose had knelt beside her daughter, hoping to relax her enough so that she would follow the doctor's orders. The doctor's cold fingers circled Signey's windpipe and he cupped his other hand at the back of her neck to hold her head securely. Staring fearfully at her mother, the girl mechanically described the paper stars she had coloured to hang on the tree.

"Good. Your voice sounds strong. And those stars sound very nice too."

He continued his examination, checking the muscles on either side of her spine. His brow wrinkled into a scowl as he compared the two shoulders and neck muscles. Again, he looked at her back, noting the contrast between the left and right sides. He turned her around so that Daniel and Rose could observe as he pointed out his deductions.

"The left shoulder hasn't improved and I don't expect that it will after this. Her voice is stronger and her neck seems to have regained its strength. Her back hasn't twisted but I want her to be encouraged to always walk with a straight back and to sit without slouching. The muscles that were paralyzed throughout the left side are still very vulnerable and the tendency of the body is to favour the weakness." The doctor showed them the variations from one side to the other. The left side of Signey's torso was smaller and, because her left arm hung due to the absence of the left shoulder muscle, her body seemed to sag towards the left. He turned her to face him again and said, "You need to keep doing all your exercises and then you will grow up to be strong. You may put your clothes on again." The medical man smiled at Signey, then turned to Daniel and Rose. "I believe she will lead a fairly normal life. She doesn't realize it yet, but she's a very lucky young lady."

"Before you leave," the man again spoke to Signey, "you should say hello to the other children. They enjoy seeing familiar faces."

"Okay." Signey answered shyly.

"Thank you." Daniel shook hands with the doctor. "We appreciate your advice."

They made their way back to the ward to find Laura and also to see the other children. A girl, who appeared to be about twelve years old, spotted Signey and pointed her wheelchair in their direction. Her smile reached her eyes as she steered the chair in front of them.

"Hi, Signey. Do you remember me? I'm Donna."

Signey returned the smile and nodded. She tightened her grip on her mother's hand, still afraid she could be left here. Laura approached the group and put her hand on Donna's shoulder.

"Isn't it nice to see Signey again?" Laura smiled at Donna, then explained to Daniel and Rose. "Donna likes to read stories and I think she read a story to Signey nearly every day she was here."

Fighting back her tears, Rose leaned over and gave Donna's arm a gentle squeeze.

"Signey loves to hear stories. It was so nice of you to read to her."

Laura went on to tell them that Donna was planning on becoming a nurse when she grew up and she was already learning a lot. "Some days around here, I don't know what we'd do without her."

Laura said she could meet them in the cafeteria in a few minutes. She gave them instructions on how to get there. They left the second floor ward behind and Signey's nervousness lessened.

"We're all done with the doctor," Rose said. "Now we'll have lunch with Laura and then it will be time to go home again."

"I thought we had some shopping to do?" Daniel joked. "Or maybe we won't buy any gifts for Christmas this year." His teasing smile had the desired effect when Signey looked up at her father and grinned.

The cafeteria was a buzz of activity over the lunch hour. They joined the queue that was formed in front of the hot food counter. With bowls of soup and ham sandwiches in hand, the family found a vacant table that had an extra chair for Laura. Rose was just tucking Signey's serviette under her chin to protect her clothes from any soup spills when Laura arrived. She had purchased a cup of coffee and a bowl of soup to go with the sandwich she had brought from home.

"I sure timed that perfectly. It usually gets pretty crowded in here during lunch break, especially in the winter months. There's a park across the street that we go to in the summer."

"With such a busy hospital to work in, it must feel good to get away from people during your breaks."As Daniel sipped his coffee, his eyes roamed the room taking in the rushed crowd. "This place looks like an ant hill with its top scrapped off."

"We are used to working with a team beside us. It sure isn't like fishing, is it?"

Daniel laughed. "Not even close. If there were this many fishermen around us, there wouldn't be a fish left in the lake!"

"Will you be able to get the time off over the holidays that you wanted?" Rose had heard from Ben that Laura hoped to spend Christmas Eve and New Year's Eve on the island.

"Yes, I will. I can hardly wait for this week to go by."

"We're all looking forward to having you with us – not just Ben. Although I guess he's expecting to have you to himself."

Laura smiled at Rose's teasing.

"What are you hoping that Santa Claus brings for you, Signey?" The girl's face lit up at Laura's question. She shyly looked at her mother.

"You can tell Laura. What was it again?" The gentle prodding from her mother gave Signey the courage to speak.

"A doll with a pretty dress." The quiet voice with a distinct Icelandic accent carefully enunciated the words. A slight flush crept over her cheeks.

"Well I know that you've been a very good girl this year. I'm sure that Santa will try to bring you a nice doll."

They talked about the tasty soup, the shopping still to be done and the hope of a favourable forecast for the weather over the holiday season. With hugs and comments about seeing each other on the following week, Laura waved them goodbye.

Chapter 10

"Silent night, holy night. All is calm, all is bright." The youthful voices reached every corner of the hall. Miss Taylor stood in front of the choir, facing the children as she conducted them through the Christmas carol. Each face watched the teacher with rapt attention, following her guidance and singing to their full potential.

In the audience, Laura sat between Ben and Anna. She was impressed by the program the school children had entertained them with. The community hall was packed with most of the island's residents. They had clapped with appreciation after the play, and after the recitations and singing. Ellen beamed at her students after the final carol.

Following the concert, everyone enjoyed a time for coffee and lunch and general glad tidings of the season. A visit from Santa Claus was a highlight of the evening. Every child received a small brown paper bag with some candies tucked inside. Outside, as Santa 'Ho–Ho-Ho-ed' his way through the door, a fresh sprinkle of snow was falling.

"What a beautiful night. Look at the snow." Laura thought the large flakes of snow went well to what she considered a magical Christmas night. It had been a few weeks since she'd seen Ben. Being with him held a magic of its own.

"It won't look so beautiful when the north wind is blowing that snow at us on the lake!" Sam saw a different picture when he glanced outdoors but he failed to extinguish the ambience from Laura's mind.

"Mr. Romantic is at it again!" Gudrun's laugh joined Laura's.

Laura felt the warmth of her new friends even though the chill of winter was all around them. It was only her second visit to the island, but she was greeted with friendliness.

Ben and his mother had met Laura with her parents the previous day in Gimli. Laura had hoped that any reservations her parents had about her relationship with Ben would be put to rest when they met Anna. The O'Neils had voiced concerns regarding the remoteness of

Ben's home and the vast difference in his livelihood to anything she was accustomed to. They liked Ben but weren't sure that he was the right man for their daughter. The two mothers had been comfortable with each other but Laura knew they both harboured similar concerns about their children. She hadn't realized that Anna would, of course, have the same reservations about her that her mother had about Ben.

Laura's father was still upset with her. He blustered on about marrying out of their community, meaning the Irish Catholic community. She accused him of being narrow-minded and unreasonable. Her mother said she was just like her father, stubborn and direct. Laura wished her parents could see Ben through her eyes.

Her parents left for home. Ben took Laura and Anna to visit Anna's brother Johannes and his family. They lived on a farm just north of Gimli. Family gatherings were few. Distance and the difficulty of travel to the island was cited as the reason for the rare visits, but Ben told Laura that it went much deeper than that. Daniel had been a baby when Johannes and his younger brother, Bjarni, had a serious quarrel. Johannes had verbally attacked Bjarni about his drinking and womanizing, strongly suggesting that he settle down and start working harder towards making a good living.

The result of the disagreement didn't go as Johannes had hoped. Instead of heeding Johannes' advice, Bjarni packed his belongings and angrily proclaimed that he'd be back 'when he made his fortune'. They never saw him again. Any inquiries had turned into dead ends.

Anna had always adored her younger brother and his leaving in haste without an explanation to her had left her bereft. And now, after all these years, she still felt it was a betrayal to Bjarni whenever she visited Johannes. Anna knew that Johannes was as devastated as she was over the disappearance. Because she had favoured Bjarni, it was easier to blame her older brother than accept her younger brother's shortcomings. The truth was Anna had difficulty accepting that Bjarni had never contacted her.

Ben explained the whole story in a letter to Laura before they met in Gimli. He wished his mother could put the hurt behind her. At the same time, if he and Daniel had a big fight and Daniel disappeared in a similar manner, he knew he would never stop searching for him. He guessed that Johannes hurt even more than his mother, but Ben would never suggest that to her.

They were all leaving the hall after the concert when Signey took Laura's hand and asked her to come and see their Christmas tree.

"I'd love to see your tree. You made some of the decorations, didn't you?"

Big, blue eyes solemnly stared at Laura as the girl nodded in acknowledgment. Then two large hands circled Signey's waist and lifted her into the air.

"Are you trying to steal my girlfriend away from me?" Ben tickled the small figure, sending her into peals of laughter. Laura remembered how silent Signey had been in the hospital and she couldn't help but smile as she noted the improvement in the soft spoken voice.

Rose had heard the exchange and invited them to come and see the tree and have another cup of coffee.

"You'll find out, Laura, that Icelanders are never satisfied when it comes to drinking coffee. There's always room for one more cup!"

A few minutes later they all crowded into Rose and Daniel's kitchen. The new oil heater threw off some welcome heat. The temperature had dipped to -31 degrees Celsius after the sun went down. Daniel stoked the embers in the woodstove and added a couple of logs to create enough heat to boil the kettle. Signey stood in the living room doorway, patiently waiting for their guest to follow her.

"I'm coming Signey." Laura hung her coat by the back door. She placed her felt hat on a bench nearby. Laura held the girl's hand and approached the decorated tree. "It's so beautiful. Which ones did you make?"

Signey pointed out the brightly coloured stars and explained how she'd made them. Rose and Karen had wrapped the gifts and tucked them under the tree. Signey picked up a small parcel to show Laura.

"This is your present but you can't open it yet." A teasing sparkle lit the youngster's eyes.

"Don't tell her what's in it." Daniel cautioned his daughter. "Mama won't be happy if you give away any secrets."

"What secrets? Signey, shush about the presents. We mustn't spoil the surprise." Rose had set the table in the kitchen for a coffee lunch. Still waiting for the kettle to boil, she'd gone into the cellar and brought out a special Christmas treat.

"You have to try some of my chocolates, Laura. I hid this box so well that no one has found it." Rose passed the sweet candy around. Laura heard how it had become a contest to Adam, Karen and Alexander to find the hiding spots. At first, when Adam was younger, Rose had joked that she'd have to hide the chocolates so he couldn't eat them all. Over the years the challenge grew and now checking all the little nooks and crannies for special hiding places was part of their Christmas tradition.

Rose collected the boxes that store-bought chocolates came in, as well as the miniature paper cups the candy came adorned with. Each year she made the chocolates using mashed potatoes and icing sugar. Eggs, butter and flavouring completed the candy filling. She rolled the mixture into tiny balls and chilled overnight. She melted semi-sweet chocolate with a small amount of paraffin wax in a double-boiler pot on the stove. Then she dipped each candy into the chocolate and placed it on wax paper to harden. Rose had tried a variety of flavourings but she usually used peppermint, almond and maple.

"This year I diced cherries and put a drop of red food colouring in some of the filling." Rose waited for Laura to choose a candy. "I rolled the filling with a piece of cherry in the middle."

"This is delicious, Rose!" Laura sampled the home-made chocolate. "I can't believe you make these. You should open a candy store."

"I only make them for Christmas. Half the fun is outsmarting these detectives and keeping the chocolates hidden." She gave the children a smug, self-satisfied grin. She set the box down to remove the brown paper separating the upper and lower layers of candy. The smug grin quickly turned to a gasp of dismay when she realized that every chocolate from the bottom layer had vanished. Daniel and Ben both saw the empty box and the wary glance between Adam and Karen at the same time. The two men howled with laughter.

"You've been had, Rose." Daniel glanced at the chocolate thieves. "All I can say is, there better be another box somewhere." His wife nodded as she agreed that her detectives had indeed duped her. There was nothing to do but join in the merriment.

"*Komdu inn*, come in." Malla slipped into English when she caught sight of Laura standing next to Ben. The couple was dropping in early on the morning of Christmas Eve.

"We wanted to catch you before your grandsons pick up you and Olivia." Ben knew the sisters would be spending the following few days with their families on the mainland.

"It's so nice to see you again. Ben was telling me that you'll be in Riverton for Christmas." Laura gave the old woman a warm hug.

"Yes, the boys will be here in a couple of hours. I hope you have time to stop for coffee." She ladled water into the kettle. It would be futile to think this was going to be a short visit.

"It wouldn't be Christmas if we didn't get a taste of your fruitcake."

Ben smiled. Just before arriving, he'd filled Laura in on all the years he'd stopped in for Malla's baking. At this time of year, it was her fruitcake. Currants, dates, walnuts, almonds and maraschino cherries were mixed into the sweet batter and baked at a low temperature for over four hours. The cake pans were lined with wax paper to prevent the outer edges from becoming too dark.

"I made some cinnamon buns. You'll have to try them."

"Malla, you don't have to give us anything. You have them all wrapped and ready to take with you." Ben's hand on her arm stopped Laura. Malla smiled.

"Shush, Laura, wait 'til you taste them. Besides, look at the size of the pan. There's plenty for her family!"

"You are spoiled rotten! Malla, how do you put up with him?"

The elderly woman's face creased into smiles. She warmed the buns on the woodstove while she waited for the kettle to boil and admitted that 'putting up' with Ben was one of her favourite pastimes.

In a few minutes they sat down to coffee, buns and fruitcake. Laura wondered why she had eaten a bowl of porridge with toast before they came here.

"It must take a long time to prepare such a big batch of buns." Laura spread a dab of butter on the bun she'd cut in half on her plate.

"I make them the usual way, by rolling out the dough with a rolling pin, then spreading butter, brown sugar and cinnamon over the surface." Malla gestured with her hands. "Then I roll, slice and place the dough in a baking pan to rise. After the buns have risen, I add my personal touch to the recipe. I pour rich, fresh cream over the buns."

"Okay, Ben, you were right. Malla, these are the best cinnamon buns I've ever tasted. I just hope Anna doesn't have a big lunch planned for us."

"No, there won't be much for lunch, but you'll have to be ready for a feast later."

With that in mind, Laura sampled a small piece of fruitcake. It, too, left her mouth watering for more. Distracting herself from the food, Laura reached into a bag she'd brought in and pulled out a gift for Malla.

"My goodness, what is this?" The bright Christmas paper and the attractive ribbon caught her eye immediately.

"You'll have to open it to find out." Ben grinned at Malla..

Under the gift wrap, Malla found a colourful book commemorating the Coronation of Queen Elizabeth ll. She gasped in delight. She'd followed the news broadcasts of the death of King George Vl, and the crowning of his daughter which had occurred on June 2, 1953. Scanning quickly, Malla noticed that the book chronicled the young queen's life in glossy, colour photos.

"This is beautiful. How did you know I was interested in the Royal Family?" The question was put to Laura, who Malla was sure had purchased the gift.

"Ben told me to look for something like that. He told me about sending you clippings from the London papers when he was overseas. As soon as I saw this book, I thought you would like it."

"It's perfect. I'll be spending lots of time looking through it. Thank you."

"Thank you, too, for the presents under our tree." Two days earlier, Ben had delivered gifts to various homes on the island for Malla and Olivia. "And now, *kaerasta min*, we should be on our way." Ben pulled out Laura's chair. They were planning to drop in on Sam and Gudrun for a few minutes.

With hugs and good wishes for a happy Christmas season, the young couple bid Malla good-bye.

"She's such a terrific lady. I can't get over her zest for life. And those buns, my God, they were so good." Laura rubbed her full stomach as they drove out the driveway.

"Didn't I tell you. And you were going to let her family have them all. Good thing I put a stop to that."

"You are such a brat." Laura shook her head and smiled. Then she slid across the seat and kissed him on the cheek.

Sam opened the door as soon as Ben and Laura reached the back steps.

"We've been watching for you. Gudrun has coffee made already. Hurry and get in out of the cold."

"We were just at Malla's having coffee. But I'm sure we have room for another cup. Isn't that what you Icelanders say?" Laura laughed and took off her coat. She'd brought a fancy tin of shortbread cookies for Sam and Gudrun. After work one night she had baked several dozen cookies to bring for Anna, Rose and Gudrun. She had wanted to bring something homemade to these women who so capably could make anything they set their minds to. She admired the confidence they had in themselves to tackle anything. This confidence may have been borne out of necessity, but it still inspired them to face any obstacles in the way.

"She may be Irish, but we're turning her into an Icelander." Sam patted Ben on the shoulder.

"These look delicious, Laura. Did you make them?" Gudrun had opened the tin and discovered the shortbread cookies with white icing and pieces of cherries on top.

"Yes, I did. I hope you like shortbread."

"We love it. Thanks so much. I have something for you, too." She took a gift off the table and handed it to Laura. "You have to open it now."

With Ben looking over her shoulder, Laura gently removed the tissue paper. The two folded paper frames opened to reveal pictures that Gudrun had taken at the Hallowe'en dance. Both photos were of Ben and Laura. One, taken after dancing a polka, showed the couple with big smiles and flushed cheeks. Ben's tie had been loosened and his arm hung casually around Laura's shoulder. The second picture had caught them in a similar pose shortly after they had arrived at the dance.

"I gave you two pictures so each of you could have one."

"What a thoughtful gift. I'd forgotten that you were snapping pictures that night. Thank you." Laura was touched.

"We look pretty good. I'm still as handsome as ever." Ben puffed up his chest as Sam smirked in laughter.

"Buddy, I've gotta tell ya – what really looks good is what you're wearing on your arm." Sam pointed at Laura in the picture. They all laughed and Ben hugged both Laura and Gudrun.

"That's the truth, Sam. We're lucky to have our girls." Not able to leave it at that, he continued, "And are they ever lucky to have us!"

Sam was happy to see some of the 'old Ben' back again. As boys, they had spent so much time together. He'd never forget the day that Ben had told him he was enlisting and hoped to go overseas. Being a year younger, Sam couldn't go with him. The following year when he came of age, the war seemed to be nearing an end. He had signed up for service and was near completion in his training when victory had been declared.

When Ben returned, Sam found his childhood friend to be a very different person. The huge smile and mischievous eyes had been replaced by the dour look of a much older man. For a long time, Sam felt that he had let his friend down and he often wished he could have stood beside him for those two years.

The next few years passed with the young men of the island working hard to improve the economy. The road across the island and the sawmill had been high on the list of priorities. At the end of the day when the work was done and it was time for fun, Ben always seemed to hang back at the edge of the circle. Sam remembered the dark stare Ben had given him when he tried to include him in planning a 'Kick-up Dance'.

They had been repairing the fisherman's dock in the village one Saturday when Sam had suggested they go home and change, then meet back at the hall with a record player and some records. These impromptu dances were popular with the young couples and, during the summer when heat wasn't required in the hall, a party could be planned in a few minutes.

Ben had looked at Sam as if to say, 'Life isn't all about having a party'. Sam had been crushed. There had been other times that Sam had suffered blows to his self esteem because of a certain look from Ben. Then one day, after witnessing a similar exchange, Daniel had taken Sam aside. He, too, had felt the sting of Ben's words and glares. Daniel told Sam that Ben just needed some time to find himself again. It had nothing to do with anything that someone else said or did. Daniel was sure that time was the key and that the two of them shouldn't take his attitude too personally.

Now, looking at his close friend, Sam was a little jealous that it had taken this Irish nurse to put Ben back on track. In the eight and a half years since Ben's homecoming, Sam had gradually chipped away at the shell that Ben had built around himself. They shared many good times and Ben had learned to take life less seriously. But on that night, the huge smile and mischievous eyes were back on his face as he teased Laura, and for Sam, it was the best Christmas present he could have received.

The new chandeliers glowed in the church, welcoming everyone to worship. All the pews were filled. Laura had met many of the islanders at the Hallowe'en Dance, but some in attendance that night were family members from afar that were home for Christmas. Sitting with Ben and Anna, Laura smiled a greeting to familiar faces. Although she was still a newcomer to Hecla Island, she had a feeling of belonging to this community.

Children tried in vain to sit still during the service. All the youngsters were donned in their finest clothes, their faces lit with the wonder of the holiday. Anxious mothers attempted to maintain control of their children while solemnly bowing their heads in prayer.

In the pew behind her, Laura recognized the face of an elderly woman but was unable to remember her name. A few seconds into the first hymn, Laura knew she would never forget the woman's voice. Slightly off-key and a half a beat behind the rest of the congregation, she immodestly raised her voice to the heavens.

Across the aisle the twins, Peter and Paul, were causing a bit of a stir. One of them had hidden a candy in his pocket and in the middle of the hymn had decided that it was time to eat it. His brother protested and a scuffle was close at hand. Kristine forced the candied mouth open and scooped the gooey mass into her hand, resulting in a shift of the protest from one twin to the other.

Sam and Gudrun shared a pew with Matthew, Ellen and Mrs. Marinsson. In front of them, Jon and Elin encouraged their children, Aldis, Beth and Stefan to join in the hymn.

In front of Laura, Rose kept an eye on Adam and Karen. Adam was trying to get Andrew's attention across the room and Karen's attempt to avoid one of the schoolboys was compromised by her continuous glances in his direction. Alexander squirmed in the pew and complained about the itchy wool in his pants. Signey stood on the seat, nestled into the crook of her mother's arm.

To her right, on the other side of Anna, Laura heard both Bjossi and Kristjan add their voices to the hymn. Thora, the organist, pumped the pedals of the pipe organ with her feet to create melodious music at the front of the church.

Laura found some similarities in the church service to her family's church in Winnipeg. She knew her transfer to the Hecla church would require some adjustments. She had to laugh at herself for automatically placing herself and her future on Hecla Island. Since meeting Ben her life had become enmeshed in his. What she had seen so far was a life she could adapt to. Ben and his family and friends seemed supportive of their relationship and she was sure they'd be helpful in her adjustment to life on Hecla Island.

Laura bowed her head and joined the others in reciting the Lord's Prayer. Towards the back of the church a baby cried. The smell of damp wool hung in the air. As the pastor lead them in 'Joy To The World', the bright lights and the voices of the happy congregation reverberated far beyond the walls of the church.

Laura loved the feeling of community that surrounded her. In Winnipeg, her church was much larger and there were many members of the congregation that she didn't know by name. Here, she was probably the only one who couldn't place a name to each face. They all gathered in the sole church on the island to worship and proclaim their faith, together as one. Proud and devout, the Icelanders wore their spirituality and love of their church on their sleeves. They questioned many things in life, but never the presence of the God who watched over them.

"Look what I've got!" Karen couldn't contain her glee when she opened her gift from Ben and Laura. The new hairbrush and shiny barrettes had been a good choice.

For Adam and Alexander, Ben had found pocket knives. But it was Signey's face, quietly beaming as she unwrapped the wooden cradle for her doll, that tore at Laura's heartstrings. Signey didn't say a word, just walked over to Laura and gave her a hug.

Ben lightened the moment by tickling his niece and extracting a hug of his own from her.

In the glow of the recently wired light-bulbs, the family and Bjossi gathered around the kitchen table after the church service and enjoyed a meal of roast chicken with all the festive trimmings. Smoked mutton was a Christmas tradition in many Icelandic homes and it had been served as a second meat dish. Laura's dessert of a bread pudding with a creamy caramel sauce had been a big hit with everyone.

Now they all sat smiling over the reactions of the younger set as they continued to open gifts. Bjossi eased into a big armchair and puffed on his pipe. Chopper had also been invited in for the celebration and lay at his master's feet. Dixie and Spike were allowed, on this occasion, to sneak into the living room. In the winter, the two dogs slept on the mat near the back door to escape the freezing temperatures. Deer bones had been wrapped for each dog, Chopper included.

"Oh." Laura gasped as she opened a box to reveal a hand-knit blanket that Anna had made for her. "This is so beautiful. I don't know what to say." The warm hug she gave Anna said it all.

"It's good to have a warm afghan when you're travelling back and forth from here to Winnipeg. You never know when the car might break down."

A squeal of pleasure from Rose caught everyone's attention as she held up an electric iron. It would replace the heavy pressing irons that were heated on the woodstove.

"Keep digging, Rose, there's something else in the wrapper." Daniel grinned at Rose when she lifted her brow in his direction. "I didn't just get you something to work with." She found the little jeweller's box and discovered a pretty broach inside. The sparkles in the pin matched the sparkles in Rose's eyes.

Most of the gifts under the tree were made by hand. Sweaters, mitts and socks had been knitted, dresses had been sewn; and tablecloths and cushions had been embroidered. Laura pressed a scarf to her cheek, loving the feel of the soft yarn. Knit by Malla, Laura noticed that the fine wool matched her coat perfectly.

Ben was amazed when he opened his gift from Daniel and Rose. Daniel had carved a cribbage board out of a deer antler. With perfect precision, he had bored the peg holes into the curve of the horn.

From Laura, Ben admired a wristwatch he had immediately strapped on. Laura wore the gold locket that had been engraved on the inside with, 'To Laura, With love, Ben Christmas 1953'.

"Are you going to give Laura her present now, Signey?" Signey hurried to the tree, picked up the parcel and rushed over to Laura.

"What could it be?" Laura looked into the expectant eyes. She slowly removed the paper. It was a small piece of driftwood that had been stowed away since early summer with the idea of creating something special. With help, Signey had turned it into a pen holder. The wood was shaped in a way that it could sit on three points and offered a fairly flat top in which to drill two holes that could house two pens. With a black pen, Signey had printed 'Nurse O'Neil'. With some of the letters larger than others and the work obviously done by a young child, it was one of the nicest gifts Laura could recall receiving. And, as a nurse, she had received many gifts from her patients over the years. Laura stroked the smooth varnished finish, then gathered the girl into her arms.

"It's perfect." Laura struggled to keep her voice steady. "I think I'll put it on my desk at the hospital – you remember the corner by the telephone?"

An affirmative nod accompanied Signey's big eyes. "Then my pens will be where I need them and everyone walking by will see it. And, whenever I look at it, I'll remember Hecla Island and all of you."

Laura gazed around the room and thought how rich her life had become since meeting this family. She couldn't believe that four months ago she hadn't known of their existence. A young girl with polio had steered her life in a totally different direction from anything she could have imagined.

Chapter 11

"Make sure I have this straight. Angela is engaged to John, and Jessica's husband is Jeff?" Ben steered the car towards the Tipperary and the crowd of party-goers that would be there. It was the evening after Boxing Day. Two days earlier they had driven into the city and celebrated Christmas with Laura's family. It had been similar to Christmas Eve on the island as far as food and boisterous children were concerned. Hilary and Frank's preschoolers had provided lively entertainment and had attacked each gift with wide-eyed anticipation.

"You've got it. I know you're going to like all of them. Just don't let the girls interrogate you too much. They're a bit curious about you, you know!" Laura was glad that Ben would be meeting her closest friends. She had felt a tighter bond between herself and Ben when she met his friends. Through them she had learned about his earlier years and been given a picture of the man who was a friend, not just a son or brother or uncle.

"And if the going gets tough, I'm to call Sean to help me out." Ben smiled as he confirmed a plan of escape. Laura's answering nod and smile softened the taut features on his face.

He'd spent the afternoon with Aiden at the Legion and returned to the house wearing a solemn face. During dinner, Laura noticed that his humour and casual talk were staged. Hilary was being her usual superior self around Ben, and her father wore a judgmental air that belonged to the movies. What was wrong with them? She worried about Ben's mechanical responses and wondered why her family couldn't see Ben for the person he was. He stood miles above any other young men she'd dated.

Because she'd been at work and arrived at home just in time for the evening meal, this was the first opportunity to speak with him alone. "Did you meet many people today at the Legion?"

"Yeah, there were quite a few. I really like Aiden. He's easy to talk to."

Laura tried not to take his words too personally. She hoped he felt the same way about her, but when it came to talking about the war she knew the invisible walls were still up.

"He says the same about you."

Ben reached for her gloved hand and gave it a squeeze. His eyes conveyed the unspoken plea for understanding.

"Sitting with a group of men who were overseas brings it all back, but it's a relief in a way, too. We talked about the best pubs and laughed over some of the crazy pranks that we pulled." Ben's expression reverted back to sadness. "Then, we talked about the ones we left behind. One guy, Gordon, said we'd all lost good friends. I'll never forget what he said."

"He said, one way to honour them is always remember the men they were and the reason they died. Somehow, we came home. Why, who knows? But every Remembrance Day, at the eleventh hour of the eleventh day of the eleventh month, he's at a school telling a story about his men and what they meant to him. He said it's tough, but he wants those kids to feel that the soldiers' lives weren't lost and forgotten."

"He really made an impression on you, didn't he?" Laura sat next to him in the car.

"Next November 11, I'm going to talk to the kids at the school in Hecla about war and protecting our freedom." Saying the words out loud gave credence to the thoughts that had filled his head all afternoon and gave a definition to his purpose.

"That's a good idea." Laura squeezed his hand and snuggled closer to his side. With one hand on the wheel, Ben stretched his other arm right around Laura's shoulders and hugged her tightly against him.

"Do we have to go to this party?"

"Here comes the Viking out in you! Just hold that thought for a few hours." The mischievous gleam in her eyes had the desired effect when Ben burst out laughing.

"You can count on that, *kaerasta min*!"

The Tipperary was in its usual form when Ben and Laura walked in. Laughter and music filled the air. Sean shouted out a greeting as he topped a glass with stout. A few heads turned in the new arrivals direction, and before they could remove their coats they were bombarded by Jessica and Angela. Within minutes Ben was introduced to the two couples and the interrogation began.

"Remote? Hecla Island is so remote we thought we lived in our own country!" Ben enjoyed himself, answering the girls' questions.

"Quiet? It's so quiet you can hear a muskrat shiver."

"Eww!" Angela shuddered. She'd never been an outside-type of girl and the visual in her head wasn't comforting. "It sounds pretty lonely to me."

"Lonely? It's so lonely we swim with the fish – not gangster style, but literally. The fish are our friends." This lament was met with bouts of laughs and Sean playing an invisible violin.

"Good grief, Ben! I'm glad I'd already told them about Hecla. You really are the limit!" Laura punched him in the arm.

"You'll have to come and see the island for yourselves. Now that we have a ferry crossing the channel, you can come anytime in the summer. We always have room for company." Ben's invitation was taken to heart. Everyone was talking about when the trip could be made.

It was just past midnight when the party broke up. Most of the group would be at work in a few hours or it would have gone much longer. Laura was one of those who had to be at work, and since Ben was dropping her off at the hospital he offered to help Sean with the cleanup in the morning.

"No need Ben, but you're more than welcome to come by."

"Laura's house will be empty tomorrow. Colin and Laura are working and Katherine is babysitting at Hilary's. So, I'll be here to give you a hand." Ben put a pathetic scowl on his face and said, "You wouldn't want me to get lonely, would you?"

Laura dragged Ben outside amid another uproar. Everyone left in high spirits.

Back at the house, cuddled on the couch in the living room, Ben told Laura that this had been an eventful day. He liked her friends and said he would enjoy seeing them again. His tone turned quiet and a little sad when he described some of the men he had met at the Legion. And then, after a long reflective pause, he told her about the night raids the aircraft crew he was with had flown. How they had huddled in their places on the way to their mission, barely daring to breathe as if the enemy might hear them. The drone of the Halifax Bomber's engines was the only sound. Then on nearing the target, how each person had followed the detailed orders to ensure the mission was completed as planned. The bombs would be dropped and the plane would head for home.

"Our reactions became automatic. I remember the night we bombed Dresden, a city in eastern Germany. The night was aglow from all the explosives. Much of the city was destroyed. We finished our drops and headed for home, trying to put the images of devastation out of our minds."

"One night we flew farther than necessary and when we backtracked to head for home, we saw the most amazing fireworks. It was in the Ruhr Valley and the targets were the many factories that were built there." He stood and slowly paced as he continued. "The colours of the explosives were incredible. All of us watched in wonder, and then someone asked how could something so beautiful be so destructive."

There were tears in his eyes when he looked at her. Laura beckoned him to join her on the couch again. He lowered himself on the sofa. Laura knew there was more he wanted to say.

"We felt so guilty. Not for bombing, that was our job. But for enjoying the fireworks display. I always believed in what we were doing. If the outcome of the war had been different, the world would be a different place today. I'll always believe in fighting for the freedom of people. But sometimes, after coming back from a mission, I would wonder if some of the people living near those targets were just people like us. They must have believed in what they were doing, too."

"I guess we all have our beliefs and principles." Laura stroked the hair on the side of his head. "It's how we accomplish them that can cause all the trouble." She was reluctant to say too much. This was more than Ben had ever said to her about his time overseas.

"I was one of the lucky ones. We came back from our missions to good food, comfortable beds and safety. Aiden was on the ground. He spent many a night wondering if he dared to close his eyes and sleep. Their food was barely substantial and they never felt that they were out of harm's way. They were never sure if the country people were friends or foes."

"Both of you came home again, and that's the important part."

"Some of the guys today were talking about liberating the concentration camps. They didn't know the camps existed until they came across one. Some prisoners came running to embrace them, while others didn't have the strength to stand. Many were mere skin and bones, but at least they didn't die in captivity."

"I know the memories, good and bad, will always be a part of all of you. I'm glad you met some of Aiden's buddies. I know they've made a difference in his life."

"It was great meeting them. I'll see them again when I'm in the city." A sense of calm seemed to settle inside Ben. The visit to the Legion gave him a much needed emotional release.

"If only my friend, George, could have been able to sit with us today.

Then it would have been perfect".

Laura wished she could wipe the hurt away. She was glad Ben had met the squad leader who had spoken of losing some of his men. He had turned his anger and sadness into something positive by speaking to school children. And she was proud that Ben had vowed to emulate him.

Laura stirred and yawned. "I'd like to stay here and talk all night, but I'm afraid my shift would feel very long tomorrow. I guess I should say today. It's long past the bewitching hour."

"We could just stay here and rest."

"There's that Viking again!"

"How many hours was I to 'hold that thought'?"

"Time's up. You missed your chance." Laura giggled as Ben stopped her flight. "Maybe it's not that late!"

Later, when they decided it was very late, they said good-night.

"I understand it better now, Ben. The war, I mean, and the way you hold those thoughts to yourself. In a way, it's like the polio epidemic. There are times when we nurses want to just crumble and cry. And the fear on some of those children's faces is so hard to deal with. But, we smile and keep doing the best we can because those kids are counting on us." Her eyes had misted over. "Sometimes the nurses talk about it, but mostly we just exchange looks, because we all know what the other is worried about." Ben's thumb rubbed the top of her hand as she continued, "I just want you to know, I understand. I'll always be here for you, to listen when you want to share, but, I'll understand if you don't."

"Thank you." Ben eyes appeared darker when he was serious. "And likewise, I'll always be here for you too. Until now I hadn't realized how often you need an understanding ear. You have many patients who aren't as lucky as Signcy, don't you?"

Her nod and grim smile was answer enough. Ben held her for a few moments, then lifted her chin so their eyes met. "I have no idea what you think you're doing, Nurse O'Neil, staying up until this hour!" His softly spoken reprimand eased the sadness from her features and they both smiled.

"You're the best, *kaerasta min*." He kissed her once more before leaving her for the night.

After dropping Laura off at the hospital the following morning, Ben knocked on the door of the restaurant. He knew that Sean would be there, preparing for another day of work.

"G'mornin' Ben! Come on in. There's fresh coffee on."

"You know how to treat an Icelander!"

Laughing, they sat down for a quick cup before tackling the morning chores. Ben once again had to reassure Sean that he truly wanted to help but after mopping the floor and washing some dishes, he begged for mercy.

"You better not be offering me any watered-down stout after this. I'm gonna need some real sustenance."

"You'll have to do some bar duty if you think you need a nip of the good stuff."

"That sounds better than more kitchen duty." Ben laughed. It occurred to him that something didn't sound right. "What happened to your Irish accent?"

Sean winked at Ben with a mischievous gleam in his eyes. "Didn't you ever wonder why I'm the only one in the family that has an accent?"

"I assumed you'd been in Ireland."

Sean grinned. "No, my patrons expect it."

"You had me fooled. Laura never said anything about it either."

"M'Laura wouldn't be tellin' m'secrets."

Ben shook his head. He was having a great time. He'd never worked in this type of establishment before. "Don't you be letting on to Laura that I do dishes."

"Aye, we best keep you manly. It's bad enough that ya have no Irish blood in ya."

"Not you too, Sean. Laura's father has a problem with me not being Irish. And Catholic. There lies another problem."

"No, Ben, I don't mind you being who you are. Ya make Laura happy, and that's what's important."

By the time Ben met Laura after her shift at the hospital, he had served several drinks and learned how to make some fancy ones. And, he had an ally in Sean.

"If you ever need a job, m'friend, check with me." Sean grinned. "I guess first impressions aren't always right. I was sure ya were a pirate."

"I know this is going to sound crazy, but, I've been homesick for Hecla." Ellen had been relieved when Ben and Laura had driven up to her parents' home on the morning of December 29. The three of them sat side by side in the roomy front seat of the car and left the streets of Winnipeg behind.

"Were you missing Matthew so much?" Laura asked.

Ellen smiled, "Yes, I guess I did. That, and the fact my parents were still harping about my 'lost opportunity'." She realized as she spoke that Ben and Laura wouldn't know about her broken engagement. "It seems my old boyfriend has found a new girl."

A look of concern crossed Laura's face. Ellen hastened to explain. Before she knew it, she was telling them the whole story. "The funny part is, I went to Hecla to get away and lick my wounds. Truth is, I found what I was looking for there. Richard didn't want a working wife. I'd have hated to miss these past months in the classroom – and Matthew!" Her face lit up in excitement. "Can't this jalopy go any faster, Ben?"

It was nearing noon by the time the trio reached the Narrows. A northeast wind was drifting snow into the snowplow trail across the ice. The snowplow had left ridges on either side of the trail that caught the blowing snow. Some of the island men had hewn spruce trees and left them as markers across the ice, indicating the safest path to follow. In the case of a white-out, when visibility was limited, the evergreen trees were easier to see than the white snow ridges.

"Here we go!" Laura and Ellen had a firm grip on each other and Ellen's right hand clutched the door handle in the event of a quick escape. Ben shook his head and let out a big sigh.

"Do you really think I would risk driving across the ice if I wasn't sure it was safe?" His remark was meant to relax the two passengers but neither one had lessened their holds. "We've tested the depth of the ice right across and it's anywhere from fourteen to twenty-four inches deep."

"But how heavy is this car? What if..."

"Laura, don't you trust me?" The teasing glint in his eye left little room for argument. Laura agreed he wouldn't risk the crossing if he wasn't sure of their safety. It still didn't mean that they shouldn't be prepared, just in case. They maintained the position and were ready to spring out if need be. Ben gave up trying to reassure them.

The plowed road arced around the island in the channel. In some areas the snow had already drifted in badly and previous drivers had left ruts in their wakes. Ben carefully maneuvered along, sometimes almost coming to a standstill. The spinning tires always seemed to catch enough grip to keep moving. The trunk of the car was equipped with survival gear. A strong shovel headed the list of supplies.

After they had rounded the channel island, the remaining stretch of ice road appeared to be clearer, and Laura and Ellen were beginning to let their guard down when the car hit a large bump and dropped with a splatter. Ben immediately stepped harder on the gas pedal and the car spun, fishtailing forward. He didn't say anything until he had reached the shoreline and drove up onto the road by the ferry landing. On solid ground, he dared to glance at the two women and smiled at the huge eyes staring back at him.

"That was a hole." Ellen's voice was low.

"No, it was just a slush pit."

"Just a slush pit!" Laura sputtered, "What's a slush pit?"

"If there's a crack in the ice, the water pressure pushes some water up through the crack and then the water mixes in with the snow and turns into slush."

Laura and Ellen both laughed nervously, happy they were back on land.

"I'm glad you girls are taking it so well."

"Taking it well. Ben, in the hospital we call this silent hysteria. If we were armed, you'd be a dead man!" Laura's outburst seemed to settle her nerves and she glanced at Ellen to check on her state of mind.

"I think I'm breathing again," Ellen said. "You're a nurse, Laura, am I breathing?"

Both women heaved a sigh of relief and smiled. Laura said, "We survived our first slush pit. At least, I think we did." They were still rookies when it came to travelling on ice roads. It must take many crossings before a person began to consider the ice road as just that – a road. It was easy to visualize the water beneath and the danger it held.

Ben smiled and continued to shake his head as he put the motor back in gear. He complimented the two city girls who had passed the test as far as he was concerned. Even the long-time islanders were wary of the slush pits, that caught you by surprise. But it was as he had described, slush on top of thick ice. And if you were able to drive through it without stopping, that was considered a bonus. If the vehicle got stuck, it meant some heavy shovelling to get out.

Bjossi was sitting in the sunroom when Ben drove by. A wave of his hand in greeting indicated that Ben had spotted the old man in the window. Lifting his arm to respond in kind, Bjossi grimaced in pain. Arthritis had started in his knees and hips but it had found new territory to bring discomfort to him. His shoulders ached every day now. He still had a few traps set in the bush just beyond the farm yard. Each day he made the short trek to check on those traps. Some days he laboured over the wood chopping block in agony. Due to his age and habits, Bjossi wasn't planning on purchasing a new heater. He failed to feel the excitement of the younger people. He was happy to carry his old hardship stories with him into the future. He had opted for electric lights, but drew the line there. Ben and Daniel were suggesting other conveniences to him, but for the time being he would make do.

Adam and Andrew needed more traps. When Bjossi had spent Christmas with the Bergurssons, Adam had been asking him if he would sell some traps to them. Daniel had piped up, "Do you boys think you can afford to buy more traps?" Adam was convinced their fur pelts would fetch high prices. The young entrepreneurs were at a confident age, so a good argument would be required to thwart their dreams.

"Maybe you boys can work for the traps, if Bjossi has some chores for you to do," Daniel had wondered aloud. Now, sitting in the sunroom, Bjossi guessed that Daniel had noticed his awkward movement in trying to hide his aches. The arrangement they made suited both parties. Every two days the boys were to split enough wood for the next two days, then carry it inside and make neat piles of wood beside the wood heater and the woodstove. For payment, each week they would earn a trap. The coffee and stories that went with each trap would be free.

So far, the boys had come once and Bjossi was pleased with the work they provided. He especially enjoyed the trappers conversation that had accompanied the afternoon coffee. Glancing at the clock, he rubbed Chopper's head, "Those boys should be coming soon, Chopper. Maybe we better put some water in the kettle for coffee."

Bjossi's house met the needs of a bachelor, offering no frills or any extravagances. The crude but sturdy kitchen table served as a workbench for sharpening saws and fixing greasy motors. Wild meat was cut and wrapped on the table and fish was filleted there. Three coffee cups, chipped and stained, were set on the table in readiness. A tin of cookies that Thora had given him lay open in the middle of the table.

Chopper perked up his ears when he heard the axe splinter a log. His tail had been wagging at the first sounds of the boys' voices. Bjossi pulled the door open to let the dog take part in the backyard activity. Because both boys were experienced at splitting the logs, it wasn't long before Bjossi was holding the door open for them to bring in arm-loads of wood. As to the verbal contract, the boys neatly stacked the wood for easy access and swept up all the wood chips that had fallen on the floor.

Coffee conversation centred around the fur bearing animals and trapping. Andrew had brought over a coyote pelt that had scars along its belly. The welts were old and Andrew wasn't sure what might have caused them. He'd been careful when scraping the fat off the hide to avoid tearing it.

"Looks like a lynx." Bjossi recognized the marks left by a big cat. "Another animal must have helped this guy. With claw marks like that I'm surprised he got away."

Bjossi complimented Andrew on his work preparing the pelt. Then he entertained the young trappers with stories of tracking and trapping the large lynx on the island. They choked down the strong coffee and ate several cookies, all the while absorbing the knowledge the old man imparted.

Thora was glad to see Ellen returning. After Ellen had confided in her, she had worried about the young woman. It had upset Thora to think that Ellen's mother had been so cold toward her daughter. She couldn't imagine believing that financial security was the main basis in finding the right husband. Thora smirked. Money wouldn't hurt, but only if that 'lovin' feeling' came first, was the way she looked at it.

Maybe she should give the woman a benefit of the doubt. In all likelihood she was a mother like herself, and simply wanted her child to be happy. Another thing, Thora mused, maybe I'd feel differently if my girls hadn't married their childhood sweethearts.

"Welcome home, Ellen." Thora held the door open for her. "It's been far too quiet around here without you."

"It's good to be home." Ellen's cheeks were flushed and her eyes sparkled. "Winnipeg is way too noisy for me now. People are always in a rush and don't seem to have time for each other. I guess that's the way it's always been. I just never noticed it before." She shrugged out of her woollen coat and hung it in the closet near the back door. "How have your holidays been, Thora?"

"Very nice. We had a big meal at Elin and Jon's house on Christmas Day. I've been rubbing my stomach ever since. Why do we eat so much?" She stroked her hand over her stomach and groaned for emphasis. "Since then the days have been quiet. I started working on some woollen socks again. It's nice to put the knitting machine away over Christmas, but I don't want to fall behind on my orders."

Thora supplemented the household income by selling mitts and socks knit in gray fisherman's yarn. On a small table in the corner of the kitchen, the circular knitting machine was bolted to the side. Turning the handle in a steady circular motion caused the needles to go up and down in sequence. As the rounds were knitted, a woollen tube emerged from the bottom of the machine. Thora would knit an entire skein in this fashion.

Then with a tube that was several feet long, she would snip it into the right length for a sock. Picking up the ravelled stitches, she would hand-knit the toe, heel and cuff.

The mitts were done in a similar fashion. The top, thumb and cuff were hand knit after unravelling a tube at the measured lengths. A tube could be machine-knit in a smaller size by eliminating some of the needles.

"You didn't take a very long holiday." Ellen said to her landlady. "You work much too hard."

"Never mind, young lady," Thora said. She motioned Ellen towards the table. "Let's have a late lunch. Kristjan ate a while ago, but I thought I would wait for you in case you came home hungry."

Ellen told Thora about her holiday in Winnipeg. She mentioned seeing her friends and spending Christmas Day with her family. They chatted about city traffic and some of the clothing styles seen in shop windows.

"I was telling Laura and Ben that I've been homesick for Hecla Island, and I truly meant it. I don't know when it happened, but I really feel at home here. To think I'd always lived in the city and thought that was what life was all about."

"You make an old woman feel good. I'm glad you like us and our island. And don't short change yourself. You're a very good teacher and you've become a special member of our community. And that's not just from Matthew's standpoint!"

Ellen marvelled at the comfortable ease with which Thora did everything. In her quiet, yet unassuming way she made each person in her life feel special. There was nothing calculated in her approach, just warmth and understanding.

Her mother, on the other hand, seemed to have a set purpose in everything she did. Ellen had argued to go into teacher training. Her mother thought a course in secretarial work would be far more advantageous in meeting the right husband. After all, the only men to be met at a school would be fathers of the children and male teachers, who really didn't make a lot of money.

Sitting at Thora's table with a relaxed ease she hadn't felt in the last few days, Ellen found herself mentally comparing this kitchen to her mother's kitchen in the city. So many luxuries were taken for granted. Her mother had a modern work space filled with the latest utensils for making household chores as easy as possible. She didn't know if her mother appreciated what she had, or if it was simply considered her right to have the best. One thing was lacking though, and that was the warmth and sense of sincere welcome that abounded in Thora's kitchen. Her mother would never understand that and therefore never offer it in her own.

She never mentioned Matthew over the holidays and Ellen was ashamed of herself for the omission. Matthew was the kindest man she had ever dated and she hoped for a future with him. She had to smile, imagining her mother's response to this insight. Her mother had merely tolerated the notion of her teaching in the backwoods, since she would come home at the end of June. No, it had probably been wise not to mention Matthew. There was plenty of time to put that storm on hold. It just didn't seem fair to Matthew.

Chapter 12

"You'll warn me if you see a slush pit, won't you?" Laura's eyes were as round as saucers when the bombardier left the shoreline and proceeded across the snowdrifts on the lake. Heavy skis on the front of the vehicle were steered from inside by a steering wheel and propelled by caterpillar-like tracks. Inside, only the driver held the luxury of a cushioned seat. Wooden benches along the sides of the interior offered seating for the remainder of the fishing crew. On the horizon she spotted small white mountains.

"Is that a mirage or is there a mountain range in the middle of Lake Winnipeg?"

"That's just some pushed up ice." Daniel acted as tour guide. "When the ice cracks, it moves apart and then in a shift of wind and water current the ice crashes together again with tremendous force. It piles up and in the distance looks like mountains."

Ben, Daniel and Jon worked together during the winter fishing season, the same as in the summer and fall seasons. Two years earlier, they had purchased the bombardier. Prior to that, they had harnessed two horses to pull a caboose and sleigh. The caboose housed a wood heater and provided shelter from the wind. Fish boxes were loaded on the sleigh, along with ice picks and shovels. The bombardier replaced the horses. The caboose and sleigh were now pulled behind the bombardier. Some fishermen still used dog teams for this job.

"That's ice?" Laura tried to suppress a shiver. "Are there many cracks on the lake?"

"We usually don't have to cross large cracks." Jon commented in wry humour.

"Don't worry, Laura. He's just bugging you." Ben was afraid of that silent hysteria surfacing again.

"You drive across cracks, where you can see the water?"

"Relax. We don't believe in putting our lives at risk." Ben gave her a nudge as the tracks rotated in the snow. "Sometimes we have to drive along the crack to find a good place to cross over."

Daniel was driving and as they neared the first net, he angled the bombardier so it would shelter them from the wind while they picked the fish.

"I don't think we'll have to cross any cracks today." Jon scanned the lake's surface and their nets seemed to be on that side of any visible ice ridges. He laughed as Laura let out a heavy sigh of relief.

Each man had designated duties. As soon as the bombardier came to a standstill, they set to work. Jon took one ice pick and shovel and set off toward the other net marker. Ben took the other ice pick and began chopping a hole near the stake which marked the end of the net. The ice was over two feet in depth. In a matter of a few minutes the hole was filled with slush. Ben grabbed a shovel and dispensed with the slush. Daniel had a fire going in the wood heater. He'd lined up some fish boxes in anticipation of a good catch.

"Jon has the line attached. We can start." Ben adeptly swept the long handled hook into the hole and under the ice to grasp the line holding the net in the water. He then pulled the line hand over hand until the net came into view. At the other end, Jon had also chopped through the ice, shovelled the slush and had tied a long rope to the other end of the net. Then the net would be gradually pulled out one hole and the fish would be taken from the mesh and thrown into a fish box. As the net came out, the long rope attached at the other end eased into the other hole. When the net was emptied, the rope would be pulled back out, hence pulling the net into the water again. The lines were put in place again and the fishing crew moved on to the next net where the procedure repeated itself.

Laura forgot the cold wind and her apprehension as she watched the men work. With fluid movement they went about their tasks. By the time Ben and Daniel had pulled the first net under again, Jon had opened the next hole which had a net linked to the hole they were at. The nets ran in a straight line. After the initial two holes were chopped they only had to chop one hole to retrieve a net.

"How do you set those nets in the first place?"

"Chop a couple of holes in the ice, grab a net, take a deep breath and swim as fast as you can to the other hole." Jon was having fun with the rookie.

"Watch it, Jon. She's not gonna believe a word we say if you keep this up." Ben was anxious to explain the fishing industry to Laura. It was important to him that she understand how he made his living.

"We use a jigger to set the nets under the ice. It's sort of like a teeter-totter. It crawls on the underside of the ice. We tie a rope to it, push it through the hole and then gently tug on the rope to get it started. It clicks and clacks as it crawls along so you can hear it. After it has travelled as far as we want it to, we chop another hole and pull it out." Ben glanced over at Laura to make sure she was following his description. At her nod he continued.

"Sometimes it's hard to hear it, so one of us tries to follow and listen carefully. Otherwise we'd chop the hole in the wrong place. Matthew has a dog, Misty, that goes on the lake with him. Old Misty is his jigger follower, she barks and dances on top of the ice as the jigger is moving along."

"That must be neat to see." Laura laughed. She rubbed her hands together, trying to keep the blood circulation flowing. Her toes were feeling chilled too, even though she was dressed in warm clothing and lined boots. Rose had lent Laura her boots which were large enough to fit heavy woollen socks into.

"How big is a jigger?"

"They can vary a bit, but our jigger is eight feet long and about eight inches wide."

"So you can use it for skiing after the nets are set." Laura joked as she pictured the long piece of equipment.

"Not likely." Ben quickly corrected. "It's far too valuable to play with, but the thought has crossed my mind."

By the time they reached the fourth net, Laura was familiar with the steps involved in ice fishing. They had made several trips into the caboose to dip the woollen picking mitts into boiling water in a pail on the wood heater. The mitts were frozen so stiff that it was difficult to move the hands inside. The water on the fish and net mesh quickly dampened the picking mitts, so this dipping ritual occurred often. Leaving the warmth of the caboose, Laura was amazed at the steam emitting from the warm mitts.

She had decided it was time to try her hand at picking fish. Ben outfitted her with a pair of woollen mitts that he warned would be too large for her hands. "It's much harder to get a good grip on a fish if your mitts are too big."

"That's fine. I'll use that for an excuse when you guys start bugging me." Her eager eyes sparkled at Ben. "I know you make this job look easy, but I have to try at least one fish."

Laura realized quickly that her words, 'you make this job look easy', were right on the mark. The first fish she grabbed slid out of her hands. Then Ben coached her step by step. Gripping the fish in one hand while the other hand squeezed it through the mesh was awkward. The fins were sharp and ripped the mesh if care wasn't taken. Minimal damage to the net was important. Laura discovered that the net wasn't the only thing the fins could harm when she felt the stinging poke in one finger. "Ouch, it got me!"

"You okay, honey?" Ben's concern wasn't missed by Jon and Daniel. A look in their direction confirmed that Ben would definitely be hearing more about the 'honey' remark.

"It's alright. You weren't kidding about those fins. That hurt."

The next fish was handled firmly, but with care. Laura knew she was very slow, but she was determined to get the job done. When she threw the first fish on the ice, that she had completely picked by herself, the rest of the crew let out a cheer. This spurred her on to pick some more.

Laura wanted to ignore her frigid hands, but Ben was keeping a watchful eye and made sure she didn't get too cold. "Your hands aren't as calloused and thick like the rest of us. It's taken us years to grow our thick skins. Go and warm up in the caboose when you need to."

"Besides, Rose and Mama will skin our hides if you go home frozen."Daniel wasn't about to compromise the mood in his household.

"And it's tough to dance on frozen feet." Jon added his two-cents worth.

Thinking about the New Year's dance the following night, Laura nodded in agreement to the string of advice. She made her way inside the little caboose and absorbed the warmth it offered. As the chill began wearing off, she started to shiver. She hadn't realized how cold she'd become. When the men joined her a few moments later, she camouflaged the chills and handed each of them a sandwich from their lunch boxes.

"You've got the chills, haven't you?" She might have known that Ben wouldn't miss anything.

"Just a little. I'll be fine." Her teeth were all but chattering.

Jon laughed. "Are you sure you aren't at least part Icelandic? The Irish couldn't be as stubborn as us, could they?"

Ben smirked and raised his eyebrows in an expression that clearly stated 'Yeah, they are!'. The look earned him a punch in the arm and a look of reproach.

"Try calling her 'honey' now, Ben!" Daniel laughed out loud, slapping his knee. The couple shared a smile and Ben pulled Laura closer to the heater.

"You're probably chilled right through. You don't realize how the cold can work it's way down to the bones. Those chills will stay with you for awhile, but you'll warm up again."

Unaccustomed to being outdoors in frigid winter temperatures, Laura hadn't built up the same resistance that these fishermen had. She was sure it couldn't get much colder than out on the ice of Lake Winnipeg. Still, she was determined to be a part of the fishing crew for the day. When they had eaten the sandwiches and finished their coffee, the rookie left the shelter of the caboose with the men and took her place beside them.

That day, they lifted ten nets before returning home. Jon, Daniel and Ben had over fifty nets in the water over the winter season. Some days they lifted more than ten nets, depending on the weather and the amount of fish they picked. Each net was checked once a week. The temperature of the water was much colder than during the open water seasons, so the fish didn't spoil as quickly. The season lasted until the lake quota was reached. Quotas weren't allocated to individual fishermen. Once the lake quota was reached, the fishermen were notified to pull all their nets out of the water.

It was mid-afternoon when the bombardier headed toward home. At one point, they crossed an ice ridge that had been caused by a crack that had rammed its edges together. Laura was amazed at the power wielded by the ice. She was also amazed at the work she had witnessed throughout the day. The next time she sat down to a meal of fish, she would respect the undertaking it took to bring it to her plate.

Back at the village, the three fishermen unloaded the fish boxes at the packing shed to await the tractor trains that travelled up the lake with supplies and returned south with fish. Times were changing though. The islanders were rapidly adjusting to the new mode of travel. It was now feasible to operate a truck to transport the fish to market. Ingvar, at the packing shed, could offer the sale of fresh fish in winter instead of just frozen. He was looking for a truck that could move the fish on a regular basis from the island. Over the ice road in winter and on the ferry in summer, the truck would provide a means for better prices. In the winter, fresh fish cashed in much higher than frozen fish.

Anna was waiting with a warm sampler quilt for Laura. She had known the young nurse would be cold after a day on the lake. A few hours later Laura was sure the shivers had subsided and she felt warm 'to the bones' as Ben had said. Even though she had felt discomfort, she wouldn't trade the day's experience for anything. Ben continued to open up a whole new world to her – a world she was falling in love with.

Rose was tired and worried. She knew the fatigue came from lack of sleep. And the lack of sleep came from worry. For the past few days Signey had been listless and droopy. She seemed to need more rest and Rose had noticed that Signey's left arm was slightly weaker again. The girl still played as usual but her appetite had waned. Her naps were longer these days and her movements were slower.

The doctor had warned that over-exertion should be avoided. Too much excitement and not enough rest could result in a relapse. Polio symptoms didn't just go away, they could reappear at any time. It didn't mean the polio was actually coming back, but the body needed a lot of time to recuperate from the disease. Progress could be halted and maybe a step would be taken backwards instead of forwards.

Rose was hoping that the Christmas holidays were at the root of it. With the other three children around every day, it was difficult for Signey to have the quiet time she needed. Keeping an eye out for the returning bombardier, Rose had decided to talk with Laura about Signey. Earlier that morning Rose had expressed her concerns to Daniel and he had agreed that speaking in private to Laura could be a benefit in learning more about Signey's condition.

When Daniel came home, the family sat around the table for coffee. Signey had just woken up from a nap. After coffee, it was time to do the evening chores. Adam, Alexander and Daniel dressed in their winter-chore gear and headed out to the barn. Rose left the coffee clean-up for Karen and asked her to read to Signey.

"I'm going to Amma's for a while. I won't be long." Bundled in her warm woollen coat, Rose walked over to the other house. There she found Laura still clutching the quilt. "Are you still cold?" She asked, remembering how cold winter fishing could be.

"I've never been so cold. And I spent half the time by the heater!" Laura glowed as she laughed at herself. "But I really enjoyed learning about ice fishing. I had no idea how much work was involved."

Ben was outside helping with the barn chores and Anna was bustling in her kitchen. Anna shooed the younger women into the living room so she could continue quietly with her supper preparation.

"Laura, I wanted to ask you about Signey." Worry was etched into Rose's features. "She seems to be losing ground. Could it be the excitement of the holidays?"

"Yes, it certainly could be that. If she gets over-tired her whole body feels it. Strange as it seems, we've noticed at the hospital that it isn't only the paralyzed muscles that suffer. I'm not sure why, but we think that the polio has affected the whole body. Yet it attacks some muscles more aggressively. We take more notice of the visibly affected muscles, but I believe the other muscles are weaker also."

"That sounds right to me. I know how active Signey used to be. And I can tell you that her right side, which wasn't paralyzed, doesn't seem to have the same strength as before. Everything is in slower motion than usual, even her right hand."

"One thing you have to remember, Rose, is that it takes a long time to regain that strength. I know it must be hard to be patient, but I'm convinced that Signey will be strong again. Except for her left shoulder, I don't expect much improvement there. It's been too long and the muscle has shrunk right down."

"We've accepted that." Rose spoke softly, "I just got scared seeing the weakness coming back."

Laura slid across the couch and wrapped her arm around Rose's shoulders, giving her a hug. "Try not to worry. I'm sure it's the holidays and the extra activity in the house with all the family at home. Signey will rest and on Monday when school starts again, the house will quiet down. You'll likely see results quickly."

"I know I shouldn't be bothering you with this. You see so many children that have more problems than Signey."

"Rose, you can talk to me any time. You're right, Signey is lucky that it wasn't worse, but that doesn't lessen a mother's concern. She still has more recovery to make and then to adjust to her handicap. There's still a long road ahead, but she's doing very well."

"Thanks, Laura. You always make me feel better. I just got scared when she was so tired and lacked energy."

"Just keep an eye on it. If she doesn't get better after the holidays, then take note of that and discuss it with the doctor at her next appointment. And I mean it when I say you can talk to me any time. I don't have all the answers, but if I can help I want to."

Rose smiled her thanks and nodded. Just addressing her fear to Laura gave her a boost. Laura could be brisk in a matter-of-fact kind of way, but Rose trusted her advice and was grateful for her friendship.

On a lighter tone, they described the dresses they would be wearing for the New Year's Dance the following evening. The whole island would be in attendance, adorned in their finest.

When Rose went home to start her family's supper, Laura shrugged out of the quilt and lent a hand to Anna in the kitchen.

The following two days flew by for Laura. It seemed one minute they were twirling around the dance floor and bringing in the New Year, and the next it was time to drive to Riverton to catch the train into Winnipeg.

The dance had been similar to the Hallowe'en Dance as far as the music and high level of stamina were concerned. But this time, instead of creative costumes, the women wore fancy dresses and the men's shirts were extra starched to maintain a gentleman's stance. The children showed off new clothes as well. Christmas was a time for receiving gifts of clothes, even though toys were more popular.

It had been fun to see everyone again. Laura was feeling protective toward Gudrun, whose pregnancy was becoming more prominent. She'd been gasping for breath after some polkas, but when Laura suggested that she might sit one out, the rebuke was quick and to the point. "I might be clumsy, but as long as I can keep up with the music, I will!"

Laura had laughed and kept on dancing herself. There would be a Valentine's Dance on the island in February that Gudrun would likely have to miss since her baby was due in early March. She was making up for it now.

After a very late night, the New Year revellers were sleepy and groaning about sore feet when the Bergursson family sat down to a special meal toasting the beginning of 1954. The adults reflected on the good fortune and the hard times that had occurred in the previous year. Electricity claimed highest marks for newsworthiness. Polio ranked as the toughest ordeal. They were thankful to be together and able to enjoy the feast before them.

"I'm praying for a smooth crossing." Laura broke away from her day-dreaming just before Ben drove off the shoreline onto the ice road. The snowplow hadn't pushed the snowdrifts aside since before Christmas, and winds since then had produced some new drifts. Bright sunshine glistened off the ridges on the lake. The dark power lines and poles stood out in starkness with a backdrop of white snow and pale blue sky.

"I know what Ellen meant when she said she'd been homesick for Hecla. I'm sad to be leaving." Laura smiled at the glimmer of teasing in Ben's eyes. "It's not just you, you know! This island has a way of wrapping itself around your heart. I love it."

Ben's eyes smoldered to the dark intensity that Laura was familiar with, as he drew the car to a stop and turned to face her. "Remember what I said to you the first time you came here?" He didn't wait for, or expect, a response from her. In a velvety voice he answered his own question. "I told you that when you say 'I do' to me, it's not just me but my island that you'll be saying it to. I come in a package. Telling me that you're sad to be leaving is better than the sweetest candy, *kaerasta min*."

"Ben, don't you think we should keep on moving. What if the ice cracks?"

"It's not gonna crack." His lips found hers as he encircled her in his arms.

"I think someone's coming."

"It's not gonna crack."

"You're not listening to me."

"It's not gonna crack." He couldn't stop the muffle of laughter. "I can see for miles, there's nobody coming."

"It's gonna crack!" Laura giggled and leaned into his chest, knowing that

she was safe and – what was the hurry anyway!

"I miss you already." Her hand caressed his cheek.

"I miss you more." His lips covered hers again.

Approaching from the mainland, a car came into view on the ice road. Ben followed its progress, his expression becoming grim when he recognized the red sedan. He stepped on the clutch and put the Chevy into gear, preparing to angle off the main roadway to meet the oncoming vehicle. As the car swerved to pass by them, its tires caught in a snowdrift and was pulled into deeper snow. Peering through his rearview mirror, Ben saw the car come to a standstill and the four occupants stumble out. Shifting the car into reverse, Ben backed up.

"Stay in the car, Laura." He pulled on his cap and mitts and got out of the car.

Ben knew instantly that the four men were still on a drinking binge since the dance at New Year's. When Ben and Laura left the dance, these men had been jeering and laughing at them as they passed by. Their taunts had reached Ben's ears but he'd quickly steered Laura to his car to avoid any confrontation. He wasn't sure he'd escape this time. He would have preferred to keep on driving and leave them to find their own way out of the snowdrift, but that went against the code of an islander. You never left anyone stranded.

"Should I get my shovel? Looks like you need more than a push out of there." Ben turned towards the trunk of his car.

"We don't need any help from a big-shot." Jacob slurred in Icelandic, looking at Ben with contempt. Two of his buddies were mainlanders. They twittered behind Jacob.

Helgi, another islander and the vehicle's driver, wanted Ben's assistance. "We could use another shovel, Ben."

Jacob moved closer to Ben and said in Icelandic, "Get out of here. And take that outsider with you." He glared at Laura. "She's not welcome here."

Laura, standing midway between the car and Ben, hadn't understood the words.

"Ben?" Uncertainty clouded Laura's face.

"Get in the car, Laura." Ben looked over his shoulder at her. Jacob took the opportunity to take a swing at Ben, striking him below his right eye. Laura gasped and came forward.

"Get in the car." Ben's words shouted at her as a blind rage overtook him. He slammed his fist into Jacob's mouth, ceasing any further tirade from him. The two mainlanders jumped in to help Jacob. Fists were flying in all directions, but Ben's punches successfully connected with more than those of his intoxicated opponents. Helgi pulled Ben away when it was apparent the other three were done with the scuffle. Standing by the car, Laura's face was as white as the snow. She quietly sat back in the car and waited for Ben.

Ben wrenched the car door open, slid onto the seat and turned the key in the ignition. He didn't say a word, just put the car in gear and revved the motor, spraying snow and ice in his wake. His knuckles were white as he grasped the wheel. In the rearview mirror he studied the damage done to his face and hastily wiped some blood off his cheek. Some swelling stretched the skin below his eye. His temper subsided slightly when he looked at Laura. Her face was still pale but her hazel-green eyes were sympathetic.

"I saw those men at the dance."

"They were there."

"What was that man saying?"

"Nothing you need to know."

Ben wasn't feeling so proud anymore. He would've ignored Jacob, if the stupid drunk hadn't hit him. It wasn't easy to walk away from that and still feel like a man.

"I know he was saying something about me. He was glaring and pointing at me."

"Let's forget about it." Ben steered the car toward Riverton and hoped for a change of topic.

"Forget about it! How can you say such a thing. You were fighting like some wild hooligan, and I need to know why."

"No, Laura, you don't. Just leave it alone."

"No, I won't."

Ben let out a heavy sigh and glanced at her. He'd lost his temper and used his fists on three men who'd been drinking for three days.

"What did he say, Ben?" Laura's voice pleaded in a softer tone.

Ben slowed the car and pulled to a stop at the side of the road. He turned in the seat and reached for her. Her head nestled under his chin and his arms went around her.

"I should've walked away, but when he hit me, I couldn't stop myself. I'm not in the habit of fighting." He hesitated for a moment, kissing her forehead. "He called you an outsider. That's what he said."

"I've got news for you. I am an outsider."

Ben held her for a few seconds, then he slid his hands back to the steering wheel. Laura sat next to him and they drove the remaining miles into Riverton with little conversation.

He saw the sadness and doubt in Laura's eyes when he kissed her before she boarded the train. The conductor took her suitcase from Ben and assisted Laura up the train car steps. Ben waved as the train started to move away. He wished he could snatch her off the train and take her back home.

Sean stood on the platform when Laura arrived at the Winnipeg train station. She couldn't even pretend to be brave and burst into tears in his arms.

"What is it, Laura? What's happened?"

Between tears and blowing her nose she told Sean the story of Ben fighting the men on the ice road and how angry he'd been.

"Ben must've had a good reason. He doesn't strike me as a brawler. And I know brawlers." Sean tried to lighten the mood but it didn't work.

"It's because I'm an outsider. I didn't grow up on the island."

"I think our Ben took care of it."

The story was retold at home to Colin and Katherine. Katherine, like her daughter, was upset at the violence.

"Was anyone seriously hurt? Is Ben alright?"

"They were bleeding, but they seemed okay. I'm sure that Ben had a shiner by the time he got home."

"I figured he was a man of principle." Colin sat up in his chair and nodded. "I respect a man who takes care of his own."

"Dad, they were pounding each other with their fists."

"But he took down three of them."

"They were half-drunk."

"He wasn't backing down and he was taking care of my girl. I say, good for him."

Laura knew there was no point in trying to rationalize how men went about proving their brawn and chivalry. She just knew that something had happened today to cause a feeling of unrest within her. She'd never experienced Ben's rage before and it had frightened her. She wasn't convinced that Ben had been completely truthful about the Icelandic words that were spoken about her. Everyone seemed to welcome her to the island, but obviously there were some who wanted her gone.

Chapter 13

Mid-January brought frigid temperatures, cold north winds and the annual visit from the school dentists. Dental hygiene was considered important in most homes. Teeth were brushed, if not regularly, quite often. Sweets blamed for tooth decay, were scarce to the island youngsters. Still, the news that the dentists were setting up in the community hall caused a nervous stir among Ellen's students.

Adam and Andrew considered sneaking out to the bush to check their traps rather than take a turn in the dentist chair. However, the plan was doomed when they were told their help would be required on the drill pedal.

"I've never done that before." Adam tried to excuse himself from the dreaded task.

"You've seen the others work the pedal, haven't you?" Ellen asked in light of the apprehension that went with the comment, but it seemed that age dictated who would help the dentists, not strong stomachs. "If enough people take a turn it won't be a long shift." Her words brought little relief to the boys.

Because electricity was relatively new to the island, the hall only had electrical lighting, not the plug outlets needed for the dental equipment. The dentist drill was operated by a pedal similar to the pedal on a treadle sewing machine. The pupils took turns pumping their feet on the pedal as instructed by the dentist. The faster they pumped, the faster the drill was able to do the job.

Ellen accompanied the boys to the hall and discussed schedules with the dentists. The equipment the older dentist and two young men in training were using was dated. But, unless the people on the island were prepared to drive into Winnipeg for an appointment with a dentist, this arrangement would have to do.

Adam, Andrew and their friend Philip took their positions. The older dentist showed them how he expected them to pump the pedals.

When the first three children arrived and sat in the chairs, the boys awaited further orders. First, the dentists made quick calculations and the gums were frozen. When uncertain, the apprentice dentists would ask for confirmation from their advisor. The freezing used was sparse. Time wasn't a commodity the dental crew enjoyed. Another school full of children in another community was waiting for their arrival.

"Okay, pump." Half an hour into his shift, the dentist barked at Adam. His legs were tired. The pedals didn't have to be moving all the time, only when the dentist used the drill. He pedalled as fast as he could so Edith, who was in the chair, would be finished sooner.

His shift on the pedal was nearly over when he looked up to see Beth sitting down. His stomach rolled. It was impossible to miss the panic written on her face.

"Open wide, young lady." To Adam, the dentist spoke too loud and just seemed too gruff. He shouldn't use that tone with Beth. The knot in Adam's stomach tightened when the dentist administered the freezing. Moments later he got the nod to commence pumping. All the strength that he could muster poured into the see-saw motion of the pedal. His legs were now beyond tired. But, he wasn't slowing down until Beth was finished. He glanced over and saw a tear drop from the corner of Beth's eye. His hands clenched into fists and he fought the urge to jump up and plant one of his fists into the dentist's face. Pump faster, he instructed himself, get it done.

After Beth, it was Adam's turn in the chair. The old dentist smiled and complimented him on the good job he'd done on the pedal. "I rarely see someone who can work as fast as you. It makes a difference to the patients when the drill rotates quickly." The old man scanned the inside of Adam's mouth and was pleased with his findings. "You have no cavities. Try to brush these teeth every day so I can say the same thing next year." He sent Adam off with a pat on the back, again thanking him for his help.

Walking back to the school, Adam felt guilty. Beth had to have two fillings and he didn't even need to get jabbed by the needle for freezing. Prepared to lay down his life for her, he would gladly have taken the pain of the two fillings for her. At least he had tried his best to minimize her agony.

Lodging was offered to the dentists. It took a good part of two days to see to all the students. When the vehicle was loaded on the second day and leaving the hall yard, cheers erupted from the classrooms. It would be another year before they would have to endure another dental visit.

"To celebrate, I'll give you the last half-hour of the day to complete any homework. If you've already finished, find a library book to read." Ellen's announcement was met with wide smiles. There wouldn't be any schoolbooks to carry home tonight.

Ben milked the cows with mechanical movements. He'd been scowling for days on end. Truth be told, his mood had gradually deteriorated as January slipped by. Conversations with Laura on the telephone left him feeling hollow. Since the ice road squabble, Ben had seen the four men and made amends. They blamed the incident on alcohol and claimed they hadn't meant a word of it. Although Ben doubted that, he accepted their apologies and spoke of his regrets for losing his temper. The subject was closed between the men, but kept alive through gossip on the party lines.

"You should go into Winnipeg and see her, you know." Daniel took the milk pail from his brother and poured its contents into the cream separator.

"I'm not sure she wants to see me."

"It's better to wallow in self-pity? I never thought I'd see the day that you'd let someone like Laura slip through your fingers."

"Maybe I'm being selfish. I'm expecting her to move out here where people treat her like she doesn't belong. How many people will I have to beat-up?" Ben set the milk stool down beside another cow.

"As many as it takes. Isn't she worth it?"

"The question is, does she think I'm worth it?"

"There's only one person who can answer that, Ben. And you better ask her."

The ice road fight was never mentioned in Laura's letters. She wrote of the hospital and her co-workers. More of her polio patients went home to continue convalescing with the hope of gaining muscle strength. Ben read about Sean ordering some new tables for the restaurant and Katherine hanging sheer drapes in the living room.

The letters arrived regularly and although they contained the events in Laura's life, Ben could read the coolness and growing distance between the lines. He was angry that Laura had to witness the bigotry of some islanders. But if it happened again, he knew he'd react the same way. Was it fair to ask her to become part of this community? Did she love him enough?

Daniel dropped the mail off, leaving it on the corner of Anna's kitchen cupboard. Anna was upstairs sweeping the floor and responded in kind to Daniel's shout of 'Hello'. By the time she finished going over the upstairs floors with the broom, Daniel had vanished and she'd heard Ben come in. He'd picked out his letter from Laura and was stretched out on the cushions of the living room couch, where he could read in comfort and privacy.

"There's a letter for you, Mama." Ben had called and then forgot everything else as he tore his envelope open and settled in to read Laura's news.

Anna found her letter on top of the weekly Icelandic-Canadian newspaper, *Logberg*. The unfamiliar handwriting had addressed the envelope to Anna Bergursson, Hecla Island, Manitoba. The return address was Chilliwack, British Columbia, a place that Anna hadn't heard of before.

Anna cautiously opened the letter without understanding why. Something told her this was a special letter. She unfolded the handwritten pages. After reading the first few lines, she sat down at the kitchen table to take a much needed deep breath before she continued reading.

Several minutes later, Ben responded to her sniffle. "Mama, are you alright?" When no answer was forthcoming, he rose and walked into the kitchen. He found his mother with tear stained cheeks still clutching the pages. "What is it, Mama?" He sat in the chair next to her and placed his hand on her arm.

"It's Bjarni. It's a letter about Bjarni." Anna could barely speak as she gave her son the neatly handwritten letter. Ben looked again at his mother and began to read.

> Dear Anna,
>
> I am writing about your brother, my Dad, Bjarni. Just recently, he told me about you. It's hard to know where to begin, as I'm sure you'll be just as shocked to hear from me as I was to hear about having a family in Manitoba.
>
> We have always lived near my mother's family, so I've had lots of cousins and aunts and uncles. As a child I never questioned the fact that they were all on my mother's side and as I grew older, it simply never came up. I just assumed, from what little was said, that Dad didn't have an extended family.

Two years ago my mother passed away. My Dad insisted that he would manage on his own so I finished my training as a teacher. I was teaching in Vancouver when my aunt informed me that Dad was ill. For the last three months I've been at home with him. He has cancer. The doctor told me it's a matter of time. There isn't anything we can do but make him as comfortable as possible.

I was reading to him last night when he said that I sound just like his sister. Confused, I asked him, 'What sister?' And then he began telling me the whole story – how he had left in anger and never been in contact again.

My Dad sent me to the bank this morning, where he has a safety deposit box. I found his family history folded up with his will, his intention being that I would find out about my family one day. There was also a letter for you. He told me how he had regretted losing touch with you.

I don't know if you are able to travel, but if it's possible we would love to see you. We live just east of Vancouver. The train has a stop very near to us. I'll print our mailing address and phone number on the bottom of the page. I hope to hear from you soon.

Your niece, Anna

Ben placed the pages on the table and looked at his mother. She seemed to be frozen to the chair.

"He named her Anna." Her voice was so low and grief-stricken that Ben instinctively put an arm around her shoulders to comfort her.

"After all these years, and now to find out we have more family." Ben couldn't conceal the amazement from his words. "And of course he named her Anna. Weren't you always his favourite?"

A teary smile emerged as she asked, "What will I do?"

Ben rose from the chair and walked to the telephone. "I'm going to call Daniel and tell him to come here and then we're going to work out a plan." Waiting for an answer from the other house, Ben checked the letter for the date it was mailed. "This was written two weeks ago. I think we should phone the number she gave us to see what his condition is. And also to let her know that you received the letter. Daniel? Come over right away. You won't believe what Mama got in the mail." He hung up the phone, leaving his brother dazed.

While Ben and Daniel talked about train schedules and the three days it would take to reach Chilliwack, Anna was in a dream of her own. Bjarni's face was so clear to her, even after thirty years. But the face in her mind was also thirty years old. Her thoughts took her back to their childhood, when she'd often looked after her beloved little brother. Her niece had written that she sounded like her aunt. How often she had read stories to him. Even when she had struggled over long, difficult words, he would sit patiently waiting for the story to continue. They had done farm chores together and forked hay in the summer. So many memories, so long ago.

"Mama, you'll have to talk to Johannes." Ben seemed worried about her reaction, but he didn't need to.

"I know. First, I want to phone out to British Columbia and talk to Anna." The name made her smile again. The simple fact that Bjarni had chosen her name for his daughter gave her strength to face any problems in the days to come. She knew, without her son's advice, what she was going to do. "Then I'll phone Johannes. As soon as I can get on a train, I'll be gone." Her hand came up to stop any argument from her sons. "I can make the trip on my own, but I will need a ride into Winnipeg."

Daniel and Ben hadn't heard that tone in her voice for a long time. They knew they wouldn't argue with her. They nodded their agreement and Anna set her mind on the conversation she would have with her niece.

Every time the telephone rang, young Anna hoped it would be a call from Manitoba. She wondered if her letter had reached her aunt. It was so strange to think of her new family. Thirty years was a long time to be estranged and then suddenly reappear. Maybe her aunt was no longer living, or was unable to make a trip across the prairies and the Rocky Mountains.

Since her father had told her, she had been filled with questions. Questions that he couldn't answer. Did she have cousins? Were they around her age? But the most burning query was, would they want to have anything to do with her?

Her new family might not be in the least bit interested in meeting her. After all this time, her father may have a different perspective of his leaving and never returning. It was possible that her uncle in Manitoba still harboured angry feelings and wasn't prepared to forgive. Listening to her Dad though, brought a warm nostalgic sense of his family life to Anna's heart. There was a restlessness within him that diminished when he spoke of growing up with his brother and sister and when he described farming in the Interlake region of Manitoba. She loved to hear his stories but they left him saddened.

It had been two weeks since she had mailed the letter. Surely someone had received it by now. If it went unclaimed, it could be on its way back to her. Then she would have to find another way of making contact with the family. She was wondering what her next step might be when the phone rang. A pang of anxiety jolted her as she reached for the receiver and answered.

"Hello, is that Anna?" Tears sprang to the young Anna's eyes when she heard the soft maternal voice.

"Yes."

"This is your aunt Anna calling from Manitoba."

"I know. I mean, I hoped you'd call."

"How is Bjarni?"

Young Anna explained his condition, which was deteriorating rapidly. She could hear the concern in her aunt's voice as she inquired more about his day-to-day activity.

"Anna, I want to thank you so much for writing to me. I've been waiting for news of Bjarni ever since he left. There's so much I want to know."

"I have lots of questions for you, too. Dad said you had a son and his brother had two children. I would love to meet them one day." Standing in the kitchen, all by herself, young Anna blushed and hoped she hadn't overstepped. "Will you be able to come?"

"Yes. Daniel and Ben, my two sons, have already been checking train schedules, but I wanted to talk to you before making more plans. I need to know where to get off the train, and do you have room for me to stay?" The older Anna was comfortable enough to take charge.

With assurances of spare rooms, young Anna gushed over the upcoming visit, bringing both women to laughter.

"I'll let you talk to Ben about the train. He'll understand it better than I will. So, I will say good-bye for now and I'll be there as soon as possible."

"I can't wait, Auntie. Good-bye."

Ben retrieved the phone receiver from his mother, who was blubbering over being called 'Auntie'. Because she didn't see Johannes' children very often, it was a title she seldom heard. And to hear Bjarni's daughter use it so warmly had set her off.

"Hi, Cousin." Ben's tone put Anna at ease immediately. Any fears of not being accepted by this family were cast aside.

"I can't believe it. Thank you for being so kind."

"I just said 'Hi'," Ben laughed. "But the thanks are all from this end. You have no idea what your letter did for Mama. I'm sorry about your father, Anna. I wish we could have known you sooner."

Ben and Anna talked for several minutes. Anna felt as if she had known Ben for years. He was kind and forthright. He was also sympathetic about her father's illness and wanted to help her in any way. When she hung up the phone, she immediately went to tell her father the wonderful news.

Bjarni had told her that he wished to make amends for the foolish silence he had bestowed on himself, his wife and his daughter. But after all these years, what could possibly come of it? In many ways, Anna knew he regretted having told her. It would've been soon enough for her to learn of her Manitoba relatives after he was gone.

"Dad, they were so nice to talk to. Anna has two sons, and the younger one, Ben, came on the phone after I spoke to Anna. He was funny and sweet. I love him already."

She fussed over his pillows, fluffing them up, and told him all about the conversation. She knew her father so well that she sensed the misgivings he was experiencing. Wanting to protect him, but also do the right thing, she wondered how the visit would go. Anna had seemed to genuinely want to come, and she had only received the letter today. Noticing a tear slip from the corner of her father's eye, young Anna knew he needed to see the sister he had left behind without a word. She was determined to make things right for him, before his demise.

After speaking with her niece, Anna quickly formulated her next step. Calling Johannes. She thought of all the times she'd missed Bjarni, and how she'd blamed Johannes. She still blamed him, but she'd realized a long time ago that Bjarni had a wild streak in him that had provoked Johannes into attempting to stop the unacceptable behaviour. Anna herself had tried to settle her young brother down, to no avail.

She placed the call and caught her brother indoors, just about to head for the barn and the evening milking. When she explained the reason for her call, he was incredulous. Anna didn't remember the last time she had heard such a lilt to his voice. Then he realized that their brother was dying, so the euphoria was short lived.

"Would you come with me?" Anna asked. At the table Ben looked at her sharply. Then he smiled and nodded when her eyes met his. At the other end of the line, Johannes didn't hesitate.

"Yes, I'll be ready to go with you."

The next morning Ben and Anna left before six o'clock. They were picking up Johannes and hoping to be at the train station in Winnipeg by ten o'clock. The train was due to leave before noon. Arriving early would give them a chance to have a relaxed lunch prior to boarding. The travellers would be on the train for two and a half days and two nights. Coach was comfortable, but Ben had insisted that they book berths to get a good night's sleep. Anna knew Ben was glad that Johannes was accompanying her. It was a long trip with a lot of anxiety awaiting them at the last stop. The train trip would give them time to reconcile their feelings toward each other and to Bjarni.

Earlier, when Anna and Ben were at home eating breakfast, Anna had looked at Ben and said, "What will I say to him? It's been so long."

Ben had reached for his mother's hands and turned her slowly to look at him. "It will be fine, Mama." He let out a deep sigh before continuing, "I remember when I was coming home from overseas. I came into Winnipeg on the train with a bunch of other guys. I remember thinking the same thing. I felt like I'd become another person in the two years I was away. The teenager that had left was long gone, and I wondered if I would ever fit in again. Then I saw you and *Pabbi* and we didn't have to say a word. We hugged and hugged and I knew that somehow, everything would be fine." He gave her a hug and they both smiled. "And that's how it will be with Bjarni. You'll give him a hug and then you'll find the right words."

Now, as they embarked on a trip they'd waited thirty years to go on, Anna hoped his premonition would be accurate. Maybe at long last they could put the past where it belonged and move forward.

"Give my best to Laura when you see her." Anna kissed her son, hoping that he and Laura would get past the rough patch they seemed to be going through. Ben hadn't told his mother that in yesterday's letter, Laura had written how her being an outsider was putting him in a awkward position. Rather than cause disharmony in his life, she suggested they end their relationship. Before he'd had time to react, he'd heard his mother weeping at the kitchen table.

Margaret was in a state! How could Anna have kept such a secret from everyone? This morning the party line was abuzz with the story of a missing brother, who was found but was on his deathbed. There was mention of a child, a young daughter, motherless. Margaret had been forced to ask Rose for information because she'd only heard part of the conversation on the phone.

"Thora, have you heard? Anna has a brother dying in British Columbia."

"Doesn't her brother live near Gimli?"

"Oh yes, but this is the brother that's been missing for thirty years."

Margaret didn't like to tarry when there were so many calls to make. Each call varied slightly from the original, depending on who took the call.

"Hilda, you won't believe what I just heard!"

"Isn't it sad, Malla, that poor Anna has to make such a long trip. And the brother is dying, you know!"

At one point Bjossi asked for the line. He wanted to catch Fred before he made a trip into Riverton. "Could you take a breath for a minute, Margaret. I need to use the phone."

"Did you hear Bjossi, about Anna's brother?"

"If you know, I imagine everyone on the island has heard." The tartness of his comment wasn't missed by Margaret. "Daniel mentioned it this morning. Now, can I have the line?"

Bjossi was able to make his call and Margaret heard his relief when Fred hadn't already left for Riverton. Fred promised to pick up the oil that Bjossi needed. The line cooled off for a few seconds and then Margaret made her next call. This new gossip would keep the telephone lines sizzling for days to come.

Bjossi remembered a day many years before when Anna had talked about her brother. He'd stopped to have coffee with Anna and Ben Senior and he was surprised to see how upset Anna had been. She explained that it was her brother's birthday and she didn't know where he was. The story had come out, about the fateful argument and his subsequent disappearance. Anna had been very distressed and eventually left him alone with Ben Senior. It was a story that Bjossi didn't share with anyone, knowing that Anna valued her privacy. This was definitely a private subject. He hoped that during this trip, she would find the closure she had been yearning for all these years.

"You broke-up with him?" Jessica was shocked.

"It's for the best, Jess. I can't put Ben in a position of having to choose between me and his neighbours." Laura was miserable and exhausted. She'd barely had a wink of sleep since dropping the letter in the mailbox.

"And you think he'll accept that?"

"I think he'll understand." She answered quietly.

"He fought three men on your behalf. He's tall, dark and handsome. He lives an exciting life on an island you love. Aren't you raising your expectations a tad high?" Jessica attempted to joke, but any humour was lost on Laura. The two nurses unwrapped the roast beef sandwiches that were the advertised lunch special in the hospital cafeteria. They were lucky to find a table at midday.

"What are you really afraid of, Laura?"

"What do you mean?"

"You defied your parents, choosing this man who sets your heart aflutter. You've travelled to his island, learned his dances, gone ice-fishing with him, and met some wonderful people. Then someone calls you an outsider and it's all over?"

"You weren't there, Jess. It was awful, and Ben was so angry."

"Of course he was angry. He didn't like what those men were saying."

"I'm just not sure that I'm the best choice for Ben."

"I've known you a long time, Laura, and I've never seen you step back from anything before. When the going gets tough, the tough get going. That used to be your motto. Are you saying that Ben isn't worth it?"

"No." Laura studied her clasped hands. "I'm saying his life would be less complicated with someone else."

"Ben doesn't strike me as someone who's afraid of a few complications."

"He hasn't mentioned anything about the fight with those men."

"And you think he hasn't mentioned it because..." Jessica waited for Laura to complete her sentence.

"Because I'm an outsider."

"Oh, Laura. You don't really believe that?"

The answer was written in the devastation on Laura's face. Jessica slowly shook her head. A movement over Laura's shoulder caught her eye. She looked up to see Ben approaching the table.

"You need to tell Ben how you feel. As luck would have it, he's here." Jessica beckoned over her shoulder.

"What?" Laura swivelled in her chair and met Ben's eyes.

"We need to talk, Laura." Ben's face softened when he saw the pain in her eyes.

"What are you doing here?"

"Did you really think you could send me a 'Dear John' letter and not find me knocking down doors to see you?"

"That's my cue. See you back on the ward, Laura." Jessica smiled and went to join some other nurses.

"Let's get out of here. Do you still have a few minutes before going back to work?"

Laura nodded and they made a hasty retreat.

Inside Ben's car in the hospital parking lot, the couple found some quiet privacy. Ben eased Laura into his arms and kissed her. She relaxed and wondered how she thought she could live without him. The air outside the car was frigid, but she felt warm and loved pressed against him.

"Why Laura? Why did you write that letter?"

"I thought – I thought it was for the best," she stammered and met his eyes.

"No, it's not. Not for my best, that's for sure." He stroked her cheek and tilted her face to maintain eye contact. "If you can't live in Hecla, maybe I could get a job in Winnipeg."

"No, Ben. I would never ask you to do that. Your home is on the island."

"And yours?"

She smiled as tears filled her eyes. "Why haven't you said anything about what happened at New Year's?"

"Is that what this is about?" His eyes reflected a dawn of understanding "Something Jacob said?"

"How many islanders feel the same way as Jacob? I don't want to be the cause of problems between you and your friends."

"I told Daniel that I wasn't being fair to you. There are some judgmental people on the island. How can I ask you to live in a community like that?"

"What did Daniel say?"

"That I was a fool."

"Daniel's right."

"I'm a fool?" A smile crossed his face.

"I know life will be different for me on the island. I'm not afraid of the changes I'll need to make. I'm afraid of how my being there will change your life."

"That change will definitely be for the better." Ben caressed her cheek. "Maybe it would be easier for us if I settled down with an island girl and you found an Irish Catholic to marry. Would we be happy? I think we'll be much happier together facing whatever it is we need to face."

"You make it sound easy." Laura said.

"It is. We need to forget about opposing influences." Ben shifted in the seat.

"What about those men?"

Ben rolled his eyes and raised his eyebrows. "Actually, I've been wanting to hit Jacob for quite a while. No, I'm just kidding. They made me mad and I responded. I saw them a few days later and it's all been resolved."

Laura finished her shift on the ward, then met Ben for an evening at the Tipperary.

As soon as they walked in, Sean glanced over and looked apprehensively at Laura. When she smiled a warm greeting, a grin appeared on his face.

"Good ta see ya, Ben."

Dining on their evening meal, their conversation took them back to that fateful day on the ice road.

"I know some people need to adjust to an Irish lass on Hecla's shores, but they will. And if they don't, I'll beat them up." Ben laughed. Laura grimaced. "Your family isn't crazy about me, but I'm bent on changing that. I know you've stood up to them on my behalf Why can't I do the same for you?"

"Simple, isn't it?"

"Actually, it is simple. As long as we're always sure of each other, the rest will take care of itself."

Ben had regained his confidence the moment he saw the look of misery on Laura's face. The nod of approval from Jessica had confirmed how Laura was feeling. Now, sipping their coffee, Ben took her hand.

"We're okay, aren't we?" His eyes burned with love for her.

"Yes, Ben, we're okay." She wouldn't let doubts hinder this relationship again.

Chapter 14

"Has everyone got a song sheet?" Ellen used her teacher's voice without batting an eyelid. She passed out the words to all the songs in the singing play. This was their second meeting to prepare for the Help-in-Emergency concert. They were meeting at Thora's since she'd be playing the piano for the tunes.

"Not me, Miss Taylor." Sam mocked in a young boy's tone.

Ellen gave him a light slap on the arm with a song sheet and then asked if everyone had been given a copy of their roles in the play. Thora indicated that she was ready to practice the songs if the troupe had their singing voices tuned up.

The group surprised Ellen with their singing and acting abilities. They were so lively and enthusiastic that the roof of the house must have been hopping. The very good singers raised their voices to cover up the not-so-good singers, resulting in a director's dream. Ellen had been named 'Director'. This troupe wasn't in the habit of selecting a leader, but following the performance of the children's Christmas concert and seeing the excitement the city-girl teacher had shown in helping with this play, it was decided unanimously to give the young teacher the esteemed title.

Ellen was enjoying helping with the play. She admired the fund-raising idea to have a purse of money available when someone had a health emergency. Few islanders had the means to put savings aside for such a purpose, but they had money to put in the plate at the concert. When all the dollars were added, it amounted to a sum that could be beneficial for someone in need. It was also a good way to combat pride. It wasn't considered a charity when everyone contributed and anyone could use it when needed.

Because it was a singing play, the acting scenes were short. They fumbled through the lines and planned the entries and exits off the stage. In two weeks they would meet again at the hall for their next practice.

"Let's go over costumes before we finish off tonight. Does everyone know what type of outfit you need?" Ellen's request was met with mutters and questions. "Okay, let's go over each one quickly."

Ten minutes later, the cast of the production knew what was expected for the next rehearsal and the director dismissed them. Ben and Sam left singing one of the phrases from the play. Ellen smiled, thinking that this play would be a lot of fun.

She couldn't help remembering the first few months that she'd been here and how she had longed to be a part of the community. She was feeling that sense of belonging now, especially when they called her by her first name. It had taken time, but she was making headway.

For early February the temperatures were reasonable, which meant you needn't fear frostbite unless you planned to be outdoors for a few minutes without proper winter wear. The skating rink behind the hall was a popular place on the weekends. Adam and Andrew were starting a fire in the wood heater in the skating rink shack. The little shanty had been pulled in to warm hands and toes feeling the cold while skating.

"Are all the guys coming?" Adam asked Andrew.

"Enough for a hockey game. The North Gang think they'll beat us today." Andrew smirked as if that would never happen. Those who lived north of the school formed a team to play against the South Gang, which were those living south of the school. Sometimes they chose captains who would take turns choosing a team, and sometimes they just split into two even groups if only a few players showed up. But, when they could it was fun to get the old rivalry of north versus south going.

"Those buggers can dream all they want. Are Philip and David coming?"

"Yeah. We'll kick their asses, alright!" The boys felt free to use 'barn talk' until some of the girls came. The kindling caught fire with the first match and in a short while the boys could feel the warmth reaching out. As soon as the chill was out of the air, they slipped out of their boots and pulled on their skates.

The door of the shack burst open and several more school children jostled for seating space on the old benches. As soon as skates were laced on, the skaters were out the door and on the rink. The first ones out scrapped off the fresh snow that had fallen since the last skating party. Hockey sticks were well scuffed from repeated use and most of the skates had been handed-down several times.

The young men on Hecla Island had an organized hockey team and sometimes travelled to Riverton to play. Ben and Sam spent extra time setting the rink up, but when it came to flooding the ice surface or any major maintenance they had lots of help. Now with electricity on the island, they were talking about stringing some lights next year. The rink would be used much more if skaters could lace up after the sun went down.

The goals were set up at each end of the rink with goalies in place. Everyone took turns minding the net because it was too cold to stand in one spot for any length of time. There were no referees in attendance for these fun games and any disputes were settled by the oldest players. Foul language was frowned upon because some of the team members were girls and the boys feared their mothers would find out.

From listening to hockey games on the radio and from watching the young men on the island play, the youngsters knew how to take their positions before the puck was dropped. After that, it was every player for themselves. Little regard was placed on strategies and game plans. The object of the game was simple – score on your opponents.

"Keep your stick on the ice!" Adam hollered when he got slashed by a younger player who missed the puck and slammed his stick into Adam's shins.

"Ah, poor Adam can't take a little hit." One of the North Gang was quick to retort.

"Shut your mouth. You wanna know what it feels like?" Adam swung his stick around menacingly.

Before things got out of hand, Andrew yelled at Adam to take a pass. The play moved down the ice with some serious glares following. Three grade one children appeared from the rink shack with a mother right behind them. Their presence was enough to defuse the fiery tempers and the game proceeded at a friendlier pace.

Beth had a chance to ask Adam how his leg was, but all he had the time to do was blush before someone yelled out, "Hey, Lover-boy, are you still in the game?"

Embarrassed to be teased and angry for the interruption, Adam skated into position for the next face off. Beth also put her stick down, ready for a quick pass when the puck was dropped. She'd like to give some of the big-mouthed boys a slap across the shins and see how they'd like it.

The game went on for two hours, until it was nearing chore time. Evenly matched, both sides seriously vied for victory. On this particular day the North Gang scored the final and winning goal. They gained bragging rights for the week ahead.

Adam and Andrew walked with Beth and some of the other South Gang home. Their scarfs were frosted from their steamy breath during the game and everyone had rosy cheeks. There was little thought given to the cool temperatures when the skaters raced up and down the ice surface, guided by the fierce competitive quest to win. Because they were all used to walking to school from their homes every day, they were accustomed to sharing the time along the way. It had become a habit for Beth to stroll beside Adam. Andrew noticed that Adam was carrying Beth's skates, but there was no way he was commenting on that.

Signey enjoyed going out to the barn for evening chores. The smell of hay and straw met her at the barn door when Alexander opened the door and let her go ahead of him. Three cats greeted her with loud 'meows' and Governor, the horse, whinnied in his pen.

"You're getting a real welcome, Signey. I think all the animals have missed seeing you." Ben gave her toque a tweak. She had regained a healthier glow in her cheeks. But, it seemed to take a long time to bounce back. Her thin limbs were fragile and she tired very quickly. To come out to the barn she had to wear heavy clothing and big, warm boots that were cumbersome to walk in. After she wore the big boots for a while, she dragged her left foot. She could use her left arm sparingly, which was an improvement compared to before Christmas.

"Can I try feeding the cats, Uncle Ben?"

"How about if you tell me when they're hungry." Ben instructed and laughed when he saw the twinkle in her eyes. He set the milk stool beside one of the cows and cleaned the cow's teats and udder with a wet cloth. Then he tilted the milk pail under the cow and began the rhythmic motion of milking by hand. Ben glanced at his niece who was standing a few feet behind the cow with a cat on either side of her. He raised his eyebrows in silent question and Signey grinned broadly as she nodded her head.

Instead of milking into the pail, Ben aimed the milk flow toward the patient felines and sprayed first one cat, then another, directly into their mouths. The third cat came running for her share, and was rewarded. Because the force of the spray was strong, the cats got a mouthful but also had milk all over their faces and fronts.

Signey laughed so hard she had to hold her stomach. Then, when her giggles started to subside and the cats had washed their faces, Ben squirted them once more and the entire procedure was repeated. It was a ritual morning and night to feed the cats in this way and Signey loved watching.

Four cows were milked. They were Holsteins, which is the breed known to produce the most milk. Adam was across the centre aisle of the barn milking the two cows that were stalled there. Ben and Adam usually competed for the fastest time and the most milk, turning the tedious task into a game.

Next to the cows on Adam's side of the barn was Governor, the horse. His winter job was to pull the manure sleigh out to the field twice a week. Prior to purchasing the bombardier, Ben, Daniel and Jon had harnessed Governor to pull the caboose and sleigh out on the lake. Now the horse lapped up the luxuries of semi-retirement. Whenever Signey was in the barn she would crawl onto Governor's feed trough, near his head, and hand feed him some hay. The old horse nuzzled her arm with his velvety nose and took each stem of hay from her hand as if it was the best candy in the world. The tiny hand never flinched when the horse's lips parted and nibbled the feed from her palm. Then he would lick her clothing and softly snort like they were sharing a secret, as she stroked his soft nose.

Alexander had fed the chickens some grain and then he treated the cows and Governor to a few handfuls of chop, which was ground mixed grain. Signey liked to watch the cows eat their grain, waiting for them to clean out their nostrils with their tongues. She was always amazed at how long their tongues were.

Because there were so many hands to help with the chores, it didn't take long to complete them. Signey watched Uncle Ben pour the milk into the cream separator. Two and a half gallons in size, the storage bowl sat atop a rotating bowl that had two spouts and a handle. The bowl was rotated by turning the handle, resulting in a centrifugal force that separated the milk from the cream. The cream went out one spout and the skim milk out the other.

The Bergursson family drank lots of milk, but the four cows usually gave them more than they needed. Some excess milk was fed to the young calves and the remainder was shared with Bjossi or Malla and Olivia. The cream was stored to be sold to the Riverton Creamery. Before the ferry the previous summer, the cream was consumed locally. Often the various commodities on the island were bartered, either for other goods or, on occasion, for labour. But now with the regular ferry service all summer, the cream could be shipped all year, with the exception of freeze-up and break-up.

In Chilliwack, British Columbia, Anna and Johannes were reuniting with their brother. Their niece had stood on the platform of the train station. Anna recognized her before the train came to a stop. She looked just like Johannes' daughter. She had greeted them shyly, unsure of their reactions to meeting her and also to having finally heard from their brother.

Bjarni was frailer than Anna had expected. His face was gaunt with heavy lines around his mouth and eyes. The first moments were very awkward with none of the siblings knowing what to say. But then Anna smoothed her hand over Bjarni's forehead, combed his sparse hair with her fingers, and lowered her face to kiss his brow. So weakened that he couldn't raise himself from his bed, Bjarni clutched his sister's hand and reached the other out to his brother. No word had yet been spoken. They smiled and stared at each other. Young Anna brought extra chairs into the room so they could sit near the bed.

"I never made that fortune." The humble but amusing tone of Bjarni's comment was the ice-breaker they needed. Anna was quick to berate him and remind him that none of them were tripping over any vast wealth.

They talked about their families and old friends. Anna told them about the ferry to Hecla Island and the industries on the island besides fishing. The sun was dipping low in the west when young Anna set up a little table in the bedroom for them to enjoy dinner together. She assisted her father by adding more pillows behind his back and head and then she fed him. More stories were brought to mind about their childhood, bringing many smiles to their faces.

Young Anna was relieved to see the reunion going so well. It appeared that forgiveness wasn't necessary to any of them. They all harboured a heavy guilt in what had happened so long ago. Being together had diminished its importance. She had worried how this visit would affect her father, but she realized that she had worried for nothing. Her aunt and uncle were the best medicine he could have at this time. When her uncle had stepped off the train with her aunt, she had felt tricked and had wished she hadn't contacted her aunt and invited her to come. But she'd come to realize that her uncle needed this reunion more than anyone else. He was the one who carried the greatest burden of guilt.

Late, on the third night after Anna and Johannes' arrival, the household was wakened by a weak cry from Bjarni. Young Anna called for the ambulance to take him to the hospital, but he died shortly after reaching there. She was shocked that it happened so quickly when he had rallied for the last few days.

Four days later, Bjarni was buried beside his wife in the community cemetery. The next day, Anna and Johannes boarded the train for the return trip home. Anna had been reluctant to leave her niece alone so soon after her father's death, but her namesake was insistent that she had lots of support from her family and friends there.

"It'll be hard to get used to the idea that he's gone." Young Anna lamented as she hugged her aunt. "I'll always remember his last days and the contentment your visit gave him."

"I can never thank you enough for getting in touch with me." Trying to stop the flow of tears Anna held onto the slim figure. "You will never know what this meant to me and to Johannes."

Before leaving, Anna extracted a promise of a summer visit to Manitoba. "It's time you met all your cousins."

"I'll be going back to my teaching job, but I will have two months off in July and August."

"That might be almost long enough to get to know everyone," Anna said. "Now that I've found you, I never want to lose touch again."

It was clear that the two Annas had formed a bond. Bjarni had left this part of his daughter's legacy in the safety deposit box hoping that the day would come when the two women would find each other.

Laura had her suitcase packed and waited in the front room of her parents' home. Ben would be picking her up before meeting his mother and uncle at the train station. The Valentine's Dance on the island would be on the following night, so this extra trip into Winnipeg made it possible for Laura to attend.

Because there was to be a lunch-box auction at the dance, Laura decorated a cardboard box with red paper and ribbon and cut out some cupids to impress her sweetheart. She had rolled out some sugar cookie batter and cut heart-shaped cookies. Liberally iced with pink icing, the cookies lay in a neat row beside squares of matrimonial cake which was also called a date-bar. Laura had grinned as she thought of Ben's reaction to her lunch. She had toyed with the idea of hiding a note inside the box asking for his hand in marriage. The covered box was tucked into a brown paper bag to conceal its glamour. The other nurses on her shift thought the auction was a great fund-raiser and Hecla Island might be a good place to scout out a husband.

The train had come in right on time. Both Anna and Johannes were exhausted from the travelling and also from the emotional toll of the visit.

"It's good to be closer to home, but I wouldn't trade this past week for anything in the world." Anna's tired words prompted a knowing nod from Johannes.

"It's too bad you couldn't have had more time with Bjarni." Laura said, hugging Anna.

"Well, at least we had three days." Anna was solemn then brightened when she added, "And we met our niece who is coming to meet all of you this summer."

The ride out of the city and to Gimli was accompanied by the steady description of the sights the travellers had seen and the reunion with their brother. The expanse of prairie and the majestic heights of the beautiful Rocky Mountains were described in great detail. Waterfalls cascaded down the snow capped peaks into rivers of rushing rapids. Train track tunnels through the rock and bright sunshine glistening on the snow in the valleys painted a pretty picture to Ben and Laura, neither of whom had ever been west of Manitoba.

In Gimli, they bade goodbye to Johannes who was so grateful to his sister for inviting him.

"I know I wasn't included in the invitation." He leaned toward her and kissed her cheek. "And I know it was hard for you to include me. Thank you for letting me go with you."

Laura was caught up in the emotional farewell of the brother and sister. It was difficult to imagine what these last days had meant to them. One thing was certain though, this trip had brought them closer together.

The cold weather, very common for this time of year, hadn't abated for several weeks. Sometimes February brought a slight reprieve in the form of a mid-winter thaw, but there was no evidence of that at the moment. Ben reassured Laura that there wouldn't be a slush pit to cross. It was so cold that in the event of a crack, the water would turn to solid ice immediately. Somehow, instead of envisioning a slush pit, she conjured a picture of a crack swallowing them up, car and all. When they reached the island side of the channel she couldn't stop the heavy sigh of relief.

"You'll get used to it in time." Anna patted Laura's hand.

"I hope so. I can't stop thinking about cracks and how deep the water is under the ice."

"It's perfectly safe. I'd never drive across if it wasn't." Ben sounded impatient and annoyed that she thought otherwise.

"I know that, Ben. But it still gives me a scare." Her tone equalled his in impatience and annoyance.

"Now, now, you two! If you're going to have a fight, wait until I'm out of the car." Anna teased and earned a chuckle out of each of them.

Laura rested her head on Ben's shoulder. "We aren't fighting." Then she raised her head again and looked at Anna. "And we aren't going to fight."

"That's 'cause I always let you have your way." Ben grinned.

"Oh, right." Laura sputtered. "My complaisant Viking!"

They were all laughing out loud as the car turned into the driveway. Rose had asked them to have supper with them, so Laura's suitcase and gingerly handled brown paper bag were stowed into the house and the three of them walked next door.

Laura had grown accustomed to the warm welcomes she always received when she was on the island. She knew the family was aware of the tension between her and Ben in January, so the hugs felt even warmer than usual.

Throughout the meal, Anna recalled her experiences of the past days. She had pictures that the young Anna had given her. Pictures that told some of Bjarni's story. He'd worked in mines and later in logging camps. On a visit to a dentist he'd met his bride. He'd continued working in the camps, going home at irregular intervals. His daughter had been a teenager before he took a job at the local pulp and paper mill on the Fraser River near Chilliwack. Bjarni had told Anna and Johannes that he'd been hiding, but couldn't explain why. Then, later, the reasons didn't seem to matter anymore. He thought too much time had passed to make amends.

"The saddest part is that he felt like a failure. I hope his last days with us gave him a better feeling about his past. I told him he could've come home at any time to open arms. He told me that he knew that. He just couldn't make himself do it." Anna shook her head slowly, "Pride can cause so much heartache."

Laura understood that sentiment very well. Her father still made comments about Ben's background, even though he liked Ben. She was afraid his pride was causing him sleepless nights. Instead of being sympathetic, Laura was annoyed that her father couldn't see past the Irish Catholic argument.

"Tell us more about our cousin." Ben was eager to hear about the girl who would be coming in the summer.

"She's a lovely girl. She's a teacher in Vancouver, but took some time off to be with her father. She looks just like Johannes' daughter, Fjola, but with Ben's dark colouring. I was very impressed with her. I really hope she'll come in the summer. It's strange for her. A few weeks ago she had no idea that any of us even existed. Now she has a pile of cousins." Anna grew wistful as she glanced from face to face around the kitchen table.

Ben took the cue, "Mama, I think it's time for you to get to bed. I'm sure you're exhausted." Everyone rose from the chairs circling the table and bade each other good-night. "We'll hear more tomorrow."

Laura had been careful to keep her decorated lunch box well hidden from Ben's inquisitive eyes. Because he'd been the one to explain the lunch auction to her, he knew what she was keeping secret about and couldn't help but tease her.

"So, how much do you think I should bid? You know you have to be nice to the man who pays to share your lunch with you." There was no mistaking the steely glint in his eye.

"Really, don't you think my baking and decorating skills will be nice enough?"

"Oh no. You have to serve the gent as if he were a king, and compliments – lots of sincere compliments are important." Ben twinkled as Laura shook her head at him.

Anna chose not to go with the young people to the Valentine's Dance. Too tired and still grieving the loss of the man she had mourned for so long, she wasn't ready to face the community and the barrage of questions they'd ask.

Everyone at the dance had left their cold weather doldrums at home and were ready to have a good time. As usual, the band had alternating musicians and short refreshment breaks outside. Laura had become familiar with the varying dance steps including the 'Seven Step Waltz', the 'Schottische' and the 'Heel-Toe Polka'.

"Don't worry, Laura. Ben won't be in any fights tonight." Gudrun, in the waddling stage of her pregnancy, consoled Laura when she noticed her nervous looks in Jacob's direction.

"I know. I wish I hadn't been the cause of the argument."

"Don't be blaming yourself, for heaven's sake. Jacob has always been jealous of Ben. I can't believe it took Ben so long to clobber him. Ben always turned the other cheek until you were involved." Gudrun smiled. "He's got it bad for you, my girl."

Laura was grateful for Gudrun's reassurances. She had difficulty understanding how the men seemed to forget past indiscretions. They didn't feel the need to avoid each other at community functions.

"Single ladies. Calling all single ladies who brought lunch boxes." One of the band members acted as emcee and asked the participating women to come forward. In the line at the front of the hall, Laura studied the other lunch boxes and was pleased that hers fit in. She'd never been to anything like this before and hadn't been sure how plain or how ornate the other boxes would be. The auctioneer for the proceedings embellished on each box, striving for a high bid. Ellen laughed and blushed when Matthew was teased for bidding the highest for the honour of sharing her lunch. Then it was Laura's turn.

"What am I bid for this beautiful box made by our Irish lass?" Laughter and more teasing erupted around Ben.

"Ten dollars." Ben shouted and winked at Laura.

"Have another look, man. Ten dollars? You can do better than that."

"Twelve dollars." A voice in the back called out. Everyone turned to see who would dare to enter into a bidding war with Ben. And there, at the back of the room stood Bjossi with a big smile on his wrinkled face.

Ben smiled back and yelled, "Fourteen dollars."

In a split second Bjossi countered with, "Fifteen dollars."

Ben laughed and shrugged. Bjossi was having the time of his life thwarting him. A look at Laura told him that she was enjoying the escapade far more than she should be. She was trying to hold back her laughter.

"Ben, come and have coffee lunch with me." There was Malla, coming to his rescue. She was laughing as hard as the others.

Laura set out her lunch to share with Bjossi. On Christmas Eve he'd been with her at Daniel and Rose's but she hadn't spoken to him except to wish him a merry Christmas and regards for the New Year. He had seemed shy and very quiet around her, so this bidding display had taken her by surprise.

"Ben told me I'm to treat my lunch companion like a king, so be sure to let me know if I'm doing everything properly." She smiled and offered him some cake.

"Sharing lunch with a beautiful young girl makes me feel like a king, so everything is perfect."

Their conversation was a bit stilted and awkward at first, but soon they were sharing entertaining stories. Bjossi told her about the various birds he watched and the changes he had experienced on the island in his lifetime. He spoke of Adam and Andrew and the work they did for him.

She described her work as a nurse and gave him some of her insight into the polio epidemic. The coffee remains in their cups had long gone cold when Bjossi saw Ben approaching.

"Okay Bjossi, should I be asking what your intentions are?"

They all laughed as Laura and Bjossi rose from the bench. Laura gave the old man a hug and thanked him for buying her lunch. Inwardly she was chuckling, thinking that she'd assumed Ben would be the recipient of her lunch and had almost tucked a marriage proposal in with the matrimonial cake.

Dancing resumed with an old-time waltz. Ben held Laura close, as they moved in perfect time with the rhythmic melody. Benches around the hall were vacant, with everyone on the dance floor. On the stage, Bjossi winked at Laura, as he kept his violin in tune with the other band members. She winked back recalling his words. "Anna's boys are favourites of mine and I want all the best for them."

On Tuesday morning, Fred made his bi-weekly trip into Riverton to pick up the mail. Laura travelled into town with him so she could catch the train into Winnipeg. This was her second rail ride. The first time she'd been too preoccupied with the ice road mishap to enjoy stopping in all the small towns along the way. This time she planned on making it a fun adventure. It took several hours to make the journey by train so she hoped to have other passengers to converse with.

Fred tried to hurry back to the island with the mail each Tuesday and Friday. By two in the afternoon everyone expected the mail to be sorted and ready for pick-up. After leaving Laura at the station he completed all his errands and collected the island mail at the Riverton Post Office.

The drive home was uneventful until he reached Horseshoe Bend. Out of nowhere a bull moose charged out of the ditch, right in front of Fred's truck. Unable to stop in time, the truck caught the back leg of the animal throwing it off balance. Because the truck had slowed considerably, the impact was lessened. However, the moose rolled onto the hood of the truck and in slow motion slid into the windshield. Fred was sure the animal was coming in, but everything came to a standstill. Miraculously, the moose rolled off the hood again. After a sound shaking, the animal limped into the woods. Close scrutiny revealed little damage to the truck, just a few dents in the hood and some scratched paint. Fred didn't mind some battle scars as long as the truck was in working condition. He heaved a huge sigh of relief. The moose had been large and heavy and had he been travelling faster the outcome might have been very different.

In the afternoon, when the islanders stopped for their mail, every conversation started with an inquiry about the dents on the truck. At one point, Fred considered putting up a sign telling the whole story to avoid the repetition.

"Was it on the way there or on the way back?" Ben rushed into the store, worried about Laura.

"On the way home. Don't worry, Ben, I took good care of your girl."

"She's still terrified crossing the ice so I can just imagine if she saw a bull moose up that close..."

"How close? What happened?" Ellen walked in just in time to hear this exchange.

Once more Fred told the story, this time downplaying the encounter.

"A moose was on top of the truck?" The incredulous teacher gasped in shock. Driving through the marsh at Christmas, when she'd been with Ben and Laura, Ben had pointed to a moose running towards the bush. That quick glance before the animal disappeared, and served up on her dinner plate were her only bouts with the moose of Hecla Island.

"Don't worry. Everything was alright."

"Does that happen often – colliding with wildlife, I mean?"

"No, there aren't that many vehicles on the island that can go fast enough to hit anything." Ben joked, but was unable to obtain the response he wanted from Ellen.

"Unless you're running down telephone lines!" One of the islanders laughed and punched Oli in the arm. That comment brought a round of guffaws from the group of men with Oli. He, in turn, shook his head and wondered when they would forget about it. It had been months ago.

"You could have been seriously hurt." Ellen refused to be distracted.

"Nay, I'm way too hard-headed for that. Really Ellen, it wasn't so bad." Fred knew that Kristine harboured similar concerns. Two years earlier, he and Kristine were taking the boys to visit his parents in Selkirk when they nearly hit a deer on the west side of the island. Fred had opted for the ditch at the last second to avoid an accident. The deer was in flight from a timber wolf and wasn't aware of the truck. It followed the truck's movement and seemed to stay right in front of them. By the time the truck had stopped, both boys had bounced off the dashboard and slithered down to the floor. Kristine had also smashed her head and ended up with a gash on her forehead. Because Fred had the steering wheel to hang onto, he hadn't suffered any physical harm.

Fred had been able to drive the truck onto the road since the truck hadn't slipped into the depths of the ditch. No damage was evident to the vehicle, but there was plenty of trauma inside. It had taken a long time for Kristine to settle the boys down. Thankfully they came out of the incident unscathed, their fear diminishing into a fitful sleep. Fred's concern was for his wife, who had blood down the side of her face and on her clothes.

In Selkirk, Fred had taken her to the hospital where a doctor stitched up the gash. By the time they reached his parents home, they'd relaxed enough to laugh it off as an adventure. Since then they'd minimized the accident to 'just one of those things that happen'.

After today's brush with a moose, Fred knew that Kristine would be reliving that previous day. The fine-lined scar under her bangs would always be a reminder of how things can change in a heartbeat. They'd been lucky, as today, he'd been very lucky.

"I'm glad it wasn't worse. And I'm glad that Laura was on the train already. I know I'd have been terrified." Ellen visibly quivered down her spine. Fred knew she was imagining being in the truck with the moose on the hood.

"I'm glad too. I remember the two of you crossing the ice with me. That's what I was telling Fred – that Laura didn't need a scare." Ben had relaxed as soon as he knew that Laura was safely on the train.

During the next days, Fred's trip to Riverton was retold many times. By Friday and his next mail run to Riverton, he had heard via the grapevine that 'he was so close to that moose he could count the hairs on its back'.

Chapter 15

"I don't suppose you've had a change of heart?"

"Dad, you know I don't want to argue with you."

"There are lots of nice Irish men. Why couldn't you find one of them?"

"I've always tried to please you, Da," the childhood name came out. "I know you think I'm making a mistake, but I know what's right for me." Laura spoke in earnest, trying to reach her father. "I've never felt like this about anyone else. Ben's the one I've been waiting for."

"But, he's..."

"Please, Dad, let's not fight. You raised me to be strong and independent so I could make my own decisions. And I thank you for that. I've made a decision. Please don't make me choose between you and Ben." Her expressive face pleaded for his understanding.

"Is it so wrong, Dad, to marry someone who isn't Irish and Catholic? From the first day that I met Ben, I've been 'me'. I've never worried about talking too much or having my hair in a mess." She tucked a copper strand behind her ear. "He loves me, whether I'm perfect or not."

"I know," he acknowledged. "I just want my little girl to be safe and happy. When you have children of your own you'll understand. I don't know much about Hecla Island and the people who live there. How can I know that you'll be alright?"

"Just know, Dad. It'll be better when you meet some of the islanders and see the community." The father looked into the face of the daughter who most resembled him, in looks and especially in temperament. How could he explain to her that what he feared the most was losing her. He was so proud of her and her strength of character. The thought of her living so far away and relying on someone else wasn't an easy pill to swallow. She'd always been his little girl.

"I love working as a nurse, because my patients need me. No one else has ever really needed me. Until I met Ben. He needs me, Dad, and

I need him. I'm only half a person without him. I found that out last month."

"Oh, m'lass, what's a Da to do?"

"Just be happy for me."

It was at that moment that Colin O'Neil knew he'd lost. He wouldn't make her choose between her family and Ben, because he knew who'd win.

Anna had difficulty settling into her everyday routine after returning from British Columbia. She wanted to be alone, yet yearned the understanding comfort of a friend. When Margaret came to call, Anna was reluctant to share too much. She knew Margaret meant well, but the woman could no more keep things to herself than fly to the moon. Bjossi simply knocked on her door, gave his condolences and asked about the trip. Then with a brisk 'Take care' he was gone.

"Anna, would you like some company?" Thora telephoned and the tone of her voice reached Anna in a way none of the others had.

Anna only hesitated for a moment. "Yes, Thora, that would be nice. I'll put the coffee pot on."

The two women had shared confidences before and Anna knew that if anyone could put themselves in her shoes it would be Thora. The water was boiling in the kettle when Thora knocked on the door. As soon as Anna opened the door and saw her friend, she felt her eyes welling up and was at a loss for words.

"Anna, I'm so sorry about your brother. Here, let me help with the coffee." Thora finished pouring the boiling water into the coffee 'sock'. When they were both sitting and the coffee had been poured, Anna began telling Thora the whole story.

The words flowed out of her. The disagreement between the brothers and Anna's sense of loss in the years that followed came out. Thora hadn't been aware of this other brother, so the story astounded her. She mumbled soothing acknowledgments when Anna paused, but let her spill all the hurt feelings she had bottled up for so long.

"I've thought of him many times and wondered what had happened to him. On his birthday, at Christmas, and on days when we were celebrating a special event – I've seen his face in my head." She blew her nose into a handkerchief. "When Ben died, I remember wishing Bjarni was there to hug me and tell me everything would be okay." Anna rose from the chair to refill their coffee cups. She needed to take a deep breath before continuing.

"It just seems so unfair to have found him and then only having three days with him. It's been over thirty years. Why couldn't we have had more time with him?"

"Try to think of it the other way. You had three days with him before he was gone. That was three days more than you expected, wasn't it?" Thora usually saw the bright side of things.

"True. Still, it isn't fair." Anna had to smile at her friend. She had found the right words to say.

"Tell me more about your niece."

Anna's face brightened at the mention of the newest addition to the family. "She's planning on coming this summer. I loved the way she looked after her father and how she wanted to know all about us." Anna went on to explain how young Anna had learned of her father's family. She spoke of her teaching career and her resemblance to Johannes' daughter.

"Do you think you can forgive Johannes now?"

"It was a long train trip there and back, so we had lots of time to talk. Things are better between us now, but we've never had the close relationship that I had with Bjarni. Forgive him? I'm not sure. I've always blamed him for Bjarni's leaving." She paused to reflect. "Maybe I needed someone to blame for my little brother's actions, and Johannes seemed like the one to take the brunt of it. Bjarni forgave him so I should, too."

The two friends nodded in understanding. And later, when Thora was going home, she said, "If you look long enough, there's a silver lining in each cloud. You lost your brother, Anna, but you found a niece you didn't know you had."

Her heavy heart lifted, Anna brought some paper and a pen to the table. Thora's parting words had given Anna the idea of writing a letter to her new niece which she immediately set out to do.

Islanders filled the community hall to capacity and the nervous director was taking care of last minute details. Ellen was annoyed that her cast wasn't displaying any jitters. Oh well, she guessed that she was tense enough for all of them.

At every piano recital, speech presentation and play role that she'd ever been a part of, she'd been fraught with nerves. Her mother was a stern taskmaster and her motto of 'if you're going to do it, you must do it well' had nearly crushed her daughter on many occasions. Ellen had grown up believing that if it wasn't perfect, then there was room for improvement. With those lessons in her head it was difficult to be patient when her troupe found humour at every turn.

"Is everybody ready?" Ellen tried to keep the shrill panic out of her voice.

"Don't look so nervous, boss, we're gonna make you proud!" Sam said. He glanced around to ensure that all the cast members were in place, then gave Ellen a nod.

She slipped around the edge of the drape and asked for everyone's attention. The crowd quieted and listened to Ellen announce the play and give an introduction to the plot.

In a flourish, the drapes opened and Thora began playing the first tune on the piano. Ellen didn't have a speaking part in the play, but she sang every song as part of the ensemble. In between songs, she followed the progress of the play with the play book in her hands, prepared to give a cue when needed. After all the joking and laughter at the practices, Ellen was amazed that not one member of the crew needed prompting.

When the cast took their final bow, Ellen realized that not only were they avid performers, they had thoroughly enjoyed taking part. Sam had been right, they had made her proud. If only her mother could have seen this success. No, on second thought, she would have found fault somewhere. The costumes wouldn't have been right or a song could have been improved upon. Helping pack the props in the background, Ellen heard her name called from the stage.

"Come on out, Ellen." Sam was standing at centre stage and beckoning to her to come forward. In the front row Ellen overheard some of the students snickering about Sam calling her by her first name. "Boy, is he going to be in trouble!"

"On behalf of all of us in the play, I'd like to present you with a small gift to say 'Thank-you'. I don't think we've ever put on such a good performance." The crowd clapped and cheered as Ellen accepted a fancy tin with lemon drop candies inside.

"Thank you." Ellen was overcome. Sam walked with her off the stage to more cheers from the cast. Winning an Oscar at the Academy Awards couldn't feel any better than this.

Coffee and lunch was ready to be served. Ellen was surrounded for the rest of the evening with praise and the anticipation of next year. Comments varied from, 'never sang so well' and 'it was so organized' or 'best concert ever'. It wasn't until Sam patted her on the back and said, "Told you we'd make you proud," that she felt nauseous, wondering if she was turning into her mother.

Later that night, after they were home again, Thora congratulated Ellen on a job well done. The director decided to air her uncertainty.

"Do you think I expected too much from the cast?" The distress in her round eyes reached out to Thora.

"Oh Ellen, you're always so hard on yourself. Didn't you notice how much fun everyone had? You only expected what they could give. But, I'll tell you this – it was the best play we've ever done and your directing was the reason why."

"You don't think I was too demanding?"

"Good grief, no. Do you honestly believe you could demand anything from Sam and Ben that wasn't to their liking?"

"Well, when you put it that way..." Ellen smiled but her expression still held a trace of vulnerability.

"There's nothing wrong with expecting people to give their best. It's only wrong if you criticize their 'best' for not being good enough. And you never did that." Thora had spoken so often to the young teacher about such an array of subjects that she had guessed where the insecurities came from. Too much had been expected of her and now she was afraid of imposing the same expectations on others.

"I just don't want to be bossy."

"You're not! Now, show me that pretty tin they gave you."

Thora had a way of settling Ellen's mind and dissolving her worries. It truly had been one of the happiest days of Ellen's life. And Thora's lesson that it was fine to aim high as long as you didn't hurt anyone in the process, was well received. They all performed well, never missing a line, and they all had a great time doing it. Thora was right. Ellen was much too hard on herself. She needed to learn to take things less seriously and enjoy things more. Easier said than done, she thought to herself. But one thing was clear. In the presence of the islanders she couldn't help but have fun. The lemon drop was tart on her tongue but the gift of candy would always leave a sweet taste in her heart.

Gudrun woke up early in the morning of March 12, a week after the Help-in-Emergency Concert, and knew it was time to get to the hospital in Gimli. They had left the island long before anyone was stirring. Sam had been worried as they drove, not liking the painful look on Gudrun's face when she had a contraction.

"We're having a baby, Sam, not flying to the moon. I'm fine, and I'm sure it will be several hours before this baby makes an appearance."

"Whether it's a baby or flying to the moon, it's our first time. Let me enjoy some panic." Sam had smiled. She was right, it would probably take some time before their heir apparent was born. He'd known that he would just feel better once they reached the hospital.

Sam paced up and down the hallway and drank many cups of coffee when finally a nurse came to tell him that he had a son. He'd always remember walking into the hospital room to see Gudrun lying on the bed with their baby nestled in her arms. She looked both exhausted and exhilarated. In that moment he knew that their lives had changed forever and he didn't know how to express the rush of pride and love he felt.

"Isn't he beautiful?" Gudrun beamed.

Sam could only nod and smile as he kissed his wife and stroked the cheek of his son, Mark Kristjan.

Saint Patrick's Day had been just around the corner when Ben had to tell Laura that he might have to miss the party at the Tipperary. They still had nets in the lake and some of the cows would soon be calving. It wasn't the best time to be away from home. At the same time, Ben argued with himself, he hadn't seen Laura in a month and he missed her. He had been weighing the pros and cons of driving into the city when his mother called him to the phone.

"What's this I hear, you're not coming to m' party?" Ben laughed when he recognized the Irish accent.

"Now, don't you be taking it personally. I hate to miss a party you're throwing." Ben tried to explain his dilemma to Sean.

"I guess I understand, but I hate to see m' Laura cryin' and sure as there's a Blarney Stone that can turn you into a sweet talkin' man, she'll be cryin'."

"If I knew for certain that the cows would wait until I got home again, I wouldn't hesitate. But they seem to have a mind of their own when it comes to calving."

"We forgave the Viking raiders when they tried to defeat us a thousand years ago, but this is too much." Sean was giggling into the phone. Ben guessed correctly that he was entertaining his patrons at the bar. "You're sayin' some cows come before m'party? Don't ya know? Not celebrating Saint Patrick's Day s'like sayin' there's no Ireland." Ben could hear laughter and some other comments that Sean was to use next.

Ben was still chatting with Sean when Daniel walked in. Anna told him that Ben was talking to Laura's cousin. When Daniel heard enough of the conversation to comprehend the gist, he waved his hand at Ben.

"I can spare you for overnight. You can go to the party. Then I won't feel so bad when I go muskrat trapping in a couple of weeks."

Ben gave Daniel a quizzical look as if to say, 'Are you sure?', then responded to Sean's invitation when he saw the confirmation on Daniel's face. "It appears I have the night off, Sean. Looks like I can make the party." Ben nodded in Daniel's direction.

"Ah, I knew I could persuade you. Maybe I could twist yer arm in ta takin' a shift behind the bar, since yer all trained now."

"You cagey old Irishman, that's why you called in the first place."

"Ah, m' Ben, I was born in the night, but it wasn't last night!" Another spurt of laughter erupted through the telephone receiver.

"If I'm there, I'll work a shift for you – as long as m' Laura doesn't cry," Ben mimicked. He wanted an opportunity to see Laura before break-up began, which would be in early April. Then it would be another month of not seeing her. He felt lonely every time he left her. One of these times he'd have to just keep her here.

Three days later, Ben was on his way into Winnipeg. He grinned thinking that the car could almost drive itself to Laura's house. Because Laura's family would be at work, he had called Aiden and was happy to hear that he would be finished work early that day. They had made arrangements to meet at the Legion. Ben had been there often enough that many of the veterans he would see there would know him by name.

Welcomed into the fold as soon as he arrived, Ben sat down at a table immediately. In a way it was like it had been overseas. Soldiers and airmen had gathered when off duty and enjoyed a few beers to go with the storytelling. Strangely, Ben was very much at home with these men. When he had first come home from the service, he never wanted to hear about war ever again. But he now realized that it would always be a part of him, as it was for all veterans. When he was here he felt whole, and able to talk of experiences that only others who had walked in his shoes could understand.

Aiden walked in and clapped Ben on the back, happy to see him. They had become good friends through their association with the Legion.

"So, are you doing bar duty tonight, too?" Ben inquired.

"Don't tell me you got talked into that! That silver tongued fox of a brother of mine could sell raincoats on the desert. Make sure he pays you dearly, my friend."

"A few drinks on the house is all the payment I need."

"Lordy, he saw you comin'," Aiden said, knowing full well that he would be paid the same way and be expected to work a longer shift.

After an hour of visiting, Ben left to meet Laura. He waited in the car, keeping it idling for warmth. She ran out of the hospital, jumped into the car and was in his arms in a heartbeat.

"Would you rather be with your cows now, Mr. Bergursson?" Liberally kissing his face, Laura unsuccessfully tried to sound sarcastic.

"I'm not sure. I may need more convincing." The glint was back in his eyes, the eyes she had learned to read. He didn't have to tell her how much he had missed her.

They had dinner with Laura's parents. Ben regaled them with news from Hecla Island. He told them about the play and how it had surpassed previous performances due to their capable director. Laura and Ellen exchanged letters, so they'd heard her version of the concert. Ben also reported that Sam and Gudrun had just come home with their new son. Laura was sad that it would likely be May before she could come to the island and see him.

At the Tipperary, Ben and Laura joined the other party-goers by wearing shamrock hats and sipping on green drinks. As always, the festive atmosphere chased away any worries one might have. An Irish band reeled off an Irish jig, while at the bar, Sean encouraged everyone to toast all the lasses in County Cork, then in Dublin town, and so on.

Later, when the band toned down to a slow waltz, Ben and Laura swayed together, her head tucked under his chin. His lips nuzzled her ear and he said, "Where do you want to marry me?"

Half asleep, she wasn't sure she had heard him correctly. She tipped her head back and looked into his eyes. Reading the serious innocence there she knew what he had said. They'd often discussed the differences in the Catholic and Lutheran churches, but she knew their future lay on Hecla Island and she was prepared to make the adjustment to the Lutheran faith.

"The church in Hecla. The same church we'll baptize our babies in and where we'll take them to worship."

"Sounds good to me." He smiled and kissed her forehead. "Are you sure?"

"As sure as I can be."

Then he led her over to the corner with the fireplace. There, at the same place where they had shared their first meal together, he opened a velvet box to reveal a diamond engagement ring and slipped it on her finger. A silent promise sealed with a kiss set the couple in their own world, oblivious to the party raging around them.

"I don't think my family will be surprised. They like you." Laura didn't want Ben to be concerned about her parent's reaction.

"No, your father seemed okay with the idea."

"My Dad knows?"

"Yeah, I went to see him at the office this morning."

"To get permission? Aren't you the gallant one!"

Ben grinned and fixed his steady, intense gaze on her. "I wanted him to know my intentions. Your parents have met Mama, but they've never met anyone else from Hecla. They've never seen the island I want to make your home. Another thing, we'll be living in the old family home with my mother. I know you are agreeable to that arrangement, but your parents might have reservations. I hope that you and Mama will always get along, but there will have to be some give and take from both of you. I just wanted your father to know that I'll always put your well-being and happiness first, well," he smirked with that so familiar glint in his eye, "after mine, of course." Then he became serious again. "We had a good talk, Laura. I told him that I may not be an Irish Catholic, but I'll always respect your roots. Our home will be on Hecla Island with the traditions that are upheld there, but I want our children to be familiar with your family's traditions too." He held her ringed hand up to his lips. "I know we can make it work."

Before she could respond, Sean shouted, "What's that on your finger, lass? It's a diamond!" Comprehension dawned and with a cheer he shouted, "Everyone, to Ben and Laura – may they be blessed with many bairns!"

The celebrations went on with Sean taking full credit for the engagement. "If I hadn't put me foot down and made him come to town..."

Ben and Laura had their picture taken wearing their shamrock hats and toasting each other with green drinks. Sean sighed, "Saint Patrick would be so proud!"

Daniel and Jon had been muskrat trapping every spring since they were old enough to tag along with their fathers. Ben had trapped with them when he was a teenager. After coming home from the war he'd been more interested in the cattle business than in camping in the marsh. He went for a day once in a while to help the trappers with the skinning, but the farm held more appeal to him.

On weekends and during the Easter school holidays, Adam and Andrew were members of the muskrat trapping crew. Jon's son, Stefan, now turned nine years old, had also joined the ranks. Alexander was old enough to go with Ben for the day but he still preferred his own bed than a night in the marsh.

It was the end of March and the nets had all been pulled up. After the winter fishing season, the nets were cleaned and re-boxed for the next season. Any nets that needed some repair, or needed corks and leads to be redone, were hung in the net shed and would be dealt with as time allowed.

"Couple of more feet, Jon." Daniel issued the directions to place the caboose evenly on the ridge where they had made their camp for several years. The 'Flamingo Motel' didn't appear quite as exotic as its name implied. The caboose boasted four built-in bunks, table and chairs, a wood heater and a two-burner gas campstove. A flat deck to step out on at one end of the caboose was large enough to sit on while skinning. Two windows let the sunshine in or the heat out if the fire outdid itself. On the windowless side was the sign 'Flamingo Motel' in bold, brightly painted letters.

"Whoa, that should do it." The two men were like a couple of boys skipping school. To them, muskrat trapping was their holiday and the marsh at this time of year was like the tropics. Hence, the colourful sign. Three years earlier, Ben had been shopping in Gimli and spotted some plastic pink flamingo lawn ornaments. He couldn't resist. They'd been hooked on the outside wall of the caboose on either side of the door ever since.

The tractor stopped and Daniel removed the bolt from the hitch. There was still snow and ice in the marsh, but the sun was higher in the sky now and the days were getting longer. Water sat on the ice road, in between the ridges created by the snow plow. The ice was still solid and vehicles were still crossing, driving slowly through the water caused from the melting ridges. It was deemed safe to cross until the water started to seep through the ice. Then the ice was termed 'rotten' and impassable.

"Back in heaven again, eh Daniel?" Jon slapped his friend on the back as they gazed over the marsh. "It doesn't get better than this!"

"So true, so true!" Both men inhaled the near-spring air of the marsh. Clumps of brown reeds speeded the process of opening the marsh waterways. As the reeds swayed in the wind, the snow and ice surrounding the plants were dislodged with help from the warm sun. Later in the spring, several men on the island would organize the burning of the marsh, to make room for fresh growth and to remove the danger of a summer fire hazard.

"We still have some light left. Let's get a few traps set before supper."

Jon was eager to start the much anticipated vacation.

"You bet. Let's set some out towards Hargraeda." Daniel pointed northwest towards a treed knoll in the marsh that was shaped like a hair comb. In a few minutes they walked out towards the closest muskrat houses, laden with traps, a spear and an axe.

At the first house, Jon drove the spear through the outside wall. When the spear found the soft interior, he nodded at Daniel that the house was inhabited. If the inside was frozen, that meant the house wasn't in use.

Pulling the spear out, Jon stepped back and let Daniel use the axe to chop a hole large enough to set the trap inside. Then, with the trap set, some of the soft interior was rearranged to cover the hole. Because it was the first day and they only planned on setting a few traps, the two men worked side by side. In the following days they would each set out on their own, to lift traps and set more.

The 'Flamingo' was parked on a ridge that was central to the area they trapped in. It was convenient to stop for midday lunch and coffee. When they were at the peak of the season, they would try to lift all the traps by lunch time. They would skin the caught muskrats and stretch them on boards to dry in the afternoon sun and head out for an afternoon lift. They usually had four dozen traps between the two men, and averaged twenty muskrats per day. Fur prices for this product fetched between one and two dollars per pelt, so Jon and Daniel considered these working holidays very profitable.

After supper, when the pelts were all stretched, it was customary to pull out the cribbage board and a deck of cards. No, life didn't get better than that!

"Remember when we first learned how to play these things?" Daniel strummed a guitar and checked it for any moving scars.

"You mean when we played for Uncle Sigfus?" Jon grinned in remembrance when Daniel nodded.

They had been fourteen years old and both had received guitars for Christmas. After practising the chords, the two aspiring musicians walked over to Jon's old, eccentric uncle's house and broke into song when he opened his door. Completing the tune, Jon had asked his uncle if he'd like them to play another one. In his slow heavily accented Icelandic tone he'd replied, "I didn't ask for the first one." And he'd closed the door!

The men enjoyed this trapping season for approximately three weeks, dropping in at home periodically, until the ice and snow in the marsh turned into slush. Then the 'Flamingo Motel' was hauled home again to await another year. Some years, they went back after the marsh was thawed out and made open water sets. This depended on the number of muskrats that were in the marsh. It was important not to deplete the population for future trapping. It was also important to monitor life in the marsh so that it could sustain all the creatures that depended on it.

Malla was excited about the wedding set for August. Although it was only early April, she had pulled her carders out to prepare some wool for a wedding blanket. Hearing of Ben and Laura's engagement had been very welcome news. Not that she was surprised. The couple was made for each other. She'd often wished for the right woman to come along for Ben, and Laura was just right.

Last summer, Malla had acquired some wool fleeces when one of her neighbours had been shearing his sheep. She had washed all the wool and then been gradually carding and spinning it into yarn. The carders were two flat boards that were eight inches long and six inches wide, each with a wooden handle. Along one side of each carder were dozens of short wire bristles, resembling a brush. The washed wool was matted in clumps that needed to be smoothed. The wool was brushed from one carder to the other, spreading it into long, wispy sheets. These sheets were then spun into yarn on the spinning wheel.

Malla loved spinning the wool. There was something about the rhythmic whir of the wheel and the wool flowing through her fingers as she twirled it into a fine string that took away her arthritic aches. Add a cozy fire in the woodstove and a cup of coffee near at hand and all was well in the world.

To make a woollen comforter, Malla carded the wool into many wispy pieces. Her aim was to have the wool brushed into even thickness so the blanket would be uniform in shape and size. She had already sewn the unbleached cotton fabric to fit a double bed, leaving one end of the cover open. After she had enough carded wool to lay inside, the end would be stitched up. With heavy crochet cotton, Malla would quilt the comforter in large basting stitches so the wool would stay in place. To finish the wedding gift, she would sew a slipcover for it. The entire process would take a long time, but for Ben and Laura, Malla had all the time in the world.

Some islanders were sceptical about the city girl Ben was marrying, but most people were happy to hear of the wedding plans. The ceremony was to be in the village church with a reception and dance to follow in the hall. Another party would be held in Winnipeg at the restaurant owned by Laura's cousin.

There had been lots of excitement for the islanders in the past few weeks. Thora had hosted a bridal shower for Andrea, Hilda and Oli's daughter. Hilda had confided in Malla that Andrea had brought home news at Christmas that she was pregnant. The previous summer Andrea had left the island heartbroken over Matthew's lack of interest in her. Now, she and her new husband had eloped and surprised everyone. Andrea had finished her hairdresser training and she was opening a little shop in the new home the couple had purchased. With comments like, 'you lucky duck!' and 'wow, your own shop!', the new bride was beaming, but some of the women noticed the fleeting look when Ellen Taylor was teased about also becoming a bride one day soon. Malla hoped that Andrea had forgotten her infatuation with Matthew and moved on with her life.

Elin was planning a gathering for Sam and Gudrun's new son. "Everyone wants to see him, and we need a party during break-up to get everyone's mind off break-up!" Her reasoning hadn't been questioned. It made perfect sense.

Malla laughed when she heard Elin. Break-up reminded her of the way life used to be all year round. In days gone by they had rarely left the island. An 'outing' was having a visit with a neighbour or walking to the store. Now, it seemed, if there wasn't a trip into Riverton every week it was the end of the world. Ah, these young people with ants in their pants thinking the grass must be greener somewhere else.

Break-up was a special time to Malla. It heralded the coming of spring and new growth. Pussy-willows and flowering fruit trees gave colour to the landscape as the woodland creatures shook off their winter coats. New life was apparent all around. Meadows turning green and the trees showing off their budding leaves were always a wonder to Malla. The ice on the lake turned gray as it became porous and broke away from the shoreline. In a couple of weeks the lake would have resumed its summer colour, sooner if a strong wind came along and pushed the ice around. The movement broke the ice into chunks that would melt into the lake faster than a solid sheet would.

No, Malla didn't mind break-up at all. She had never felt like a prisoner on Hecla Island. As long as she had a warm home, food to eat, and her spinning wheel, she was content.

Chapter 16

Laura looked into her purse while she waited for the light to turn green. Several other hospital workers joined her on the street corner. Laura's head was full of wedding plans that morning because after work she was seeing her mother's friend, who would be sewing her wedding gown. Inside her purse, she located the swatches of white satin that she had feared were still on the dining room table. She had narrowed the choices down to two fabrics. After work, the decision needed to be made. Laura had selected the pattern for her gown and she'd found the perfect crown-shaped adornment for her hair.

"Are those for a wedding dress?" A lady who worked in the hospital cafeteria spied the swatches. "They're both beautiful."

Laura nodded and smiled at the lady. "It's so hard to decide."

"You can't go wrong with either. Someone said you were leaving the hospital after your wedding."

"Yes, I'll be moving away from Winnipeg to a place called Hecla Island."

"I've heard of it, but, I've never been there. I have family in Gimli and they've mentioned the island."

A sudden shriek from a woman near the curb startled everyone in the vicinity. A car raced through the intersection, rushing to beat the red light. In its haste, the car went into a skid as the driver lost control. Not knowing which way the car would go, everyone was in a mad scramble to escape. When the car lurched in their direction, the people around Laura screamed in alarm. She was so taken by surprise that she didn't react as quickly as the others.

She tried to leap out of the way, but the front fender struck her solidly, sending her flying into the wall of a storefront. She heard glass shattering, and metal crunching, and then – everything went black.

Two new calves were born that morning and Ben and Daniel had just come into the house for coffee when the telephone rang. Anna handed the receiver to Ben and went back to setting some fresh tea biscuits on the table.

"Ben, this is Colin O'Neil calling." His voice betrayed his uneasiness and Ben stood very still. "It's Laura, Ben. She's been in an accident."

"What happened, is she alright?" Ben grasped the telephone in his trembling fingers.

"She was hit by a car on the street near the hospital." Straining to keep his voice even, Laura's father continued. "The doctors are still with her. She has a broken arm and collarbone and they're checking for any internal bleeding."

"Have you been able to talk to her, is she alright?" Ben asked again, sensing there was more.

"No, Ben, she hasn't regained consciousness yet. Her head was hit quite badly. The doctors will probably tell us something soon. At least I hope so."

"I'm on my way, Colin. Tell her I'm on my way."

Urgency replaced all other emotions as Ben hung up the telephone receiver. Daniel and Anna listened to the grim details. Ben mechanically went into action mode. Asking his mother to pack some clothes for him, he motioned for Daniel to follow him outside.

"Help me load the boat into the truck."

"Ben, I can get a couple of the guys. We can cross with you." Daniel offered.

"No Daniel, I'll cross myself. I'll take the little duck boat. Let's go load it."

In case of emergency, there was a boat at the ferry landing that had long skis attached to its base. Four men, two on either side of the boat, would walk across the 'rotten' ice, pushing the boat along with them. In open water areas, they would jump into the boat and row until they reached more ice. Then the boat was pulled on top of the ice again and the trek would continue to the mainland.

The duck boat was loaded and while Ben went to grab his clothes, Daniel quickly told Rose what had happened and instructed her to call the family that lived nearest the ferry landing on the mainland side. If Ben insisted on going alone, Daniel wanted someone waiting at the other side if help was needed. In that family home near the mainland ferry landing, many weary travellers had found a warm fire and good food over the years.

The truck had never moved so fast. Daniel's comment on the boat bouncing right out of the truck box was lost to deaf ears. Ben was so focussed that he didn't hear his brother.

At the ferry landing the men unloaded the boat and Ben tossed his things in alongside the oars. He shook his brother's hand and Daniel drew him into a rough hug.

"She'll be fine, Ben. You travel safe, brother."

Ben looked his brother in the eye and with a solemn nod, turned and pushed the boat onto the ice. It was less than an hour since he'd spoken with Colin O'Neil.

The sun was warm but the slush was cold through Ben's rubber boots. It was slow going, even when he tried running and pushing the little boat. The boat skimmed the surface, but the ice collapsed in places below Ben's feet. He hadn't gone far before the dampness was reaching over his boots, soaking his clothes.

He was overcome with fear and anger. This couldn't be happening. Not to his Laura. When the fear became too much, he relied on the anger to propel him. Pictures of George in the hospital flashed in his head, but he angrily blurred them out. He was not going to lose her, he mustn't. Her bright smile and laughing eyes were in his vision giving him the rush of adrenaline he needed. He reached the island in the middle of the channel and dragged the small craft through the dead grass and reeds.

On the mainland side of the channel island another boat with skis was anchored in the grass. For approximately a week during the last part of break-up, it was easier to go across the island in the channel, but difficult to drag the larger boat across. So, they would leave Hecla Island, pull the boat onto the little channel island, walk across the little island, and push the other boat to finish the crossing. While the ice covered the whole area, with no open water, then it was easier to push the boat over the ice and avoid the little island altogether. The islanders had all these safeguards in place, but they were seldom put to the test as Ben was on that day.

Daniel studied Ben's progress and noticed a truck stopping on the other shoreline. At the mainland ferry landing, four vehicles had been parked since the ice became too dangerous to drive across. Ben's car was one of them. The islanders didn't make a habit of using the vehicles during this time, but the cars and trucks offered a means of security in an emergency.

Across the island, Ben pushed onward. He was gasping for air after pulling the boat through the grass. 'Just stop for a minute, Ben,' he told himself. 'Only a minute.' But he couldn't get his legs to listen. Back on the ice, he stumbled and fell. He was soaked to his chest. Dragging himself upright, he kept going. He had to get to Laura.

Silently, Ben coached himself over the last stretch of ice. The wet clothing and cold breeze didn't register in his mind. Just a few more yards. Keep moving. Hands grabbed the bow of the boat and pulled it onto the shoreline, dragging Ben with it.

"I got it. You better get out of those soaked clothes." The man took the suitcase out of the boat and handed it to Ben, saying that he'd pull the boat onto dry land. While Ben changed into dry clothing and dry boots, the man signalled to Daniel that Ben was safe.

On the island side, Daniel acknowledged the truck's blinking lights by answering with the lights on his truck. Three times the lights were turned on and off. Daniel maintained the vigil until he saw the man's truck and Ben's car drive down the road. Then, he too, turned around and drove home to await any news from Winnipeg.

By mid afternoon Ben walked briskly into the hospital. Laura's parents had been watching for him and spotted him as soon as he arrived on the Emergency Ward.

"How is she?"

"We're still waiting for her to regain consciousness. There was a little internal bleeding which they were able to fix and they put a cast on her broken arm. Her fractured collarbone has been taped." Colin and Katherine both looked weary. Katherine gave Ben a hug, trying to keep her emotions in check.

They accompanied Ben into Laura's room, where Hilary sat beside the bed coaxing her sister to wake up. She arose when she saw Ben and motioned for him to sit down.

"Ben, maybe she needs to hear your voice." Hilary prayed that he'd have the solution.

Without saying a word, Ben slid into the seat and gently wrapped the limp hand into his. Her pale face was swollen and bruised on one side. Above the distorted eye, a dark gash had been stitched. Her copper curls were matted with blood. A nurse came in to assess Laura's condition and noted that there was no change. Colin, Katherine and Hilary left the room with the nurse, but Ben was oblivious to anyone around them. He shifted in the chair, leaned over her face and left feathery kisses on the unharmed area. Then, in a dreamlike voice he began speaking to her.

"Come back to me, Laura, come back." During the war, Ben remembered how he would think of exotic places while the air crew was on a mission. It was a trick someone had shared with him in the barracks. "Think about good things, like home or a tropical island. It helps to shorten the time." And, Ben had found the advice to be true. Now, he hoped he could will Laura to dream with him until she woke up.

"See how white the sand is? Let's walk under the palm trees so we don't get sunburned. I think we should come here again someday, don't you? Did I mention that I love that bathing suit you're wearing. The colours match your hair and your eyes perfectly." His soft tones were directed into her ear as he rubbed her arm. He continued weaving the story in a slow drawl, wanting to relax both of them and hopefully urge Laura into opening her eyes.

"I don't think there's anyone around. We could sneak behind that palm tree and make love. It's so warm and you're so beautiful." Ben stopped and kissed her cheek when the doctor came in with Laura's parents and sister.

"All indications are positive. When the head suffers a severe trauma, it needs quiet and rest to recuperate. In Laura's case, it's like she's in a self-imposed sleep." The doctor concluded, trying to sound convincing to the ears of the frightened listeners.

"How long do you think she'll be like this?" Ben asked.

"It's difficult to say. We'll have to be patient."

Katherine persuaded Ben to go with Colin and have something to eat. Ben called home to relay the news and the doctor's prognosis.

"I'll call before midnight if there's any change. Otherwise, go to sleep, Mama, and get some rest. If you don't hear from me tonight, I'll call just after eight in the morning." The island telephone operator turned the switchboard off from midnight until eight a.m. The telephone could still be used on the island without the help of the operator, but not for long distance calls off the island.

"Take care of yourself too, Ben. Try and rest. Laura is strong and she'll be fine."

"Yeah, I hope we have good news soon." Ben tried to sound upbeat, but he had a tough time believing himself. She was so battered and bruised. And if he was truthful with himself, Ben had to admit he was terrified. He'd seen too much in hospitals overseas not to be afraid. He'd heard doctors say things they thought you wanted to hear, only to have hopes die.

He resumed his position at her bedside. Stroking her cheek, he murmured in a quiet voice telling her about the new calves. The ashen face displayed no sign of having heard. Ben kept talking to her, paying no attention to the staff members who checked on her. Later, he instructed the O'Neil's to go home and rest. He would call if there was any change.

Still, he used his voice to try and reach her. He didn't know if he was helping her or not, but he continued. At ten o'clock in the evening, Laura hadn't opened her eyes or moved a muscle. Ben had told her about everyone on the island by then and he was struggling to stay awake. He'd been up several times the previous nights to check on the cows that were close to having their calves. He catnapped when possible during this season, but he'd become very tired before Laura's accident occurred.

Throughout the day, Ben had silently prayed for Laura's recovery. During the two years he had been overseas he had felt the presence of a guardian angel, but the absence of a higher power had also been felt. Many times he had battled with his beliefs. Again he asked, 'Why is this happening?'. Just when they had found such happiness, why was Laura being made to suffer so. Ben continued to pray, but he was also in mourning. He mourned the young man he had been, excited to see the world. He mourned his friend, George, and his other acquaintances whose lives had been lost. And he grieved for the man he'd been when he returned, sullen and angry and sad. Then he made a pact with God. If Laura could come back to him, he would forgive those absences and consider the score even. If he could just have his Laura back, he would protect her forever.

With one hand curled against her cheek and the other holding her hand, he laid his head down on the side of the bed. Jessica had brought a comfortable chair for him to sleep in during the night, and he'd pulled it as close to the bed as possible. In a moment he was asleep.

News of Laura's accident spread quickly over Hecla Island. Everyone remembered the copper-haired nurse with the big smile from the three island dances. And for those who knew her personally, it was a solemn day.

Daniel and Rose's children heard before they went to school. They told Ellen as they slid into their desks. A cloud settled over the classroom, setting the mood for a long day.

Malla and Olivia consoled each other and shed some tears for the couple they admired so much. They worried about Ben if the outcome wasn't favourable. He loved Laura so much and the change in him since she had appeared on the scene was remarkable. Malla recalled his letters and the day he came home from the war. He'd been serious to the point of being morose. These past months with Laura had brought joy back into his life.

Baby Mark was having a bad day. Thora explained to Gudrun that babies pick up on the moods around them. Breast feeding the baby had become the new mother's favourite times of the day, but on that day, she failed to find contentment. Visions of Laura in pain plagued her. Sam prowled around, not able to settle down to his chores.

In the afternoon, Bjossi and Anna met at Daniel and Rose's for coffee. Bjossi couldn't believe that anything would happen to his Lunch Box Social date. He was adamant that all would be well. She was a strong Irish girl and she'd be fine. It was difficult to imagine the girl who'd sat across the table from him coming to any harm.

Anna, too, was hopeful. If there was a will, Ben would find the way. She felt that Ben and Laura could accomplish anything they set their minds on. With Ben in the city by Laura's side, things had to work out.

Daniel had worried all day about Ben. It was true that Laura was the one in physical danger, but Daniel feared for his brother. If he were to lose Laura, it would destroy him. The single-minded determination that Ben had demonstrated in crossing the channel had frightened Daniel. It was as if Ben had to do this alone. Daniel didn't want to even think about the consequences if the worst case scenario occurred.

Fred spent the day listening and reflecting on the news with all his patrons. The store had always been a meeting place and that day was no exception. Everyone was anxious to hear the latest news and they waited for a call from Winnipeg.

Margaret, so fond of gossip, was heartsick. She found no pleasure in dallying on the telephone discussing Laura's accident. Even though Margaret criticized the upcoming nuptials of mixed faith, she didn't wish any harm to them. She tried to pass the time baking cookies, but nothing could fill the void created by this tragedy.

Ben may have felt lonely as he slept in the quiet hospital room, but back home on Hecla Island everyone tried to be optimistic for the couple. Evening meals were subdued and the family time following was spent with thoughts of hope. In each home as Heclingers prepared for sleep, prayers for good news in the morning were carried to bed.

Some time later, Laura was able to lift her eyelids a fraction. Motionless, she tried to understand the situation she was in. Closing her eyes again, she attempted to put the pieces together. Her head throbbed and she again willed her eyes to open. Gradually it all came back to her.

The street light, the car, and the smashing glass. She studied the plaster cast weighing her arm down and she felt the constricting tape around her shoulder and chest. Why couldn't she open one eye wider? Trying to lift her other arm up to check on her eye, she wondered what was holding her hand back.

Then she realized she wasn't alone. The hand that cradled hers was rough and calloused. The face was relaxed in sleep. The sun and wind had left tan lines that smiled out of the corners of his eyes. Rugged stubble covered his jaw line and his unruly dark hair appeared to have been hastily finger-combed. Laura decided it was the handsomest man she'd ever seen. Her heart swelled as she moved her fingers in his hand and his eyes flew open.

"Laura." His voice was so gentle. He touched her cheek and kissed her. "I'm so glad you're awake." Relief and strain collided on his emotional face.

"Ben, I can't believe you're here." She grimaced in agony as the movement of her mouth sent shards of pain through her head.

"Shush, your head must hurt. You have a bruise on the side of your face and your eye has some swelling." Ben minimized the extent of her injuries in order to comfort her.

"I feel like I've been hit by a truck! I guess I should say car." She attempted to laugh at her own joke, but that caused her more discomfort.

A nurse approached and Ben stood back, but continued to hold her hand. After examining her, the nurse was able to update the doctor who came in next. Leaving Laura with them, Ben went to call the O'Neil's and his mother in Hecla. He just made the connection in time to call the island. When the operator heard Ben's voice, she berated him for not informing her earlier. She would have gladly left the ringer on overnight so he could contact his family anytime.

Jessica walked back into Laura's room with Ben. She informed them that the man driving the speeding car that morning had been arrested. The drunk driver was facing many charges.

Later, when Ben had taken his position again in the bedside chair and Laura was resting, the couple shared a comfortable silence. He had briefly described his channel crossing and she had been anguished thinking of the danger her accident had put him in. Both of them thought of the relationship they had. Ben said he loved her deeply, but that day had made him realize his love for her was far greater than even he had guessed. Laura had also had a revelation. In the dark recesses of her unconsciousness, it was Ben's voice that she had fought back for. She couldn't imagine anyone else having the power to draw so much from her.

"I had a wonderful dream." Her mouth quirked up on one side to smile. "We were on a sandy beach with palm trees and there were sailboats on the water."

"You heard me."

"Yes. I remember your voice. Promise me, Ben, when I'm feeling sad, promise you'll talk to me."

"I promise." His eyes smoldered as they looked into hers. "I want to take you home to Hecla Island and keep you safe."

Chapter 17

Signey ran around the back yard chasing the two dogs, Dixie and Spike. With the carefree attitude of a preschooler, she paid little attention to favouring weak muscles. Her left leg had recovered most of its previous strength and she was able to use her left hand with restrictions. The shoulder muscle had shrunken out of sight causing a permanent handicap, but the forearm could still be manipulated to limited use.

After school each day, Karen made her exercise as the doctor had stressed. Signey often grew impatient with the repetitive drill and gave her older sister a hard time. At first, the exercises had been painful, but as spring arrived the pain had lessened. With everyday activity, the muscles weren't as stiff and became more toned.

Squealing in delight, the girl rolled over the grass with Dixie. The dog sprang up again, licking her face and caused a fresh flurry of giggles. Rose was hanging freshly laundered sheets on the clothesline and smiled as she watched. She teased her daughter that she'd never tire of hearing her voice. It was a miracle that Signey had regained so much, when the previous September had threatened to take away so much.

"Stop, Dixie, stop!" Signey laughed and tried in vain to push the dog away. Then Dixie was distracted by Spike's barking, and the two dogs dashed off to meet Bjossi coming across the field. Chopper and Billy flanked his sides. Billy strutted in a haughty gait, happy to be out with his summer friends again. The old goat glowered at the two dogs as they romped with Chopper, clearly stating that he was above their juvenile behaviour. The three dogs got together in the field or along the shore road each morning to have a gossip and a tail wag.

"Hello, Bjossi." Signey had walked toward the visitor.

"Hello, Signey. Do you want to look at the geese? I just spotted them this morning." He had brought his binoculars with him. The previous summer, Signey had been interested in looking at the birds with him and he'd wanted to share the return of the Canada geese with her.

"Where are they?"

"Over there, on the other side of my house." He leaned over to her level and pointed at the small flock near the beach. "Here, look through the binoculars and you'll be able to see them up close."

It took a bit of adjusting to get the right angle for Signey to see the birds. At first everything was a blur, but it was really the sky the magnifying glasses were focussed on. Bjossi knew the instant she saw them when she quietly gasped. In a whisper she told him they were near.

"They just seem to be close because you're looking through my magic glasses." Bjossi told her he was happy she was interested in bird watching. She was someone he could share his knowledge with.

"Do you have time for coffee, Bjossi?" Rose had picked up the clothes basket and was walking toward the house.

"Not this morning, Rose. I wanted to show the geese to Signey. Oh, and I was going to ask if you have enough seed potatoes. I have extra if you need."

"I guess it's time to start thinking about the garden. I'll have to check. The potatoes wintered well this year, so I might have enough. Mind you, the boys eat twice as much it seems." Rose shook her head telling him about the growth spurts both her sons were experiencing.

Crows cawed overhead. They had been back for a couple of weeks. It was said to expect a winter storm after the crows returned and another one after the geese migrated north. The second storm had occurred that morning when there had been a brisk wind accompanied by sheets of cold rain. Then by the time the school bell tolled, the sun was shining and the wind had diminished to a soft breeze.

Spring had definitely arrived. All the ice floes had vanished, leaving the brilliant sapphire hue in the water. Leaves were budding and blooms were beginning to open on the fruit-bearing bushes and trees. The early morning rain, along with the sunshine that had followed, brought out the lush green colours of the vegetation. All these vivid colours softened the craggy limestone cliffs as the island officially declared that winter was over.

Laura leaned on the upper rail of the *S.S. Keenora* as the steamship moved away from the pier in Winnipeg. It was a warm morning late in May and Laura was travelling to Hecla Island for the annual Spring Picnic. Ben had offered to come for her, but she knew he was busy preparing for the fishing season that opened in a few days. Besides, ever since she had heard about the passenger boat she had wanted to sail aboard her. On the Monday of the long weekend, Colin and Katherine planned to make a day-trip out to Hecla Island to pick her up and also to see the community their daughter would call 'home'.

The *S.S. Keenora* had been built in 1897 and was used to transport passengers and carry freight on Lake of the Woods. In 1917, the vessel had begun its next chapter when it was moved to Winnipeg. The steamship had been employed since in the same manner on the Red River and Lake Winnipeg.

Sean had driven her to the pier and waved as the boat steamed into the current of the Red River. Past Selkirk, the boat would continue its voyage into Lake Winnipeg. On that particular morning, they would dock at Gimli and Hnausa to unload provisions, before stopping at Gull Harbour.

Sean had boarded with Laura and taken a quick tour of the boat. In the dining room on the main deck, Laura checked the brief menu and wasn't surprised to see a meal of fish as an entree. The passenger deck emitted an elegance befitting high-class travellers. Wood floors shone with glossy varnish and a wide staircase with polished wood rails led to a stately lounge. In the lounge, a piano was placed in one corner. The perimeter of the room offered seating for the guests and the centre of the room was clear for dancing.

The hallway on the passenger deck was very wide and Laura guessed that travellers would gather there if the weather wasn't good. A glance into an open door of a cabin exposed a small space with two built-in bunks and a little stool that was fastened to the wall. There was enough room to accommodate sixty-five passengers at a time on board, but on that day Laura was one of twelve voyagers and she didn't require a cabin. In the peak of the summer season, tourists were more apt to fill the cabin capacity.

Striking up a conversation with two other women, Laura discovered that one was returning home to Pine Dock after a visit to a dentist and the other had needed surgery and was sailing home to Berens River. They were happy to share their experiences of travel on the lake. It shortened the trip for them and their listener was completely rapt in her eagerness to hear their stories.

Time passed quickly for Laura. It was mid-afternoon when someone pointed to the shoreline and announced, "That's the south end of Hecla Island." Laura didn't leave the upper deck after that. She studied the landscape, impatient to see the first houses and the village. Her face was beaming as she indicated the homes she knew and the various buildings in the village. Then the lighthouse at Gull Harbour was just ahead of them. Around the point and into the harbour, the *S.S. Keenora* came to rest at the pier. Ben stood there, with a big grin on his face.

"He's a looker, my dear," one of the women commented. "I can see why you've been so anxious to get here." Both of the women bid the bride-to-be a sincere farewell. "Good luck to you, and maybe we'll meet again."

Ben grabbed Laura in a hug and spun her around in his arms, much to the delight of the two ladies watching from the upper deck. Laura was able to throw her arms around him without the cumbersome cast she had worn previously. She had spent eight days in hospital after the accident and then been off work for another five weeks. During one of those weeks, Ben had brought her home to recuperate on the island. She'd felt like a celebrity with all the attention she'd received.

Anna had suggested a sewing lesson, if the plaster cast wouldn't hinder her. It had been a week that melded the relationship between Anna and Laura. With Anna's help, Laura mastered the pedal on the treadle sewing machine and had sewn a duvet cover and matching curtains for the master bedroom. There would be a shuffle in bedrooms when the married couple took up residence.

Laura learned the fundamentals of cooking on a woodstove and had observed the barn chores. Her laughter had joined Signey's when Ben fed the cats in the customary way. It had been difficult to work with the cast on her arm, but she'd managed to maneuver her arm to achieve several tasks. The only remnants of the accident were a scar over her eye and an occasional headache.

With one arm around Ben's waist, Laura waved to the remaining passengers as the *S.S. Keenora* steamed on its course to the northern destinations.

"What an amazing trip!" Laura gushed and told Ben about the stories she'd heard and the interesting conversations she'd taken part in.

"It's a pretty big tub, alright. I've only sailed on her a couple of times, but we've often had to unload some freight she brought in. Two years ago a shipment of desks for the school came on board the *S.S. Keenora.*"

"Someone said that tourists travel up to Norway House and back in the summer months."

"Yeah, that's right. And the summer people here at Gull Harbour have always used the boat for their transportation. I guess that will all change now, with the ferry operating all summer. They'll be able to have cars out here."

They arrived home in time for afternoon coffee. Laura loved that time of day at Daniel and Rose's house. The school children were home and relating the incidents of the day, and the adults joined in the lively discussion.

"Who are you running the Three-Legged Race with, Karen?" Alexander, as all the children on Hecla Island, couldn't wait for Sunday and the Spring Picnic.

"Probably some boy, uh, Karen?" Ben teased, giving her a little nudge.

"Am not!" Indignance turned to a smirk on her face. "It's Adam you should bug. I bet he'll be asking Beth."

"Do you have many races at the picnic?" Laura attempted to divert the conversation to a less personal one. Rose nodded her thanks to Laura. Alexander accepted the task of informing Laura, explaining how two legs were tied together between two people to form three legs. Also, the Wheelbarrow Race consisted of two people, one walking on his hands while the other held his legs up and ran as if pushing a wheelbarrow. Adam and Karen tried to demonstrate, but ended up in a heap on the floor.

"These are tough races." Laura laughed with the others. "I hope they're just for the kids. I don't think I'd be very good at them."

"And the Sack Race." Alexander continued, "You get into a big burlap bag, usually up to your waist, and hop as fast as you can to the finish line."

"It sounds like lots of fun. I can't wait for Sunday to get here." Laura grinned at Alexander, whose facial expression echoed her words.

"We have pies to bake before then." Anna stated with her eyebrows arched in a question.

"I'll help. I remember everything you taught me last time." Laura exclaimed excitedly. "How many pies are we making?"

"Just four. Some of the other ladies are bringing pies, too. What are you taking this year, Rose?"

"I'm making sandwiches."

"I can help you, too." Laura's eagerness spilled over.

"How about me?" Ben muttered. "Now that you have both hands working again, I think it's time you learned how to milk the cows."

"And break a nail before the Picnic?" Laura fanned out her hands to show off her newly manicured fingernails.

"Bet you didn't see that one coming, did you, Ben?" Daniel slurped some coffee from his cup to hide the grin on his face.

"I may have a solution." Laura looked thoughtfully at the faces lining the kitchen table. "If I have a cow milking lesson tonight, maybe Karen and Signey can help me with my nails. In exchange, I'll do their nails. I brought a new bottle of nail polish especially for the picnic."

Two faces lit up at the plan. Rose smiled, thinking that Laura knew how to please everyone.

"Actually, I have enough nail polish for you too, Rose, and Anna."

Laura noted the satisfied gleam in Anna's eyes. Ben had written that since returning from British Columbia earlier in the year, Anna had been different. There was a new serenity about her. She had received three letters from her niece since the train trip and the young Anna was planning on coming for the wedding. Ben had also noticed that his mother spoke more often to Johannes now. Even though they had lost their brother, they had learned of his life and gained a niece. And in doing so, had begun resolving the invisible barrier that had grown between them.

"So you're going to milk the cows, eh?" Ben was triumphant.

"Well, I'm not going to listen to you calling me 'city-girl' all weekend!"

Everyone laughed as Laura mocked him. Chairs scrapped backwards as each person focussed on the evening chores. It was time to get started.

Sunday arrived with bright sunshine and heightened anticipation in every household. No one required reminding to get all the chores done early. Light lunches were eaten at home and then it was time to go to the village hall and the nearby school grounds.

For Laura and Ellen, it was another first. They had been told so much about the picnic that they had a good idea of what to expect. The school children spoke of little else the previous week, so Ellen was familiar with the agenda of the day. Laura, too, was informed from Ben and the Bergursson children.

Laden with pies, Anna and Laura joined the other ladies in the hall kitchen. As usual for a community gathering, the room was overflowing with food. Trays and large plates held assorted sandwiches and dainties. Kettles were heating on the woodstove. Some of the older ladies took command and issued instructions to the others. The kitchen was alive with spontaneous chatter and warmth.

Outside, various sports events were organized. Ingvar and Kristjan looked after the Icelandic wrestling, while Fred monitored the pole-vaulting. Daniel and Jon were in charge of the children's races. The entire yard encompassing the hall and school was alive with activity.

"We're lucky with the weather. Actually, I think the sun always shines for the picnic." Gudrun had baby Mark wrapped in a light blanket. At just over two months old, he wasn't very interested in all the bustling around him, but everyone was interested in him.

"Let me give your arm a rest, Gudrun. I haven't had much chance to hold this little man." Laura gently took the baby into her arms. "It's your first picnic, too. What do you think of it, so far?" Her sing-song voice drew Mark's attention immediately. He started cooing and pouting his lips. "That's how I feel, too! It's lots of fun."

"I hear your parents are coming to the island tomorrow." Gudrun commented.

"Yes, they haven't been here and they are anxious to see the island and meet Ben's family. They did meet Anna in Gimli one day, but otherwise, they only know everyone from stories that Ben and I have told them."

"I can just imagine the stories. Are you sure they want to meet all of us?" Gudrun giggled. "Listen, why don't you bring your mother and Anna over for coffee tomorrow afternoon. I'll ask my mother and maybe Rose and Elin, too. It'll be fun."

"That sounds great. As long as we can bring something. I don't want you to have extra work for us." Laura knew that her mother would like Thora and the others.

"Perfect! And inviting friends over isn't work."

The sun was angling toward the west when some of the men were leaving. Laura was sad at the thought of the day coming to an end. She had visited with so many people. It was always a marvel to her how the islanders exerted such effort and amusement into the island's events.

"I wish it wasn't over already. This is the type of day you wish would never end." Laura's laments were met with a surprised look from Gudrun.

"Are you kidding! The best part is coming up."

"But people are leaving."

"They're just going home to do chores. They'll be back. The baseball game between the married men and the single men will start when the chores are done and everyone's back. Believe me, you don't want to miss it!"

It had been a long-standing contest – the baseball game pitting the married against the single. Ben and Sam were on opposing teams which created a rivalry of its own. Each year there was a teasing build-up prior to the game, including small time wagers. Bragging rights were held for an entire year, so athletic prowess was displayed to its full extent.

"That's right, Ben mentioned something about a baseball game."

"There's a lot at stake here, especially with our guys on opposite sides. You'll be hearing about this competition all year."

As Gudrun had indicated, the crowd merged around the baseball diamond in droves. After the rosters were set and the umpires in place, the game began. The cajoling between the teams provided entertainment for all the fans. Laura had wondered if her nursing skills would be needed when Fred ran to catch a fly-ball in centre field and stumbled on a gopher hole. He went down in a dramatic rollover, then sprang up to retrieve the bouncing ball. His aches and pains would have to wait. There was a game to win!

The innings went on with several plays that were performed for the audience. Just when Laura thought she couldn't laugh anymore, there was a foul ball hit into the adjacent pasture. Matthew, on first base, yelled "I'll get it" and ran toward the barbed wire fence. Laura had never seen him run before and starred at his rubber-legged approach to the fence. With one hand on the top wire, he vaulted over the barbs, arm and legs flopping in all directions. Holding her breath, Laura was sure he'd shred himself into pieces. He cleared the fence, picked up the ball and flung it back to the pitcher's mound before he lopped toward the fence again. This time she was certain that he'd wrap himself around the wires. With awkward agility, Matthew repeated the jump, never endangering any body parts. Laura had to wipe her eyes, she was laughing so hard.

After the game, in which the married men proved victorious, Laura consoled Ben, "You're a super ballplayer."

"Next year, Ben, you can play on a winning team." Sam added some salt to the open wound.

"I don't know which is better, living with a winner or a loser. Both are hard to take!" Gudrun shielded Mark's face from the setting sun.

"Win or lose, that was fun to watch."

"Winning is better, but when the umps are against you..." Ben shrugged having already found his team's excuse and grinned as Sam slapped him on the back.

"See what I mean. This will go on all year." Gudrun said to Laura.

It was time to gather in the hall for the evening dance. The children were full of sweets and ice-cream and tired from a day of playing in the sun, but they would find more energy to dance. The Spring Picnic was a day for everyone. And as usual, with everyone's participation it was always a success.

Colin and Katherine O'Neil arrived at the house by ten o'clock on the Monday morning of the long weekend. The ferry ride and scenic drive had overwhelmed them. It was even more beautiful than they expected. Before lunch, they met Daniel and Rose and their children.

"I feel like I know all of you already. Laura has told us so much about you and about the island, too." Katherine was comfortable instantly. Anna wanted to show her the house and also show her the sewing that Laura had done on the treadle sewing machine.

The men ventured outdoors and Colin was taken on a tour of the farm. He had promised Katherine that he wouldn't bring up any sensitive subjects. Laura had made it abundantly clear that her life would be on this island. And after hearing about Ben's long-lost uncle, Colin and Katherine didn't want an estrangement in their family.

Being a news reporter and a soon to be father-in-law, he was interested in everything. He asked several questions about their cattle operation. Then he saw the bombardier and fishing boat. One thing led to another, and soon they were in the net shed, studying the mesh sizes.

After lunch, Ben and Laura took the O'Neil's for a ride through the village and down to Gull Harbour. Along the way, Laura pointed out the few dwellings of people that she had previously mentioned to them. Her enthusiasm flowed as she introduced her parents to the island. Laura was explaining the hatchery's background when Ben interrupted, "You were listening to me." His eyebrows arched in a taunt. "Here I thought you just wanted to be alone with me." He laughed as Laura's parents realized that he was referring to Laura's first tour of the island.

Gudrun opened the door in greeting when Laura and Rose, along with Anna and Katherine, climbed up the back step. Inside the kitchen, Thora and Elin repeated the welcome to their new visitor.

"Oh, Laura, we need another chair. Could you grab the one in the living room?" Gudrun requested.

"Sure. I wanted to –"

"Surprise!"

Laura nearly jumped out of her skin as complete bedlam broke out. In the living room, a group of ladies burst out of their hiding spots. Still reeling, Laura saw the decorated chair and several gift-wrapped boxes on the table beside it.

"Welcome to your Bridal Shower, Laura. Did we surprise you?" The look of total bewilderment on Laura's face answered Gudrun's question. "I guess we did!"

In a flurry of introductions for Katherine, the bride-to-be was escorted to her chair and instructed to open her gifts. Gudrun stood to present a toast to her friend.

"Remember the first time we met, Laura? I was just past the morning sickness part of my pregnancy and Sam was a witch! We knew Ben was bringing someone new to the Hallowe'en Dance, an Irish nurse from Winnipeg. Believe me, we were nervous. Then you walked into our lives, and we became good friends.

"Now I don't want to cry on such a special day, but I want you to know what a difference you've made in our lives. You've adapted to life on Hecla Island like a real Heclinger and we know that you'll be involved in all our undertakings. In fact, I believe that Ellen already has a part for you in the next Help-In-Emergency Concert!

"Ben has always been one of our bright lights of the island. He works hard to achieve his goals and the goals of our island. We've always counted on him. But there was something missing, something he found on a hospital ward in Winnipeg last September. You have brought such joy into his life, Laura, and seeing the two of you together has brought joy to all our lives.

"And so, on this day we shower you with gifts and good wishes. Welcome home, Laura!"

With her eyes brimming over in tears, Laura hugged her friend and thanked her. All the ladies cheered and clapped their hands, in support of Gudrun's words.

The pile of gifts revealed tea towels, a cushion, embroidered pillow cases, a crocheted doily and an apron, all made by hand. Laura was overcome by the generosity of the ladies. Coffee and dainties were passed around the group of nearly twenty women and the room was filled with spontaneous chatter.

Katherine felt better about her daughter moving to Hecla Island. This place had sounded so remote and she worried that Laura would miss her family and various aspects of city life that she was accustomed to. Sitting next to Malla helped alleviate her concerns.

"You know, Ben has always been a favourite of mine. He can be a cheeky brat," Malla's eyes shone, "but he's also someone I'd trust with my life. Your Laura is a strong woman and that is exactly what Ben needs. And a sense of humour. She has that, too.

"I'm sure you're worried about her moving so far from home, but we'll take good care of her. Life on the island can be very challenging, but I've found that the best things in life usually come with a challenge."

"That's true. And I can tell you that Ben has become a favourite of mine, too. At first, I wished he lived closer to Winnipeg. Now that I've seen how Laura is thought of here, the distance seems irrelevant." Katherine was grateful to the wise, old woman who Laura had spoken so fondly of.

Scanning the living room, Katherine noted all the people that Laura had told her about. There was Ellen, the city-girl teacher, who seemed to have found her niche. Then Gudrun, who had taken Laura under her wing on her first visit to the island and continued to do so. And Rose, who Katherine was sure would always be supportive to her daughter. Then her eyes rested on Anna. She was already showing maternal protection and respect in regards to Laura. During lunch preparation, Katherine had noticed how Anna and Laura worked together in a comfortable partnership.

Katherine knew that there would be times when Laura would miss Winnipeg and her family, but after meeting some of the islanders, she felt more confident that life on Hecla Island would be good to her daughter.

June and July were busy months and went by quickly. In June, the fishermen were on the lake. Last minute details, like painting the boat and boxing the last nets, were done by the end of May. As for fishing routines, this season was the same as the fall season. The fish camps were opened and Ingvar had stored ice in the packing shed in readiness for all the fish he would pack and transport to market.

Laura made one trip out to the island in June. She painted the master bedroom and the bedroom that Anna would be moving into. Because Ben was fishing, he wasn't able to go into the city. Laura had convinced her father that she could drive his car out to Hecla Island on her own. And after making the trip once by herself, she knew she could easily do so again. She had loaded the trunk and the back seat with some of her belongings. A storage trunk that had come from Ireland years ago and a small armchair that she planned to put in the front window of the bedroom, were crammed in with the rest.

Laura spent some time with Ellen, who had worked hard to fulfill each grade requirement and then plan the end of year School Picnic. With all the picnic planning and final report cards to complete, Ellen hadn't given much thought as to how she would spend the summer holidays. She told Laura she had signed on for another year of teaching on the island, much to her family's dismay. She'd also told her family about Matthew, promising to bring him into Winnipeg for introductions sometime during the holidays.

Spring housecleaning was done and the gardens were sown early, as soon as the risk of frost passed. As the wild berries came to fruit, plans for berry picking were made. Islanders usually went in groups to pick, just in case some bears were thinking along the same lines.

Laura planned her next visit for the third week in July, to coincide with blueberry picking on Deer Island. Ben had sparked her interest when he described the berries as the hugest he'd ever seen. She didn't question his apparent vast knowledge on blueberries; she simply made sure she was in the boatload of pickers late in July. Laura wasn't disappointed. The berries were plentiful, huge, and very tasty.

"If you're going to eat them, try not to squirt juice all over your face. It's a dead giveaway." Ben teased her. She smiled, revealing blue teeth, which sent him into more hysterics.

"As if you're so innocent, Mr. Bluebeard!"

Laughing, the couple turned back to the job at hand, quickly filling their pails. Later, the berries would be cleaned and readied for pies or enjoyed with sugar and cream.

Laura learned first-hand how to make hay. Ben cut the meadow grass with a sickle mower. Then, when the sun had dried the winter feed, Laura took a turn sitting on the hay rake. The large circular forks gathered the mowed grass. Getting the nod, she pulled hard on the lever which lifted the forks and left the bundle of dried grass in a roll. With careful navigating of the tractor, the rolls were amassed in a line, then picked up and forked into a haystack.

Fishflies and bulldogs were new to Laura. She had arrived in time to see the clouds of fishflies attach themselves to everything. At first, they were intimidating, but Anna showed her how to carefully pluck them off. They didn't bite, but if you were to sit on one, it would leave a stain that no known soap could penetrate. The life span of a fishfly was very short. They blew in, settled in every possible spot and then died. Islanders had learned to leave them hanging on the houses until they dried up, thus eliminating stains.

The bulldogs were bigger than any fly that Laura was accustomed to. And they were vicious biters. They especially liked to attack the damp skin of a swimmer, so when the bulldog season was at its peak, it wasn't advised to loiter on the beach after a swim.

The forlorn calls of the seagulls and loons grew familiar. Listening to the quiet ripple of the waves on the shoreline acted as a lullaby in the evening. All these sounds and the smell of the lake and freshly cut hay were recorded in Laura's mind.

Wedding preparations were well underway. The next time Laura travelled to Hecla Island, it would be for her wedding. She'd been living in anticipation for so long, that it seemed strange that her new life was about to begin. It would be different, living here, rather than just visiting. Who could have guessed when that serious Mr. Bergursson had walked onto her ward with his demands, that her life would take this path? A path with an exciting future as Hecla Island would continue to progress and flourish. Laura's eyes scanned the horizon over the waters of Lake Winnipeg. She took a deep breath and exhaled slowly. The peace and serenity she always felt on the island engulfed her. Yes, she thought, I've come home.

Chapter 18

The church bell tolled and organ music drifted through the church door as Laura stepped out of the car with her father. She gazed over the landscape that she would wake up to every morning. The picturesque village which served the needs of the community, and the bountiful lake which provided a living. This was her new home.

With a smile of resignation and approval, Colin O'Neil walked Laura down the aisle. She looked to the front of the church for Ben. Hands clasped in front, he stood with a ramrod straight back and she thought, those intense eyes of his. As soon as their eyes met though, his face softened into the confident assurance she had come to know.

Sam and Daniel stood next to Ben, and Jessica and Hilary had preceded Laura down the aisle. The pews were filled with family and friends. Sean and Aiden, along with their parents, had come for the day. Jessica and Angela had brought their spouses for the event, and, of course, the remainder of Laura's immediate family was in attendance.

Beside Anna in the front pew, sat the younger Anna from Chilliwack, British Columbia. She had been a guest on the island for two weeks. They would both be going to Gimli with Johannes and his family following the wedding reception. Anna wanted the newlyweds to have the house to themselves for a few days, and it was a good excuse to visit with her brother. Young Anna was scheduled to board the train on the following Thursday, so Sean had made plans to have a wedding supper for Ben and Laura on Wednesday night so she could be included.

Meanwhile, Sean had been drawn to Ben's cousin from the west. He mused as he sat in the second pew that even for an Icelander, she was a 'bonnie lass'. Maybe she would spare him a dance or two.

Adam only had eyes for Beth. She had combed her hair into a new style with pretty barrettes. By hook or by crook, he would ask her to dance with him tonight.

In his well pressed suit, Bjossi beamed his approval as Ben and Laura exchanged vows. Yes, Ben had chosen well. Bjossi looked forward to having Laura take up residence in his neighbourhood.

Near Bjossi, Malla and Olivia sniffled into their hankies. This was perfect, absolutely perfect. Malla hadn't realized how much she had yearned for Ben to find such happiness.

Gudrun rocked Mark in her arms, trying to hold back her happy tears. She knew Laura would become an even closer friend in the years to come as they raised their families together.

Thora played a wedding march on the organ. The church bell tolled for all to hear. Mr. and Mrs. Ben Bergursson led the way to the hall. Refreshments and dancing awaited the wedding guests.

To the strains of the couple's first waltz as husband and wife, Ben circled the floor with Laura. After one circuit around the dance floor, Ben beckoned to Signey. He lifted her with one arm and she draped her right arm around his neck, while he kept his other arm around Laura's waist.

"You're the reason we're here." Ben kissed the girl's forehead and the trio continued circling the floor. Signey didn't understand what her uncle meant, but she felt like a princess in the arms of the uncle she adored and the nurse who had always been so kind to her.

Author's Note:

The early settlers on Hecla Island overcame many hardships and tragedies. Their resourcefulness and determination paved the way for future generations to continue the work they had begun. Each generation accepted the challenges, intent on seeing the island progress to its potential and provide a fine community in which to raise their children.

Islanders witnessed many changes to the face of their beloved island. The school closure and land expropriations forced them to relocate in 1969. In 1970, Hecla Island Provincial Park was born, and in 1971 a causeway was completed across the channel, replacing the ferry. The village they had relied upon gained heritage status and became a tourist attraction.

With mixed feelings, the people of Hecla Island took up residence elsewhere. Some were employed by the Parks Department, some continued fishing off the island, and some only managed to return for an occasional visit. No matter where their lives led them, they would always be proud to refer to Hecla Island as 'home'.

Every summer my family enjoys all the recreational activities that Hecla Island Provincial Park has to offer. My daughter was baptized in the Hecla Church in 1970 during the same service that the church key was given to the Parks Department. My son was born in the fall of 1971, when the causeway was completed. Today, my four grandchildren love the sandy beaches, heritage village, lunch at the marina and ice cream at the village store. I felt it was important for them to have a sense of the unique community Hecla Island was before it gained park status.